MA

K-MACHINES

K-MACHINES

Book Two of Players in the Contest of Worlds

DAMIEN BRODERICK

THUNDER'S MOUTH PRESS • NEW YORK

K-MACHINES

Published by
Thunder's Mouth Press
An Imprint of Avalon Publishing Group Inc.
245 West 17th St., 11th Floor
New York, NY 10011

AVALON
publishing group incorporated

This project has been assisted by the Australian government through the
Australia Council, its arts funding and advisory body.

Library of Congress Cataloging-in-Publication Data is available.

ISBN: 1-56025-805-5
ISBN 13: 978-1-56025-805-6

9 8 7 6 5 4 3 2 1

Book design by Maria E. Torres

Printed in the United States
Distributed by Publishers Group West

For my sister and brothers:
Della
Tony
John
Frank
Mick
and their families
with love

I like a look of Agony,
Because I know it's true.

—Emily Dickinson

I dislike Nietzsche, because he likes the contemplation
of pain, because he erects conceit into a duty, because
the men whom he most admires are conquerors, whose glory
is cleverness in causing men to die.
    —Bertrand Russell, History of Western Philosophy

When the universe plays hide and seek with itself, it
plays to win.

—Stuart LaForge

It's like watching a dance, or listening to music. It's not plot,
it's pattern.

—Robert B. Parker, The Judas Goat

There is no end. There is no beginning. There is only the
passion of life.

—Federico Fellini

ONE

"NAME AND DATE of birth."

"August Se—" I began.

"Name first." The overweight clerk was testy and trigger happy. She'd been sitting all summer morning on a sweating plastic seat at this counter, had probably munched a brown-bag lunch high in sugar out back in some cramped room filled with mops or dusty filing cabinets crammed with yellowing records that nobody ever looked at because it was all in the database, and now her blood sugar was plummeting perilously.

"My name," I said patiently, "is August. My birthday is—"

"Surname or given name? I haven't got all day."

Actually she did have all day. What else was she going to do except punch in this information that was already contained in the documents I'd handed her? She had pushed them to one side, naturally, without a glance. I could have strung this game out for a while, for the amusement value. But when I turned my head a fraction, I saw the line of bored and irritated students snaking away behind me. I'd been creeping forward in the same line myself, developing much the same mood, for about half an hour, after two hours first thing in the morning in another interview with the police concerning the disappearance of Great-aunt Tansy and the death of her friend Mrs. Sadie Abbott in the freak accidental destruction of our

Northcote house. They wanted to know where I was living now, and my current phone number, as did the insurance assessor, and I could hardly tell them that I was sleeping in a different universe where the phone company's service didn't yet extend. My temper was frayed.

"Listen to me carefully," I said. "My name is August Seebeck. I was born—"

"Zayback with a zed?"

"You spell my surname *s-e-e-b-e-c-k*. It's Estonian."

"Kid, I don't give a rat's ass if it's Lower Slobovian. D.O.B.?"

"My date of birth," I said automatically, as you do, "is also August, the—" I broke off, shook my head in confusion. What? *Wait* a minute. I flipped out last year's laminated student ID card. Back then I hadn't known I was a Player in the Contest of Worlds. It showed a slightly grim picture of me beetling my brows at the digital camera, above my name, spelled correctly for a change. The date embossed on the background security hologram was February 12. *What?* Seamlessly, then, as these things do and the rules change, the fact retrofitted itself into my memory. Hot high-summer Southern Hemisphere birthday parties, splashing in the plastic pool, laughing a lot as Aunt Tansy looked on from the shade of the veranda, shoving and hugging Dugald O'Brien the golden Lab who was . . .

Who was my father Dramen, actually, under a kind of disguise, but weeks earlier that ludicrous and impossible truth had worked its way neatly into remembrance past with no further bobbles or boggles, however dismaying it seemed. I pushed the card back in my pocket, a bit shaken by a different impossible thought. I'd started to tell her I was born in August, which was no part of any calendar I'd ever heard of until this moment when it tumbled out my mouth. It was ridiculous, like imagining a month called "Steve" or "Bruce." There were eleven months in the year, always had been. Ask anyone. Now there were twelve. Shit, they'd *squeezed in an entirely new month*. An extra month, named after me. I shook my head, trying not to grin. Up came more facts, unbidden. On February 12, 1809, Charles Darwin had been born in this Earth, and a few thousand kilometers away, in Kentucky, so had Abraham Lincoln.

You know, Lune had said something along those lines. And I hadn't understood her. Who would? It was insane. More symmetrical that way, she'd said. Revise the Seebeck family rhyme, not to mention . . . what, the seasons? Or had she said the calendar? And something more, something scary as shit, my unconscious told me, scuttling away from it, eyes closed. Six doughty women—but I only had five sisters. I slammed the door shut on that before it got a foot in. All this in a long moment, with the clerk tapping her toe impatiently.

Okay, anyway, so that meant—given the precession of the equinoxes, the fact that the seasons were reversed here in Australia, so local February was the new astrological August—that I was now an Aquarius, perhaps the paradigmatic Aquarian, and so—

"Date. Of. *Birth*."

"Twelfth of February," I told the clerk, and added the late-twentieth-century birth year embossed on the ID card. Of course, who could possibly know if that year meant anything, truly had anything to do with my birth? As far as I could tell, I might indeed be twenty-something years old, which is how I looked and felt, or half a million. Half a trillion, maybe, long before this world's Sun had coalesced out of frigid interstellar gas, long, long before the planet under my feet accreted from cosmic leftovers and started spinning days solar and sidereal. I felt a jolt in my gloved right hand, shook my head, waited for my pulse to come back under control.

She was looking indignantly at the top sheet I'd passed her. "This says you've completed three years of your medical degree and now you want to change your major."

"I do."

"Damn it, you only have one more semester before you graduate as a Bachelor of Medicine. Six months. What's wrong with you kids today?"

"I don't seem to have the patience and human kindness to be a clerk, let alone a medico."

The clerk narrowed her eyes. Perhaps she detected some tincture of irony, or even of sarcasm. I gazed back blithely. She shook her head, clicked keys, peered at the flat screen.

"The philosophy courses you have listed here are all filled, you'll have to go back to the department and choose a different schedule. Next."

I stayed put. "Dr. Blackford has confirmed my standing with his graduate program. I'll be taking an accelerated bridging semester. His signature is on the second form."

"Philosophy! What sort of job do you think you're going to get with—All right, that's in order." She scribbled an initial, clicked more keys, stamped a form, passed it back to me. "Take this to room 102 and get two photographs. They'll prepare a card for you, Mr. Zay-back. And don't come back moaning to me when you're flipping burgers and watching all the young doctors cruise by in SUVs. *Next.*"

I nodded to her with a certain sudden access of respect, taking my forms. Maybe she *did* care about her faceless, ever-changing temporary charges. Maybe her own heart's desire had been medical school, but she simply hadn't made the cut, hadn't scored highly enough on rigid tests designed, apparently, by nerd-clever Aspergers. Poor woman. Ah well, there were trillions more like her, breaking their hearts in menial jobs, grousing behind stained counters and eating themselves sick on a billion worlds, a googolplex of worlds maybe, and all of them, when it came down to it, no more significant than scene-setting in the greater scheme of things. In the Contest.

Whatever that was.

Room 102 and its jaded photographer could wait. I went out into the blazing cloudless summer sun, looking for Lune.

She leaned against the bole of a tree in the courtyard, the milk coffee perfection of her skin freckled by a thousand shady leaves. Lune seemed utterly relaxed, arms loose, hands clasped easily in front of her. Another woman stood half in the sunlight, eyes squinted against brightness, speaking with apparent urgency. I loped across the grass, glare from the Edward Kelly Law Library windows spearing my eyes.

"Ah, the wonderboy." The woman seemed to be in her mid thirties, mature but attractive, dressed for a day of the office, probably behind a large polished executive desk.

Lune lifted her right hand with a kind of carefree grace, took my left, aware of my sensitivity or, more exactly, residual anxiety about my own gloved right hand. I squeezed her fingers. "More bureaucratic bullshit, and miles to go before I sleep," I told her. To the woman I said: "Hello, I'm August Seebeck."

"August, this is Morgette Smith's Daughter, the Custodial Superiore of the Ensemble. My boss, you could say. Or my adoptive mother."

"How do you do?" When I extended my gloved hand, Morgette shook it firmly for the shortest possible time. Maybe she knew what it could do. "So you're the Mother Superior, so to speak?"

"We're hardly a celibate order of nuns," Lune said in mock reproach. "As you have reason to know." She sent me a dazzling smile. "Morgette is the founder of the Ensemble."

"Not exactly," the Player woman said. "That was the work of your young friend's sister, Superiore Septima. A very long time ago, far before your time, child. Do you think we could get out of this wretched sun now?"

Septima? Did that ferocious old warrior Septimus, guardian of the hellmouth or Gehenna or what vile plenum of pain and horror it was, have a twin sister? Yet another member of my monstrous, profligate family? A month ago I had supposed that I was an only child, an orphan, yet already I'd collected more than a double handful of siblings, not to mention two recovered parents, now vanished again. What was another sister in that rowdy pack? The more the merrier. I put the question out of my mind for the time being.

"There is a coffee shop at the entrance to the student union building," I said. "Quite good latte, if that's your poison. Or iced tea, probably better in this weather."

"Lay on, Macduff," Lune said. Morgette said, "You're training him quite nicely. I appreciate thoughtfulness in a new Player." She strode along beside me and Lune, and I saw her frown. "I have to caution you against undue familiarity, Lune," she said. "It's obvious that you two are intimate; you must understand that I disapprove, although of course it's your own business."

I opened my mouth, closed it again. As usual, I knew too little to say anything sensible. Superiore Morgette was getting under my skin, but there was little advantage in making this obvious to her.

With some asperity, Lune told her, "Butt out, Madam." She paused, a breath, added, "All due respect, and like that."

I held a smile from my lips, squeezed her hand. Morgette gave her a hard sidelong glance, flicked her eyes at me, burst out laughing. "Very well, you bad girl. I understand that the child has been promoted already, and at the hands of our Founder, no less?"

"Madame Morgette, I am not a child," I told her. "I am a stranger in a very large number of strange worlds, and probably many centuries younger than your good self—" I gave her a bland glance of my own. "Or am I being inexcusably rude in mentioning your age? I must say, you're very well preserved."

I pushed open the heavy glass door to the union building. A gust of cold conditioned air swirled past us, escaped into the sunlight. Several spotty students tripped over their own feet, instantly smitten. Lune smiled at them in a friendly and utterly sisterly manner, and followed me into a small space of Formica tables and steel and plastic chairs, redolent of third-rate coffee. Behind us, one of the young men dropped his pile of books. It must be like this when you stroll around in the company of a movie star or some radiant fashion model. The difference, thank God, was Lune's wondrous intelligence. I pulled out a chair for her, something I never would have dreamed of doing for a woman a month ago; but a month ago, I'd never have dreamed that someday I would meet a woman like Lune. For a moment, I stood there behind her, dazed by a rush of emotion.

"Charmed," the Ensemble woman said, an edge to her tone. She stood beside the square table. "If you please."

"Oh. Sorry." I drew out another chair, settled her in place. Three or four younger academics watched us with guarded interest. A young woman student in what looked like a cheerleader's uniform, except that we didn't have cheerleaders in my version of Australia, stared at Lune with a kind of shameless envy. Once, I'd have stared at the cheerleader in her skimpy skirt and perky sports bra; no longer. "What can I get you both?"

By the time I returned with my laden tray, they were in some sort of voiceless standoff. I unloaded an iced tea for Morgette and two cans of frosty Dr Pepper, plus a lamington on a paper plate for Lune. "It's probably stale," I said regretfully. Fresh and fluffy from a pastry chef's hands, layered with strawberry jam, coated in a soft surround of dark chocolate sprinkled with coconut flakes, a square block of lamington is the food of the gods, if we exclude the pavlova, another Australian confection, all crisp egg-white shell, whipped sugary cream innards, sliced strawberries and spooned passion fruit on top, the thought of it made me weak with yearning, with longing for my lost Great-aunt Tansy, the finest cook I knew, gone forever, never more than a mask for my hidden mother Angelina, she gone in her turn, once again, with my father Dramen. This particular lamington, I could tell, had not been fresh for several days. No doubt a fly or two had strolled upon its dried chocolate crust. I sighed, sat down, popped the tab on my soda.

"So how about them Bulldogs?" I said.

"Frivolity," the superiore said in a flat tone. "How refreshing."

I looked at Lune; she gave me a bland glance, and I felt my tightening muscles relax. There were plenty of ways to play this, although I felt like grabbing my beloved's hand and walking back out into the sunlight, or opening a Schwelle into a more hospitable world. That would leave the people idling away their noontime in the coffee shop in a state of shock, confusion, and disbelief, which would be unkind and quite possibly attract attention from those I was eager to avoid, so it didn't seem like the best plan. I let the fuzzy bubbles slosh around my mouth for a moment, then put down the can.

"I'm new at this game," I said. "Until last week, I didn't even know it was a game. That was before the deformers killed me, of course." I could hear the brittle edge in my voice. It's no fun, remembering the vile moment of being torn into shreds and then reconstructed by an Angel from the Omega Point, even if you end up in better shape than you started, which maybe was the case, although I had my doubts. My right hand clenched inside its leather glove.

"New." Morgette regarded me steadily. "So I'm told. I find it hard to believe."

I laughed. Lune didn't seem interested in her lamington; I pulled the paper plate in front of me, and started to peel off pieces of coconut-sprinkled chocolatey cake, popped them in my mouth. I was right: stale. "Frankly my dear," I said, "I don't give a shit. Believe what you like. Lune, I hate to eat and run, but I think I'm wasting my time with this old harridan." I pushed back my chair, stood up. Someone screamed. Something tore like old canvas, noisily. Lots of people screamed. All this in the moment of my rising. It seemed a disproportionate response, somehow. As I turned, the heavy glass door to the coffee shop ripped away from its hinges, and a terrible thing came in to join us.

Lune kicked away her chair, became very still. Morgette, I saw from the corner of my eye, was reaching into her purse. Everyone else was yelping, crouching under tables, sitting frozen in disbelief. My right arm was instantly rigid, outthrust. A word of fire hung upon my tongue; I withheld it. Nothing would be gained in setting the union building ablaze with a lick of plasma from the edge of the Sun. There were more ways than one to skin a monster.

I muttered, "Hard wind." And instantly regretted it as the leather glove was torn off my hand by a blast of foul-smelling air stinking of sulfur, captured, as far as I knew, from the dense atmosphere of some nameless world in a galaxy far, far away. A millimeter wide at my palm, it was a hose-stream of force equal to a battering ram. It caught the creature in the center of its breast, where three or four crusty nipples stretched vertically, like buttons on a vest, from throat to thorax. The blow flung it back into the smashed doorway, where its bat wings tangled on the damaged aluminum frame. Its muscular tail thrashed, catching a bearded intellectual who held a copy of Derrida's final book before him like an amulet, laid him flat on the vinyl tiles. The dreadful scaled neck, cabled with muscle and sinew, flung forward the thing's vile head, all gaping jaws, snarling teeth like rusted knives, forked blue-gray snake tongue, eyes boiling in rage. It drew in its wings tight against its body and flung itself toward me.

A line of brilliant light stabbed across the room, cut a jagged, blood-gushing, instantly cauterized incision in the thing's breast, where my air blast had already broken ribs. The monster screamed, high-pitched and ear-splitting as a factory whistle, hesitated only for a moment, crouched back upon its two great scaled legs, leapt again. Morgette's weapon fired a second time, but the thing was armored like a tank. Lune said in my ear, "Burn the fucker, August," so I did. No time for niceties. The back of my hand still stung where the glove had torn and blown away. At least the leather wouldn't catch fire and singe me. I spoke of sunfire to my Vorpal implant. Plasma from the surface of the Sun scorched the air. Actinic radiance splashed back from the plate-glass windows. When you need a pair of Ray Bans, you can never find them. I squinted, blinked, and saw the thing catch fire, the fat under its scales igniting. Bat wings frizzled, stinking like toenails dropped on coals.

Its screams were ghastly, set my teeth on edge. The slaying brought me no pleasure other than the satisfaction of not dying myself. I played flame upon its head, which exploded into steam and greasy smoke, putting an end to the racket. There'd been not the slightest sign of intelligence. Whatever it was, this was some adjacent world's version of a feral tiger, a Kodiak bear, a pack of pit bulls, dropped into this world to do harm to me, to my love, or for all I knew to Superiore Morgette. The fire went away from my hand. My arm was shaking, my whole body was shaking. I was drenched with sweat. I saw that Lune was safe, reached behind me for the chair, leaned on it a moment. Its rubber feet squeaked in the silence on the floor. I sat down at the table. The lamington was smeared across the Formica surface. I glanced at my left hand; chocolate and cake everywhere. I rubbed it off on my jeans. The Ensemble woman was tucking away her weapon. Not a hair out of place.

"Someone up there doesn't like us," I said. Around us, and outside in the lobby, people were starting to sob and mutter.

"The contest is hotting up," Lune said, "no pun intended. Thank you."

"My pleasure. I hope the vice chancellor doesn't send the insurance bill to us. My God, I'm famished." I licked my dry lips. "Fighting monsters certainly takes it out of a man."

"I don't think you should expect quick service today," Lune told me, glancing at the unattended counter. An open door showed that the serving staff, no fools they, had swiftly found discretion the better part of valor.

I really was abruptly very hungry. I sniffed, caught a tang of freshly cooked meat. I picked my way through broken glass to the fallen monster. Its flesh was charred, smoking still. One hefty thigh had a nicely glazed look to it. In a fit of silly bravado, aware of Morgette's gaze upon me, I seized the great three-taloned foot, jammed my boot against the fire-blackened breast, ripped. The cooked limb resisted at the joint. I twisted it, fingers sticky with monster juice, tore it free. It smelled okay, a bit gamy perhaps. I took a bite.

"Needs salt," I said.

The Ensemble woman regarded me with disgust. "That was a damn fool thing to do. You don't know where it's been. You don't know where it's come from. Its biochemistry could be enantiomorph—"

"Here." Lune threw something; I caught it in my left hand. Salt cellar. I sprinkled some on the warm flesh, took a second bite.

"Thanks. Care for some? Breast or leg?"

"I think not," she said judiciously. "What's it taste like?"

I mused, flung the gnawed meat back on the carcass.

"Chicken." I grinned at her. "Tastes like chicken."

TWO

THERE IS ONE who asks: What is the document whose name is called *SgrA**, and how is its name properly pronounced?

One answers: We speak this name thus: "Sag-a-star." The multiform document, whose name is called thus, is the sacred Scripture more properly known as *Sagittarius A Star*, revealed in its infinite variations throughout the Many Worlds to the blessed and accursed human Eric Linkollew.

There is one who asks: Is this "Sagittarius A Star" a Revelation, an observed reality, a literary device? Is it animal, vegetable, or mineral? Is it bigger than a bread box?

One answers: O Fool! Read the Words and know Truth. All Knowledge is in *SgrA**.

THREE

HE RUNS ACROSS the room, short legs pumping, arms outstretched to the shiny pots inside the kitchen cabinet. He stumbles as he grabs at the open cabinet door, it swings shut, for a moment jams one finger painfully. The impulse to scream pulls his mouth wide, draws in his furious breath, but wait, as he jerks from the hurting thing, the door swings open in his grip, he totters backward, the door swings wider, he falls to the linoleum floor on his padded backside, and light gleams and beckons and shouts its joy. In go his hands, grasping the heavy, shining pot, pulling it onto the floor. The lid clatters wonderfully, slides free, bangs on the floor. He grabs at it, gets his fat fingers around the knob on top, strikes the pot with the singing lid, the sound of it, the cry of it, rings in his ears and dances in the bones of his arms. Rapture! He beats the pot, slam, bash, banging, crash! Holding the pot by its long handle, he stumbles to his feet, runs into the front room where Mummy is sitting in her big chair in her robe and nightie, asleep. But she is not asleep. She looks at him with wet eyes, without moving. She tells him to be quiet.

"No!"

He runs back into the kitchen, slamming his aluminum drum. The jagged clashing crash is pure happiness. "No!" he cries again. Bang, bang. He laughs and runs. Mummy stands in the doorway. She bends forward. "No! No! No!" Has she said it? Has he said it? She bends forward and puts her hands upon her belly, and goes to a chair beside the kitchen table, and puts her head on the table. Mummy is making a terrible sound. Mummy is crying. He drops the pot. He watches her, and feels hot tears burst from his own eyes. He clutches her knees in sorrow. Mummy draws him against her, lifts him up on to her lap, rocks him.

"Don't cry, Mummy," he says in anguish. "I'll help. Where you hurt?"

She cries and cries, drenching his hair. "Your poor little sister," she says at last, muffled against his head. Her breath. He hasn't got a sister. Jealousy burns in him. He pulls away. Mummy says, "You would have had a little sister or brother."

FOUR

THE SMALL PORTHOLES in the control cabin of the vimana were annoyingly blurred, not quite translucent, like an out-of-focus lens. They were designed, of course, for the cryptic optical system of ambulant vegetables, their Venusian designers and crew. Face pressed close to the damnable quartz, Jan Seebeck snarled under her breath, wishing for the intuitive interface of her dark energy craft, *The Hanged Man.* Soon enough, she assured herself, I'll be back in my own ship. It should have repaired itself by now.

She stepped back to the controls, which looked simple but were only marginally more intelligible. The flying saucer sauntered in its leisurely fashion toward the orbit of Mercury. She and a team of vegetable engineers had modified the vimana's operating system in a way she still didn't understand, because really it had been *The Hanged Man*'s suggestion that somehow rewrote elements of reality's core rules, briefly opening a Schwelle large enough and weird enough to let through a spaceship from the Venusian galaxy to this universe of Son o'Star and its riled inhabitants. The limitations were severe, though; they'd had to start from Venus, there was no way to jump straight from Earth to Mercury. The Shintoists must surely be in hot pursuit by now, but they were running very silent indeed.

"Two more hours," her tattoo told her. At the corner of her eye the fairy nudged itself free of her bare upper arm, luminous blue wings beating into a blur, hovered above the controls. At some level below her conscious awareness, the vimana's cybernetics were linking with Jan's Vorpal grammar. Thought control, in effect. She shrugged. Easier than trying to conn by hand while peering through what seemed to be the bottom of an old Coke bottle.

"Thanks, sweetie," she said. She settled uneasily on a stool designed for a calla lily with legs, sort of, hitching up her short skirt. Sylvie floated across the panel, settled on a plastic nipple jutting from the surface, caked with dried ichor, bent as if to drink. "Honey, I don't think you'd like it. It's sort of plant fertilizer."

"Give me a break, Toots," the fairy told her, looking over a slender shoulder. "Not as if I'm really here, you know. We're both going cabin crazy." The psychonic projection bent its head again, sipped at the foul stuff, or seemed to. Jan shuddered, squeezed her eyes tight. Her familiar was right; cruising from Venus to Mercury in a flying saucer that seemed to have been snipped out of sheet metal and soldered together by a class of incompetent slum technical school fourteen-year-olds was far less enthralling than screaming at close to the speed of light back to the Solar System from the enigmatic Xon star her family had once mistaken for the appalling black hole at the center of the galaxy, *Sagittarius A**. At least then you had temporal dilation to help the time pass or at any rate to squeeze time into a smaller package. She sighed, put her head in her hands. Bristles stung her fingertips; her hair was growing out, and she didn't know what to do with it.

A rustle like dry leaves blown by a damp breeze, or perhaps wet leaves blown by a dry breeze, brought her head up. The

Venusian Stalwart entered from the cabin where it had been estivating. It had a certain military bearing unusual in a tuber. Jan gave a languid wave.

"Warrant Officer Pjilfplox," she acknowledged. "Had a nice rest? We're nearly there. Couple of hours at the most."

The faint smell of manure was stronger now, and she tried not to wrinkle her nose. One man's meat, she told herself. Still, it was unnerving; the thought of her sister Maybelline locked in sexual embrace with one of these creatures was positively disturbing. The fairy darted at her ear, whispered, "While we're doing clichés, live and let live, huh?"

"All right, all right, already, Sylvie," she muttered. Sometimes the psychonic projection was as irritating as having a dime-store psychoanalyst perched on your shoulder.

"I am refreshed," the saucer's pilot told her, the sibilant mushy. "Has your vessel communicated with you as yet, or you with it?"

"*Hang Dog* remains stealthed, as instructed," Jan said, slightly testy. "The last thing we need at this point is a squadron of Zealot warriors buzzing around us like wasps." She hopped off the stool, jiggled her gold Lurex tights, looked around for her jacket. "I hope the same proves to be true of this old tin bucket." The jacket, soft pale-blue baby Ichthyosaur leather scaled so finely it gleamed even in the saucer's dull light, lay wadded up as a pillow at one end of her inflated sleeping bag. She knew perfectly well that the vimana was undetectable by any technology likely to be available to the Bar Kokhba culture, but something perverse in her drove Jan to goad the plant when it went military on her ass. Turnips and asparagus in uniform, it was like something out of Charlie Dodgson, how could you take it seriously?

"This humble vessel," said of the Venusian warrior

reproachfully, "is a state-of-the-art war machine. It is true that our methods of construction are not as—"

"Now look what you've done," Sylvie said. The tattoo settled on the console, and folded her head under her wings, as if embarrassed.

"Oh, shut up." But Pjilfplox could not see the fairy, except as a motionless tattoo on Jan's arm, and was now doubly affronted. "No, no, not you, sorry, look I'll just go away and have something to drink until we get there. Give me a yell, okay?"

"But there is nowhere to go outside this cabin," the warrant officer said. Clearly there was more it would have liked to have said, but it was unused to civilians. It blustered on: "And it would not be wise to partake of intoxicating—"

Jan put her hands over her ears, pulled a face, and took herself off to the sleeping bag. It was maddening beyond measure to have Schwellen closed to her, but what could you do? Try to open a doorway to another world this far into empty space, and the unimpeded Xon radiation flooding from the direction of $SgrA*$ would block your effort like a palm shoved in your face. You can't get there, anywhere, from here, that was the rule. Generally speaking, anyway. She'd done it once, somehow, utterly mysteriously, escaping to Juni's nano-encrusted retreat from a previous engagement in this Solar System with the children of the Bar Kokhba civilization that had built her dark energy starship and then, frightened out of their wits at her return, had tried to nuke her into oblivion. Sometimes she wished she were clever, like that Lune girl. One of these days, she'd have to find out how that had worked. Maybe good old *Hang Dog* had been thinking about the problem, whiling away the boring hours on orbit near Mercury. Or maybe that kid August would provide some fancy answer. She snorted, face turned to the hull, eyes closed. Fat chance, the boy was green as a spring apple. But cute. Very cute.

From her shoulder, the fairy Sylvie said: "Bad girl. He's your brother."

"Nag, nag, nag," Jan murmured, drifting already into the sleep of the terminally bored. "So he *claims*. Never heard such a whopper . . ." Her whisper faded into silence and the rustle of leaves going about their business.

Something wet and rather disgusting brushed her ear. Jan jolted up.

"Kindly attend," the vegetable said diffidently. "Our craft is under attack."

"Oh goodie." She struggled to her feet, recoiled instantly from the manure-scented damp of the deck, scuffed the soles of her tights on the sleeping bag, and jammed her toes into her boots. Pretty boots, but perhaps not ideal for combat. Still, it was all in the wrist these days, machine against machine, nothing to do but watch, half the time. "Action at last," she said anyway, just to suit the mood of the moment. "Have we heard from the *Hanger* yet?"

"The ship is probably masked by Mercury, perhaps at the libration point. To be short: might be unable to see us."

Something smacked the vimana hard, like a firm clip over the ear from an old-school disciplinarian. There'd been plenty of them plying their trade in the yeshivas last time she visited the Messianic Shintoists of this universe. No reason to suppose they'd have mended their ways in a mere two or three generations; these guys were traditionalists to a fault. The sleeping bag skidded away around the curve of the cabin. Jan and the warrant officer tottered, managed to remain upright without clutching at each other, to Jan's considerable relief. The psychonic fairy came off her shoulder, hovered in her left visual field.

"The old bucket won't last ten minutes with the stuff they're throwing at us," Sylvie informed her, patched into the control system of the Venusian flying saucer. Of course Jan could have bypassed the interface, plugged her own Vorpal grammar directly into the system, but she hated to have other people's software squirming around her brain stem. Especially when the other people were aliens. Friendly aliens, true; allies in the Contest, standing shoulder to shoulder, or shoulder to pistel, or whatever, against the K-machines and their presumptive gamemasters or mistresses or whatever the hell—

"Well, come on, *show* me!" All Jan could see projected in the three-dimensional bubble that now filled half the cabin was a blur of scribbles, something a child might have done with crayons, a whole box of them. The visual system of the tubers operated by different rules. Presumably all this was a magnificent tactical and strategic map laid out for the benefit of the warrant officer. If so, that worthy was instructing its craft by more subtle means than speech. Or speech that she could understand. The bubble seemed to clear as Sylvie performed prodigies of transformation in the map state-space. The saucer icon hung in the center of the display, surrounded by grid lines, astronomical reference points, indices of the planets and moons and asteroids and dust lanes of the Solar System, with a muted icon showing the Sun altogether too close for comfort. Five attack craft moved on vectors that were not at all encouraging. A list of the weapons being deployed snapped down as Jan ran her eye from one enemy vessel to the next. Particle beams, lasers, rail-gun bombardment (that had been the impact, she saw, deflected at some cost by the vimana's mercury-orichalcum defense field array), maybe even the craft themselves if they were in suicide-martyr mode. Shit, surely it hadn't come to that. But they'd been pretty pissed when she stole their Kabbalah ship and took off for a little trip to investigate the Xon star.

The charged particle beam locked on to the saucer and would not be shaken off. In the display the saucer tilted; despite gravity adjustment, Jan tottered. A line suddenly joined her borrowed craft and one of the enemy: she knew the great crystal at the base of the saucer, between the three landing balls, was blazing its terrible weapon. The red enemy ship jerked visibly, could not evade the beam. Abruptly, it was gone. Jan felt sick. She was glad the display was decently schematic, that the portholes did not show her the destroyed vessel, the expanding shell of gas that had been human lives. Yes, they were trying to kill her, but really they had every reason to be pissed. Four lines struck from the remaining war craft, touched the icon at the center of the display. Instantly, the wall of the hull began to glow: dull red, crimson, yellow, white. It started to dribble, blazing droplets splattering on the moist deck. Jan gave a yelp, flung herself into complete registration with her psychonic projection, and through Sylvie with the saucer's communication and command structures. The pilot was there already, of course; she apologized hastily, stepped sideways in the virtual command tangle, sent out a shout at the speed of light for *The Hanged Man*.

The hole in the hull went violet, burning her out of focus, wide open eyes, and peeled into blackness. Air rushed out with a whistle, then a whine, then a howl. Even in her distraction, Jan's habits reached again and again for a Schwelle, an opening into one of the infinite number of universes where she was not under attack. Nothing happened. She shook her head like a small dog savaged by a large dog. Light-years distant, unmasked by a planet's bulk and atmosphere, the uncanny radiance of the Xon star clamped its prohibition upon her.

"Trapped me, eh, you motherfuckers? We'll see about that." She clung to the crystal pole in the center of the flying saucer, gasping for breath as air rushed into vacuum. Frantically, she sought for emergency life support. Nothing, not even a glass bubble to pull over her head or a brass bra and panties to keep the airlessness at bay. Her shout to her starship continued in a roar of radio frequencies and modulated light. The illumination inside the vimana, always dim, wavered and seemed to fade. No, she thought, that's just me.

"On his way," the fairy told her, and folded up limply into a tattoo on her arm.

Light exploded inside the display bubble. Mother Angelina, she thought, the bastards are hitting us with everything they've got. No quarter given. Who needs K-machines with refusnik allies like this?

She lunched away from the crystal pole, eyes streaming and bulging, chest aching, wrapped her arms around the startled warrant officer. "It's been fun, toots," she said. Her voice sounded thin and unconvincing in the thin and almost unbreathable partial pressure. "Too bad we—"

Four red stars bloomed and went out. The great light flared a second time. Something struck the flying saucer hull, which rang like a great bell. The deck jolted, throwing Jan to her knees.

you appear to be having some difficulties, the voice of her Kabbalah ship said inside her skull. *i am bringing you aboard.*

"You do that, you great lug," Jan said. "I hope you haven't been wasting your time out here. I expect a full report on the Xon—"

In the display bubble, *The Hanged Man* floated above them like an elaborate golden Menorah ablaze with candles, or a Tree of Life. It wrapped arms about them.

Jan allowed herself to pass out.

FIVE

ENSEMBLE SUPERIORE MORGETTE Smith's Daughter scowled, took a small vanity mirror from her shoulder purse, propped it on the table, muttered. The mirror curdled. Something unnerving happened. Here I was in the room of hysterical people crouched under tipped tabletops, weeping, gasping, out cold, with the doorway blocked by a large smoldering heap of scorched Chicken McNuggets, redolent of frizzled bat wings, and really that was nothing special, just a ferocious carnivore of unknown species put out of its misery in double-quick time, but what set my teeth on edge and raised the hackles of my neck was a blunt-fingered hand, nails not especially clean, poking up out of the mirror and reaching around like Thing in the Addams Family. It's strange, in retrospect; I'd seen people come through mirrors before, I'd done it myself for that matter, but this was utterly out of context. This café was a place you dropped into for a quick Dr Pepper and a lamington.

Before I could utter a moan, Morgette had hold of the fingers, gave them a tug, seized the emerging wrist with her left hand, and put her back into it. An entire arm jerked forward across the table, jammed at the shoulder, and then did the thing that actually freaked me out. Somehow without the frame of the mirror changing its dimensions, the shoulder came through, an ear, part of a badly unshaven chin, and now there was the whole head, neck, shoulder, arm, cloth cap jammed down over the eyes. The hand pulled free, reached up blindly, pushed the cap back, and a pair of whimsical eyes regarded us.

"Come now, this ain't very comfortable," said James Cooper Fenimore, the Disposal Man. He caught sight of me with my mouth gaping. "Ah, the Seebeck lad. I was sorry to hear about your great-aunt's demise but cheered by the return of your parents. Always a silver lining, eh? Now come along, if you please, there's work to be done."

Doubting my own sanity, I grabbed the machine under the arm and helped Morgette haul him into the coffee shop. At the interface with the mirror, his torso distorted like an image in a different sort of mirror, the kind they used to have in funhouse tents, according to Aunt Tansy, who was old enough to remember such antiquities, except that she wasn't, she'd never really existed, she was some sort of imposture, a mask my mother had worn in her period of hiding from the deformers, as my father Dramen absurdly wore the implausible likeness of a gruff old Labrador dog. The Fenimore caught for a moment at the hips, gave a wriggle, popped out and slid across the Formica table, much heavier than a man of his size, and crashed to the floor. Morgette put away her mirror. The machine got to his feet, straightened his cap once more, made us a bow.

"Another fine mess, eh?" He cast a swift look around the room, took in the pile of cooked offal, drew a familiar gadget from one baggy pocket. "Nothing we can't set right in a jiffy," he told me, reassuringly.

"You're rather quick to assign blame," I said irritably. The few remaining customers were clambering over tumbled chairs and tables, past the counter with coffee machine and stale treats, headed for the staff exit. I wondered why campus security wasn't here already, sticking their noses in. The hubbub grew louder in the foyer. "It's not as if I invited the damned thing in."

"As to that," the superiore said with a sniff, "I rather think that's exactly what you did. Rumors abound, young man. You're making rather a name for yourself as a troublemaker."

I stared at her. "Good God, Madam," I said. "If you cast your mind back thirty or forty seconds, I think you'll find that I was the one who just saved you from being eaten by that thing."

"Jammervoch," the disposer said, whatever that meant. He sounded like a man with a cold clearing his throat. Yammervogk? "You'll find the beastie had *you* on its menu, 'less I miss my mark." He did little hop, touched his cap, muttered, "Beggin' your pardon and all." He fired up his gadget, which this time emitted a harsh red beam. With practiced ease, his hand played the beam back and forth, up and down, paring the remains into seething blocks of muscle, melted and concealed fat, bone blackened at the marrow, scaly pelt peeling and worthless.

"Why don't you just, I don't know, make it disappear? Haven't you got a ray for that? Something green or indigo perhaps?"

"All in good time, sar," the machine said, patient as ever. "Neatly done is how it's done."

"*Bewahre doch vor Jammervoch!*" Lune said in a sepulchral tone, eyes dancing. "*Die Zähne knirschen, Krallen kratzen!* Good advice at any time, August, but you seem to have done just fine without any tips from us." She took up my left hand, the one still sticky with chocolate, and licked it clean, while the Ensemble woman turned away with an air of unendurable tedium. I felt my heart melt and had to force a certain gruffness into my tone.

"You're talking nonsense, love. Unless that's Russian. I speak Australian and a word or two of American, but no Russian." I knew as the words came out of my mouth that I was the one talking nonsense. The Vorpal grammar that suffused my nervous system had been my on-board Babelfish in more than one alien and indescribable universe. It was all too new. We put up barriers of inattention and denial when shock grows too grievous. I knew that was what I was doing now; something in me sensed the need to distance myself in facetiousness. Lune responded to my mood.

"It's not Russian, you fool, it's Estonian. I thought your family were Estonian aristocrats back in the day?"

"Peasants, I reckon. Piss-ants. Not a president among them." But that was the old August's history, the tissue of lies that had wrapped me safely for two decades in a grimy Melbourne suburb at the top of the hill in an old house where sometimes, in the evening or the dark of the night, people like Lune and my sister Maybelline lugged dead bodies of machines somewhat like James Cooper Fenimore but less polite and far less agreeable, and left them in my great-aunt's bathroom. I sighed.

"Allow the mirror again, would y' kindly?"

Morgette fetched it out again with an ill grace. "I don't want it covered with blood," she said.

Coop shoveled the seeping stuff, bit by bit, through the mirror and into some other universe. I couldn't work out why he didn't open a large Schwelle in the floor and kick it in. I could probably have done it for him if he'd asked. The situation was beyond me. I watched the machine push the last of the guts into the mirror, handed him a paper napkin to clean the glass and the plastic rim. His hands were bloody up to the elbow. Out from the anodized tube burst another handy ray, slurping away the sticky mess from his fake skin, then the disposer was spraying the floor and walls. Where the beam bathed the remains of the Jammervoch, an invisible brush seemed to paint the last of the flesh, blood, and lard into nonexistence, like a wonderful household detergent as advertised on TV. I'd seen it before; I still didn't believe it. Weary enough to tumble straight into bed and sleep for a day, I watched blue light play over the smashed and splintered door, repairing it like a double exposure. I took Lune by the hand, pushed open the repaired door, pulled her after me into the lobby, where, for some reason, everyone stood or sat in a sort of unattending daze. I knew that when the machine was done, none of them would remember anything of their fright, the monstrous thing that had walked among them, the still more monstrous beings who had confronted it. The green ray would see to that. They were pieces in the game, nothing more. I refused to accept that. A month earlier, that had been me. I felt sick, and it wasn't from the meat of the Jammervoch.

"I have to spend time by myself," I told Lune.

What were my emotions? I could not have told you. A mixture of anger without a target, vexation, frustration, bafflement to the very edge of a nervous breakdown, maybe. I loved her wildly, I knew that much, she was the center of my life, somehow, and I had to be apart from her, at least for a time.

"Let's meet at Toby's," I said. My brother Toby—part of me knew, shiveringly—had died, as had my brother Marchmain, as had Lune and my father Dramen and my mother Angelina, yet now they lived, somewhere, enigmatic as ever. I had been the target of deformer malice, yet they had died, as I had died, in dreadful pain, and then been snatched back from death. So now I proposed airily to meet up with a dead man and a dead woman, this dead woman in front of me, alive with a brilliant joy. It was impossible. It was the case. "Give me an hour. Or two."

The beautiful woman kissed me lightly on the lips, her fragrance in my nostrils dizzying. "Okay, my best beloved," she said, not looking a whit put out. "I'll make sure his back garden is clear of termagants."

SIX

AUGUST RAIN SLAPS the louvered windows of his back veranda sleep-out, cold Melbourne winter wind bangs at the tiles on the roof, slips chilly tendrils through the edges of the rippled pebble-glass louvers. He has jammed them as tightly closed as possible, pushing the flat aluminum levers, but they are not designed to be airtight. Not like a spaceship air lock, he thinks.

In his woolen pajamas, snuggled under sheet and blankets, he leafs again and again with unbelieving joy through the pages of his birthday present. He'd asked for it by name, knowing there was almost no chance they'd buy it for him, despite his artful mention of the title at key moments of opportunity. He turns swiftly past the opening pages with their boring chapters and drawings of ancient war rockets fired by absurdly clad Chinese and Indian soldiers from ships and boats crewed by men in mad squashed hats, past the chapter on jet cars and Robert Goddard's liquid-fuel rocket, past rocket launchers slamming into Nazi tanks and U-boats, the V-1 flying bomb streaking across an English town, modified to become the U.S. Navy "Loon" hurtling like a fat bird from the deck of a ship, and finally, finally the marvelous V-2 rocket, blazing fuel, tearing into the sky. And then, flip, flip, the Moon!

A great winged spaceship braking in flame and debris upon

the Moon's scarred surface. A spherical space station hanging above the mighty curve of the cloudy Earth. Rapturous joy, that incredible spaceship canted on its landing props upon the ruptured surface of Phobos, the immense glowing peach globe of Mars filling a third of the sky, vast blurry dull-green webwork of canals, small men in space suits setting up their instruments. What a spaceship! Like an Aussie Rules football, a double-pointed oval but with the ends squared off, a rocket engine at each end for ease of maneuver, four great landing legs tipped with shock absorbers. It was like nothing you had ever seen.

And at last, explorers laden with equipment treading into the frozen methane of the moon Titan. Saturn and his tilted rings glow like gold in the green sky, three quarters of a million miles away. He closes the book, closes his eyes, draws in a deep, cold, winter breath. That's where he is going.

How many more years before he can grow up and become a spaceman, before we'll have these great ships? Ten? Twenty? What if he must wait until the year 2000? Impossible! Almost half a century off in the future. He'd be an old man. He'd be . . . fifty-six years old. For a moment, the pressure of that thought seizes him. He clutches the book, at its stiff cardboard cover. How old is Grandpa? As old as fifty-six years? Mummy is . . . thirty-six this year, so Nana and Grandpa must be even older than fifty-six. It is impossible to imagine them wrapped tight in glass-fiber spacesuits. Impossible to see them on the icy-cold surface of Titan. It will happen sooner than that. It must happen sooner than that.

The wind rises outside, pulling at the empty branches of the fruit trees, knocking them against the wooden fence. When he was a little kid, he thought that sound was ghosts or monsters. He'd hidden under the sheet, pulled up the blankets around his head, breathed his own hot breath into the safe, dark space between his chest and the bedclothes. He'd muttered prayers to ward off those menacing creatures. When he made the mistake of mentioning this, they'd taken his comics away. *Superman, Batman, Strange Adventures*—thrown into the garbage bin, they'd rot his mind, they'd make him nervous, maybe it was true, after all, he did have nightmares, he did fear the things under the bed.

So now he kept his favorite comics hidden away in the narrow space between the top of his wall-mounted cabinet and the low roof of the sleep-out. He could push his treasures back out of sight, and only his own small hand, reaching in carefully, fingers extended, could hook them out.

He opened the cabinet door, carefully put away his birthday copy of *Rockets, Jets, Guided Missiles and Space Ships*. He listened keenly; no voices in the kitchen. He drew out his stolen copies of *Brick Bradford*. It made him guilty to pilfer them from newspaper stores all along the tram track from school to home, although he made sure to replace all the other stolen comics within a day or so, read so carefully, never bent, that nobody would know they were not brand new. The newspaper stores really lost nothing, he'd worked it out in careful detail, except for these ones that he could not bear to replace.

Suppose some other kid came in wanting the latest *Superman* comic, and it wasn't there because the day before he'd slid it into his bag. Well, true, the man lost that sale, so it looked like his sin of theft had hurt the newspaper seller, stolen his profit. But wait a moment. There were always other kids coming into the shop, and who was to say that this second kid, the next day, two days later, wouldn't be just as anxious to buy the copy just returned? Newspaper sellers only ever ordered one or two copies of any single issue, so if someone *had* bought that copy, if he hadn't stolen it the first day, the other kid would've just gone to a different shop to buy his copy. It all worked out, as long as you read it and returned it very quickly, before it was out of date.

He teased out his six or seven guiltily prized but truly thieved, unreplaced, copies of *Brick Bradford Adventures— The Greatest Adventurer in All Space!* He'd already read these same stories in the newspaper, where you only got one strip each day, alongside Dagwood and the others, and he'd carefully scissored them out and glued them into a large scrapbook, making his own comic. But some days the newspaper wasn't brought home, or the comics page was used to wrap up vegetable peelings, despite his stricken cries, and sometimes his scissors slipped and made a bad cut, or glue leaked out from one edge and stuck the pages together, so they tore when he opened it next.

No, there was nothing like the real thing, page after page of beautifully printed pictures and words, the dream of flying the Time Top from star to star, world to world, flinging the great, red, whirling spaceship forward into the future or backward in time, or maybe into worlds that went sideways. Brick had a young friend on his adventures, a stowaway kid called Cricket, a bit of an idiot really, but about his own age. So it was possible. You could go into the Chronosphere—that was the correct scientific name chosen by the inventor of the Time Top, Dr. Horatio Southern and his daughter April—and leave everything familiar behind you.

He spread the comics out across his bed, pulse beating. The wind clattering at the louvers were the time winds. Here was "The Monsters of Planet Plattner," with a dreadful creature displayed in the great, spherical visiplate, above the levers and dials of the controls. Here was a thrilling underwater realm of aqua people with fins and gills, riding great fish. Here was a cover and story that truly had terrified his nightmare mind: "The Quest for Crystal Q," with its little oriental men rising out of the stark landscape inside hidden glass-and-steel watchtowers that resembled mushrooms, their great sucker weapons flung out to capture Brick, snapping on to his back and clinging like those leeches in the warm summer dam water, ugh. "The Prince of the Black Planet." The world of pirates, where one entire continent on an alien world stared blindly out at space like a skull, with islands below it shaped like crossed bones.

And most dizzying and delicious of all, "The Sargasso of Space," an astonishing and dismal place where spaceships and jet jalopies of dozens or hundreds of different worlds had become trapped by the flat gravity of two competing stars, unable to break free. And yet you could fly there, light as a butterfly. See, there was Cricket on the cover, arms extended, zooming above the access deck of the Time Top, weightless, delighted, astonishing Brick. I could do that, he thought. I could fly in space. Well, in fact, anyone could, without gravity. That was the trouble with comics, they weren't really accurate. Those controls, those levers—would they really work?

His movie projector hadn't worked, not the way he planned. He thought of the convalescent hospital where they put him because of the polio scare when he was five years old, after his tonsils were taken out, he turned six while he was there, no school for months, wow, that was exactly half his life ago, he was way behind in reading when he got back, didn't really understand what they were doing in add-ups. He hated it. He hated being there. They made you wear a sort of dress or nightie, not even pajamas, except for the older boys. Nobody came to see him, it was too hard to reach, the train didn't run that far, they had to wait for Grandpa to drive them in the car he used for work. One of the older boys wrote a letter for him, because he didn't know how to do writing yet. *BRUNg mE a KAr.* They came on his sixth birthday and gave him a beautiful, red, tin, double-decker bus with real wheels that turned, and one of the big kids grabbed it the moment the visitors left and used it as a skate, so it got all crushed down and bent and the wheels were broken, and everyone screamed laughing. Things like that always happened, and they did rude things to each other's bottoms, and the nurses didn't even notice.

He got them to move him into the next room when a kid in there got better and went home. He was tired of being in a cot with barred sides that pulled up, like a baby, and wanted a real bed. Finally they let him switch rooms, but two strong nurses came in and pushed him in his old cot into the new room, where some other kid had taken the spare bed already. So now he had to make all new friends, and he was still in the cot. But he did get one of the nurses to help him build a movie projector, because he'd designed it and he really, really wanted to try and see if it would work. First he had to get some paper you could shine the light through, and all they had was this thin, gray, waxed-paper stuff, so he cut a long strip of that and drew stick figures one after the other down the length of it, each one slightly different, and he got an empty bathroom tissue roll, and then he had to get the nurse to bring him a lightbulb on a cord, and she said he was a silly thing, but he said the light would go through the paper and down the tube and out onto the wall, but they'd have to do it when it was getting dark, and she brought the lamp in and they set it up while all the other kids peered at him, and he dragged his drawings down in front of the light, and all you saw was a stupid blur. Oh well, said the nurse, I never thought it would work. It should have done, he was sure.

Now that he thought about it, he felt embarrassed. How stupid. Obviously, he needed a lens to focus the light, and a shutter, and transparent stuff to draw on, and probably other stuff. But he'd only been six, after all. He had much better ideas now. Him and some other kids had worked out how you could build a gun and get your enemies without anyone knowing. You made this thing sort of like a slingshot, but it would have magnets all the way along, electromagnets that only went on when you connected up the battery and pushed a button, and the magnets would drag a metal nail along a groove faster and faster, and then the magnetism would switch off when the nail got to the end, and the pointy nail would shoot away without any noise and get your enemy. First of all, they had to get some wire and some batteries. Next week.

Footsteps in the kitchen. He scooped together his comics, jumped up at the foot of the bed, pushed them into their hiding place, skinned back under the sheet as the door opened and Mum said, "What's this light doing on? You're meant to be asleep. You have school tomorrow. Don't think you can stay home because you're too sleepy, either." But she gave him a quick kiss, tousled his hair, flicked off the light, shut the door.

In the darkness, he wished he had a little radio. A crystal set. There was a place in the vacant lot where you could dig down and make a tunnel, and nobody would know it was there, and you could imprison your enemies. You probably needed concrete, because otherwise the tunnel might collapse, but one of the kids said his dad had some in bags, you just had to mix it with water, so that would be easy. When you had your enemies down there, you could try shooting them with your gun.

SEVEN

EARLY FEBRUARY AFTERNOON sun was broiling hot, as you'd expect, and I found myself wishing for a straw hat of the sort common in bush paintings of the Heidelberg School. I was quickly sweating under my dark shirt and jeans. Goth black is stylish enough, but not especially adapted to Melbourne summer. I found a shady tree beside the South Lawn greensward that covered the staff parking lot, sat on a handy chunky hewn stone, pulled off my shoes and socks, dumped my feet in the recirculating channel of faintly chlorinated water. The cool ripples soothed me.

Once is happenstance, twice is coincidence, or so an overweight old vet named Mike had told me in Chicago during my year of high school there. But three times, he said, index finger pressed knowingly against the side of his nose, is enemy action.

Yes.

"Enough," I said. "Enough already."

I raised one bare foot, placed it against the hot, rough stone, gripping its pitted surface with my toes and hiding the sigil impressed into the flesh of the sole, propped my right elbow on my knee, my chin on the knuckles of my gloveless hand. Auguste Rodin's *Thinker*. Enough-ish thought.

A native bird was making a noise above me, shaking the leaves. I scarcely heard a note, then noticed the fact. I snorted at that reflection; it seemed to me that I'd been doing a lot of that lately: ignoring things, putting aside all the absurdities great and small, the glitches, the changes that snuck past me (dear God, a whole new month, named after me), everything except Lune and me, in bed and out of it, walking the worlds just for the fun of it, in love for the first time, for me, at any rate . . . shoving it all into the too-hard basket.

An epithalamium forbidding sadness, Lune had told me one day in a sweetly melancholy mood that somewhat undercut her meaning. I didn't actually take her meaning at the time, having no idea at all what an "epithalamium" might be. Medical studies were rather narrow in my time and place. I looked it up later, of course, yahoogled it off the Net: a rather recondite wordplay on a couple of poems common to my world and one at least of hers. ("A Valediction Forbidding Mourning" by John Donne and a wedding poem for some chums by any number of old dudes from Sappho and Catullus to Edmund Spenser, if you must know, and I'm damned if I'm going to quote any of them now. Well, maybe a piece or two from Donne. "So let us melt, and make no noise," was sort of our motto during those horny, besotted days, except for the part about making no noise. He had some other wise words that seemed freakily appropriate to our peculiar situation as Players in the Contest of Worlds: "Moving of th' earth brings harms and fears; Men reckon what it did, and meant; But trepidation of the spheres, Though greater far, is innocent." The earth moved all right, and not just under whatever bed of opportunity we found ourselves hot and sweaty and languorous within, atop, beside. Every choice to be made, it seemed to me in my fright, shook an earthquake or tsunami through the very spheres of heaven, innocent or otherwise, that all-but-infinite plenum choking the four Tegmark levels of reality with their seething abundance of

life, of suffering, of joy. End of parenthetical aside.) Our epithalamium had just about run its course, it suddenly seemed to
me. The verse was broken. The gaps in the logic were showing
through. For a ferocious moment, I felt like finding Lune,
grabbing her by the shoulders, and giving her a good shaking.

"Something funny, lad?" A shadow fell on me in the mottled
shadows of the tree's leaves. I looked up, still chuckling.

"Just imagining myself covered in bruises, Coop," I said.

The machine regarded me without further comment. A
human might have asked for elucidation or, embarrassed,
changed the subject. James Cooper Fenimore, by profession a
disposer of slaughtered machines, or so I'd understood from the
little I had seen of his work, stood in the hot sunlight in com-
panionable silence. After a time, he plucked out a stinking old
briar, thumbed in a plug of his rank tobacco, snapped a match
against his thumbnail, fired up blue smoke. One or two students sunning themselves on the grass a good dozen meters
away wrinkled up their noses and stared angrily. Coop was
blithe. I choked a little myself, withdrew my hand from my
chin and waved uselessly at the polluted air. Just another
absurdity, a machine sucking down the poisons and stimulants
of a drug designed for organisms. But then, what did I know
about the internal workings of a mechanical being like Coop?
I'd seen part of the robot guts of a flayed despoiler stretched on
an autopsy table in my sister Ruth's mad-scientist laboratory,
and the thing seemed a blend of subtle mechanism and flesh,
bone, blood: an android, perhaps, as they use the word in TV
shows. A K-machine, I had been informed. The foe. Maybe the
Red or Black team in the Contest, if we were the White pieces.
That's what it was, the dead thing Lune and Maybelline had
dumped in my aunt's bathroom for disposal by Coop—a
K-machine, or at any rate that's what it was called. M y ignorance

was all but universal. Here was the chance to remedy at least part of my defective understanding of the many worlds.

"Coop, what's the *K* stand for?"

Instantly, the machine told me, knowing exactly what I meant: "Killer. Killing machines. Foul things."

"Hmm." It seemed unlikely, somehow. Too easy. Like a children's cartoon. A shiver went through me, despite the sweaty heat. That was pretty much exactly how my own life had been turning out. Deliberately, I turned my thoughts away from that direction. A melodious note rang out overhead. I glanced at the golden sandstone pinnacle of the clock tower above a heavy, granite, Gothic cloister built in, oh, 1930. One o'clock. Hickory dickory dock. The clock struck one, I thought inanely, and down it run. I shivered again, and another little convulsion went through me. There it was again: I was nothing better than a mouse, a blind mouse, on the run, and the farmer's wife was running after me, menacing and terrifying and not at all comical, waving her sharpened knife.

"So was that Yammer thing one of them? I didn't see any—"

"No, sar. Wild beast from an ugly world, 'tis all."

"So someone picked it up and put it down next to me, next to Lune, just to be a nuisance?"

Acrid smoke billowed about us, trapped by the leaves overhead. Coop regarded me with a friendly eye, fake teeth clenched on the meerschaum pipe's stem, said nothing. All hints and no substance, like some sort of damned programmed learning course in how to fight demons.

Really, I knew nothing about my foes other than scraps and hints. No killing machine had presented itself to me like some two-handed engine from a special effects movie or the pulp magazines. Something had smashed Tansy's house, the sweet center of a turning world to which I'd returned again and again, growing up, after my parents had died in Thailand. Except that they hadn't. A snare and a delusion. But something had broken that house open and slaughtered Sadie Abbott, an innocent woman I'd once suspected of being just such a foe. Instead, she'd been nothing more than what the theater students call a spear-carrier. A placeholder. A Pawn or less than a Pawn in the Contest of Worlds. Except that, again, she wasn't; she was a human being, with memories, grouchiness, devotion to her silly church, and to my aunt. And someone or something had swatted her like a fly on a kitchen table, no, worse than that, had killed her without noticing, without caring, without pity, without anger as far as I could tell. And yet they thought of themselves as exquisitely emotional beings, more so than humans.

As an afterthought they'd killed my faithful old dog, Dugald O'Brien, dear faithful Du Good, and then I'd—and then I'd—brought him back to life. The least an honorable son could do for his father. And a while later I'd blown a dreadnought crew of the bastards out of the sky. Presumably. I never saw them, just the boiling mist of volatilized metal. In a different sky. A sky of a variant Earth where the Players of the Contest of Worlds, as far as I could tell, went to school under the tutelage of an artificial intelligence called the Good Machine which once had done genocide upon all the humans of its own world, Ember's home page, so to speak. My mind jumped away from the lunacy of it all.

I glanced up at Coop, standing placidly in the sun. What's a nice machine like you, I thought, doing in a place like this? I remembered Ruthie's derelict factory full of odd robots like lethal toys in what seemed to be a deserted city in a recently deserted world where the wind blew old newspapers and candy wrappers in the dusty streets beyond the grimy windows. And understood in a moment of shocked clarity that the disposer device standing before me was no construction of Ruth's nor the work of any member of my family, despite the fact that the Good Machine was the evolved fruit of my brother Ember's feckless research in manufactured minds. If so—the implication caught me like a blow to the belly. I hunched for a moment, pressed my forearms to the muscled flesh under my ribs, drew in a gasping breath. I wanted to run away, run away.

"You were one of them," I said. My tone sounded flat in my own ears, not accusatory, not terrified. "You were a K-machine. Whatever the fuck that is. And my family turned you."

For a moment Coop stood silently. He knocked out his dottle, then, on the lawn beside the cool, flowing water, trod out its coals with his heel, replaced the pipe in his pocket.

"I don't remember, young fella." He started to walk away from me across the grass, jerked his head in an invitation to me to follow. My feet had dried in the sun; I dragged on my socks, slipped on my boots, followed him down the steps to the library. Maybe he meant to show me some ancient manuscript that would explain it all. Or perhaps he was heading for the lavatory, where he'd find a mirror large enough to walk through without needing someone to lever him. I caught up in the main Ned Kelly lobby, where jaded legal students sat at catalog terminals and a fat librarian in a Simpsons T-shirt scanned bar codes and stamped out unreadable tomes. Coop set himself in front of a monitor, placed one small, strong hand on the keyboard, and did invisible electrical stuff that made the screen forget it was part of a library. Images came and went on the flat screen, vividly colorful geometric shapes like the noise you see if you press your thumb into your eyeball. I watched over his shoulder, forcing patience upon myself.

I was teetering on the soggy end of a diving platform that

seemed to be about one hundred meters above a handkerchief-sized bright-blue swimming pool full of screaming, hooting, riotous children who splashed, dunked each other, dive-bombed from the edge, while one or two adults in rubber hair restraints swam doggedly up and down the center lanes and a bored safety officer in a bright-yellow cap sat in a plastic chair and did nothing to quell the bad behavior. I squeezed my eyes shut, opened them again. In actuality, the water was probably no more than five meters below me, but from here it looked like the wet, open mouth of hell. When I turned my head, someone was standing directly behind me.

"Come on, numb-nuts," a boy's voice rasped. I lowered my eyes automatically to meet his, found myself staring instead at a pouty navel. What the hell? I swayed, sense of perspective completely shot. I raised my eyes to the horizontal and found myself staring at James Davenport, who was about twelve years old. He waved his arms in front of my face in a derisive gesture, and my hands came up automatically fend him off. They were a child's hands. I went stock-still, air cold on my wet body.

"You've gotta be fuckin' kidding," I said. My voice was eerie, high-pitched, trembling.

"Hey Miss," Jamie piped, mockery rich in his tone, "August said a bad word. It's all because he wouldn't wear his uniform, don'cha know."

This isn't happening, I told myself. I'm in the Kelly law library. It's all the fault of that—I couldn't decide whose fault it was. Law library? What was that?

"Kick the little pussy off," said the kid at the top of the ladder behind James. His voice broke at the end, cracking into a laughable squeak. He flushed. I recognized him: a fourteen year old, in the class a year ahead of us, Bruce something. He was a nasty shit, and sometime soon, it came to me, he was going to chase

Davers around the playground because Davers was wearing his sister's tutu and pink pom-poms in a gesture of solidarity with my refusal to wear the school uniform. My head spun. Stupid. Hadn't happened yet. So how could I know about it?

Davers muttered quietly, "Come on, August, it's no big deal. Just shut your eyes and jump. We don't want that Brucester prick on our tails."

It came to me as well, then, standing beside the computer monitor, that I love diving, that I spent hours beside the pool in Chicago, and before that in Adelaide, or was it in Melbourne, day after day during school holidays, learning the mass and balance of my growing flesh and bone, the springy bounce of the board, the magic lift into air, body jackknifing, head down, arms like wings or thrust ahead like a plow, flying without wings, eyes open, watching the blue, slicing into water, swallowed up by its womb, pressure in the ears, pressure on the pent lungs, delicious joy, kicking like a frog, bursting upward into air, stale wind gusted out, sweet fresh air drawn in, buoyant in water, stroking effortlessly to the pool's edge with newly strong muscles already starting their growth spurt into adolescence, vaulting up and over, quick, hot-soled, bare steps back to the foot of the concrete and steel diving board installation, waiting my turn with a sort of relaxed eagerness, climbing back into the air, into the sky, into the expectation of joy. It had happened, it was part of me, part of my sinew, part of my very self, it hadn't happened yet, it would happen, I knew precisely what to do. I gave Davers a thumbs-up and a wink, turned to face the water, saw nobody in the water beneath me, bounced in the perfect moment on my toes against the unyielding platform, soared, turned upon my own axis, fell like a bullet, went into the blue. Hardly a splash. Maybe not a perfect ten, but pretty good for a kid having an insane hallucination.

I came up out of the water into my adult body, shaking imaginary or remembered wetness out of my hair, staring at the darting sigils on the monitor screen. My ears still rang with the slight pressure change. Now I recalled that first astonishing, life-altering dive from the high platform into the municipal pool. It had seemed at the time as if I'd been gifted with some peculiar grace, some awareness of the body and its powers attained without learning, maybe somehow just by watching all the experts do their stuff at the pool and on TV. Certainly our swimming coach was taken aback and wanted me to start training in earnest. Mention was made of Olympic prospects. It excited me a little, but my parents told me, regretfully, it was out of the question. I guess they didn't want me to draw any additional attention to myself. When you're flying through the air like a blend of Superman without a cape and Aquaman without the scales, and photographers are taking happy snaps, it's hard to hide or disguise the silvery hieroglyphs that have always pierced the bottom of your foot. Swimming, even diving, at the local pool were okay; gladiator sports were *verboten*. It turned me inward a little, I guess, as loneliness will, but then again, I don't suppose the obsessional life of a career athlete is necessarily a barrel of laughs. And with swimmers, it's a career that runs out of puff long before you reach your full maturity. So I'd had to settle for being whatever I was, I thought with a snort. Shapes twined, spun, danced like a Rucker animation of creatures from the fifth dimension. Maybe that was me, too. A Vorpal homunculus, Lune and my siblings had called me. Whatever the fuck that was.

I still couldn't see what this had to do with the K-machines. I bent down to lean across Coop's shoulder, and a fizzywig of light burst across the center of the screen and took me into a dark, dark place.

Wasn't as dark as I'd thought. The huge movie-ratio flat-screen TV display was showing a sitcom or series drama, and I slouched back in a comfortable leather chair with something cold in my hand. It was a beer, I saw, in a pop-top can. I brought it closer in the dim room, identified it as a Foster's Lite Ale. Not my favorite drink, but good enough for television viewing. There was no laugh track, so this was series drama. I watched for a while. It was *The Gilmore Guys,* an episode I hadn't seen. Loutish Jack was up to tricks again with the girl next door, Robbie was working feverishly to cement his position as class captain or valedictorian or president of the Young Democrats local, while fat Ed was trying to avoid exercise on the high-tech stationary bike Rose had given him for his birthday. As satire, it was middlebrow but not exactly lame; as drama, it was *Leave It to Beaver.* I reached around for the remote, sighing, and a man in a beautiful dark suit with the palest-blue shirt and a narrow silk tie bearing unicorns and lions *couchant* stepped in front of a camera, in the middle of the screen, and said, "August, you're the sorriest excuse for a Godiva ever seen."

I blinked, as you do when someone addresses you from the TV set, unless you're dreaming, of course, in which case it seems perfectly normal, and glanced down at myself. Fully dressed: T-shirt, cargo pants, track shoes. I blinked again, taking it in on internal replay. Not "Godiva." The man in the TV screen had called me "the sorriest excuse for a god I've ever seen." It made me angry, perhaps unreasonably angry. I took one more swig from the nearly full can, belched, pulled back my right arm with its gloved hand and threw the can as hard as I could at the screen. I winced as it struck, expecting glass everywhere. No, that was old technology. The Fosters can rebounded from a sheet of robust plastic-covered pixels, flew across the room spraying beer and foam, clattered on the floorboards. The shot angled on the man's hard, classical features. He shook his head slightly, disapproving or disappointed. His gaze was radiantly intent. I couldn't look away but I was still furious. I reached around blindly for the remote, found it. My thumb hammered the off-button. At the edge of vision, I saw the remote's red light flick off, on again, off, on again. The man watched my antics as if he could see me from the far side of the screen.

I found my voice. "What bullshit is this? Has Somebody up there given me a promotion? Med student one day, Vorpal homunculus the next. Then on the third day, after rising from the dead, they decide he's a god." I laughed, and it instantly stuck in my throat. After all, hardly more than a week earlier I had indeed been killed, then salvaged, somehow, in disgusting pain and anguish by a real god or reasonable facsimile, an Angel from the Omega Point at the culmination of a collapsing cosmos somewhere in the heartland of the Tegmark manifold. I wondered briefly where Cathooks had got to. Still running backward to the dawn of time, I supposed, like Merlin in that old book.

"The new improved edition." His scorn was withering. I leaned forward, squinting.

"Okay, I get it. You're one of these KKK-machines. Hey, aren't you morons meant to be wearing white sheets?"

I guess I knew that he couldn't reach through the screen, seize me by the throat with hands and sinews of steel, and choke me until I was dead (again).

"Impertinent insect." The K-machine was female, her face unchanged except for the subtlety worked in humans by the possession of an extra X chromosome rather than a Y, somehow crueler, more implacable and, if possible, still more ardently ferocious. Her hair was pulled back from her forehead, businesslike, and her dark suit fitted her exactly over a white blouse buttoned at the neck. It was frighteningly apparent that she still wished me dead. Passion blazed in her machine eyes. "The worlds are in a condition of Theomachy, and you attempt your feeble wit."

"I have no idea what you are talking about, but you look to me like something a human being with feeble wits like mine cobbled together on a bench, then threw out in disgust, and it wandered off before the trash guys could haul it away." The thing said nothing. I said, "You still haven't told me what the *K* stands for. Our friend Fenimore here tells me it means *Killer*; it seems appropriate enough, you cold bitch."

"Interesting. Perhaps you know more than your apparent ignorance discloses. We K-machines descend from Arbeiters, nanotechnological cornucopias, Santa Claus machines—"

I think it was about to go on and tell me about its famous lineage, but, scared as I was, I burst out laughing.

"Oh my God. You're *K* for *Kris Kringle* machines! This is like, what? Earn good money in computer repairs? Home study for the New Era?"

"We are *Kriegspiel* machines," she told me, ignoring my feeble wit. "In that respect," she added, "you and I are alike. In no other." She shook her head in disbelief. "'Cold' . . ." I could hear the inverted commas. I had no idea what the thing was talking about. For that matter, I had no idea what a Kriegspiel machine might be, except that it had a Teutonic sound to it, maybe Nazi, or maybe that was just my prejudice against killing machines showing. Schwellen. Jammervoch. Kriegspiel things. It was like a nightmare from the middle of the twentieth century. Fuck it anyway, this was all some sort of dream. Nightmare. Virtual performance conducted by James Cooper

Fenimore—ridiculous, laughable name—in the lobby of the law library where I had no business being, halfway as I was between medicine and philosophy. Oh. Oh shit.

"I was right. Fenimore *is* one of your creatures." No, really *not*, that made no sense at all. All right: "Was. Then he came over to our side, maybe the pay is better, excellent conditions, good working hours lugging machine corpses back to Ruth's lab through the mirror, but even so, you've still got your little back-door links tucked in there under his rug. Poor devil. I'm starting to seriously wonder about my family."

"Stop your maundering, Mr. Seebeck. Shut up and listen. This is information you need and that we wish you to possess. A most unusual concurrence of interests. It is unlikely to recur."

I stayed perched on the padded edge of my imaginary chair, leaning forward in the dark, fascinated and repelled. This was something, sort of   I couldn't put my finger on it. Milton, maybe. Satan yacking to Archangel Michael or Uriel, whatever. Or perhaps an upmarket executive business negotiation. The thing had the appearance now of a small, feral, ten-year-old of ambiguous gender, which slightly undercut the effect, but it still wore the suit for the role.

"Yeah, yeah. You've got ninety seconds to make your pitch, then I'm switching back to *Gilmore Guys.*"

"Memorize this." A complex image replaced the machine's face. There was no obvious focal point. I saw a bunch of circles annotated with words in different colors, lines connecting the circles. No time to take any of it in, although I had an instant, creepy, unconscious sense that names were there inscribed, names I recognized, or ought to. Decius, for one, in the upper-right corner. I had seen Decius just once, wrapped in what looked like a sheet from the bed, ablaze in glorious reflected light from the singularity at the end of time, the Omega Point, the fount of the godthings, the Angels. He had been a man of middle age attended by another, younger man, presumably not of the Seebeck clan, although who could say—our parents had apparently proliferated like rabbits.

The image vanished. It hung for a moment in reversed afterimage against the empty screen. An instant later, the display flickered, showed me a library menu. Coop rose easily from his chair, pushed it aside, said, "Thank ye, sar. I'll be on my way now. If I see the cat, I'll be sure'n let him know you asked after the old fleabag."

I let him go. Why not? I needed to do some more maundering, as the K-machine had called it, before I returned to Toby's world, and Lune. A young woman in pink overalls and a pink-edged overbite was waiting rather impatiently for access to the catalog and rather too closely to my elbow. I nodded to her, stepped away, bit my own lip, and went back out into the sun. The clock was now striking three; it was hotter than ever away from the shade, and the hard, dark shadows had lengthened visibly.

Being footloose in infinite worlds was undeniably fun, and sharing the company of a brilliant, beautiful woman who gave every indication of being as madly in love with me as I was with her—what's not to like? A life of adventure, a whole new family of squabbling maniacs, creatures trying to kill me at every turn—who could wish for a more bracing fate? I had fallen into a comic strip. And nonetheless, something nagged at me, some foolish scrap of dissatisfaction. I stood stock-still, looked it in the eye, recognized it for what it was: homesickness. All this headlong rush and excitement and danger and passion, not to mention startling and unexpected insights into the nature of reality, it wore upon a man. I wanted to go home. And I couldn't. Yes, I could revisit that old house in Northcote, but all

I'd find was ruin piled on ruin, smashed timber, shattered glass, piles of broken brick, and large pools of water where the aged pipes had snapped like old bones. Nothing there of home.

I wandered in some confusion through the paths and one-way internal streets of the campus, head down, lost in a turmoil of thoughts and feelings that had no obvious resolution. I walked along Monash Road, headed east, mid-afternoon shadow preceding me, turned right instead of crossing into Faraday Street. A large, green tram rattled past in the middle of Swanston Street. That was comforting, somehow. It was a sound I associated with childhood, with my parents, with a safer time. My hand felt bare without the glove. I glanced up briefly to take my bearings at the Grattan Street lights. Green; I crossed. An uneasy sensation went through me like a chill. I couldn't put my finger on it. Chicago . . . ? Up ahead, a van was parked outside a needy office, sliding door pulled back. Two men struggled with some white-goods item, a refrigerator, maybe. I trudged along in the hot sun, glad that it was their job and not mine. One of them was short, stocky, dark-haired, the other was pudgy, red-faced, balding—incompetent, by the look of things. A dolly sat uselessly on the pavement. They had their tilted cargo jammed into the van's side opening, the back edge firmly planted in the black asphalt. They struggled frantically with it as I approached, muttering to one another, plainly at their wits' end. A familiar silly impulse took command of me. As I passed them, I leaned my head confidentially toward them and said, "You want to be careful there, fellas, you wouldn't want that thing to get stuck."

I heard a noise like an explosive sneeze, glanced back over my shoulder. The red-faced man had let go of the equipment, which remained jammed in place, and was leaning forward with his hands braced on his knees. The short man stared at him, then at me, and burst out laughing as well. They roared together. I gave them a cheeky wave and kept going, flushed with a curious gratification. Had I tried that little stunt in Chicago rather than Melbourne, one of the guys would have hit me or, worse still, said in a tone of affronted menace: "*Excuse* me?" I heard the last gusts of laughter at my back and knew I was home. My tight shoulders relaxed; I had not realized my tension. I needed a beer and maybe a game of pool with some guys I'd never met before upstairs in Johnny's Green Room. I glanced left, started to cross the road, and somebody tried to run me down.

Even before I identified the car coming directly at me on the wrong side of the street, I was crouched, right arm extended and braced on my left hand, a word of power at my lips. A millimeter-wide beam of Force 12 wind struck the left front wheel, flung the car sideways. Another vehicle hit it, passing the wrong way on the other side of the street, flung it back toward me before veering away to pile into a parked car pointed in the wrong direction. Everything was wrong. I said the word that opened a pathway to the Sun. A middle-aged woman passenger was staring in hysterical fright at me through the windshield as the dented car came at me. The driver had disappeared. No. The numb, white-faced woman whose mouth was opening in a scream I could not hear *was* the driver, her hands gripping the driving wheel. I jerked my own hand aside, shut down the scorching solar fire, but the briefest burst of plasma at twice the melting point of steel had already licked one back wheel. The hub and axle glowed incandescent. Rubber and polyester cord burst into flames, evaporated instantly into stinking fumes.

Somehow the gasoline tank failed to tear open and explode. The car crunched past me with millimeters to spare, hit the curb, bounced, spun away, jammed the fused, cooling wheel rim onto the tram tracks. A Prius. On the far side of the street, light traffic veered to avoid the Silver Top taxi that had hit my would-be murderer. I found myself back on the sidewalk, legs trembling, making sense of the senseless. *Everyone* was driving on the wrong side of the road. Nothing else had changed. The buildings were familiar, the overhead power lines, the neon signs on the scruffy shops, the tall spires of downtown office buildings a kilometer or two to the south. And people were driving on the left, like the Brits do even to this day, instead of the right—as *we'd* done, for that matter, before the Australian Republic was declared in the excitable days following the assassination of the American president, Bobby Kennedy.

Whatever. Somehow I'd got myself in the wrong universe, and in my paranoid carelessness had come close to killing an innocent. At least my stupid mistake had not occurred in two or three hours' time, when this road would be thrumming with traffic heading in both directions as fast as they could manage. This time I looked right instead of left, saw an approaching car slow to avoid hitting the brutalized Prius, and then I ran to the driver's right-hand door. I wrenched it open, reached across her lap, slapped the release button on her seat belt, dragged her out of the car. The back axle was still dull red with heat. If the goddamn fuel tank had broken open during the several impacts, it could explode at any moment, just like in the movies. Luckily, I couldn't smell volatiles.

I dragged the shocked, weeping woman across to the sidewalk, propped her on the ground against a dirty brick wall. People were coming out of buildings, agog, avid for some afternoon excitement. One in a cardigan and sensible skirt appeared to be a nurse, probably from the nearby school of nursing; she took charge of the distressed woman with a curt nod of thanks in my direction. A tall redhead youth in a backpack and a T-shirt informing us of the exploits of MUFF DIVERS—an engineering student, by the look of him—was explaining to a storekeeper that the car had been hit by lightning. The storekeeper glanced derisively at the empty blue sky. The student asked him haughtily if he'd ever heard of heat lightning and static discharge. I decided there was nothing I could do. I couldn't give the poor creature a new car, but probably her insurance would cover the damage. I walked away, feeling sick, wondering how the rules of the world could be changed behind your back, no notification required, history rewritten. For God's sake, it wasn't just the traffic regulations and rules of the road, somebody had jammed a completely new month into the calendar, and they'd named it after me.

This wasn't my world any longer. And I missed my dog, Do Good, terribly.

I looked around for a telephone box, but they don't make those anymore. I found a shadowed alcove, made sure nobody was watching me, opened a Schwelle, and stepped onto the low hill overlooking Toby's dwelling. Nothing tried to kill me, which made a nice change. I walked shakily down the hill, looking forward to a pot of tea and some scones. My brother Toby—assuming he were still alive, assuming he were at home, assuming he was still talking to me—had an arrangement with an excellent pastry cook in a conveniently time-dislocated world, and his strawberry jam and whipped cream were to die for, almost.

EIGHT

THERE IS ONE who asks: What is the Tree?

One answers: In the multiform variora of the Linkollew Scriptures, a single icon persists as universal, central, august in significance, potent in force: the Tree.

The Tree is the *Axis Mundi,* the Omphalos or Navel of the Many Worlds, the Yggdrasil. It is the font of existence, the exfoliation of infinite realities, the trunk against which the Child braces his back, from whose great branch dangles the sublime and indifferent Hanged One.

The Tree is the Tree of Knowledge of Good and Evil and the Tree of Life.

The Tree is the algorithm and the expression of healthful growth, of computational complexity: the essence of the K-machines.

In the Tree is combined burgeoning abundance and responsive selection, activity and rest, left and right, back and forth, the uppermost and the lowermost, the green in the blue, root and leaf, death and life.

In the Tree is joined Past, Present, and Future.

The great Tree, the Yggdrasil, is the single thread winding through the haze of probabilities that is the greater Cosmos.

The Tree is the Xon.

There is one who asks: In whose martyred blood, ichor, and other circulating fluids is the Tree watered?

One answers: Oh, get a grip.

NINE

A YELLOWED SCROLL, possibly in vellum, unrolled at both ends and pinned to the wooden door of Toby's cottage by bright, new thumbtacks, asked me to forgive my brother's absence and invited me to make myself at home. The calligraphy was beautiful, hard, masculine, flowing without fuss. Beneath his words, Lune had added in ballpoint: "Sorry, called away on duty, back soon. I love you. L."

I glanced over my shoulder at the autumnal peace of the glade. Nobody in sight, Golden, brown, yellow-green leaves blown everywhere, no sign of footprints or worse. I put my hand to the carved wooden doorknob, entered the place carefully. Too many people and things had been trying to kill me lately.

An odor of black tea, warmth of coals in the fireplace. The indefinable emptiness that speaks of a deserted house. My mouth tasted sourly of burned Jammervoch, faintly disgusting now the humor of the moment had passed. I threw myself down in a well-padded leather armchair, drew my knees one after the other up against my chest, unlaced my shoes, kicked them off. My socks stank, and so did my armpits, now that I thought about it. Fright does that to you, I've found. It has nothing to do with courage or resolve; the juices of the body rally to our need, and good for them, I say. I thought of taking a shower in one of Toby's miraculous bathrooms, but it wouldn't be as much fun without Lune. She didn't mind the stink of combat; actually, I think it turned her on. Nothing fastidious about my warrior love, I told myself, for all her doctorate in ontological computation, or computational ontology, whatever the hell that was. I reached down and peeled off my socks as well, wrinkling my nose. Sweat and a faint tang of chlorine. The air lazing from the fireplace felt good on my spread, naked toes. I leaned back in the armchair.

I woke with a jolt, looked about. Afternoon light came golden through mullioned windows. A lick of red flame stood above a fallen log in the fireplace; the crash of its settling had awakened me. The room smelled of me. Still nobody home. I went to the bathroom adjoining the guest bedroom Toby had made over to Lune and me, threw the rest of my clothes in a heap, doused myself for a quarter of an hour in warm down-flooding water from some tropical world far, far away.

Toweled to a fresh rush of blood in my tingling skin, wide awake and hungry, I padded back naked into the living room. It was strange; I'd spent only a day or two in this household, had learned here my passion for Lune and hers for me, fought a creature at least as terrible as the Jammervoch, a thing built like a storm of wasps from a million small feral parts that came together in a single cruel mind, blew the filthy fucker into soot and stench with the power of the dreadful thing that had been embedded into the flesh of my palm. Yet the place already felt like home, or as near as I'd come to finding one since the deformers had destroyed the old house where I had lived with the being—could she truly be my mother?—masquerading as my Great-aunt Tansy. That was before I had learned that I was a lost piece, or perhaps Player, in the Contest of Worlds. Whatever *that* was. Too many unknowns. Nothing but confusion.

No, unfair. Far more than that. My flesh sang with my infatuation, my besottedness, my love for Lune. That made it all worthwhile. I would pay the price of confusion, gladly.

At a loss, unclad, I wandered through Toby's unexplored house from room to room, opening doors, glancing inside, learning again how much larger this small cottage seemed on the inside. Away from the fire, the air was cool on my skin. I frowned. Why doors anyway, why corridors? Toby was a master of Schwellen, those gates between realities and parts of realities. They had fetched the machine Fenimore through a mirror, like some robotic Alice in Looking Glass territory, had brought me here from my own Earth. The shower I'd just enjoyed, for that matter, was a Schwelle artifact, gushing sweet water from some alternative reality that Toby had found and turned to his use. Why, then, build a house with doors, when the utterance of a word of power might take you anywhere you wish? Maybe the place was not of his design, perhaps it was a delightful *objet trouvé* abandoned, with this whole Earth, by its owners and inhabitants. And yet the watery domain of the Sibyl Avril, my creepy astrological sister, was surely tailored to her every specification.

I turned at an L intersection, found myself in an unexpected nook framing a large, plain, pale door without a knob or keyhole. A triangular copper or perhaps bronze plate stood embossed in its center. Well, hell. I poked it with one stiff finger, like a doorbell. Nothing rang. No gigantic mastiffs bayed on the far side of the door. My fingertip tingled. I pressed my whole palm to the plate, felt a jolt from my Vorpal implant. Soundlessly, the door slid open.

Impossible morning light flooded across the great cedar staircase extending down from the landing beyond the door to a floor of polished white and burnt-sienna stones in a chessboard array, a large, formal space decorated principally with suits of mediaeval armor catching glowing light from the immense leaded windows to left and right. Beyond, I saw lovely formal gardens. At the far end of the space, a pair of great doors patterned with the pyramidal heads of iron bolts stood closed.

I was hardly dressed for the occasion, but I felt as if I were in a dream. I went down the cool steps, crossed the marble silently, stood before the doors. Again, why doors in a world of Schwellen? Symbolism, I told myself. Ancient and grave. Once more I found no latch, doorknob, keyhole. Knocking on those great timbers with my knuckles was not going to cut it. The nearest plate-steel suit was outfitted handily with scabbard and sword hilt. Probably purely decorative, but hey. I flipped up the visor of the empty suit. Sightless eye sockets of white bone looked back, toppled toward me, skull clunking against the inside of the helmet. I dropped the visor with a clang.

"Christ! Don't *do* that!"

After a shivery moment I reached out again, raised the visor, prodded at the skull. The jawbone had fallen down into the neck of the suit; all sinew, gristle, skin had been eaten by decades if not centuries. Maybe the soft tissue had oozed and dripped down into the leggings and armadillo footwear, greaves, sabatons, whatever they were called. Must have read that somewhere. He'd been dead a long time, although his suit gleamed. I closed the visor again, left him to his long sleep.

So it wasn't really theft. I took the sword's grip in my right hand, lifted the blade against slight scabbard resistance, felt the sword slip free and come beautifully into my grasp. Good grief. "My name," I muttered sarcastically, "is *not* Arthur. Trust me." Nobody said anything. Nobody home. Okay.

I raised the wonderfully balanced mass of the sword, making

sure not to slice off any tender parts, brought it above my shoulder, and beat thrice, heavily, on the closed double door.

It opened like the wings of a bird in a dream.

Darkness was all, within.

I stayed where I was, at the threshold.

Of course, some light entered in there from the great windows. I narrowed my eyes. Something hung in the middle of the air, in the midst of the darkness, above an expanse of deep-varnished wooden flooring smooth as silk. It glowed with an uncanny radiance close to the end of the visual spectrum: ultraviolet, something like that. It was a polygon of rare device. It reminded me weirdly of a shape I'd seen during my high school year in Chicago.

"Good God," I said, and lowered the sword by my side. "It's a Susan B. Anthony dollar coin."

It wasn't, of course, but I had recognized the form. Josie Todd had teased me with it, since its design seemed so abnormal for a piece of negotiable currency designed by the severe custodians of the Mint. Approximating a circle, one vertical line running across the top, straight lines of equal length tracing the rim, to the flattened V at its base. Now my eyes darted, counting the number of sides; eleven, as I'd thought.

I stayed put, skin growing chilly. You'll never get me into one of those newfangled devices, I thought in a dizzy moment of self-mockery. Or perhaps I muttered the words aloud, because the polygon—what had Josie called it? an undecagon? a hendecagon?—tilted in the air, obtuse angle toward me, hardened like glass or crystal, hung waist high. Ghostly figures sat on simple benches, one at each sharp-drawn edge of the floating polygonal table. Was it brighter now inside that room? Had my eyes adjusted? The figures were clad in antique apparel, some fanciful blend of Elizabethan finery and moody *fin de siècle* styling from Aubrey Beardsley. There was nothing of the twenty-first century, at least of my version of it, in their 'dos.

It was jolting. These were my brothers and sisters. My eyes darted, and I caught my breath. They were motionless. A sort of hologram or diorama, a high-tech family portrait. My parents— *our* parents—were, I saw, absent. Nothing new in that. I gazed from face to face, putting names to those I'd met, however briefly.

At the far side of the room, facing me directly from what I couldn't help but regard as the head of the table, was the Seebeck sibling everyone had kept assuming was my father. Really, I didn't see the resemblance. Good-looking, I guess, in a sly and self-satisfied sort of way.

To Ember's left, from where I stood, which is to say at his right hand, sturdy Toby sat. Dread Septimus, all shoulders, wild gray hair restrained by a gold circlet, pent ferocious masculinity, stared into his golden chalice. A premier vintage presumably, or maybe some roughgut more appropriate to a warrior in charge of a hell world. At my leftmost, Marchmain gazed at his siblings in a fine ironic humor. The Reverend Jules, arrayed as a bishop in some gaudy Eastern rite, completed the male contingent to my left.

Directly before me, where the great hendecagon came to its closest angle, I looked across the shoulders of a woman I took to be the one they called Juni, and beside her the stocky young woman named Maybelline, whom I'd caught lugging a dead body in through the window of Great-aunt Tansy's upstairs bathroom. It seemed a lifetime ago; in reality, whatever that meant—well, by my body's own clock—I'd found Maybelline and Lune about their gruesome business with the terminated Deformer no more than two weeks ago. Incredible.

I squeezed my eyes shut. I was naked, and cold, and holding

a sharp sword in my lethal right hand, and I couldn't make all of this go away. I clung to the image of Lune, the one person I didn't see at this spectral table. Well, of course, luckily, my beloved Lune was not a Seebeck. Incest, at least, was ruled out. I glanced again at Maybelline's beefy shoulders and smiled. No temptation there.

Avril, at Maybelline's right, appeared to be addressing what remained of a large steamed fish, reduced to bones, head, and tail. To my rightmost, Ruth, the forensic librarian, maker and unmaker of robots and strange whimsical mechanical things of all kinds, carver of dead deformers, sat straight and gazed to her right with a look of intense disapproval. Understandable enough, in such a tight-ass: Jan, my wonderful space pilot sister, was the only one not dressed for the table. Her ensemble appeared to be something she'd thrown together by grabbing at random in a thrift store run by and for tasteless blind holdouts from a half-century ago.

Admittedly, that was a very provincial assessment. For all I knew, her garb was the height of fashion in whatever strange cognate Jan made her home, when she wasn't tearing around the Solar System in borrowed flying saucers or hunting for her lost dark energy starship. I liked her a hell of a lot. Actually, about that incest thing—if I weren't madly in love with Lune . . .

Beyond Jan, and bringing us all the way around once more to Ember, I recognized with a jolt the man I had last seen transfigured, wrapped like some damned prophet in a white bedsheet blazing with a reflected light of Angels, in the high places of Yggdrasil Station, at the boundaries of spacetime where time and space closed in on themselves, smashed together into Xon foam, birthing the godthings that had retrieved me from pain, anguish, death. And those I loved with me.

I squeezed my burning eyes shut, heart clutched in

remembered terror and gratitude. My mother and father, Dramen and Angelina, lost and found again, had died with me, broken in the colossal firefall of one world flung into another by the might and deranged hatred of the K-machine deformers. And now were gone again. Players in the game, the Contest, the enigma at the heart of the computational cosmos. Or maybe just scurf and trash flung on the surface of the frothy and entangled quantum foam. I supposed that Decius remained pent there, at the fountain of reality, basking in the worshipful vision of the godthings born from that Omega Point catastrophe. Or triumph.

And where was I supposed to sit, with no place for me at the table of my brothers and sisters? On the floor with the cat? Oh, that's right, they hadn't known about me back then, when this family shot was taken. Well, fuck that. I stepped across the boundary into the room. It was cold, cold.

"Why, hello, folks," I said cheerily to the holograms. None of them looked my way. You couldn't blame them, they were only photographs, after all. But I was pissed. "I had to step outside for a moment, you know, a decade or two while I was growing up. Allow me to introduce myself. I'm August. Not Augie, nor Gus. August Seebeck. Your brother, can you dig it?"

Something terrible happened. The world crushed shut like a deck of cards and splayed open again, as if a cardsharp had riffled through the stars and plucked a spare one from his sleeve, adding it to the pack. The Joker, I shouldn't be surprised. The table contorted, bulged slightly, like an optical illusion opened a new angle between Avril and Ruth. An empty bench stood before the empty space in the . . . what was it now? Dodecagon.

Oh dear Christ. The great floating crystal table now had twelve sides. Had *always* possessed twelve sides. Just as the calendar had always owned and displayed twelve months.

I leaned forward, dizzy and sickened, leaned with two hands clenched on the hilt of the sword. After a time, I straightened, walked further into the darkly ultraviolet room, stopped before the empty bench. A golden plate was in place there, with silver utensils, a crystal chalice awaiting wine, another filled with clear water. I looked across the table into the ferocious gaze of Septimus. It'd be enough to put a man off his meal, I thought, and found myself grinning.

"That's mighty neighborly of you," I told the diorama, or the entity or subsystem or whatever the hell was behind it. "I'd love to stop for a chat, but I don't seem to be dressed properly. Have you ever had that dream? You know, late for the exam and you've forgotten to put your pants on. Time to wake up now, August."

Like a cunning illusion in two parts, the second more subtle and extraordinary than the first, the diorama flickered. Septimus was gone. In his place, directly across the reconfigured table from me, sat a small woman in dark robes, heavy long black hair piled in a bun and clipped with silver. Her eyes gazed into my soul. An instance later, the second part of the illusion caused me to blink and grunt. Avril had been seated at my left, Ruth at my right. Now they sat across the table, flanking this woman I had never seen in my life, presumably one of the family. I glanced incredulously to either side. Marchmain now at my right hand, Toby at my left. What the *fuck*?

Morgette had mentioned the name Septima. Superiore Septima, one of the founders of her own order. Of course this was her. Sister of Septimus, presumably. Perhaps his twin. I glanced again at Marchmain. Now he appeared to be smiling directly at me with a look of faintly disdainful pleasure. His work? Not impossibly: he had taken my parents, Dramen and Angelina, and torn them in four. Had rebuilt their segmented psyches into illusionary partial manifestations designed to evade the scrutiny and malignity of the K-machines. Presumably, then, this was his doing as well.

Was it possible that Septimus, a walking archetype of potent masculinity, was Septima in a new guise? The idea made me dizzy.

The diorama folded together, then, cards back into their box, and the table floated vertical, symmetrical, twelve-sided, hung there for a moment like a highway sign that some idiot had forgotten to paint the directions on, and faded into the darkness. I pulled the tip of the sword out of the timber floor— I'd been leaning on it pretty hard there for a moment—and took myself back through the great doors to the place of marble and light, tipped my nonexistent hat to the bone man in the suit of armor, retained his sword for good luck, and tramped upstairs to look for some clothes. With any luck, Lune would be back in time for dinner. Not that I had any objection to Toby as a dinner companion, but it's just not the same, probably not even at a dodecagonal table with gold and crystal settings.

TEN

THEY HAVE DRUNK deep, dancing like fools at a campus ball in the company of giggling and flirty girls in black wispy garments. This is not, alas, *Brideshead Revisited,* nor is it Oxford in the 1920s, *the rare glory of her summer days . . . when the chestnut was in flower and the bells rang out high and clear over her gables and cupolas, exhaled the soft airs of centuries of youth,* but then he was half a world and more from Oxford, burbling as a passenger down Burke Road, Melbourne, in a topless Goggomobile at the height of winter, rank smoke pouring from the driver's briar. The giggling girlets have been returned to their chaste habitation. Burly Dale is crushed into the backseat, tweed-capped Thomas at the wheel. Stunned pleasantly by beer, he gazes with distant terror through the scratched plastic windshield as Thomas accelerates, turning from one major thoroughfare into another, tram powerlines glinting overhead in the frosty sky, the Goggomobile relentless in its trajectory as a huge truck or two bears down upon them, the motor mower engine uttering its roar, the car turning to the right, lights smeared by motion, turning, in fact, rather more than anyone inside it might have wished it to turn, the too-abundantly quaffed booze rising to choke the gullet as the vehicle goes onto its side, sliding gracefully and at surprising speed toward the looming, immovable, steel streetlight pole, the car tipping a little more with each meter so that it is clear it will end up scratched like the blazing head of a wooden match along the road, the curb gutter, into the pole, crumpled, but not before the defenseless mammals inside its roofless fiberglass hull have been decapitated, rubbed to the bloody nubbin, headless torsos crushed into its sardine container, the urbane driver poised through all this prolepsis with perfect confidence, eye clear, pipe puffing like something from Magritte, scarf waving in the gust of their impending deaths. Lurch. Bump. Stop. There are no seat belts. Scrambling across each other, checking for blood and missing bits. There are none. They had been moving quite slowly, after all, by that point. All they had to tell their future children was the slenderest of fables, feeblest of war trophies: the shivering wait for the Royal Auto Club man, in the hungover night, while their borrowed girls, miles behind them in their narrow teachers'-college beds, slept drunken dreams of pointless virtue.

ELEVEN

OUTFITTED IN FULL clerical drag, Jules Seebeck opened a Schwelle. "Give me the bordello." He stepped into a fantasia of perfumes, pheromones, silks, satins, leather, reeking juices. For two and a half hours, he had delirious and gratuitous sex with a red-haired Irish Catholic, a brunette Jewess, a lush, whip-scarred bottle-blonde Zulu drawn from the racist imagination of a plantation cognate, and an equally imaginary choirboy in black cassock and white lacy surplice. Finally, he lay back in a pool of his own sweat and semen, drained, limp in every sense, as always curiously unsatisfied. It was like eating sixteen bowls of strawberry ice cream one after the other: eventually it just became hard work, and your tongue ended up numb. He sniggered to himself. Not so much hard work as soft, now. With a pat to his catamite's luscious buttocks, he dismissed them back into the Star Doll database from whence they had sprung.

"Bathe me," he said, and settled into steaming, fragrant water lightly frothing against a black marble jacuzzi. Two stern Swedish masseurs stood on either side of him, waist deep in the warm bathtub. They scrubbed him with brisk precision, laved his hair, cleaned his fingernails, washed between his toes, dried him with soft towels and warm gusts of air. When they were done, Jules inclined naked on a couch, toyed with the thing in his left ankle. The Xon imprint was cool to his touch, cooler than his own flesh, metallic yet yielding. He knew it was what loaned him authority in this place, among the trillions, quadrillions, whatever awful number of minds darting in the concentric Dyson swarms of the Matrioshka Brain that once, two thousand ago, had been a Solar System. The Seebeck trademark, he thought with some complacency. But no, not really. All the Players of the Contest of Worlds were pierced by such an enigma. It made no earthly difference to him what the stuff was, no, nor heavenly difference, either. He tapped at the thing with a fingernail, acknowledged distantly the temptation, the whisper, the tropism toward complicated action that would unfold as such things did, probably lethally. For some reason, the Vorpal implant fascinated the denizens of the M-Brain.

And here was one of them now, pestering him as his butler put out his fresh garments and dressed him as a lesser aristocrat of a northern Gondwana culture trapped by ice and tradition. Glaciers were funny that way. They stressed primitive humans in just the right way to drive their brains toward invention, community, murder, and dominion. And they locked more complex peoples in the bonds of routine, privation, fancy rituals frozen for centuries. Probably he would have to kill some king or ecclesiastic. Suited him just fine. And this suit of white-and-brown-speckled fur, bone or maybe tooth clasps, snug heavy boots, patiently carved ivory scrimshaw ornaments that clung and clattered, it suited him fine as well. The ambient temperature had dropped, of course, to keep him comfortable instead of sweltering, to prepare him for the transition. The M-Brain representative thing waited silently.

"What? Speak, or may the Snow Lord spit your guts." He was speaking Ungapok already.

The manifestation was slight of build, barefoot, dressed in a pale-brown robe with a hood pushed back. Its eyes were slanted, pupils slit horizontally. Possibly this was a comment on snow glare. Possibly it was caprice or an incomprehensible fashion statement. It spoke the same language in an extraordinarily deep voice that resonated like an oboe.

"The Ra Egg approaches the Omphalos. Try to be back within three days. We expect to be busy." It bowed, turned, made to leave. Jules stared at it.

"What?" The word blurred on his tongue, a bastard blend of Ungapok and his customary language. He forced the imprint to one side, slipped back into his own vernacular. The implications of what the thing had just said were dazing. "Are you telling me the Matrioshka Brain is *moving*?"

Was that a pitying glance? That in itself was hair-raising. The vast composite being which spoke to him was almost always scrupulous in avoiding hurt to his feelings. This was deliberate, then. The thing said, "Apologies, Jules. This information has been implicit from the outset. Yes, we have been in flight to the locus where the Xon star stands in all of the known universes save this one."

"You can't be fucking *serious*. You just took it into your heads to fly an embedded Dyson shell complex several, what, light-years, parsecs, whatever, dragging the Sun along with you?"

The manifestation opened a window filled with blackness and a haze of false-color light. "Rather, the Sun is propelling us." Annotations whispered in Jules's ear. His viewpoint plunged into the image. The concentric shells blazed ever hotter as he tore toward the hidden star at their core. At solar North Pole, preposterous mechanisms ripped at the photosphere with blinding laser light, slashing deep into the Sun. Churned to a fury, plasma and light gouted forth, a flame at least a million kilometers deep. Equations dappled the screen. Something loaned to Jules interpreted them. This was star-lifting; this was a focused mining operation turned to a single ruthless purpose. The star burst forth its own substance, flung forward into the darkness by the flame of its own going.

"How long has this—"

"Some two thousand years. Of course, for the last millennium we have been decelerating. Within several days, the Ra Egg will be at rest relative to the galactic coordinates provided by your sister Jan."

Jules, cold with anger, stamped his foot. Icy snow crackled and spattered; the environment had morphed into climatic agreement with his destination. "And why. The hell. Have you never *bothered*. To *inform* me. Of this small item. Of fucking *general interest?*"

The thing regarded him for a long moment in silence. "You never asked." It drew the cowl about its face, turned away again, stepped into the diagram of the terribly deformed star, left Jules staring in useless rage.

"Oh, come on. Enough of this bullshit. I have someone to kill." He opened the precise Schwelle that the Contest had stacked and queued in his memory, along with the lexicon and grammar of Ungapok and the necessary abbreviated history of those who spoke it, and his task, in fairly nonspecific terms: same old, same old. Canvas seemed to tear; he stepped through into a place, a palace, made all of carved ice. Ten thousand years of packed glacier had been hewn over centuries into a frigid miracle of scattered greenish light and shadow. He strolled from his shaded hollow to join a gathering of nobles and their carls, clad like him against the cold, faces plumper than his and breath rancid with fish oils and the fat of the creatures who provided their coats and the furs he treaded upon. To his left, an ice sculpture reared: a great bear, jaws agape, ferocious teeth transparent and dripping water like slaver. To his right, a rendering of hand-to-hand combat between two overweight thugs thwacking each other with sharp-edged icy bones from something with a rib cage the size of a whale's. He moved his head and hands in the appropriate gestures of greeting, passed with the company into another icy cavern fitted out with furry beanbags and pillows that stank to high heaven. After much rustling, and muttering, and jostling for position, a troupe of players bounded into the cleared circle surrounded by their audience.

Like the furs, the play stank.

For the first two minutes, Jules was busy snuffling after the spore of K-machines. To his surprise, none seemed to be in attendance. Presumably, then, his target was a Pawn in the Contest, one of the onlookers. As the minutes became hours, and pieces of fish and lightly roasted meat were passed among the company by the hosts who, washed down by something he learned from his imprint was fermented human milk blended with blood bowled in the skulls of small animals, he hoped that his prey was the bombastic bellowing buffoon taking the king's role. Or the simpering, fat strumpet who was either the royal heroine or the mother of the dauphin or perhaps the king's squeeze.

Jules rose and circled the audience, found the hollowed trough the men were using as a jakes, pissed into it with a disturbing sense of fragility, circled further, recognized his target. The youth sat inconveniently close to the action, but that would serve the purposes of distraction. Jules slipped in behind him, took a brimming skull of alcoholic blood from the hands of a servant, pushed forward, pressed it and a small quantity of poison upon the youth with a roar of laughter, clapped the lad heartily upon his padded back, slipped away again, took an unhurried stroll toward the shadows. Uproar. The buffoon on the stage shouted more loudly, thinking himself mocked or applauded, who could tell. Women's voices raised in an instant pitch of despair and sorrow. Jules opened a Schwelle, checked his work one final time before he stepped through. The kid was on his face, dead as a doornail, heading toward entropic equilibrium with the ice underfoot. Ah well. Death, you're soaking in it.

He walked away and closed the gate behind him. A butler took his foul, heavy garments, brought him a glass of pale, pale wine—he wouldn't be able to drink red for weeks, he thought—and said, "Can I get you anything else, sir?"

"I think I might have a nap," the augur said. After a moment, he forgot every word of Ungapok, thank God, and remembered the bizarre news the manifestation had conveyed to him. "Hey!" he shouted. "Are we *there* yet?"

TWELVE

"I SEE YOU'RE dressed for dinner," Toby said.

Straight-faced, I said, "If I'd known it was going to be formal—" I felt a jolt of happiness to see him alive, tucked it away inside.

Toby gave me an avuncular, forgiving smile. My brother, to glance at him, could easily be my father. He has a woodsman's look, sturdy and broad of chest, high, suntanned forehead that stretches all the way to a fluffy fringe of white hair at the back of his noble head. *Woodsman* captures only part of the thing, though. He reminds me a little of those Roman senators when Rome was still a republic and had not yet decayed into the temptations of empire, when the men who took their turn in the forum and the army were farmers, quite often, by trade. Still close to the earth. Toby loved his special world, I could tell that just by looking at him and recalling those couple of tramps we'd taken through the falling, mulching leaves of his woods and dales. Leaving aside the ghastly termagants he'd had to kill, once with my own help. But those Roman soldier farmers had battled with foxes and worse in the defense of their crops, their hard-won wealth, the lives of their loved ones.

"I found your sweaty castoffs and sent them to the laundry," Toby told me, then. "You'll find—"

"I'm sorry, I didn't mean—"

Toby waved my apology to silence, and his smile broadened. "Not at all, not at all. I do understand that you are new to this. I've laid out some fresh clothes in your room. Just don't expect this kind of service every day."

I had the sense to leave off my protestations and accept my good fortune and his generosity. I stepped toward him and started to extend my hand, and the weight of the sword took me by surprise. I lowered my menacing hand at once, more embarrassed by the pilfered weapon than by my nakedness.

"Not something you idly tugged out of a stone, I trust?" Toby said, glancing at the blade.

"I should get dressed," I said. I looked around for somewhere to lay down the sword, uncertain of the etiquette involved. Presumably you couldn't dump it on the table or couch, or prop it point down in a corner. "Is there somewhere I can—"

"May I?" Toby did not yet extend his hand; it came to me that a gentleman did not presume to handle another gentleman's weapons of war. But this lump of hardware was not mine, certainly not my tool of trade. I was dimly conscious, as well, of a certain phallic ambiguity in all this. It's one thing to be caught in a dream without your pants, it's quite another when it happens while you're wide awake.

"Of course, Toby," I said, and held out the sword in an uncomfortable gesture, thumb down. Toby took it from me carefully, turned aside, fell with instant grace into some fancy saber posture, sword extended in his rigid right arm. He took a couple of steps forth and back, like kata, and I left him to it.

The garments he'd thoughtfully set forth for me somewhat resembled those I'd worn in this world on my first visit: expensive underwear and calf-length silk socks fit for an Arab prince planning to attend a knighthood at Buckingham Palace, tight-fitting trousers in some impossibly soft leather, ankle boots ditto but with sturdy leather soles, buckled in brass, one of those white Hamlet shirts with baggy sleeves and wide lapels that show off as much chest as a starlet at the Oscars, an extremely handsome deep-green jacket that flared at the shoulder and tucked in snugly at the waist before falling to mid-thigh. I felt like an idiot as I climbed into this stuff, then like an impostor at the Gay Mardi Gras as I gazed into the bedroom's long mirror, checking the fit. It was impeccable, of course. I had no idea how Toby did this; maybe some sort of computerized laser scan had taken my measurements while I showered on my first visit. Still and all, by the time I'd drawn on the jacket, I was feeling pretty damned pleased with the effect. I wished Lune were with me, so I could take it all off again, and her clothes as well. For some reason excellent couture has this effect upon me. Or maybe it's just Lune, and the thought of her glowing, naked, coffee skin.

"You look well in that. I've made a fresh pot of tea," Toby told me when I returned to the living room. "I have placed your blade over there for the nonce." He gestured with his head to something in the corner that looked like a clothes drying rack crafted by a superior carpenter out of pure ebony. The sword, gleaming in firelight as if it had just been lightly oiled—and it probably had been—stretched across its diagonal. Had Toby got the stand made in one of his time-distorted universes? Maybe it was just a little something stored in one of the many rooms of this ridiculously huge cabin.

"Thank you," I said. "And for the clothes. But Toby, I'm sorry about the sword. I didn't mean to take it, it's not as if I have a use for it."

Toby frowned. "No need to apologize to me, my boy. It's a very pretty blade, I'll give you that. Whose is it? I was quite serious about the stone, by the way."

I must have given him a startled look. "Why, it's *yours*. Or the family's. I found it downstairs."

"Pardon? There *is* no downstairs, not here. Oh, you mean in some other—"

A light tap sounded on the front door; it swung open. Lune came in, looking drenched. I hadn't heard any rain. Well, no. She'd come into Toby's world from some different place, some other time, where the so-called Custodial Superiore Morgette Smith's Daughter had dragged her after our messy encounter with the Jammervoch. She shook her head, spraying mist.

"Oops, sorry. It's beastly where I've just been. I should have stopped somewhere and changed. Hello, Toby, it's good to see you again. You're keeping an eye on our scamp?" She smiled delightfully as she said it, turning her gaze to me immediately, as embracing as a hug. I was suddenly glad not to be naked. I crossed the room, caught her up, kissed her soundly. At my back, Toby cleared his throat. I released my soaked bundle.

Scamp. I wasn't really sure I liked the sound of that. It wasn't unfriendly, if anything it was *too* friendly—in the wrong way. The sort of thing a grown-up said of a naughty but promising child. A slight shiver ran through me; I recalled that despite her youthful appearance, Lune was at least twice my age, possibly more. But that was a calculation appropriate to humans, to my old life, to the illusion that was my old life. My life before I learned that I am a Player in the Contest of Worlds, as is Lune, as is my entire family. A Vorpal homunculus, Lune had called me. A construct on the computational substrate of the many-leveled Tegmark cosmoses. Whatever the fuck that meant. She was the expert. Once again, I felt like an ignorant child.

But Lune had taken up my hand, then Toby's, drawn us to the fireplace. Steam rose from her garments. She shivered a little. "I'd kill for a cup of tea," she said.

"Damn," said Toby. "I had a pot steeping. It'll be sour as a witch's tit by the time we're ready to drink it. Let me have your clothes. I seem to have become the local laundress as well as scullery maid." There was no sting in his words, merely a sort of fond amusement. Lune took off her clothes, down to her underwear, then skinned out of that as well, kicking her sandals aside, handed the bundle over. Toby withdrew without a glance. I was dumbfounded but not fool enough to make a fuss.

"I'll get you a towel," I said, and did that thing. While she dried herself to a glow, I slouched in a leather chair and regarded my stolen sword. It felt like a metaphor, somehow, but I couldn't parse it. Probably a good thing that I'd given up medicine and taken on philosophy—I might learn a thing or two. Assuming I ever got back to Room 102 and completed my admission form.

"You seem troubled, August," Toby told me.

"I feel as if I've fallen into a fairy tale," I said grouchily. "A Grimm fairy tale, at that." It was a rotten pun but it expressed my sentiment fairly exactly. I'd had the same realization when I first met my family, or a good handful of them, in Maybelline's Heimat.

"In a sense, that's exactly what's happened. But the other way round." Toby glanced across the table to Lune, dipped his head ever so slightly, as if deferring to her authority. She watched him in silence, tucking a pastry between her lips. He added, speaking directly to her, "You haven't told him much, then, I take it?"

She said, "We preferred—"

I spoke over her in a hard tone. "What we discussed is our business, Master Toby. Think of our time away as a sort of honeymoon." How we conducted our lives was our business, not Toby's, however concerned he appeared to be for our welfare and comfort. Not the Seebeck family's. Call me bull-headed, but I'd walked away before and I would walk away again if need be, if busybody interference were in the offing.

His eyes flicked, automatically I suppose, to Lune's left hand, to my own, flicked instantly to the plate in front of him. Perhaps he shook his head a fraction. Lune smiled, shook her own, said, "We are not wed, Toby. But you may regard us as a couple."

He smiled now broadly, raised his glass of rich red claret. "This much, I am happy to say, is apparent. I wish you, of course, the greatest joy in one another." He quaffed his glass. "I would not intrude upon your privacy, but I feel there are ques-tions teasing at my brother's mind. Would you care to voice them, August? If not, I have one of my own."

I laughed out loud, felt my tense shoulders relax. "I have a thousand questions, Toby. Yes, I put them aside during our . . . *idyll* is probably the word, especially in a fairy tale. Now I'm bursting with the damned things. I intended to plague Lune this afternoon, until her strange friend Morgette put in an appearance, and we ended up fighting a monster that could just as easily have come straight out of one of Grimm's fairy tales, and probably did."

"A Jammervoch," Lune explained. "I have no idea who imported it."

Toby freshened my glass. I left it untouched, tasting again the filthy flavors of the half-incinerated beast. "Madame Smith's Daughter," he said, "is sufficiently monstrous for one day's work. And didst thou slay the Jabberwock?" It came from his lips oddly, like a familiar quotation. Not one I recognized. Shake-speare, maybe? Actually it sounded like something whimsical that might have made its way into one of Lewis Carroll's Alice books in another cognate, or out of it. Hard *j* rather than *y*. *b*'s instead of *m*'s. English *w*, not Germanic *v*.

"They spoke its name differently, but yeah," I said, watching Lune. She added nothing. "Jesus Christ, what the hell is this? Some sort of goddamned fraternity initiation?" My traps, deltoids, and splenius were tight again, my thighs and calves ready to fling me angrily from the table. "Some sort of Dungeons and Dragons quest game?"

The taunt sounded feeble even as I spoke. Hadn't they told me this was a game, shown me that this entire cosmos was some sort of multidimensional board upon which we Players strutted our stuff? That was a preposterous conceit in itself, but I could not deny the memory, the truth of it. I recalled too vividly, too bitingly, our progression through the levels and paradoxes and confusions of the many worlds. I remembered the recovery of my father and mother from the revenants that had masked them in protective disguise for a generation, and their deaths under the assault of the K-machines, and my own destruction and rebirth. It was too much to accept yet it was too vivid, too stony hard, to deny and disown.

They waited patiently for me to work myself through from defensive anger to some sort of acceptance, if not understanding. My brother and my beloved. I was lucky beyond measure, I decided. If you're going to get stuck in a nightmare, make sure you have people like this at your back and your side.

I said, then, "That was petulant of me. Toby, you have a question."

Instantly, he said, "What downstairs?"

"Well, you know . . . the one at, like, the landing. The big windows, the flowering gardens, the suits of armor, the room with the Round Table with the squared-off edges, *that* bloody downstairs." What *was* this? Back to their damned mystery tour again?

Lune tilted her head. "Ah. So you found a door on this floor, and went downstairs, and found yourself on the ground floor with windows looking out onto a garden in full bloom."

It was obviously ridiculous, when you put it that way. Strange how inconsistencies even as great as the one Lune pointed out to me could skid away from your attention simply because each step of the journey had been so real, so unambiguous. In the moment that I realized the nature of the delusion, I saw as well that it was not a delusion after all. I had the sword for proof.

"The door must have been a Schwelle," I said. "It sent me to some other place. Like I said. And that table—you were all sitting around it, your images I mean, except for Lune of course—it, it . . ." I trailed off. I forced myself to speak. "There were eleven sides. Then there were twelve. An empty seat. I presume it was for me." I looked from one to the other, and saw that they were as baffled as I. More so, perhaps.

Toby rose. "Come with me, you two." He led us around a corner into the corridor where I've peeked impertinently into the disused rooms of his house. He walked briskly to the end of the corridor, spun, stood facing us with his hands on his hips. "The door was here?"

"No, I mean the one to your left, at the end of the alc—"

Rather like the jaw of my poor boneheaded dead friend whose sword I'd stolen, mine dropped.

There was no alcove. No door with a palm lock in copper or bronze. The corridor came to a dead end.

THIRTEEN

EVERY TIME HE steps from the air-conditioned blandness of Kingsford Smith airport into the sudden subtropical swelter of Sydney, his heart lifts. After Melbourne's gray-and-dusty-green sedate *politesse,* this great city on the harbor buzzes and roars. A public transportation bus lurches up, belching exhaust smoke. He carries his backpack onboard, pays the modest fee for a ticket to the heart of town. In Melbourne, it would be an airline coach or a taxicab, irritatingly expensive, as if air travel were still the privilege of the wealthy. The sky is a high, brilliant blue even through the scratched windows. They bounce across intersections, plowing through the clotted traffic. Jackhammers stammer. Angry drivers toot their horns. The bus driver sings out of tune, something Italian, something from an opera. He smiles, happy.

From the bus terminal, pack on his back, he walks the several miles through Hyde Park and along the down-and-up, swooping stretch of car-clogged William Street to Darlinghurst, to the edge of wicked Kings Cross. Even in the bright winter sunlight, the huge Coca-Cola sign mounted at the top of William Street runs through its sparkling dance. A spurt of the thirst catches at the back of his throat; he grins at his own suggestibility. He sneezes. The air in Sydney, he has to admit, is full of aerosol crap, worse than Melbourne's, trapped by some appalling temperature inversion effect despite the sea winds off the harbor. Asthma town. He jinks sideways into the maze of streets to the south of the central thoroughfare, wends his way home to Palmer Street, once notorious for its brothels and streetwalkers. History is on the move, and the trendies are moving in. He suspects that he and Em won't be able to afford to rent this big place for very much longer; the demographics are against them. Up the hill in Oxford Street, the gays are replacing the sleaze, bringing color and money to this rough old neighborhood.

Emily is working in her light-filled studio, daubed with spatters of paint, lurid bright specs of metallic confetti in her hair. Grinning, he flicks a piece or two from the tip of her nose, bends to kiss her mouth. She gives him a distracted smooch in return, careful not to get paint on his clothes. He dumps his pack on the kitchen table, brews coffee for them both. The kitty strokes past his leg, perhaps happy to see him, perhaps hoping for a treat. He lifts the cat up against his shirt, strokes her long, soft, Persian fur, checks for knots. Her purring grows louder; her eyes slit shut. It is a perfect day. He realizes, suddenly, to his intense surprise, that it's his birthday. Once, he had anticipated this annual event for weeks in advance. Now, with thirty behind him, midlife forty well off in the future, it seems that one year is like another. Everything important is the same, even as everything changes.

He takes Em her coffee, hoists his pack, runs noisily up the stairs to their bedroom. On the white west wall, where it will catch the morning light, he finds that she has mounted a large portrait of him, his birthday present, rusted old and bright new metal, blurs of paint on twine and canvas, twisting out of the frame like a proof of four-dimensional spacetime. His heart lurches. There is nothing he regrets about leaving Melbourne for this remarkable city, this delightful wife of his. By the end of the year, his protracted long-distance doctorate will be complete. He'll shake off the dust of Melbourne, complete his move to the harbor city. He opens the French doors, steps on to the wood-and-iron lacework veranda overlooking Palmer Street. After a moment, he sneezes, his chest tightens, he sneezes again.

FOURTEEN

IN A COLD passion, the Sibyl Avril Seebeck raged.

"That fool boy! Who ordered *him*?" She flung down her cards upon an onyx table covered in papers scratched with arcane symbols. Finger-worn, hues muted by years of handling, the deck scattered in the air like startled birds, spun and fell, splashed in water. Swan maidens moved to retrieve them, garments drifting behind them. "Three centuries of work! More! Utterly undone. All lost in chaos—"

Ignoring her assistants, she arose, swept like a green storm from her sanctum to the broad staircase, descended its seventy-eight steps to the Great Hall. Beneath her bare toes, the warm, soft gold of the final twenty-two steps was soothing after cold granite, but she stumbled at the final step. Cold as ice, slippery under the balls of her feet. Avril glanced down in renewed irritation. Light struck up at her, prismatic, hard. The final step had changed from gold to a pure diamond.

"Ancient *damn* it!" she shouted. "Juni, you idiot, what have your interfering little brutes done *now?*" But her sister was a Schwelle away, and her nano-offogs safely off the premises, presumably, until the Castle Keep required its next housecleaning. This change was a manifestation direct from the computational substrate. A declaration from the Ancient Intelligence. She looked away from the light-smashing brilliance, stepped carefully to the huge ouroboros pattern in the stone floor of Great Hall, stabbed by an intimation as cold and sharp as a diamond blade. Afternoon light entered the hall from high windows, dimly illuminated the tapestries hanging from the rough stone of the walls. Crossing the inscribed back of the immense World Snake gorging upon its own tail, she called for Blessing Mariel, her Principal Swan.

"Your service, Madame Sibyl?

"Prepare me for *reverie*."

Mariel, usually imperturbable, sent her a sympathetic look. "Ma'am."

Suspended between green and blue she hung, eyes half closed, arms extended, held from immersion and drowning by the lifting, secure touch of eleven swan girls' fingertips in the grand baptismal font of the chapel. Their touch was the merest breath, yet it burned like points of coal at occiput, shoulder, thigh, knee, heel. The young women sang in eleven-tone choir, eerie, atonal, elevating Avril to a mood of cooling detachment, less masking her rage than transforming it to a certain high purity. In the depths of her floating being, she sought communion with the Ancient Intelligence.

"Hear me, Great Mother."

As ever, she waited, senses straining uselessly as she commanded them to quietness, instructed her flesh in the ancient liturgy, felt her way into deep passages of mystery and uncertainty. Here, as ever, awaited the temptation of delusion, self-deception, babblings from the lost child within, mocking sneers, hopeful mutterings derived as much from her strengths as from her weaknesses and vulnerabilities. She emptied the vessel of herself into the nothingness of the void, the void that lifted and sustained her no less than the salt, watery embrace of the font, the burning coals of her swans' fingers. After a timeless time, something approached, placed its own impress upon her. She was the snake; she swallowed herself: knowledge came to her. And its price.

What will you pay for illumination?

As always, the Ancient Intelligence was blunt to the point of malice. Avril tensed, caught herself at the edge of resentment, took command once more of her breathing, slowed her heart. This was the cost; it had always been the cost. She was not sure how much more of it she could tolerate, and yet she was certain that this karmic penalty was both just and in her interests. No great truth might be had free of charge. There were no gifts, not in the Contest universe, which was the only universe accessible to her and the other Players, however infinitesimal that aperture must be—at least in the sight of the gods, the goddesses, the godthings, whatever the hell the Ancient Intelligence might be.

"I am ready to meet the price," she said, words slurred and barely audible in her profound reverie. "May I ask what it is?"

I find you more tractable than usual, the Great Mother told her, perhaps approvingly. *You may choose your fee. I offer you a choice.*

Avril's pulse quickened once more. She was frankly terrified. No rule of reason guided demands placed upon her by the Ancient Intelligence; all was caprice, all was pain or loss fancifully proffered.

"Thank you," she said, acquiescent in word but rebellious in the core of her belly. For months, she had worked in the loneliness of her fastness under the torment of daily headaches that crushed her brain, knotted the muscles of her shoulders and neck. They find me rude and unyielding; well then, let them choose such suffering. Unfair, some part of her protested. Unfair that this burden fell always upon her, never upon her brawling siblings. Least of all that brat, that absurd child of parents she had thought dead. The Great Mother ignored her inner, unspoken reservations.

Here is your choice: a gnawing and griping at your guts—

The Sibyl felt her entrails tighten, the acids of anxiety spurt into her. No! No, this Promethean agony was not to be borne. She cried out: "The other option?"

You must abandon the memory of all you have learned in the last decade. Go directly to jail. Do not pass Go. Do not collect $200.

Mystery upon mystery wrapped around an offer so cruel, so paradoxical, that for a long moment Avril forgot to breathe. And cried out, then, in agony: "I cannot! Great Mother, it is *your* work I do. It is for your glory, to bring forward the day of your triumph, the completion and victory of the Contest. How can I——" Again she caught herself. Meshed with the caprice, the cruelty, some deep, strategic essence was worked in her mind and body, in all the Players, the Seebecks, the Ensemble, the innumerable rest of them. Perhaps, she thought with a shudder, in the deformers, too. That being so, paradox ruled itself out. True, the fruits of her researches for the years passed, perhaps for centuries rather than the single decade she was being asked to forfeit, were spoiled by the appearance of the brat, spoiled and distorted in ways she could not remedy, could not yet detect. So the loss of that work was truly no loss. And yet—

"I—*can't*. How can I give it up? How can I abandon—" Tears flowed from her closed eyes, ran down the sides of her face into the salty, tear-tasting waters of the font. With a gasping sigh, she said, "Give me the pain. Quickly now."

It entered her chest beneath her breasts like a nail thrust into a bed of dragging, hurting weight.

What is your question, child?

For hours she had struggled to frame her question most tactically. Now all that pith and precision was lost. Avril blurted: "The time is out of joint. The center will not hold. What's happening, Great Mother, and why?"

Her senses shut down. She did not gasp and flail; this was her recurrent exclusion, at once a theft of world and an elevation above it, or perhaps, rather, a burrowing deep beneath it. This was not darkness and silence but nothingness. Avril waited.

The Tarot deck shuffled in her phantom hands, riffled face to face. She readied her spirit to lay out the family cards. A table extended before her made all of emptiness and stars. Dreamily, she knew that she must select and put down eleven cards, one for each member of the Seebeck family, excluding her absent parents. A shiver ran through her bodiless body. No, *twelve* cards. The brat. The wretched, disruptive—

The first card she placed directly before her, turned it over, considered its ancient design. Card 10, the Wheel of Fortune. The image swallowed her.

Hanging in space without breath, without the necessity of breathing, she studied the inner Solar System. Here was the Earth, overlapped upon itself innumerably often in the superspace of quantum alternatives, mostly blue and white and lovely, the jewel of life in an empty cosmos. Within Earth's orbit, the hot, white, poisoned globe of Venus curved away. Beyond Venus, the melting, pockmarked, lunar ball of Mercury. And at their center, blazing in brilliant power, the diamond clarity of the Sun.

This was no literal-minded telescopic image, nor was it an astrological convention of the sort she studied every day, seeking to capture vagrant wisps of insight from the deep workings of the Ancient Intelligence. Now she saw the immense, muscled curve of the Midgard serpent, the ouroboros, Typhon's scaled snake, wrapped around the whirling worlds, bearing life and extravagant complexity from the substrate to its material expression. On the far side of the Solar System, a being as great as any traditional god moved in orbit, jackal-headed Hermes, intelligence aspiring forever to attainment greater than mere cleverness. Avril shuddered. A change! Always before this had been Ruth's card; now, distressingly, she found that it was her sister Juni's. And see, here she was, sitting above the display in the likeness of a sphinx, beautifully dressed, a cloud of offogs about her head. Very well: Juni as material Wisdom. The Sibyl felt her non-self ease. This much was unfamiliar but not impossible. This, in the Kabbalah, was now Juni's grounding presence as Malkuth.

Avril drew another Tarot card, the second of the Major Arcana. Her own card, the High Priestess, Veiled Joy flooded her. Formerly, dangerously, this had been Marchmain's card, the Foundation. Perhaps all was not lost. Beyond the image, she watched herself, seated on a throne intaglioed with hermetic symbols, the immense, black-marble pillar of Boaz flanking her right hand, the white-marble pillar of Jachin to her left, life energies flowing between them, cathode to anode. The Moon placed upon her head, moving the waters of the world. On her lap a document containing that which she had always sought, which she might yet attain: the automata rules underlying all four Tegmark levels of the computational universe. Avril unconsciously took one step forward, her hand stretched hungrily toward the scroll. Instantly she shook her head in self-rebuke, stepped back from the tempting image, seated herself once more at the dark table splattered with starlight.

The third card she placed above her own and to the left. No longer Jan as Splendor. Marchmain now, of course. Hod, the

Magician. Her brother was naked under a gaping white lab coat stained with fresh blood. In his right hand he held aloft a scalpel with a red bead upon the razor edge; his left hand stretched down to toggle the controls of the magnetic resonance drum rotating at his back with its terrible noise and auric confusion. In her reverie, Avril seemed to smile. These were ancient symbols, long-antiquated yet standing in good stead for the subtle machines and instruments of which March was master. On the workbench before him stood a grail betwixt an inscribed pentacle, a wand, a gleaming sword with a jeweled hilt. Effortlessly, Avril brought to mind the symbolism: Fire, Earth, Air, Water. In their proper order, and with their proper names, Solid, Liquid, Gas, Charge. Or more exactly still, and in the reverse cosmogonic ranking: gravity, strong force, weak force, electromagnetism. All of those, in turn, unified into the profound Xon force whose embodiment was signalized by the symbol above Marchmain's head: the lemniscate, the infinity sign, the Midgard serpent yet again gulping down his own tail. A dreadful stomachful, that. Even in the nothingness, detached from the flesh, Avril felt a pang at her center. Something within her cringed at the promise of waking agony. Something within her shrugged; this was the price, she had accepted it. Live with it. For as long, at any rate, as the Ancient Intelligence deemed fit to inflict it.

She turned over the Empress card, and placed it upon the seventh node of the Tree of Life, Netzach. With a gust of relief, she found it unchanged. Who else but Maybelline stood under the sign of Venus? May reclined in a field of extraordinary vegetation, nothing of Earth, but abundant, fruitful, eagerly drawing in the light of the nearer Sun. The Sibyl had never seen her sister so arrayed in beauty in the real worlds, but the symbolism of the card suited her: a loose robe richly decorated, seven pearls at her neck, a crown of eleven stars. No, *no*. Once more this disruptive, unnerving alteration. This time May wore twelve stars woven in her hair.

Agitated, Avril found and flung down the next card upon the node of Tiphareth, at the very heart of the Tree of Life. What she found soothed her agitation. Ever before, that dubious bishop Jules had stationed himself upon the symbol, making mock, in her view, of the beauty and compassion anciently signified by the Sun, the Hanged Man. Now he was replaced by Janine, and Avril found herself smiling. Well, of course. Was not *The Hanged Man* her sister's whimsical name for her dark energy Kabbalah starship, the vessel that had borne her not to the Sun but to a greater stellar enigma, the Xon star? Yes, this was appropriate, this gave hope. Perhaps the changes wrought by the upstart were not all ruinous. Perhaps the end they portended might be turned, with her own sibylline guidance, to the Contest's end.

The next card fell upon the fifth node, Geburah, the Tower, reversed. Here, under this reversal, was a place of judgment, where a Rock might stand. Once again, to her bafflement, the identity of the card seemed an inevitable fulfillment rather than a betrayal of tradition. Always before, this had been Juni, grounded in the material world, subject to temptation and frivolity. Now brother Toby regarded her: foursquare, trustworthy, truly a tower of strength. It came to her that she had tended to disparage Toby in the past, to overlook him, regard him as a bucolic bookworm in retreat from the Contest proper. This card was an alert. She said a prayer of gratitude to the Ancient Intelligence and an unvoiced apology to her brother.

Chesed, the Emperor, mercy, leadership. Always, or at least for a very long time, this had been Septimus, indefatigable toiler in the hell worlds. Now, incredibly, *and not reversed,* it was that idiot Jules, whiling away his time in theological games, a plaything of the planetary Mind that comprised the Star Doll, the Matrioshka Brain built in another cognate by a culture old when Egypt and India were young. Sphere within sphere of whirling molecular bubbles, like Maybelline's Venusian vegetation sucking in sunlight, but ever so more efficiently, the inner shell seething with raw solar heat, running upon its own substrate minds vast, and fast, and terrible, spilling its waste heat to the next shell, and that to the next, and the next, to the frigid outermost zones of what had once been the Solar System, where Jules spun out his days, when he wasn't making a nuisance of himself elsewhere, in a sort of spinning Argentine bolo that gave him the illusion of weight along with the illusion of importance. He was a toy. He had allowed himself to become one. But then again, he treated the Matrioshka Brain and its manifestations, the whole cosmos really, as if it were *his* plaything. A fool. Not *the* Fool, that card had not yet been turned. But Emperor? Absurd.

The final node or branch of the left-hand pillar of the Tree of Life was Binah, traditionally—and uncomfortably—her own. Another change. A jolt went through her. Had she been in the flesh, it might have loosened her bowels. This was the place of death and wisdom; she had expected to find Septimus here, since he was no longer in the Chesed station. Now another stood in his place, yet *not* another. Mounted upon a dreadful killing machine, standard in hand, minatory above a wretched mother turned away in terror while clutching a gaunt babe to her breast, a woman all in black armor gazed back across the reeking battlefield of dead to hold Avril's eyes.

"Septima," the Sibyl whispered, fear coursing in her. "Great Mother, is *she* returned?"

Her trembling fingers went to the Daath pack of discarded

cards, plucked one forth. Very well. This was Knowledge, unexpected, from beyond the pale. It was, of course, Ruth, the archivist and coroner of slain K-machines. She placed it to the right of Binah, turned up the second last card, positioned it to the right of the Daath card. Here was Chokmah, in ancient times the Zodiac, now the Tegmark multiverse entire, in an infinite fractal. Inevitably, as always, this was Decius. He stood in a chariot, a burning star upon his head, representing—she now knew for certain—an entire collapsed cosmos, a cognate closed upon itself in controlled gravitational infall, guided to its central singularity by the near-godlike beings of its terminal history. Decius had spent his life at Yggdrasil Station, the vantage point created for him by the beneficence of the unborn god builders. Not even Decius supposed that he was the driver of that cosmological chariot, for all the symbolism of the card. He was an observer gifted with glory, and the lion sphinxes at his feet were the godthings born in the ignition of an entire universe crashing in upon itself. As she stood within the world of the card, one of the sphinxes glanced across at her, winked, licked its lips. It was not a lion, she realized with surprise. It was a cat, a mangy old tomcat missing the best part of one ear. She'd seen it before, in Maybelline's arms struggling to get free, cursing freely, or basking lazily in front of May's Heimat fireplace. Dear god, she thought; it's Cathooks. The foul animal is a godthing.

She closed her eyeless eyes. Ten cards had been dealt out. One remained, as always. Relief went through her. Only one sibling remained to be accounted for. There was no room on the Tree of Life for the interloper. She had known him for a fraud from the outset. Something sent by the K-machines, probably. A lure, a distraction, doubtless worse. She turned over the last card, placed it at the top of the Tree.

Kether, the Fool. But reversed. Ember, of course. Scapegrace, creator of the Good Machine and consequently an accomplice before-the-act in the most monstrous genocide any world had ever seen, even those tormented places in the custody of Septimus. Septima, she corrected herself. She reached without reaching to retrieve the pack, shuffle it anew, place it with due respect within its silk covering, its carved jasper box. Somehow one fingernail caught the edge of the Fool's card, tipped and reversed it back. Pain in her sternum tore like a ripped muscle, like a lesion exposed to acid.

The face of the brat looked out at her, not watching where he stepped. He wore a tunic of budded universes topologically connected, a rose in his left hand, a wand in his right with a swag or wallet tied at its end. Glaring sunlight fell upon him from behind; he stepped heedlessly into a precipice, plainly a representation of the Schwelle system. A dog barked at his heels, presumably the animal that had sequestered her father's essence, or part of it, during their hidden years when the brat was conceived and born on some negligible cognate Earth. In the distance far beyond him, awesome mountain peaks lifted into pale-blue sky, the computational structures that underlay reality. It was unendurable. Everything—*everything*—was changed.

August Seebeck was the Parsifal, the Tarot's Fool.

Choking on saltwater, Avril flailed, caught one of her swans a slashing blow on the cheek. She found herself sinking, thrashed in the element she had always regarded as her own. Burning took her. She doubled up, vomiting, and the price of insight burned within her.

FIFTEEN

THERE WAS NO door.

I had the purloined sword in my hand. I raised the heavy, beautifully balanced blade above my shoulder, as I had in the place that no longer existed, brought the blunt hilt crashing against the white-and-blue wallpapered plaster of the wall where an alcove and the door to a staircase had been less than an hour earlier. My blows split open the delicate patterns, pitted the drywall surface. The wall was exactly as solid and as vulnerable as you'd expect in a nicely fitted-out cottage.

In a fury, I brought the blade about, took the hilt in both hands, began hacking like a fool at the wall, as if the sword were an axe. Toby made no move to stop me. It was just as well. In my mood of despair, I might have taken a cut at him. I heard Lune's voice. Perhaps she spoke my name. I cut, I jabbed, I slashed; plaster dust flew into the air, gritted my eyes; the taste of it poisoned my tongue. Chunks of plaster fell at my feet. I was ruining the blade. My shoulders convulsed in a tremendous blow that drove the blade a good inch into the black oak of a vertical stud, where it jammed tight. I tugged at it. The goddamned thing refused to budge. I let go of the hilt. The sword hung in the wounded wall like a rebuke.

"Fuck," I said. I backed away from what I'd done until my shoulders struck the corridor wall behind me. "So much for the theory that I'm the reincarnation of Arthur bloody Pendragon."

Somehow my legs gave way. The weight of my body slid me down the wall. I took three great convulsive gasps, floating dust catching in my lungs, coughed, burst into tears. I was beyond humiliation. I was beyond sense, reason, trust; I was beyond the reassurances of love. I howled like a lost child, which I was. I placed my fists in the wet sockets of my eyes, and roared with inarticulate loss and grief and confusion. A hand touched my knee—I brushed it away, pressed my eyes against the upjutting bones of my knees, put the palms of my hands over my ears, and wept, shaking.

I do not know how long I remained in that storm of fugue. It cannot have been an hour. When I recovered myself somewhat, Toby had withdrawn, and Lune sat quietly at my side, contained, alert, legs stretched out, hands clasped lightly on her thighs. When I looked at her, shaking my wet face, she turned her cobalt gaze upon me.

"We're going to need some WD-40 to get that free," she remarked in a calm tone. "Or Teflon-Plus."

"What?"

"It's a bicycle lubricant. Pricey, but effective."

I said nothing.

"Or we could leave it there, patch the wall around it." She regarded the wrecked wall aesthetically. "A statement about, you know, Man's inhumanity to Man."

It was wry, it was funny, I wanted to laugh but there was no laughter in me, not yet. I sent her a sketchy grin, a rictus spasm of my mouth, wanting to reach for her, pull her against me, take comfort from her solidity, her steadfastness. I shook my head, shrugged, let my head fall forward again. I closed my eyes. Everything was gray. I was tumbling into the gray. I caught myself, drew back from the edge of the precipice, opened my eyes, pushed myself to my feet. I felt as if I'd been beaten by canes until my flesh was bruised and my bones near to breaking. Lune was gone. The sword hung in the broken wall. There was still no door, no staircase. Someone had revised the rules, then changed them back. No certainties.

The Contest of Worlds.

Precisely.

And we were not the Players, by Christ.

We were the Pawns.

I dusted myself off, went back to the guest bedroom. Lune was not there, for which I was grateful. From the living room at the front of the cottage I heard her soft murmur, Toby's gruff, restrained answer. I closed the bedroom door, took my clothes off, went into the *en suite* bathroom, had a very satisfying shit through a warm-breezed Schwelle into what I hoped was an empty cognate world, and got back under the shower to wash away the tear-clotted plaster dust. It seemed to me in my mordant mood that I was spending far too much time in this place under the shower. But the water was free, refreshing, and for some reason standing there under the warm rain of yet another optional wormhole into yet another Earth cleared my mind and kick-started my sluggish engagement with this preposterous reality. I had tried to batter my way through a solid wall. There was a better way. I opened a Schwelle upon a gust of hot desert wind, shook my wet head, droplets flying from my hair. What an idiot.

No point looking for new clothes. I dragged on the old ones, went straight back to the corridor. Strictly speaking, there was no need to do this, no need to leave the bedroom. But I wanted to see if the alcove and door were back. Nope. I looked ruefully at the mess I'd created. There was a grammar inside me. So I'd been told. It had not let me down yet, except when I'd neglected to access it or when someone else with authorization had indicted my requested actions. I tried to remember how I'd found my way back to the house I'd shared with Great-aunt Tansy before the Deformer brutes had smashed it into collapsing rubble. The Schwelle operating system seem to possess at least some degree of intelligence, perhaps artificial intelligence. There was leeway; probably it made its best guess at construing what you needed, even in the absence of an exact deictic address. Okay, let's give it a shot.

First, though, I tried once again to pull the sword out. It was jammed tightly in the heavy grain of the upright stud. Hey, maybe two birds with one stone.

"Give me the, uh, Round Table room," I told the system, holding tight to the sword's hilt as I did so. Canvas tore. I pitched slightly into darkness, the weight of the freed sword pulling me forward. My mood lifted, and the corners of my mouth. "Too cool," I said, grinning at myself. "Maybe I *am* Arthur, after all." But in truth I was *not* Arthur; I was myself, not about to be conscripted into some mishmash of myth. I dropped the sword on the floor with a clang and left it there.

The iconic dodecagon grew visible before me as my eyes adapted: ultraviolet, blue-tinted. It swung down, formed its table, showed me its heraldic cast of characters. I looked for its empty seat, waiting for me, and my smile vanished. I sat there at the table, between Marchmain and Toby, dressed in some sort of highly dubious tunic with long floppy sleeves and a pair of rolltop calf-high boots that you wouldn't be seen dead playing hoops in. The tunic was decorated with glittering spheres of light that budded from each other. At my right heel, crouched down with his nose on his paws, was my beloved dog,

Dugald O'Brien. For a moment, my eyes burned again with tears, but they were tears of grief. Do Good had died in the deformers' attack, and I had recovered him from death with the power given to me by the creepy thing embedded in my right hand, the X-caliber device imposed upon me in Septimus's war room. And now Do Good was gone once more, fused back into the reunified person of my father, Dramen Seebeck. Was all this, then, the work and design of Septimus? I stood behind my phantom self, resisting the urge to crouch down and cuddle my old doggy friend, gone, gone, and looked instead across the table to Septima, the twin or female doppelgänger of my hell-world brother. Her image regarded me unflinchingly. Once again, it came to me what I must do.

"Give me Septima," I said. *Septic,* muttered some idiot pun ning commentary from my unconscious, *sempiternal. Septifragal,* said another kind of voice, almost in my ear, not quite sounded, *botanical: dehiscent breaking away from a natural dividing line.*

What the *fuck?*

But the portal had torn open. A foul stench blew through, rotting meat, corroded metal, filth, and corruption. I gagged, instantly covered my mouth and nose with my hands. The small, stocky woman in black protective gear looked up from her work. At her back, a large autonomous machine delved among the protruding bones, the faces eaten to the skull, the half-decayed limbs with, appallingly, fingernails still attached to the yellowed, bloated claws. She held a child in her arms. The poor little thing was mute in its terror, its loss, skin shrunken upon its bald head, limbs like sticks, belly swollen. It gazed at nothing with its dead eyes, but it was alive. Barely.

"August," the woman said, voice muffled by her mask. "I've been expecting you, lad. Here, take this child."

The urgent need to vomit had not abated. My ears rang. I clamped shut my nostrils and epiglottis, trying to breathe without breathing. I held out my arms, and Septima lightly laid the wretched child in my clasp. He did not look at me—I saw now that the tiny, ruined body was male—and he hung limply. Sores covered his skin. His mouth opened once, and his tongue was swollen within it. My arms brought him up against my breast of their own volition. This violence was unspeakable. I felt my heart breaking. When I spoke, my voice was broken as well.

"Where can we—" I cleared my throat. "We have to get this baby to hospital."

A soft buzzing; the machine backed up, and Septima stepped down into the cavity it had opened. Something moved. Something uttered a feeble cry. My sister reached into a space between a leaking water pipe and a heap of fractured concrete, humming gently, brought out by one hand a small, shuddering girl child who held a piece of blackened rag pressed against her mouth. Perhaps it had been a bib or part of the covering of a favorite stuffed animal. The little girl whimpered. Her eyes swiveled between us in fright. Septima must have seemed to her a demon, a ghost, a monstrous enemy. Yet in her release from fatal captivity the child clutched at my sister's hand and arm with ferocious intensity. Her gaze fell then upon the bundle in my arms. She took a step forward, held out her own spindly arms, croaked a name. The baby did not move, his emptied gaze fixed nowhere. I could not make out the name; I doubt that it was one I've ever heard before, nor that the child spoke any language of my world or its nearest cognates. But what would I know? Each inhabited world is choked with the fluent grunts and clucks and pitched songs of tongues most of us will never hear uttered.

The little girl cried out that name once more, twice, looked away doubtfully, fell silent. Septima waited. The child turned back to her, wrapped her arms around one dark-garbed leg, and pressed her face into my sister's thigh.

"I have a refuge prepared," Septima told me softly. "Come with me."

She lifted the child into her arms, muttered a deixis code, opened the portal. I followed her through into a softly lit circular space in soothing pinks, yellows, pale blue. A console with a large flatscreen showed in muted colors a sleeping child, thumb in rosebud mouth, hair fluffy except where it was crushed into a pillow, presumably from an infrared CCT feed. Doors stood closed every three meters or so, decorated with green giraffes, purple lions, other birds and animals I did not recognize, including several dinosaurs merrily spotted and feathered. Septima touched a key at the console. Almost immediately, a door opened and a short man in a nondescript tracksuit came briskly in.

"Coop," I said, taken aback. His hair was neater than usual. The dreadful meerschaum pipe was absent from his fake teeth. He looked first at the children in our arms, then to Septima, finally to me. He had never seen me before.

"Oh, sorry—" I started to say, as he said to me, "Apologies, sar, we've not met. You must be thinking o' one of my fellow avatars. Here now, let me have the little one." He took the gaunt ghost of a child from my arms with the easy skill and care of a man with a dozen children of his own. It was impossible, in that moment, to regard him as a mechanism, let alone a renegade killing machine.

"August, this is Mr. Happy. Meet my brother," she told the twin of James Cooper Fenimore.

"Another Seebeck sibling, eh? Pleased to make your acquaintance.

This infant is badly dehydrated. I have to put him on a drip. Is the other child related?"

Septima had removed her isolation mask, and started to peel off her suit without detaching the older child from her leg. The girl whimpered faintly, darted glances at the dying baby. "Unknown, although that's my guess. The genome scan will tell us. Put them in a room for two, cots for both of them. Now, sweetie, you're going to have to let go of me for a moment. August, can you look after her? Happy, we'll need assistance."

I crouched down, took the little girl under her armpits, lifted her free. Or tried to. She shrieked in terror, a piercing ululation, and clung more tightly to my sister. I released her, drew back a hop, placed my left hand lightly on her back in what I hoped was a comforting gesture. More shrieks and shrinking. Septima's protective suit hung from her waist. Beneath it, she wore a ballet leotard in a surprisingly sprightly electric blue. Somehow, I could not see her variant incarnation, Septimus the Promethean alpha male, wearing such a thing. Another door opened, and the child's shrieks cut off. Me, I'd have screamed twice as loudly. I very nearly did anyway.

A clown had come through the door, a broad-shouldered, bald, blubbery man with a large red poppy nose, extravagant black liner making stars of his eyes, a padded clown suit in cavorting colors. It took me only a moment to recognize him under the grease paint.

"Mr. Fun," Septima said. "See what you can do for this poor wight. Oh, and meet my brother August."

The clown sidled up, exuding avuncular friendliness, huge flat shoes flapping humorously. He recognized me no more than Mr. Happy had.

Not surprising. The only two times I'd seen him previously, he was dead as a mackerel.

"Welcome to our hospice, Mr. Seebeck."

I kept my right hand at my side, left hand touching the child's back, shifted slightly to get my martial arts balance.

"You look better without that ridiculous comb-over," I said.

Memories, like flash cards under strobes—

Traumatic instantaneous memories, burned into the neural attractor networks of my brain—

Lune and Maybelline climbing impossibly through Great-aunt Tansy's upstairs bathroom window, lugging this man's corpse, a seeping bullet wound in his chest. Coop carrying the corpse away through a mirror.

An autopsy table in another world, accessed through an open Schwelle, this thing stretched naked, the sister I'd mistaken for a lady librarian dickering inside its trepanned skull.

"Excuse me, sir?" Mr. Fun was baffled.

"You're Devlin's little project."

Insight spilled through memory like gasoline, ignited by the sparks, burning in a display as clear as a written message.

The Deformer stayed where it was, watched me impassively. No, watched me *sympathetically*.

"Ms. Seebeck. Yes, I see, that would be your sister, Mr. Seebeck. She redeemed me. Now I have useful work. Let me attend to this child, but I would enjoy continuing this conversation with you later, if that would be convenient."

Agog, wanting to burn the thing like a pyre with my right hand, knowing far too little to make that choice in the presence of these brutalized children and my sister who days earlier had been my brother and months before that, years and decades before that, had been entirely unknown to me, I let the turned K-machine lift the child into its clown arms. It followed the Coop thing, Mr. Happy, into a room marked by a striped hippo, illuminated by a soft pink-tinged glow, and shut the door behind them. Septima kicked off the protection garment, left it slumped in a heap on the floor. She found a brown coverall in a concealed closet, slipped it on.

"You're just going to let those goddamned things take sick human children and—" But of course she was. This was her world, or some annex off it. My sister—my former brother—had evidently appointed her/himself Florence Nightingale of the Holocaust, or maybe of the Apocalypse. Clearly she knew what she was doing. Clearly, the children were in no danger, at no risk. I looked back down at the discarded clothing, changed tack in mid-sentence. "No nice, sanitizing, biohazard sluice? No check with the Geiger counter? Or am I now going to come down with radioactive boils? Hair and teeth falling out, like that?"

"Rest easy, silly puppy," Septima told me, not unkindly. "Your augmentation would have kept the Schwelle shut had you been in any danger." That raised more goosebump-creeping implications than I cared to deal with at that moment, so I followed her to the console display and watched the two machines tending to the children. Perhaps sedative drugs were being aerated into the room. The girl lay back in her cot as Mr. Fun tucked her under a bunny blanket, stroked her matted hair with delicate solicitude. I'd expected robotic nurses to bundle the children quicksmart into a bathtub, dry them off roughly, wrap them in grim institutional pajamas. No such thing. Mr. Happy was crooning some old English nursery song as he slipped an intravenous needle into the skin-and-bone arm of the dehydrated baby, deftly arranged the intubation, snugged the infant into a tiny cot that closed up and held him secure. Septima turned away from the screen after a few moments' inspection.

"You did well, boy, thanks for your help. Now—you must be

starving, I know I am. Come along, we'll shovel some nourishment into you. Growing lad, you need some filling out."

She was right. I'd missed lunch with Lune about a thousand years ago, it felt like, except for a smeary bite of chocolate-coated lamington and another of scorched Jammervoch. I grimaced at the thought, shrugged, nodded. "Sure, lead on to the . . . *mess* . . . isn't that what you military types call it? An army marching on its stomach? Septima, *are those children going to be all right?*"

My sister placed her hand on my arm, slid it down delicately to take my hand, patted it. She was almost *unbelievably* unlike Septimus. "They'll be just fine. We look after them, you see." She looked at me sidelong with her dark-brown eyes. "Your friend Lune grew up here in Iron Mountain Redoubt a good many years ago."

"Oh."

That simple fact, tossed to me without a blink, fell into place with an almost audible click. Lune had avoided speaking about parents, family, anyone other than her Ensemble associates. I'd assumed she'd grown up in an abusive family and come through it with impressive resilience. God! And this sort of horror had been her hearth. A surge of admiration and love tightened my chest. I remembered, then, what Superiore Morgette had said— that Septima, the original Septima, presumably before she became Septimus, had founded the Ensemble. Wheels within wheels.

We walked along a hallway of repeated doglegs with windows looking into classrooms of diligent children, computer dens, a huge gymnasium of training machines with an Olympic-sized swimming pool at the far end visible through foggy glass, young folks in a variety of shapes, colors, and ages doing their stuff under the guidance of adults who I'd have sworn must be apostate K-machines—some uncanny calmness attended them. Perhaps some of those guides had spent time in Tansy's bathroom, dead as mechanical fish. My gorge rose. We were walking briskly, so I didn't get much chance to make a nuanced assessment, but I didn't catch anyone horsing around, pulling pranks, drifting off or goofing off, hanging out, having a good time. Room after room, the kids looked like clips from a current affairs program I once watched about Japanese schoolchildren. Poor Lune. Then again, maybe that's what you needed to carry you from retrieved infancy in a nightmare death-world all the way to a doctorate in ontological computation or computational ontology, or whatever the hell her specialty was, when she wasn't catching and killing mechanical vermin for Ruth to fix.

Septima took me into a small, attractively presented dining room, neither a restaurant nor a cafeteria. Three young people of Chinese appearance, maybe my age or a little older, were eating and talking quietly at a table with white linen and a rose in a glass vase. They were not in uniform, yet somehow contrived to make it seem that they were.

"The senior mess, as you say."

"Septima, I just left Lune and Toby hanging. I need to let them know—"

"I'll see to it. Find a table, I'll be with you in a moment."

A young man in a beautifully starched white shirt, buttoned at the neck without a tie, pressed black trousers, gleaming black shoes and white apron, stood at the servery door. He did not approach. In the absence of a menu, I studied the single dark-red rose in the center of our own table, the large naval engravings on the pale blue walls. A mastless trireme, rowers laboring incredibly in unison at their three great banks of oars. Phoenician? Two great men-o'-war firing broadside gouts of smoke and fire and metal into each other. A sinister conning tower vanishing under a vee of its own waves. I realized that actually I really was very hungry indeed. The stench of the hell world still clung faintly to my own shoes and perhaps to my dusty clothing, but the animal needs of my belly seemed to be over-riding my more maudlin instincts. Soft music bathed the dining room. Debussy or Ravel, I felt sure, but I didn't recognize the piece. Probably from some slightly alternative cognate Earth. The thought of the untold musical and artistic riches available to us worldwalkers made my head spin.

My sister returned. Probably I should have stood like a gentleman, pulled her chair out, seated her. Nobody did that in my world, not any longer, unless they were seventy or eighty years old. The Kennedy regnancy had seen to that, and the convulsive youth rebellions that were finished decades before I was born. But refusnik attitudes had shaded subsequent generations even as the boomers bit the hand that fed them before settling down to feed the mouths that would bite them in turn. The Sir Beatles, Sir Ringo Starkey, all that. Luckily, my gaffe with the chair went unnoticed, or at least unrebuked, because the handsomely kitted-out waiter was at our table as if he'd passed directly through a Schwelle, chair withdrawn, Septima settled, menus presented.

"Toby sends his regards," she told me. "Ms. Katha Sarit Sagara bids you *bon appétit*. I'll have the *boeuf bourguignonne*, with green beans and fried potatoes. This young man will have—you eat fish?"

"I'm an Australian, are you mad, of course I eat seafood. Assuming it's fresh." August, you idiot, why wouldn't it be fresh? These people can probably open a Schwelle into the middle of the ocean and pop their catch through the hole straight into the skillet. Well, no, there'd be all that gushing water, and nobody likes their trout complete with guts. "Do you have Balmain bugs?" I said hastily.

"He'll have the grilled flounder stuffed with crab, and side vegetables. I'll have a glass of Burgundy, he can have a chilled Chablis." I shrugged, nodded. The waiter only just failed to salute and click his heels. She looked at me across the table. "You have a question for me."

I propped my elbows on the linen and leaned forward. I felt like laughing, as you do at a sour jest.

"Yeah. Or maybe a thousand. Not that I expect—" I glanced up. Astonishingly, the waiter was already back, placing our elegantly deployed plates before us, uncorking two bottles, offering Septima a taste of the red wine. She waved him on, he poured, he was gone again in his dancing black shoes. My ~~sister~~ plunged into her lunch, or her dinner, whatever, prodded me to do the same with a briskly flourished knife. I took a mouthful of fish. It was excellent. "Not that I expect any serious, responsive, um, response. You lot have been ducking and weaving like acrobats whenever I try to get a straight answer. But thank you for getting in touch with Lune and Toby."

She regarded me intently, shoveling stew into her mouth. I could imagine Septimus wolfing his food like this, getting it in his white beard. I wondered if she still slept in his martial cot, above the armory where I'd received the X-caliber Vorpal implant. At least she didn't smell like a compulsive cigar smoker. She said, "You haven't worked any of it out yet? *Where are my fried potatoes?*" she called in a piercing voice. I blinked. The waiter emerged at speed from the servery door. I noticed that the people at the other table kept their eyes front, ate without interruption, but fell silent, probably listening avidly. The waiter glanced at our table, blanched ever so slightly, muttered apologetically, was gone again.

"Worked—?"

"You are in training, little puppy. Think of yourself as a page who would be a knight, embarked upon a course of testing, exploration of your prowess and skill with weapons. As a great man said—"

"Bullshit," I said loudly. I don't know if the people at the far table picked up their ears; I was too irritated to care. "A *page?* A *knight?* You people are delusional. Contest! Knight! What I am is a Pawn, that's what I've concluded. And I'm bloody well sick and—"

"My *potatoes!*" Septima bellowed like a sergeant major. The waiter scuttled in, beet-red, with a steaming dish of fried potato chunks fragrant with herbs. She prodded them with her fork. "Too many," she muttered, looking grim. She took one on her tines, conveyed it steaming to her mouth, chewed it up, and swallowed without the gasp of pain I'm pretty sure I'd have emitted. "I'm paraphrasing: he said the military sciences have no method to distinguish a true knight from a fancy counterfeit in armor, save through the ordeal by fire. The true knights survive and meet their obligations. The phonies and slackers perish." Her gaze cut into me, relentless. "Sadly, lad, the false knights let down their sworn brothers and sisters, their companions in arms. There is no greater tragedy in war."

I shook my head, looked at my plate, forced myself to eat in silence. Septima seemed prepared to wait. She polished off her meal, quaffed her wine, took a second glass from the magically attentive waiter before I'd drunk half of mine. I chewed, and it was not my fish and vegetables that stuck in my throat. War?

Finally I pushed my plate to one side. "I know people have been trying to kill me. Or *things*. Shit, they didn't just *try*, they succeeded. Has the word on that little adventure circulated among the Seebecks yet? Dead one day, bouncing back the next?"

It sounded completely insane even as I spoke. I remembered every filthy, agonized moment of being burnt to death, smashed to atoms, clawing back from nothingness, held from extinction by the golden Xon matter of the Vorpal implant that threaded my body. My fake human body, if Lune had it right, if she and I and Toby and Septimus/Septima and the whole sick crew were nothing but caricatures, simulations, homunculi written, incomprehensively, into the computational substrate under-lying space and time. Paranoia! As bad as the blitherings of the Valisologists.

I forced words into my mouth. "They killed me, which I resent, but they killed Lune, and for that they deserve the most dreadful death I can find for them, whoever the goddamned fuck they are."

I pushed my chair back, stood up, leaned across the table with my fingers gripping its edge so tightly that the tablecloth jerked toward me, toppling the rose in its vase, Septima's empty wine glass. I noticed from the corner of my eye that the waiter had made himself scarce, and that the three from the other table were leaving discreetly. "*What* are they? *Why* are they trying to kill me? Us, all of us? Who are *we*, for that matter? What kind of war is it where a guy in college and his poor old harmless Great-aunt and their goddamned *dog*, for Christ's sake, can be conscripted in complete ignorance and—"

I was babbling nonsense, and I knew it. I was acting on the basis of the August I'd been a month earlier, the August who had grown up an ordinary Australian kid with Estonian ances-tors, spent a year of high school in Chicago after his parents mysteriously disappeared, lived with his dotty, psychic aunt in an old house high on a hill in a rundown suburb of Melbourne. That August was gone. In a sense, that August had never existed. My memories were dubious. The old lady and the dog, my aunt Miriam and her violinist husband Itzhak, were an invention, a confection, a dissociated construct created by the scientific magician Marchmain Seebeck out of the living substance of my parents, Dramen and Angelina. Dear God, the B-movie melodrama! The craziness. I felt dizzy leaning across the table. The grayness was back, the gray that had sucked at me in Toby's cottage as I crouched nerveless and exhausted and weepy in a pile of smashed plaster.

I simply don't believe this, I thought. I'll close my eyes, and when I open them again, all this will have gone away. No sister Maybelline caught in *flagrante delicto* fucking the giant vegetable next to a flying saucer. No machine corpses in Tansy's bathtub or revived for nursing duties in a hospice for the damned. I did shut my eyes, squeezed them tight, and instantly opened them again. Even if I could do that, I *would* not. It had nothing to do with Septima's preposterous tales of knighthood. Lune was central to this mad universe, or my part of it, and so long as she lived, I would stay here, fight beside her if that were permitted, hold her in my arms until the dark fell or the morning came again. I found Septima staring at me intently.

"You see, boy, you do understand. You are a Player, and this is the Contest of Worlds. All the rest is details, strategy and tactics and courage and patience. This is the heritage our parents have bequeathed us." To my disbelieving astonishment, she made the gesture with both her hands that I'd seen the assembled company of Seebecks and others make at the family moot outside Avril's Norman castle. It was like a pair of opposed sine waves or, wait, a smoothed-out version of that famous illusion they show you in Psychology 101, two faces that flip as you watch them to create a . . . a chalice. A grail. Oh dear God. *The* Grail.

"The Yggdrasil," my sister told me, instantly deflating my paranoid interpretation, and just as instantly reinflating it. Norse mythology. The great Tree stretching from the underworld to the heavens, three mighty roots driven deep under the ice and rock, something like that. Another symbol, obviously enough, the one I'd seen before. A model for the multiverse, I'd conjectured. Roots in basic mathematics and logic, branches shooting off into the T-levels, lesser branches and twigs being the cognate worlds, the variant Earths. And Yggdrasil Station—the place beyond space and time where/when I had stepped after my . . . resurrection, you might as well call it, and found my brother Decius and his lover enthralled in the glory of the godthings forged at the moment of Omega Point as an entire closed universe folded in upon itself and created a singularity so profound that its reverberations pierced all the Tegmark levels of the metaverse. All this came to me in an instant as she spoke that name. Had it been in my memory all along, lost from view? I had experienced the sublime a moment after I had suffered the torments of death and the death of my beloved Lune. No wonder I was a little shaky on the details.

Symbols. Sigils. A recalled image flashed into my mind: the curious shape the morphing K-machine has shown me on the library monitor. I realized that I was still on my feet, Septima regarding me with a certain pained irony. I sat down again. The waiter appeared apologetically, collected our dishes. I said to him, "Can you get me a notepad and a pencil?"

"Surely, my lord. Will sir and the general be taking dessert and coffee? We have a very fine—"

"Just get him a workpad, Denzel. Thank you for your service. Next time, remember the potatoes."

He came back with a wafer-thin sheet of black quarto paper and the slender black inkless stylus. I scribbled white curves on one corner, erased the lines with my little finger. Quickly, I sketched the shape the vermin had shown me.

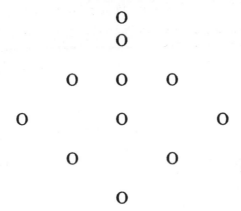

I pushed the pad across to my warrior sister and saw her go on high alert.

"Where did you see this?"

I sighed. Maybe we were getting somewhere. "I think we'll need that coffee after all," I told her.

When I was finished telling her about it, Septima stroked at her chin, for all world as if she expected to find whiskers there. "It's either a structural diagram of Jan's dark energy warship, which would be exceedingly depressing, because we didn't think the scum knew about that." Her eyes went out of focus; she steepled her fingers.

"Or?"

"Oh. Well, of course it's the Tree of Life."

"The Yggdrasil again?"

The old warrior smiled. "You could put it that way." She pushed her coffee cup away, nibbled on a chocolate mint. "No, it's a very ancient Kabbalistic formula. You say these nodes were labeled? Might they have looked like this?" She lifted the stylus to her lips, muttered a string of sounds that made no sense to me. Instantly, my sketch changed. Words appeared. I examined them, recognizing nothing particularly.

```
                              O
                              O

                           Kether

           Binah        O     O     O    Chokmah

                           Daath

Geburah        O              O              O      Chesed

                         Tiphareth

           Hod      O              O    Netzach

                              O

                           Yesod

                              O

                          Malkuth
```

"So?"

"These are the Sephiroth, the eleven great stations of the Tree. Each Sephirah is the sign and location and emblem of one of our family. Save for you, young sprat. But I see that the deformers have played a little joke on us." She pointed to the double globe at the top of the diagram. "Kether is the station of the Fool. In the great order of the Contest, I have always assumed this was Ember, our bumbling genocide of a brother who brought the Good Machine into the world. I assume you've met him?"

I gritted my teeth. "Everyone thinks he's my father."

Septima laughed. "I recall making the same mistake. You favor him remarkably. Never mind, both of you resemble our father. Dramen's not on the diagram, of course, nor is our mother Angelina. They stand above, naturally, Ain Soph and Ain Soph Aur."

I had no faintest idea what she was talking about, what the words meant that she'd just uttered, what the annotations on the diagram were meant to convey. I got this much, though. Ember my brother stood at the top, but that left one Kether empty slot. I placed my fingertip on the doubled globe.

"So the extra one is *me?*"

"It seems so." She gave me a wolfish grin. "Yes, young August. Our Parsifal. We've been waiting for you, we just never knew it. Until you took the excalibur brand, at least. You are the Fool."

I bridled. "I'm ignorant, Septima, I grant you that. It's not surprising. Our parents kept me in the dark until they . . . went into hiding, and then their revenants continued to keep me in the dark. It's not as if I——"

"No, no, my boy. I'm not insulting you. I'm identifying you in the Tarot."

The *what?* Oh, dear Christ. One of the sidelines of Tansy's hokey telephone psychic scam was reading Tarot cards. But she played fair. Phone jammed in the crook of her neck, she'd faithfully unwrap her silk-clad Tarot deck and lay out her reading. She refused to let me play with the cards, but I'd overheard her plenty of times, watched over her shoulder as she shuffled and dealt them: the Emperor, the High Priestess, the Wheel of Fortune, the Hermit, the Hierophant, the Magician . . . the Fool. Good God! What card did Septima suppose she represented? The Empress? The Chariot? Death itself? I felt a chill. Probably Death. Almost certainly.

These people were *deranged.*

Abruptly, I recalled a line of dialogue from the end of *Alice In Wonderland*. It had amused me when I was a child entertained by paradox and again later, shaded by adolescent condescension, as Great-aunt Tansy used her silk-wrapped pack to divine the present and future. "You think we're nothing but a pack of *Tarot cards?*"

"In a manner of speaking." Septima was unruffled. "You could put it that way."

"I certainly fucking will *not* put that way," I said in a harsh tone. "You might be pleased to think of yourself as a toy or a poker chip. I'm a *person.* I have memories. I know who I am." But, of course, even that was not entirely true. At least some of my memories were fraudulent. Others seemed to be traces I'd retained from the alternative selves I'd merged with briefly in Tegmark superspace. I recalled the chatbot homeboy's mocking italicized pseudo-voice and the selves I'd been with lightning-flash brevity in other cognate histories. Septima was watching me in a kind of sympathetic silence. I said, "All right, of course I don't know who I am. I know who I thought I was, and even that isn't . . . reliable." I put my head in my hands, said in a muffled voice, "How can anyone live this way?"

"We abide by the Unicorn's Bargain," Septima told me. "Speaking of Carroll."

What? I dredged my memory, my fallible memory, of childhood. Oh. "'I'll believe in you, if you believe in me?'"

"It's a rough-and-ready epistemology," Septima admitted. "And fairly dreadful as ontology. But it'll do at a pinch."

"Band-Aid philosophy," I said. I looked at her, and she looked at me, and after a long moment we both started to smile. I stretched out my lethal right hand across the table, and my sister grasped it firmly. All right. Better to be one of a pack of cards, perhaps, than an isolated, solipsistic lunatic adrift in a sour fantasy, probably in a locked ward, or lying on a filthy mattress in an alley.

And in that instant I believed I understood why the deformers had attacked and destroyed Tansy's house.

SIXTEEN

A BARELY DETECTABLE breeze carries the reek of salt and putrid vegetation. The very deck of the rotting ship stinks with decay, slopes away from her at a disturbing angle, prow sunk beneath the nearly still water, stern high and tilted. Lune steps carefully, keeping her balance with outstretched arms. On every side, matted kelp and seaweed coat the sluggish surface of the ocean between the trapped hulks that have drifted here across hundreds, thousands of kilometers, fetching up at the still center of an indefinitely slow vortex on a cognate world of oceans seized by locking land masses. Other spoiled vessels hang trapped in the feral vegetation's embrace, moving slightly, rocking against each other's hulls with low, grinding vibrations and deep clangs, scarcely audible, like the booming of whales. This ruined ship, the *Argyle*, must have dangled here in the jaws of the sea for at least a century and a half.

"I can't do this any longer," she says. "I won't."

"How touching." The K-machine wears a heavy yellow canvas mariner's coat and black rubber boots, leaning against the stump of *Argyle*'s fractured main mast. Broken spars and fragments of a fallen sail and tangled rigging cling about it. "You love him."

The timber planks beneath her foot are pulpy, sagging with every careful step she takes. The ocean has invaded the vessel from within, seeping upward through the wood, rusting and corroding the ironwork, without yet swallowing it down into the depths. Perhaps that fate is certain, but it has been delayed for many decades by the matted pelagic vegetation flattening the surface of the water, locking all these marooned vessels into a graveyard without burial. Lune grimaces. The setting is the perfect preference of the thing that regards her approach with deep, gratified irony.

"Yes. I do love him. I did not expect—"

"Because he brought you back from death. This is not love, it's supine and self-interested gratitude. Get over it."

"You would have been quite happy to sacrifice my life to extinguish his. You tried repeatedly—destroying his aunt's house, the asteroid impact. As you admit, you succeeded that final time."

"Your life, like everyone's life, is illusory. Is this not what you believe and argue, philosopher? The Schmidhuber ontology, the blasphemy that computation is the basis of reality?"

She stares at the thing with disgust and a certain enduring fright that she has known since childhood, when it first made itself known to her. The K-machine possesses power over her in a measure she does not truly understand. Perhaps it and its kin had slaughtered her parents. Or perhaps, as it argues, that destruction had been, instead, and wickedly, the work of cold humans themselves, intent upon creating their own hell world. The Ensemble instructors had evaded that issue whenever she'd attempted, as an acolyte, to raise it.

"If life is illusory," she says, "I lose nothing by living it in the way that I choose. I'm done with you." But still she stands there.

The thing reaches forth an arm and hand made all of black metal, tenderly strokes her cheek. A kind of joyous revulsion rises within her. A memory from just beyond infancy: a figure all in black, shielded against the foul fumes rising to the shattered surface from the piled dead in the concrete caverns below. Dark-clad arms plucking her up, carrying her to safety, her pulse roaring, her terrified childish voice locked in her throat. Septimus, or one of his assistants, she sometimes thinks. Or perhaps, as it claims, this thing slouching at ease before her, or one of its kindred. It is a salvation she can hardly regret either way, and yet she detests its memory. She waits stock-still as the thing draws a line down her face, withdraws.

"And you'll be telling August Seebeck about your deception, I presume?"

Coldness, dread, radiates from the center of her body.

"It is no longer a deception."

"I'm sure that will console him."

Guilt blends with detestation. She has killed these things, the stupid Pawn soldiers at any rate, and the killing has brought her satisfaction. Her sentiment toward this one is more ambiguous. Perhaps she could kill it, perhaps it could kill her if it chose. They are beyond the Accord, beyond the Contest. Her fingers curl.

It glances at her fists with amusement.

"Release the Schwelle," she says. "I cannot abide your company a moment longer."

The K-machines stretches, almost voluptuously.

"Why, no," it tells her. "I find the ambience refreshing. The sea air, the nostalgia. I believe we'll stay here a little longer. You might use the time profitably in devising an apology to the young man you have betrayed."

SEVENTEEN

HALLEY'S COMET IS back in the sky, a pale smudge barely visible even well away from the city lights, hardly worth the seventy years' wait. Not long before his forty-second birthday, drifting toward separation from his wife, he has taken up (when they can manage it) with his philosophy colleague, Dr. Moon Ku. Quite quickly the orbits of their lives spin into chaotic confusion.

His and Moon's mutually declared position includes a devotion to the ideal of existential freedom lightly leavened with promiscuity, preferably with full advance disclosure, though perhaps without the subsequent gory details. While Moon, at thirty, has always operated with fair success under this rubric (she and her partner Barnard take it in turns to look after the cat), it is somewhat theoretical for him, sustaining, as he does, a high degree of evasion on this score with his wife. Emily has made it plain that she does not wish to know. Curiously, and bit by bit, he has found that his new lover, Moon, gets oddly irritated by any suggestion that he has continued to put this program into practice—little enough of late though it's been, he acknowledges somewhat regretfully.

He is, it seems, being unfeeling and cruel.

Well, hey, fuck that, he decided. A deal's a deal. When certain other women he met on the campus expressed more than a passing interest during the brief high-profile phase when he first took up his lectureship in computational ontology, Moon made it plain that activity in this quarter would be deemed, on a number of grounds, perilously sleazy or hurtful. In the interests of his growing fondness, he has valiantly forborne, though his rhetoric continues manfully unchecked.

At one time or another, various onlookers and confidants had pointed out to him that his claims of invulnerability to sexual chagrin were predicated pretty thoroughly on his wife's fidelity. While he found this plausible, he remained convinced that even if Emily decided on a blazing affair, he'd get through it fairly smoothly. Sauce for the goose. He fancied himself a feminist, after all.

Before this theory could be tested, however, he and Emily, childless, decided that their relationship might be most easily salvaged if they lived apart—not that they were splitting up. He contrived the mortgage and moved into a depressingly motel-like apartment.

Moon, for ideological motives, had already moved into an apartment by herself ("An apart-ment," she'd said wryly), leaving Barnard *in situ*. One day she mentioned that a former lover would be visiting from Adelaide for the weekend. "You have only one bed," he observed. Of course, there was a couch. Days later, he asked if she'd screwed her visitor, now departed. Of course she had. He shrugged. Uh-huh. How was it? So-so.

During his traditional run through Royal Park with the Dobermans and Emily, a custom hardly to be abandoned merely because of their domestic separation, he and his wife congratulated each other cheerfully on having attained, with a pleasing degree of smoothness, the condition of good friends. Although Emily was as yet unattached to anyone else, their present circumstances were, she felt, tolerable enough, certainly better than the bad faith they been sustaining during recent years in their cool and untouching bed.

This concord freed his spirit to an unexpected extent. He found himself responding to his lover Moon with a new access of intensity. The shadowy influence of his moralistic upbringing, no doubt.

Two weeks later, his wife took him out to dinner.

"Something's happened," she told him. "I've been to bed with someone."

He'd had a presentiment that she might be going to ask for details of his own dealings with Moon prior to their separation, but no; quite the reverse. She was buoyant with delight. Her new lover, as it chanced, and here her voice tightened a little, was that nice young person who had been coming around to use Emily's word processor: Rene, the girl next door.

He nodded, poured out a glass of cabernet sauvignon with a certain smug satisfaction. This revelation exactly fulfilled his hunch that Emily's affections would take this direction when his absence was settled, if not before. It had seemed to him quite plausible that she might turn to another woman, at least for a time. After all, she had trodden that path briefly in her late adolescence, as had so many.

What's more, he'd rather supposed that Rene was developing an interest in Emily, and as Rene was a droll, energetic person, another artist, he thought it likely that Emily would respond in kind if and when the occasion arose. As indeed she had. Everything worked out quite nicely, although there were some tricky bits of social interfacing. Rene's lesbian chums were not entirely enthralled by the intrusion into their world of a visiting straight woman; it was hard for Emily to introduce a new lover to family, friends, and workmates—the obvious catalog.

Was he really this cool? Not entirely. A couple of shaky days found him uttering informative slips of the tongue that suggested his unconscious was up to no good. By and large, though, it was all extremely agreeable and even satisfying, for now he could surrender an admission of his own affair with Moon. His wife accepted this news in a kindly way. For a time, evidently, she had feared that he might not actually get it together with this excellent person who was, after all, a fellow feminist. Nor was the case absolutely news to her, since Rene's friends on campus had swiftly borne word to her lover's ear.

In the cleansing air engendered by this full and frank exchange of views, this inner-city *glasnost*, he found himself during the following days opening quite poetically to Moon, to her amazement and delight. All the following weekend they made love with fiery lust augmented by unbounded sensitivity and tender beauty, and after a charming stroll by the Sunday sea and declarations of mutual love, he took Moon for the first time to visit some old mutual friends of his and Emily's. They proved to enjoy Moon's company and she theirs, and when the afternoon was done, she set off to a prearranged dinner *a deux* with Harry, a fellow academic. As it chanced, he had known Harry slightly since undergraduate days. "I'd rather you kept out of his bed," he'd told her, early on. Now he saw Moon to her car in a haze of wine and love. He was rueful. "Have a nice fuck." She drove into the twilight. He rejoined his friends and drank wine.

Under the terms of their agreement, Moon called him next morning.

"I'll give you the bad news first," she said cheerfully.

His lights powered down and went out. The sea moved through his head.

It had been a pretty dull evening, all told. She'd been about to leave at eleven, in fact, and zip over to visit him, but as she drew on her coat and made for the door her colleague had urged her to stay, so what the hell, why not, she'd been wondering for months, and it was okay but nothing to write home about, truly she loved him the better for it, and the chances were she'd only fuck Harry another four or five times before she got quite bored with him.

All those things you see in movies, read in short stories, all those clichés. The last time this had happened to him was in 1971, in Sydney, when Emily told him that he would have to go back to Melbourne alone because she was going to remain with her first husband. The time before that, he was totally wet behind the ears, twenty-one years old, the start of 1966, when his first love broke his heart by responding to an offer of marriage with an announcement that she'd been screwing another guy over the vacation period and didn't wish to see him again.

He is holding the phone against his ear, attending to Moon's news. His stomach drops out, smack! Gut full of acid, muscles paralyzed. He looked it up later in his paperback medical reference. Taken aback, Moon said she would come over in a few hours for a cuddle. He hung up. He sat down in an armchair, more or less regarding the digital clock on the video machine. The little number jumped from one position to another. Hours later turned out to be five minutes. Half a second proved to be half an hour.

When Moon arrived after an hour and a half, she was fairly horrified by this bout of midlife hysteria. She was sweet and considerate, then crisp, then a touch crabby, and while he was deciding that, first, he was having a perfectly routine human experience from which he'd far too long been shielded, and hence with which he had never learned to cope, and which therefore meant nothing beyond its own description, and that, second, even so, he was, to his tremendous surprise, powerfully in love with this woman, and only cowardice could contrive to send him back within the tatters of his cool shell. Moon, in turn, was trying to deal with this unexpected reversal. Drought to inundation; neither pleasant, when all is said and done.

The next days were ruinous. Sleep destroyed, no work, commitments ignored. The sexual side effects of this grief and jealousy, as cliché and evolutionary psychology inscribed, were overwhelming: initial anesthesia pricking to priapism, teary lovemaking, coming in thunderclaps and lightning again and again and again and again—but none of it offering much guidance about what you do when you get out of bed or, more precisely, whom you get back into bed with in another day or month.

He and his estranged wife Emily attended to each other's reports, giving the odd if tentative hug when it helped. The balance sheet: Emily feels she is doing quite nicely with her new lover, although she finds the Girls somewhat irritating; lots of dogged goddess worship and do-good attitudinizing. Still, she is pleased with herself, awash with forgotten sexual pleasure. Her nails are now very closely clipped.

Moon leaves for two weeks of conferences in New York, calling him long-distance at considerable expense with messages of, probably, she thinks, love, um. He lolls on his virtuous bed reading Richard Dawkins's *The Blind Watchmaker*.

His scalding gut still bears an inner bruise. He purchases a fresh bottle of Mylanta, a liquid antacid with a chalky taste. Before her departure for the United States, Moon, with rather a lot of grumbling, told Harry that she's decided, in deference to his strong feelings about the matter, to cool it. Harry, she reports, finds this a cause of some annoyance, suggesting that he and Moon might readily deal with the difficulty by the simple expedient of keeping him in the dark. It is, of course, pretty much what he would have urged upon a new lover whose partner lodged the equivalent complaint.

He muses on his ideological inconsistencies, wondering whether one's tendency to feel at forty-two things other than one felt twenty years earlier is not necessarily a proof of the brain's softening, of loss of moral fiber, but perhaps a hint of maturity. He recalls that while Bertrand Russell swore by hearty fornication early and often, everyone else involved in the proceedings tended to think him a shit for it.

And yet, and yet—one can hardly change one's views simply because of the return of the repressed.

So he is terribly pleased whenever Moon calls from New York. Somehow he never really expects her to do so.

In Melbourne, the late-autumn night is balmy, soft, and warm, and Bach is playing on the radio. Moon keeps jumping out of the world, catching him unawares. He's been zipping along through an enchanting account of echolocation in bats, and the expression *chirp* chirps at him. One of her words. Some reverberation of her voice in the pages of science. He experiences a rush. Isn't it odd? Isn't it nice? *Isn't it sickening*, he imagines Moon saying with a wince. No, she doesn't, she yearns to hear it, but yes, surely she does wince, no doubt she'd squirm a little at the pushiness. . . .

What's happening to him, he senses, is a sort of unpeeling, exhilarating and hopeful, not just the usual trudge downhill, and if there's some risk, he thinks, even a lot of risk, and some nimble footwork, and defenses are up to be snuck through, well, okay, right now he is buzzing beautifully even if his gut still feels the bruise and the bite. And that's the thing, he tells himself, that's the difference between his cool more-or-less indifference at Moon's up-front general policy announcement (and his own) of the joys of existential zipless fucking and his present preposterous pains. He cares now, yes, the clichés inscribe and traverse him, for the first time in years he is vulnerable, and things hurt vilely that a mere week back barely registered.

Is this a by-product of his years of evasion with Emily? No doubt, at least in part. What is driving him to numbness, he decides, has nothing much in common with any dubious regressive urge to ward off the threat that the world might touch him, which he suspects is the secret of many marriages. His woundedness, it now seems to him, is quite the reverse of running away. *Not* being hurt before was running away. Hurting his wife Emily and ignoring it, often enough not even noticing the fact, was, he concludes, running away. He notes the banality of this conclusion and chooses not to give a shit.

What precisely is posed for the future by these reflections, these feelings, he cannot estimate. He is clear at least that he is neither demanding from Moon, nor offering her, fidelity in the 1950s' mold. His brain has not turned entirely sideways. What he desires above all is to continue barreling along this heart-crushingly luminous and sudden road. And yes, his love, his consciousness of Moon is central to this change. Can he tell her outright? Certainly it is news that might not please her, might seem an imposition merely, might reek of an implication that he wishes to limit her choices in the interests of pursuing his own moment (perfectly commonplace, after all) of—is it saying too much?—joyful happiness.

Eighteen

SPACE BUBBLED, RIPPED open. *The Hanged Man* fell through a hole in reality, reconfiguring the computational substrate. It wasn't supposed to be possible. Until several weeks ago, it hadn't been. A girl could get the impression, Jan told herself, that we approach the Contest's endgame. Everything is up for grabs.

A planet hung before them—not the beaten copper highlighted in sulfur yellow that her spaceship had watched without boredom during her absence, suspended between Sun and Mercury—but a world more eloquent, more nuanced, more straight-out ridiculous, really. Flying saucers! And now she had one, badly dented at best, useless for space at worst, tucked up against the belly of her craft. And below, or in front of them, was the vimana's place of origin.

Somebody had been throwing craps a billion times in a row and gotten sixes each time. How else could you explain the silly place?

This Venus, Maybelline's special and wildly improbable world, was gray ocean under streamers of gray cloud. Its twin moons hung like pale skulls in black space, each half the size of Luna. Jan's eyes went to a display where this cognate's Earth burned as a milk-bright pearl. It made her heart ache to see her world, even from such a distance, seething in its deep, putrid, poisoned envelope. In this universe, a Mars-sized protoplanet, orbit twisted by chaotic dynamics, smote this accreting twin world instead of primordial Earth, blasting off a Moon-sized lump of lithosphere that spun, elongated, tore in two, gravity flinging them into their double round as their own gravity sucked away the foul smog that in most cognates had cooked Venus to impossible hothouse temperatures. Jan winced. As Earth had cooked, in this subuniverse. No life, not even extremophile bacteria.

a beautiful planet, her starship told her, regarding Venus with a dozen diverse sensors. *shall I drop you and the warrant officer off here with your sister, or should we return to the battle?*

"Not much of a battle left back there, dude." All the Shinto craft attacking her had blazed in dark energy, then snuffed out like candles. "Let's drop Pjilfplox and the wreck off, then have some R & R." Something tickled at her mind from her implant. "No, actually, I have a better idea."

Positioned politely to one side of her control room, the warrant officer fluttered leaves in a gesture of acquiescence. They could speak human languages when they wished, but they preferred not to. A faint stench of manure had entered the cabin along with the rescued vegetable, and despite her gratitude, not to mention a tincture of guilt over the smashed flying saucer, Jan would not be sorry to see the back of it. To whatever extent it could be said to have a back or front. Presumably Maybelline could tell the difference, especially when one was in rut. Jan shuddered slightly, watched Venus turning from an etched plate to a globe to landscape beneath her, swept with blowing cloud.

They fell through moist air to a cleared place marked by immense growths—not trees, not bushes, not corals, nor mottled, soaring aggregations of multicolored fungi, but some alien blend of them all—disposed against the soil in an immense

Pythagorean theorem. *The Hanged Man* floated to the edge of the large square on the hypotenuse. The tree things were hung with vimanas in various stages of construction or perhaps deposition, like gaudy holiday decorations. Light blurred from the gray tin of their hulls, dazzled from the crystal nodes in their bellies, gleamed from the eggshell white of the landing balls. *Mazel tov!* Jan shook her head, trying not to laugh.

As the starship deposited the wrecked vimana with typical delicacy, Maybelline came through a Schwelle from her Heimat fortress to meet them. It was apparent even from a distance that she was not pleased. Then again, May was rarely pleased by anything. Jan found herself grinning. That typical dyspepsia gave Maybelline her Warrior edge. It didn't make her any more likeable but it made her a formidable foe of the K-machines, a good woman to have at your side. Like that frustrating man, Ember, a Knight Warrior, if ever she'd seen one, and a damned fool with his monstrous research into superintelligence that had blighted an entire cognate Earth. Maybe the new kid, August, would make a fourth Knight. He was still unformed, that much was obvious, but he had the 'tude of a fighter—and Septima's crystal, after all, had selected him for the X-caliber implant.

Jan rode the extruded escalator to the surface, gave May a saucy wink.

"Hey there, toots. Pity about the flying gadget, but at least this time it wasn't deformers that blew the shit out of it. We're lucky that good old *Hanger* arrived in the nick of time and saved our bacon."

Her sister scowled. She was wearing some sort of ghastly mottled-green-and-puce sack, probably trying to blend in with the natives. "You never tire of breaking things, do you, Jan?"

"It was in a good cause," she said with mock contrition. "Saving the warrant officer's life. And mine, of course."

Maybelline pushed past her, offered one muscular hand to the Venusian. "Welcome home, my lord Pjilfplox. I apologize for letting you get mixed up with this nonsense. Personal vendettas have no place in the Contest." She glanced sideways, shaking her head as the vimana was dragged off by writhing tendrils into the heart of the Pythagorean theorem, where it would be disassembled in a series of processes that would leave it reduced to molecules, and those fed, in turn, into the nano-capillaries of the great Sun-hungry Builders.

Jan could not contain herself. "Give me a break. What, are you going to tell me that flying saucers don't grow on trees? Oh, wait—they do."

"Ignore the externalities as usual, Janine. Never mind the costs that have to be borne by—"

"Lighten up, kiddo." A faint, tingly stench moved in the air, not the rank odor of blood and bone or manure but something that made her heart jump, like a whiff of horny testosterone. For a moment she wondered who or what was in heat. Not me, she thought. And remembered, an instant later, that this was the tang of Venus. Goddess of love my foot, she thought. She put her arm through Maybelline's before her sister had a chance to pull away, placed the other arm around the vegetable warrior, drew them away from the hanging *Hanged Man,* made a jaunty little skip. "Come along, gang. Let's get a drink, or an infusion, or whatever. Then after that, you and me, my love," giving her sister a sharp jolt in the ribs with her elbow, "what we need to do, we need to climb back lickety-split into my hog and get back to work."

Maybelline pulled away, gave her a resentful look. "You're getting very high-handed, missy. I'm perfectly satisfied right here, doing—"

"And *then,*" Jan said more loudly, speaking blithely over the top of her, "we can fetch our new little friend August on board, and take another run out to the Xon star."

Loud noises from inside the vimana Builder made them both grit their teeth and squeeze their eyes shut involuntarily. That was the trouble with vegetables—they could be so damned *noisy*.

NINETEEN

I GOT UP from the table, thunderstruck, thinking about Tansy's ruined house, the place I had lived for years, about dead things dropped in her bathroom while she and her guard dog slept through it, more or less, the intruders equally unaware of the sleepers as they fetched dead things to the nexus point for collection. My deathwatch sister regarded me without moving anything more than her gaze, which she now held fixed upon me. I said, "Sorry, Septima, I have to go. This has been very illuminating." I reached across the table, took her hand, shook it sincerely. "I hope those poor children . . . well, you know."

"They're human, August. They'll survive. May I give you a word of advice?" Now she, too, rose, keeping her grip upon my hand, standing beside me in her plain cover-all and her military bearing.

"I'm all ears. It's more than any of my other siblings have bothered to give me."

"Don't sulk, lad. I've offered you the reason for their evasions. Think of all this as a combination of testing and training. Being tested in fire tends to burn, August, but you will come out of it—assuming you *do* come out of it—tempered and strengthened."

I did not find her comments remotely encouraging. Nobody asked me to sign up for this; I was a conscript, a poor dumb schmuck who had wandered into the wrong universe by mistake. No, that was ridiculous and self-pitying. I was a Seebeck by birth, as were they. If Great-aunt Tansy and my poor lost hound, Do Good, were illusions, dissected fragments of my family's skittish parents, still their sweet memory remained presences in my life, urgent, talismanic. They had represented stability, kindness, love, loyalty, courage, even sharp intelligence of a rather skewed variety. I owed their memory, dubious or even false as it was, at least this much: I was the last of their children and now I must stand beside my brothers and sisters in this conflict, this absurd Contest, until we prevailed.

The problem was, nobody would tell me the rules, nobody would show me the scorecard.

I shrugged. "Whatever," I said. To the operating system I added, "Give me my brother Marchmain."

A Schwelle opened. I stepped on to hot, crunchy, dazzling-white sand. Waves boomed and then hushed, boomed and crashed and hushed, tall, blue, curling water, frothing white foam. My nostrils twitched at the spiky odors of the ocean that stretched from brilliant shoreline to a horizon of paler blue. The sun was high overhead. Marchmain lay stretched on the sand, cheek resting on his crossed forearms, naked and sinewy, brown as old oak, a battered straw hat on the back of his curls. He turned his head a fraction, slitted open one eye.

"Ah, the wonderboy. I understand that I have you to thank for my continued existence, according to the damned cat. Don't stand on ceremony. Skin down, August, pull up some sand."

Water. Always water. If they weren't trying to drown me or wash me, they wanted to invite me in for a dip. Maybe it was because I had grown up as an Australian, in the sea-girt land of 'roid-free Olympic gold medalists. Cultural stereotyping. It was high-summer hot, I'd started to sweat already, and I was dizzy with what I realized, after a moment, was the cross-world equivalent of jet lag. I looked around carefully. Nobody, nothing living other than the line of trees and low bushes at my back, nothing ferociously half-alive, half-mechanical, for that matter.

Oh, what the hell. I took my plaster-dusty clothes off, placed them carefully on the sand, weighted them down with my footwear. The sand was hot under my bare soles, too hot for sitting naked and shooting the breeze, especially since there was no breeze. I ran down to the water's edge, waded quickly across a million tiny white-and-blue fragments of shattered shell to the cold, crisp sea, plunged in, sported for a few minutes as the tension in my muscles drained away, mindless as a dolphin.

I could not stay that way. For minutes I floated on my back, paddling lightly with my hands, formulating my questions as clearly as I could. After a while, I swam back to shore and joined my brother.

"I hope you kept an eye peeled for sharks," he said lazily.

I didn't know whether to believe him or not, but my muscles tightened again. "You bastard. Couldn't be bothered mentioning it before I went in?"

He rolled over on his back, propped himself on his elbows. Glistening sand clung to his torso, stuck in his sweat and body hair. A curious emblem in gold dangled on a chain, propped against one nipple. It was a question mark inside an open circle, with an arrow pointing to the right. I knew what it meant, because he'd uttered that expression when we'd first met as if it were a mantra: *Ask the Next Question.* Well, I'd just done so, although it wasn't the one that interested me.

"Calm down," he told me. Like a gymnast, he brought one foot up almost to his waist, tapped the metal gleaming there.

"These little gadgets seem to put sharks off. Handy, really. So tell me, why are you here pestering me? Shouldn't you be out with the rest of them, killing things?"

I thumped away hot sand with my own heel, crouched, scooped some more from the top layer, carefully lowered my backside into the cooler depression. "I don't suppose you have any sunblock? Or a spare hat? I'm staying here until I get some answers, but I'm not eager to pay for them with sunstroke."

"For Pete's sake, must I do everything?" Marchmain reached out his right arm, muttered a deixis, and his hand disappeared into a narrow slot in the air. He rummaged about, drew out a spray can and threw it to me, poked around some more, leaning far to the right, dragged back something white and complicated, handed it to me with a smirk. I dropped it on the sand, stood up and sprayed myself from head to toe with sunscreen, enjoying the familiar coconut savor, sat down, and examined the thing. Linen and lightweight ropes of some sort. I couldn't help myself; I started to laugh.

"You've gotta be kidding. A burnoose? Been out riding lately with Lawrence of Arabia, have you?"

"A burnoose is a cape, you ignorant dog. This is a qutrah and a kaffiyah, and as for El 'Awrence, I could tell you some interesting stories. For God's sake, it goes on like this." He fitted the Arab headgear in place for me, tightened the two bands that held it there. I felt like a fool, or somebody posing for a gay porn Web site, or both, but I was more comfortable. I tried to look imperturbable rather than humiliated.

"I suppose Lawrence gave you that dinky little insignia?"

"This?" Marchmain lifted the gold emblem off his sweaty chest, let it drop back again. "Actually, no. That's borrowed from a sage I knew, in one of the worlds. An Auger, almost, had he been one of us and not a human. A wonderful storyteller, blessed with astonishing insights—again, for a human. I wonder if you know his work? A writer named Ed Hunter Waldo."

"Sorry, never heard of him. So let's *get* to the next question, already."

"I can loan you a copy of . . . oh, what would be the point? I might as well try teaching a turnip to tap dance." Under his straw hat, he looked sulky. "You want to know where our parents have gone this time. Answer: I haven't a clue. Last time I saw them, I was dead. So to speak."

I took a deep, harrowed breath, let it out slowly, squeezed my eyes shut. That *had* been my question, of course. One of them, certainly, the one at the top of the list. I had lost my parents once to a fatal plane crash, or so I'd been told as a child, had lost them again in my presence when the K-machine filth pounded a planet of dinosaurs with a rock half the size of an asteroid. Had hoped against hope that my magician brother might have word for me of their recovery and the place to which they had retreated once more. I should have known better.

Surely Dramen and Angelica would have been in touch with me by now had they wished to do so, if only to set my mind at rest, as loving parents might be expected to do. But then it was just as likely, precisely because they *were* loving parents, that they had chosen against their deeper instincts to sequester themselves in some extremity of the multiverse so that their dozen children might be that much safer by their absence.

It was small comfort, but it was comfort.

I opened my eyes, still dizzy with time lag and the heat. "All right. Let's go back a couple of steps. Unless," I said with some bitterness, "that'd be a shocking infraction of the rule against telling that ignorant dog August anything at all the least fucking bit useful."

Shaking his head reproachfully, Marchmain leaned away from me again, murmured to the operating system, shoved his hand into nothingness, threw me a frosty can of beer, popped the lid on one himself. I pressed mine against my forehead for a moment, then scoffed the suds gratefully. I belched, surprising myself, and my brother sniggered. He said, "I take it you've been talking to Septimus. 'Tempered by fire,' that sort of thing?"

"You know the family better than I do," I said, nodding. "But that's Septima now."

That did take him aback. "So the old bitch has returned, eh? Mark my words, young August, we're moving toward the endgame." He rose, brushing off sand from his buttocks. With a self-pitying groan, he added, "Time to kick myself back into gear, I dare say. You'd think that being murdered by a bolide would earn a man more than a week's reprieve from duty. Ah well, life is just a bowl of cherries."

I stayed where I was. "I'm so tired of this runaround," I said. "Sit down, you bloody penny-ante Frankenstein. I want some answers, and I want them now."

Marchmain stared at me in astonishment, then scowled. He flung his half-empty can onto the pure sand. It teetered, tipped over; foam gushed, drained away, like a metaphor of the sea, like a metaphor of my life. "You will not speak to me like that." He puffed himself up. I've heard of toads that do that, and then explode, spraying their guts about the place. At that moment, I would not have been surprised to see this happen. I suspect I'd have trudged down to the water, washed the crap off me, then gone home. Wherever home was. I waited in silence, staring stonily back up at him.

After a long moment, his indignant expression faded. He did the most extraordinary thing. He flipped backwards from a standing jump, knees and feet rising toward his chest as he spun upon his own axis, penis and balls jumping, landed squarely in a perfect dismount, winked at me, cartwheeled away like a Leonardo da Vinci on the move, sand spraying in his wake. He fetched up at the edge of the water, threw himself into a long, flat dive that, I swear, had him skipping off the surface once or twice like a flung flat stone. I shook my head, and my borrowed headgear clapped against my shoulders. One way out of a sticky social impasse, I decided. I realized I was grinning again. The man was clearly demented.

Dripping, he came back lightly on his toes and the balls of his feet, spraying water from his hair. He bent to retrieve his straw hat, popped it on at a jaunty angle. "All right," he said calmly. "Now that we've annoyed each other sufficiently, ask your questions and be damned. I'll answer three of them free of charge. After that, if I'm still in the mood, there'll be a penalty."

That ruined my mood. "Penalty? You think this is a fairy story, Marchmain?"

"No, I've already told you. I think this is a bowl of cherries." From beneath the brim of his hat, he gave me an arch look, and scratched his balls. "Those are your first two questions. And the third?"

I stood up. "Fuck this bullshit. I came to you for help, not to provide a chorus for your fatuous one-liners. Here's a question, you fraud." I'm sure he was enjoying every moment. "Do you know how Maybelline and Lune managed to drop off Deformer corpses once a week in Tansy's upstairs bathroom without anyone noticing? Anyone—Tansy, the K-machines, the guard dog my father. I think I do."

In the shadow of his hat's brim, his eyes gleamed with a sort of delight. "Good lad! You've finally started to think your way through the puzzle, I see. You might recall that the first time we met, I complimented you on posing the puzzle we Seebecks each wish ardently to solve."

"What?"

"'Why is the Xon star such a big deal?' I believe that's the elegant way you framed your inquiry."

"Forget that," I said impatiently, ignoring his sarcasm. "I have more pressing matters on my mind. I want to know about the nexus point that Tansy—"

"Let's get out of the sun. Don't forget your clothes." Turning aside, he opened the Schwelle at an angle that prevented me seeing more than a portion of a laboratory, all glass and gleaming steel. Again, I stayed put.

"Answer my question."

"Don't be petulant. Come with me or stay where you are. It's all one to me."

Petulant? It seemed a word more appropriate to his own changeable nature, such as I had seen of it. But I wasn't really interested in a pissing contest. I picked up my clothes and boots and followed him through the portal into a dream of 1950s sci-fi B-movies. To one side, in a farther room behind glass, a large brushed-aluminum drum thrust out a padded tongue. Some sort of physiological resonance scanner, presumably. I found a cluttered lab bench, pushed aside beakers and containers marked as reagents and more mysterious substances, dumped my clothes on the cleared bench, brushed sand all over the floor, got dressed. The temperature inside was about 20°C, wonderfully cool after the blazing sun but not cold. I found a four-legged stool, pulled on my boots. When I glanced up, I found that my brother was wearing a white lab coat over a rich scarlet robe and bare feet. Hey, it was his place, he could wear a horse collar and paisley pantyhose for all I cared. When I was done, I put my elbows on the lab bench and watched him fiddling about with glassware. I said, "Searching for a good retort?"

Marchmain raised one eyebrow, drew an imaginary mark in the air with his right index finger. "Ha, the Quip Modest! Not bad. Some of the others think you're stupid. Not me. There is an immense difference between mental incapacity and ignorance, especially when ignorance is not of your own choosing."

"Gee, thanks." Actually, that rankled. I shrugged, but I suspect I flushed a little. I remembered a conversation I'd had with something enormous and terrible pretending to be a gypsy fortune-teller in the Matrioshka Brain system, where my brother Jules seemed to hang out; I found it hard to believe that he presided over it, as he tried to imply by his lordly demeanor, or, come to that, had any significant role at all. A mouse in the wainscoting, that's how Jules seemed to me. A pet mouse fed each day with scraps of cheese, and the house cats kept carefully at bay or belled. I'd asked the gypsy whether I were a bug or a feature. She assured me, in a haze of whiskey fumes, "August, you're the upgrade." Despite rumors, I'm pretty sure Microsoft and those other guys don't release stupid upgrades. I said to Marchmain, "This is your Fortress of Solitude, I take it."

"I think we've got off in the wrong foot, August. Let's not waste our energies sniping at one another. Let me ask you—has anything tried to kill you lately?"

I slapped my hand down hard on the bench, a cracking that resounded from the crisp surfaces. "Yes. And this is absolutely typical. Evasion, ducking and weaving, anything except a straight answer. You people make me sick. You in particular."

"Brother, you wound me. Why, only the other week—"

"—you slaughtered the woman who raised me." And my beloved dog, I thought, with a spurt of anger. Poor innocent Do Good. I waved away his objection even as he opened his mouth. "Yes, yes. I know they didn't really exist, I know they were a kind of disguise that my mother and father were forced to wear when they took me into hiding."

"Half the disguise," Marchmain said pedantically. "Why, you too—" He seemed ready to go on and defend himself, his obscene manipulations with the flesh and the minds of my parents. My body ached with time lag. How long had it been since my lunch with Septima? Minutes? It felt like hours. How long since I'd slept? I spoke more loudly over the top of him, truly exhausted by the man's equivocations and prevarications.

"At this point I don't fucking *care*. For what it's worth, a thing called a Jabberwock did try to kill me and Lune a few hours ago. I burned it to death, and then I helped cut it to pieces and shove them through a mirror. How did it find me? It wasn't able to do so in all the years I spent in Tansy's house. Then people started dropping in. Brother Jules set himself up just down the road as some sort of fake cleric and inveigled my poor great-aunt and her friends into his congregation. My dear sister Maybelline, Lune, God knows who-all else, started leaving corpses for collection by that good old renovated K-machine calling itself James Cooper Fenimore. And during all this nobody noticed Tansy, or me, or Dugald O'Brien, until I woke up after a shot of patented green ray and screwed everything up by charging off through the bathroom mirror in search of . . ."

I trailed away. None of his business. "And within hours the deformers turned up and smashed the place to shreds. Why did they care? Well, it's obvious—they cared because they'd found Tansy and the dog, maybe me, too, for that matter. They'd found my father and mother, or some remnant portion of them, and they must have been out of their minds with delight. How long have Dramen and Angelina been in hiding?

Years, decades, centuries? Longer than that, maybe? Well, not in that house, at any rate, or that country. Less than a hundred years. Plenty of time to settle in, change identities now and then, move from one city and state to another. But that's not the question, is it?"

"There might have been a question buried in there somewhere," Marchmain said judiciously. He was messing about with water and a beaker. "If so, I didn't catch it."

"Why the house? *That's* the question. What was Jules hanging about there for? Why was it effectively invisible for so long? And why that place as a nexus point to lug the guts?"

"You're picking up the vernacular quite nicely," he said. "And speaking of Jules, he'd be pleased. For him, everything is metaphor. Phenomenology as semiotics. Representational ontology. He's got a point, I'll grant him that. We might as well be uttering spells when we open up the Schwellen with a code word or two." He raised his hands in mock self-defense at my impatient look. "The house. Okay, I never went there. Possibly Jules dropped everyone off there after I completed my work. Or perhaps they made arrangements with somebody else. The whole family has been discussing it, of course, since you turned up. Obviously I knew everyone was tucked away safely somewhere. I preferred not to ask for the details. None of my business, really. I'm a surgeon, not a real estate agent."

"Christ! You're all as bad as each other. This is why the house was important: it was off the board, outside your goddamned Contest arena, a small secure locality beyond the map—or was, until I fucked things up by going through the mirror and drawing everyone's attention to us." My limbs were trembling with frustration; I was a hair away from blowing a hole in his slick lab with sunfire from my extended right hand, just to wake the bastard up, just to get his attention, just to show him how very serious I was about this. I gritted my teeth, tried to keep my temper, remembering that poor innocent woman in the car I'd very nearly slain in my fit of paranoia. "I'm starting to wonder whether you've all been programmed like goddamned machines yourselves to avoid facing the real questions. 'Ask the next question' my ass! *Avoid* the next question, avoid *all* the questions, that's the way you pests prefer it. You call yourself Players, but as far as I can see you might as well be playing cards without a functioning brain between the lot of you." My nostrils twitched. The lab was filling with a wonderful odor, and a gurgling, and a hissing.

"I see." Marchmain crossed the room, found two large mugs on a bench, filled them with black coffee from the beaker. He pushed one across to me. "Can I get you cream or sweetener?"

I pulled the decorated white mug toward me. It showed a ragged old tomcat strumming a guitar. A Kliban cartoon. I looked at the verse the cat was singing. *Love to eat them mousies.* Cathooks, I thought. *Nibble on they tiny feet.* The godthing, the Angel. I shook my head, lifted the hot stuff to my lips, blew across it, wondered for a moment if it might be doped with some heinous substance that would turn me into a toad or leave me blind and deaf. I decided that was pretty unlikely, and sipped the finest coffee I've ever drunk, including Toby's. Being a superscience magician clearly had its rewards.

Marchmain said judiciously, "I take it you've not yet been initiated into the protocols and callings of the Contest?"

"All I know about your blessed Contest," I said, still testily, "is a mishmash of words splattered about by you lot. It's like some sort of moronic hazing ritual. Even Lune's avoided the topic." It hurt me to admit it, but it was true—the woman I loved had been just as evasive as the rest.

"Drink your coffee and have a breather, that'd be my recommendation. You're spinning your wheels. You're running in circles chasing your tail. A moment ago, you informed me that Septimus—sorry, Septima—had explained that you're still in page training, one might say undergoing a species of hieratic military apprenticeship. You can't expect to look in the back of the textbook for answers. What's more," he said, raising his voice as I opened my mouth, "the answers to some of your questions—in particular those you probably have not even thought of yet—are unknown to us. Has it not occurred to you, young August, have you not noticed even when we declared it explicitly, that we are in pursuit of questions of our own? That the essence of a contest is mystery as well as valor, strategy and tactics evolved in the absence of complete knowledge, which Gödel and Chaitin assure us is out of reach anyway? Oh, good grief, uncross your eyes. I see I'm back to teaching abstract expressionism to a field mouse."

With considerable effort, I clung to the small amount of information he'd managed to let slip. "What protocols? And what are *callings?*"

"Ah, the creature stirs from its sleep. A calling is a—" For a moment, Marchmain seemed taken aback, for the first time lost for words. He shrugged. "Might as well try to explain an orgasm to a three-year-old, or one's burning hunger to see the final act of *Götterdämmerung* to a twelve-year-old. Or the sweet tang of fresh honey to a fish." He shook his head, waved his hands helplessly. "You'll know it when you feel it, boy, like a tropism, like the memory of a dream where your task lay ahead of you, a pattern of bright lights in mist. Like . . ."

"My God," I said. I could not believe it, yet there it was. "I was right. You poor gullible brainwashed ninnies. You're tools. You're the tokens in the game, not the Players. Something else

147

has you dangling from strings. My God," I said again. "How trite. How pitiful. How sad." I stood up and walked away from the bench. "Count me out, buddy." All I wanted to do was head for home, but it was gone, and that hurt so bad I needed to scream. I wanted to find Lune, to hold her against me, to defend some last sanctuary of reason and trust. Yet I dared not go to her, not in my current frame of mind. It came to me with an overpowering sense of conviction that the person I needed to speak to, and urgently, was my sister Jan. I imagined her, louche and confident on the bridge of her starship, questing after this Xon star they were all obsessed by, half stoned, dressed like a Goth princess, a cheeky grin . . . she was the obvious choice. I couldn't work out why I'd bothered coming to question this dismal idiot Marchmain or Septima before him when I could have asked instead for Janine. I said to the operating system, "Give me Jan."

Tearing; a gust of freaky air, instantly recognizable, utterly unlike any place I'd ever been, in this universe or the others I'd sampled, except Maybelline's haunt. I stepped through onto a slightly raised dais of copper-gold metal. Orichalcum, probably, if I remembered my James Churchward Atlantis and Mu books correctly. Maybe that's where I was. There was a terrific clattering noise. Two of my recently discovered sisters turned as I came through, one of them with a jug in her hand, wiping her red mouth with a forearm.

"Was just about to call you," Jan said. "Good timing."

They stepped up to join me from an open scrubby place surrounded by immense growths—not trees, not power stanchions, not gigantic fungi—that poked straight up toward rushing clouds. Daylight reflected dully from metal things that looked, improbably, like flying saucers, high in the growth masses. That's not all we were surrounded by. Creatures resembling ambulant vegetables went this way and that, busy and somewhat martial. I'd caught Maybelline fucking one of these aliens, if that's what you'd call what I'd found them doing. It had been affronted and flown off in its flying saucer.

The gravity seemed slightly wrong, and I wondered what version of Earth this was. I took another sniff of the air, and felt my blood racing.

"Jan, I—" A tremendous dark shadow fell upon us. I ducked involuntarily, looked up. "*Shit!*" I said.

The thing ceased its motion, hung above us without falling. It was black. It was enormous. It was the thing diagrammed by the K-machine that had manifested its image in the library catalog screen. I wanted to throw myself face down on the ground, cover my head. A ghost of electricity flimmered about its dark form, the great tree-trunk shape of its holds, its engines, its fuel tanks, whatever those immense black spheres might be. I crouched on one knee, brought up my right arm.

"Augie, dude!" Jan stood beside me, grinning happily. She grabbed my lethal hand, gave it a shake. "No need to make a knee, just family here. And friends. Oh, and good old *Hanger* up there."

It still felt as if the terrible mass plunged down at us, about to smash our flesh and bones to pulp. *The Hanged Man* stayed put overhead, despite the illusion, like a very low thundercloud made of black metal and alive with lightning. I dropped my arm, and Jan's hand fell with it. Maybelline uttered a caustic cough, followed by a snigger. I must have offended her at some time. Maybe breaking up her tryst with the Adamski vegetable. Maybe snatching Lune away from her hopeless infatuation. I bared my teeth at her, halfway between a snarl and a conciliatory smile. She rolled her eyes and said to Jan, "Do we really have to take *him*?"

"*Take* me?"

"I hope you've got your toothbrush packed, bro," Jan said. Her tattoo, Sylvie, winked at me, put her tiny fingers between tiny lips, emitted a high-pitched whistle. The red-gold plate we stood on left the ground and drifted smoothly upward toward the vessel's darkness. "You're off for a ride in a starship."

TWENTY

EXAMINATION SEASON APPROACHES. As he switches off his overhead projector, his students shuffle anxiously in their seats, wanting to know nothing other than clues toward what will be on the paper. One or two of them, it's true, possess a spark of initiative and enthusiasm for what he still finds himself calling, with a suitably ironic cough, the life of the mind. But then, as Socrates said, the unexamined life is not worth living, and by God, these poor little devils are going to be examined within an inch of their lives in this age of economic rationalism and education geared ever more tightly to the requirements of a workforce that ever more swiftly will need no workers at all. Computers, they'll do it for you. They'll mark your multichoice exams, they'll weld your new Suzuki, and type your next essay after downloading it from the World Wide Web, they'll handle import and export of nations in a trice, they'll fuck up your credit card and ruin your rating without pausing for breath, without taking a sick day. Christ! I've seen the future, he thinks, and it's out of work.

"Okay, people." Formal lecture done, he steps out for the last few minutes from behind the lectern, man of the people, no technological barrier of sound system and overhead projectors for these few minutes. Facing them, he runs his fingers in a sort of reflex nervousness through his thinning hair. No need for nervousness, he's been doing this for years. Maybe it's that cute coffee-colored babe in the second row who's throwing him off his stride. He allows himself to glance at her, nod slightly. There's a definite resemblance to Moon Ku, he can't deny it. What an imbecile! Still mooning over Moon, even if he can't bear to talk to her for more than five minutes, the tormenting and twisting and entirely predestined loops of their flagellating conversation laid up in advance like the entrapping circuits of a maze, like the many-plied bad moves in a chess game that a computer might avoid in its blind quest through search space, while the poor benighted human player blunders on, trapped by those first injudicious moves of pawn and knight. By main force he brings himself back to focus. "Let's talk some ontology."

Of course, some jackass jumps up with an objection based on solipsism, an idea he seems to think he's invented even though he's patently filched it from a sci-fi writer. "Why should I even believe in all you zombies?" the kid says, smirking.

"You believe in me, I'll believe in you," he says. "The Unicorn's Bargain." They look at him numbly, for the most part. Maybe they don't know what a unicorn is. No, that's unlikely, most of them have their damned noses stuck in one fat, vacuous, fantasy trilogy after another, nothing but dragons and feisty princesses and more unicorns than you can poke a helical horn at. "It's a quote from Lewis Carroll, the noted logician," he tells them wearily. "It's also a sort of ontological corollary of Gricean implicature, which we discussed briefly several months ago. A Lewis Carrollary, if you like." It's a terrible pun; in evidence, nobody laughs. Moon would have laughed, or at least sniggered.

One of the few eager beavers is insistent. "But like, suppose some creep goes, 'You're a real asshole,' and you go, 'No, *you're* the asshole,'" and you like want to *obliterate* the dude, well, doesn't that . . ." The words ebb away, and whatever fraction of thought lay behind them disperses into the conditioned air. Outside, he knows, there is a wintry August chill on the breeze. He hunches his shoulders slightly, imagining stepping outside into the quadrangle, bare branches of the few trees snapping in the wind. A shot of Scotch would go down very nicely. But he needs to stay alert. There's a pile of essays on his desk in his cramped, shared office space, waiting for him to drag his Husserlian intentionality across their dismal pages. At least these days most of the repetitive gibberish and constellations of category errors are legible, banged out on the dot-matrix and laser printers that have replaced the typewriters that replaced the appalling scrawl most students of his own day had inflicted upon their long-suffering tutors. He says, "Solipsism is not an option. The world is not your dream. It's not even the shared dream of everyone in this room. That particular dead end . . ."

"How can you be so sure?" Shit, what's her name? It's not Moon. What's in a name? Ontology recapitulates philology. "What test," she goes on relentlessly, "can we apply to our construction of the world, to our experience of others, like, what *operational* test, you know, would disprove solipsism?" She closes her pink lips, regards him solemnly. There is no venom in her question. He has grown accustomed to the expectation of a barb. Has grown accustomed, indeed, to responding with one still sharper and more brutal. But that was then. This is . . . not-then. If p and not-p, then any q at all logically follows. Talk about solipsism. Talk about Lewis Carroll.

He wonders if he is losing his mind. Distraction is one thing, obsession is another altogether. If distraction is p, and obsession is q . . .

"I'll see your solipsism," he says with an artful smile, "and raise you panpsychist emergent stochastic constructivism."

This time they all stare at him as if he's just taken off his trousers and danced a jig in front of the class. Calm down, he cautions himself. These are freshmen, it's their first bloody year at university, even if the end of their first year is now near at hand, their testing time. Poor little lambs.

"Never mind," he says in a buoyant tone. "It won't be on the exam. What will be on the exam are the views of Plato and Descartes concerning—"

"Just a moment," another student says. Flattened New Zealand schwa vowels; a Kiwi, certainly. "You're saying we sort of . . . *collude* . . . in creating reality?" Big kid, Maori genes there, looks like a rugby player, broken nose, but there is no rule that says jocks have to be stupid. High probability, good Bayesian priors, no certainty. The kid—Jonathan something?— is saying, "The only common basis we could have for, you know, having this conversation is if we live in a shared world. I mean, one that came before any of us. We evolved in the real world, we're adapted to it, it's absolute superstitious bullshit to think it could be the other way around."

"But Foucault says—" another kid begins, but now he's snapped to attention and waves for silence.

"Okay, Jonathan, good point. But what if the shared world is like one of those MUDs you kids spend all your time playing in when you're not getting whacked on ecstasy?" Someone hisses. "I'm serious. Suppose the world we're experiencing is some kind of humongous computer simulation in a cosmos that's completely different from this one. Maybe it's got more dimensions. Or maybe it's this universe in a thousand billion years time. Imagine that. Intelligence has taken over matter completely and rewritten the rules. Maybe the creatures in that far future amuse themselves by reconstructing their own history, and that's us. Or they just make up some new worlds and populate them with a few billion emulated minds and bodies, and *that's* us." He pauses, lets them think about it. Maybe some of them do. The Foucault fan is looking disgusted, and seems to have flipped open a newspaper. The coffee girl—young woman—is thoughtful. The jock named Jonathan is ready to explode.

"You're saying we're just the shadows in Plato's cave, right?" It is a penetrating remark. This boy has been doing some reading. "So what, Doc? Lots of people think some God created the world." One beefy hand slaps down on the writing bench folded over his lap. The loud crack wakes some of them up. "If we're in a multiuser domain, it's exactly the same. We can't tell if we're the pieces in some game, just deluding ourselves we're playing it instead of being played. I mean," the kid rises in his place, hulkingly, at the end of his aisle, "if this is all just a simulation, why shouldn't I just come down there and smash your head open like a fucking coconut?"

Audible gasps. He steps forward from the lectern, narrows his eyes at the young man. "I don't appreciate threats, Mr. Wilson." Amazing how the name comes to his lips when he needs it. "Even in a gedanken."

Lazily, the kid sits back down, not even slightly discountenanced. "See? Even the imaginary threat of violence cuts through the bullshit. The world's real. That's ontology enough for me, dude. Next topic."

He sighs. "Kick the stone. Thus you and Dr. Johnson refute Berkeley. How delightfully simple. How simply delightful." He needs that Scotch. The kid is right, of course. Three thousand years and more of arcane bullshit and tortuous logic-chopping. What the hell's the point? It's a job, dude, he mocks himself. It's a paycheck. He glances at his watch, and the date catches his eye for the second time today. Time to wrap this up anyway.

But he can't leave things dangling like this. In a rush, he says, "I believe your real concern, the concern we all feel, is less a matter of ontological vertigo and more one of ethics. The problem with smashing somebody's skull to prove a point is that outside a lucid dream you can't be sure you're only pretending an action in a simulated arena. Listen, here's the bottom line. If people in the far future do somehow create a simulated world and move themselves into it, or they create fake people to live there, there's only one rational and ethically prudent way to go about it." He pauses. They are restless, delving in their bags. "Build a whole array of customized universes, share them out among those of like mind. Put up firewalls between them. Tailor them to whatever standards appeal to those choosing to live within them. No fuss, no strife—" No Moon.

"That's apartheid, isn't it," the beautiful young woman says reproachfully. "We won't kill the Jews and the Gypsies and the Arabs and the blacks, let's just shove them off into some imaginary world where the sight of them no longer offends us."

"No, no," he cries vehemently, "of course that's not what I—" But amid the rustling of paper and the slamming of books and the clatter of seats springing up as students begin to straggle out at the end of the hour, his voice is lost. He shrugs, steps back behind the lectern, looks for his briefcase and its copy of Frank Tipler's new book, *The Physics of Immortality*, mailed to him by Emily in Sydney. No hard feelings. For a moment, he places his face in his hands. Happy birthday, dude. When he looks up, the room is empty.

TWENTY-ONE

SOMETIMES RUTH SEEBECK felt like a kindergarten teacher surrounded by gaudy toys. A knitted snake wriggled across the floor from her mail-drop Schwelle toward the escritoire, a large white envelope clamped in its woolly mouth. Ruth suppressed a smile, found a blunt-edged letter opener, tore the seal, drew out a crisp sheet headed in gold embossed cursive script. Great heavens, the self-indulgence of the woman! Yes, Juni was mistress of an entire world smogged to choking point in her wretched floating nano-gadgets, her offogs, so there was scant effort involved. It would be the work of a moment, of a word—of a thought, very nearly—to run up whatever fancy item of self-amusement took her caprice. Ruth rattled the heavy sheet, reading the invitation, looked away, frowned. Actually, she told herself reflectively, that wasn't quite it. The offogs in Juni's world might assemble a sort of tempo- rary *faux* of this document out of their own substance, but it would not endure passage through a Schwelle to another cog- nate Earth. This had been compiled with molecular assemblers, or—amazing thought—Juni had sat down with a fountain pen and *written it* on *paper* by *hand.*

> My dearest Sister
> You are cordially invited to a T-party, to be held

tomorrow afternoon in the Thyme Garden. I do hope
everyone will come. Please bring an amusement to
share with your fellow revelers. Dress in costume (I
shall be coming as a Faerie!) or if you'd rather, as you
are. All shall have prizes!

I do hope to see you there tomorrow, along with
every one of our brothers and sisters. Of course you
may bring a friend!

Your loving sister, Juni Seebeck

Ruth placed her invitation to one side, shook her head
minutely. A Faerie. How precious! A Tegmark-levels party, at
this moment of impending crisis. Her family was corroding like
the inner workings of an old clock left too long unwound. She
sighed, rose, called a handful of her assistants, and set off down
the empty corridor to her nexus collection point.

The most recent Deformer trophy lay stretched and inani-
mate but carefully restrained on an autopsy table close to her
array of tools. A robot like an especially mobile Calder mobile, all
wire coat hangers and boxes, clattered and jangled to her. Ruth
took her white lab coat, drew it over her neat afternoon-wear. A
drawer slid open, disclosed surgical gloves and mask; she slipped
them on, dismissed the machine. Through the eyepieces of the
mask, she dispassionately examined the motionless, terrifyingly
dangerous thing on the table. After a moment's study, she found
a scalpel and took its face off.

Time to learn as much as she could of what the damnable
thing and those who manipulated it understood concerning
recent developments in the Seebeck family. She twisted its neck
cruelly, clamped the head in place. With probes positioned as
delicately and exactly as acupuncture needles, she closed down
potential pathways in the spine. When she had done all she

could to protect herself and ensure the thing's responsiveness, she switched some of its brain back on.

Of course, it shrieked most foully. Ruth observed with quiet satisfaction that she had not recoiled in the slightest, although muscles in her chest, bowels, and throat tightened. A touch with another probe hushed the racket.

"Speak to me and tell the truth," she said. "Tell me: What is the number and clade formation of your principal Opponents in the Contest?"

With plain reluctance, the Kurzweil spiritual machine told her, "Two of three, and two of two, and one each of two." It ground its fake teeth.

"A certain ambiguity attends this response." Ruth performed an excruciation. "Which are the three, the two, the one each?"

Answers came grudgingly, but they came. "The three are Rocks, each of Solid, and Augurs, each of Liquid."

"Yes, Earth and Water, and?"

"Two are Warriors of the Gaseous Realm."

"Air," Ruth said.

"If you will. Two are Warriors of the Energy Realm."

"We call that realm Fire."

"You may call it what you wish, witch, bitch."

"Indeed I may, and do. Keep a civil tongue in your mouth. But wait, you have no mouth." She made it scream. After a time, a robot assistant crossed to the table, dabbed at the faceless face with tissues. "You have not completed your roster, I think."

The thing gasped and groaned, as if it were alive, as if it were human, as if it possessed in truth and not merely in name some spiritual call upon her sympathy. She had seen the work these foul things did. When it quietened, it added reluctantly, "One is an Augur, of the Gaseous Realm. One more is a Rock, of the Energy Realm."

Ruth regarded it reflectively. So they knew already. "That makes twelve, not eleven."

The dead machine said in a tone of flattened fury, "Update— One is correct."

"Provide the identities of these opponents."

"You know them. You're one of them."

She made it scream again. It broke both legs against its restraints. "Provide the clade table of your principle Opponents."

"You are Ruth Seebeck, a Rock."

"This is correct. Continue."

"Ember Seebeck, Warrior. Toby Seebeck, Rock. Maybelline Seebeck, Warrior. Avril Seebeck, Augur. Juni Seebeck, Rock. Decius Seebeck, Augur. Jules Seebeck, Augur. Septimus Seebeck, Rock. Marchmain Seebeck, Augur. Janine Seebeck, Warrior.

"Still only eleven."

It cried out in a fury.

"Curse your jackass ears! Update—August Seebeck, Warrior."

"Ah, so this much is known to you. And if to you, to all of your number, via contagion."

The faceless face tried to scowl, by heavens. "This is a calumny!" She touched it once, twice. It leapt against the metal bands. "He lay in hiding in the shielded place. Now he carries the X-caliber scar. The letter and spirit of the Accord are breached."

Ruth felt her own lips twist. This was not a convenient line of investigation. She said, with a prod, "You neglected to specify Realms. Never mind. Now we come to the interesting part of this conversation. Tell me without prevarication the equivalent names and stations of *our* principal Opponents." She made a calculated move with a probe.

The machine, stretched powerless upon her table, cursed her vilely, and all her clade with her. "Begone, soulless churl." But it started to speak, and Ruth listened with the greatest interest. Finally it fell silent once more. It seemed unlikely that the thing would provide her any more insight into the range of its apprehension. She shut it down completely, took the top off its head, and went to work taming it and bending it to her purposes.

"Give me some music," she told a robot hanging like a scarlet spider from the wall. Instantly, hidden speakers bathed her in the Lacrimosa from Mozart's *Requiem in D-Minor*, K. 626, the version completed in a cognate Tegmark world where the composer had recovered from rheumatic fever but died two years later, still penniless, after a fall from a fractious horse. It seemed like a metaphor of some sort, Ruth decided, delving into the machinery. She murmured, "I'll go to Juni's T-party as Constanze Weber Mozart." Everyone had hated her, too. The thought made her smile.

TWENTY-TWO

DESPITE MY SATISFYING leap at the age of twelve from a diving platform at mad Jamie Davenport's urging, I never grew to like heights. When there's hard-packed soil down below, rather than water, I'm even more reluctant to look over the edge. Even so, when I peered across the lip of the levitating metal coin carrying us up smoothly toward the dark opening in a darker starship built like a Tarot Tree of Life, I felt a powerful pressure to jump off immediately and take my chances. Minimize the damage. Annoyingly, we were already too high for that sort of theatrical getaway.

"A little starship adventure, eh? Not on your bloody life, mate," I said. "Jan, take me back down. You idiot, if we start tearing around in this thing, we'll be marooned." I was thinking of the Xon star and its apparent inhibition of Vorpal abilities. Jan should be the last person to let that factor escape her attention; hadn't she been stuck inside this very spacecraft for decades of rest-frame time, her access to the Schwellen portals blocked, limping home at a substantial proportion of light speed?

"Marooned?" Jan, though, elected to be blithe. "Nobody gets marooned *in* a starship. It's when they push you out the airlock and—"

The metal surface under our feet bore us irresistibly into a shadowed cavern, slipped snugly into a prepared cavity. Lights glowed on, filling the space with glare-free illumination, as heavy doors to the hold slid noiselessly into place, shutting off our view of the surface below.

I was in a curious frame of mind, some disturbed part of me noted. I knew with certainty that it was a very good idea to be here with Jan and Maybelline. Hadn't I been planning to join them from the outset? Our task—The details, admittedly, were a little unclear. That puzzled me, in a remote way, because it was obvious what we needed to do, or at least that we had to do something specific, pursue a path toward—

I felt a buzzing sort of tingling in my right hand, then, and glanced down at the X-caliber implant. While it was not glowing white hot or flashing in rainbow colors, certainly it was trying to tell me something.

A tickle in the back of my mind, a stirring in my chest. I was starting to get mad, but I didn't know why.

I followed my two sisters through a circular doorway that sealed cozily behind us, along a companionway as bland and reassuring as a Tokyo high-rise corridor or, indeed, a similar passageway aboard the starship *Enterprise*. My god! A genuine starship. It was mind-boggling. Somehow just being here was more ferociously exciting than sampling the infinite variety of the Tegmark levels in my rite of passage with Toby and Lune a thousand years ago, or two weeks, or whatever.

I tripped, tangled in my own clumsiness, caught myself, felt a burst of—felt something. Unaccountable anger. It seemed an odd emotion to be subject to at a moment like this. The women, up ahead, were arguing about politics of some kind, their dispute made incomprehensible by the tongue-twisting names they flung back and forth. Wait a minute, I'd heard one of those names the first time I stumbled upon Maybelline having her way with an alien from a flying saucer. Pjilfplox. No, wait a moment, her vegetable love had been Phlogkaalik. My baffled tensions increased. I was angry, could feel my anger surging but blocked, and I didn't know why. I wanted to discuss it with Lune, and she wasn't here. I stopped dead, and called after my sisters, "This is far enough. Take me back down to Earth. What the hell am I *doing* here?" I fell silent, frowning. Surely it was obvious why I was there. I knew perfectly well—

"If you wish to get back down to Earth," Jan said, laughing, looking over her shoulder at me, "I'd strongly recommend staying aboard."

I stared at her. "Now you're *threatening* me?"

"Don't be ridiculous, you little prick," Maybelline said, looking ready to punch me. "Where do you think you are, anyway? Just down the street from the strip mall? That's not Earth down there, you idiot, it's Venus."

Oh. I stood where I was, squeezed my eyes tightly, probably swayed back and forth a bit. A sort of memory from my Vorpal grammar clarified itself, not very much like a voice whispering in my ear, more as if I'd known this all along but clear recollection had managed to slip my mind. Yes, of course. Maybelline's Heimat, her comfortable quarters and home away from home, was not on one of the variant Earths but on some incredibly unlikely boutique Venus. I started to laugh, not happily, and the sound of it grated in my ears. Voyage to Venus. Easy travel to other planets. I joined the navy to see the sea, and what did I see? I saw the—

"Take it easy, kiddo," Jan told me. She walked back toward me, held out the jug she was still clutching in her right hand. "Have a snort, you look as if you could use a heart-starter."

The liquid burned the back of my throat, numbed my tongue, made my ears ring faintly. Or perhaps that was some sort of pressure change. An ambient, directionless machine voice told us, *welcome back aboard, Commander. we are returning to venerastationary orbit. no enemy forces are apparent at this time. good afternoon, August Seebeck, i for one am pleased to make your acquaintance finally. i am* The Hanged Man, *and i'll be your starship transport today.*

Wonderful. A robot spaceship pilot with an impeccably dry sense of humor. And what the hell was "venerastationary"? Up popped the answer, like a remembered translation: stationary in relation to the surface of Venus. Oh—as in "geostationary," like a satellite in Clarke orbit, hanging above the same place on the Earth, except this time we really *were* talking about Venus. You might suppose I'd be beyond astonishment by this point, but that sent me reeling into a moment of dazed confusion. I really *had* been standing on another planet. Not the Venus of my own Solar System, obviously, as that was a poisonous, blazing waste land ruined by its own runaway greenhouse effect. Or so I'd once read in *Scientific American*. Now the lunatics wanted to kidnap me for a flight to some unknown destination in the wrong universe. No. And again, no.

"Ladies, obviously we're talking at cross-purposes. I don't even know what convinced me to come here. Some sort of bloody mental programming, that's what I think." I looked with disgust at the thing piercing my palm like a stigmata where they'd gone wrong and left the nail in. "I don't like being pushed around. And that's all any of you seem to be doing to me. In future, I'd recommend asking nicely." I addressed myself to the deixis operating system. "Take me back to Toby's."

Nothing happened. I said it again, more sharply, and then once more, using Lune's name. Nothing happened.

I looked angrily at the women. One of them was blocking me. I hadn't yet learned that trick, but obviously it was possible—

Toby had shut out the rest of the clamoring pests the first time Lune and I visited his private universe.

we are in direct line of sight to the Xon anomaly, the starship told me in its strange voice. *normal service will resume when that object is occulted. regrettably on our current orbit this would not occur for seventy-nine hours. we will not still be here at that time.*

"Seventy-nine *what?* Take us back down to the surface, I'm not waiting here for—"

the planet Venus in this cognate has a slower rotational period than the main-stem twenty-four-hour period of the planet Earth, but it is considerably faster than the standard retrograde Veneran diurnal period of 243 days.

"The kid doesn't want to know that sort of tedious crap, *Hanger*," Jan said. "Bore-*ring.* C'mon, team, come through to the control deck and I'll show you around. And try to play nice—we're going to be here together for way longer than a Veneran day, so let's settle down, huh?" She started to put her arm through mine, and I pulled away sharply. That earned me a hurt look.

"I don't recall signing on to any mission, Commander. Put me down on the surface immediately. This is kidnapping. It's blackbirding."

Now my sister the spaceship driver looked more baffled than hurt. Peering at me from the corners of her eyes, Jan frowned, shrugged, opened her lips as if to speak, thought better of it, shook her head, turned away, and started back along the corridor.

Maybelline stayed put, blocking my way, said to me, "Shut the hell up, you idiot. This woman has brought us back the most significant information about the Xon star that we've ever . . . How do you think we managed to reprogram the vimana you somehow managed to bumble into saving from destruction, back on Ember's world? How do you think *The Hanged Man* got *here*? You just don't have a clue, do you?" She, too, shook her head. The curls bounced. I felt angry enough that I was tempted to grab her by the shoulders and give her such a shake that her teeth would bounce as well. Luckily, I'm the courteous type, plus I remembered that May was some sort of Warrior Princess, probably able to rip me into bleeding chunks. That realization just made me more cautious; I was not mollified.

"*I* don't have a clue? Why should I give a flying fuck? I'm not part of your brainless game or contest or whatever it pleases you to call it. You and Lune and your robot pal Coop hijacked me. You pestered poor Tansy with your bloody corpses until the K-machines came down and destroyed everything she loved. You might as well have tapped the deformers on the shoulder and waved a Judas flag, then handed them a map marked with a big red X, you careless bitch."

"I can't see you whining about this to your beloved Lune, somehow," Maybelline said. She flushed angrily. Jealousy and rejection, surely that was it, as I'd once suspected. I could not find it in me, at that moment, to feel sympathy for her. Truth be told, I was rather glad that Lune was millions of kilometers and several universes distant from us at that moment. I loved her wildly, but just now I had more than one bone to pick with her. She knew much more than she'd told me, and I felt like a manipulated fool whenever I stumbled into a gap of logic or family history that might have been filled by a sentence or two of considerate explanation, and be damned less with Septima's nonsense about knights in training.

So, of course, "Leave Lune out of this," I said, equally angrily but rather feebly. "Ship, why are we not yet on the ground?"

authorization has just been received from vimana control to break from orbit. we are now accelerating out of the solar equatorial plane toward the Xon manifestation at right ascension seventeen hours forty-six minutes, declination minus twenty-nine degrees. point 866 light velocity will be attained when gamma equals two within 144.7 hours. assuming no further attack, we should arrive at the star in—

"What!" We entered a spacious elevator without elevator music. The doors opened almost immediately, and I followed the women into a huge space of comfortable chairs, consoles, large screens portraying data icons in vivid detail, several showing a black starfield. In one, Venus was the smallest shrinking half-orb almost lost in darkness. I blinked, and it was gone.

"Cool it, dude," Jan told me, popping herself into a large, comfortably padded chair and pulled her legs up sideways under her. She had good legs, I couldn't help noticing. Sister or not. "What's with the attitude? You know what we've got to do. There's no point acting like a resentful, spoilt child." She gave me a gamine grin. "Hey, listen to *me*. Like some schoolmarm. Listen, August, stick your butt in one of these seats and lean back for the ride of a lifetime. Or do you want me to get back to the guided tour?"

Diagrams formed in large three-dimensional displays, rotated, sketched lines presumably of trajectories, mapped celestial bodies. Labels appeared whenever my eye rested upon some portion of a display. A month ago, I would have found this astonishing technology. In fact, I still did, but in the meantime I'd met the Good Machine, blown a Deformer dreadnought out of the sky by sheer force of personality and the sunflame from my good right hand, visited my brother Decius in an environment bubble poised within an Omega Point cosmic collapse . . . I felt tired.

"This is completely ridiculous," I said. "You can't just *do* this to someone. I mean, just drag me in off the street in a faster-than-light craft that looks like it was designed by someone with a Tarot fixation. I'm not going to put up with—"

slower than the velocity of light, the spacecraft told me. *it is dangerous for macroscopic objects to travel faster than our optimal velocity of under 0.9c. ablation due to impact with electrically neutral interstellar media has the potential to obliterate—*

I tried to take in what the machine was saying. Impossible. Grotesque. *The Hanged Man* seemed to be telling me that I was stuck inside a prison cell moving at relativistic speeds all the way to the bloody Xon star. I clawed at my memories of physics classes. As you got close to the speed of light, your local time slowed down in relation to the rest of the universe, wasn't that it? Shit. And the bloody spaceship had just said that it was aiming to haul its ass at 90 percent of the speed of light. For how long? Everyone I'd left behind—Lune! Lune!—would be sundered from me not just by the distance we covered but by a worse dislocation, a gulf of dilated time. In a strangled voice, I said, "How far . . . I mean, how long . . . goddamn it, *how much time are you planning to steal from me?*"

Both women regarded my outburst with apparent surprise. They glanced back and forth, then at me. Maybelline said, "Pods above, you're a whining brat! You've been watching too much sci-fi. Time is a nonissue for us Players." With a conspicuous shudder, she added, "Luckily, we won't have to spend the next thirty years listening to your bellyaching." She crossed the control room to Jan, adopted a formal posture before her. "Commander, I request permission to withdraw into an Entertainment for the duration."

"Aw, honey." It seemed to me that Jan made an effort to look crestfallen. "C'mon, we hardly ever get to hang out together.

Let's at least have a meal together, two sisters and our new brother."

"Frankly, I can't imagine anything more tedious. With your permission?"

Jan's lips tightened. With a wave of one hand, she settled back into her padded chair. "Granted. *Hanger* can direct you to your quarters." Immediately, she turned her attention back to me. "You're not going to run off on me too, are you?" Her eyes danced with recovered merriment. "I mean, I know you'd *love* to, but you can't get there from here, sorry. August, get that ramrod out of your ass and sit down over here next to me, for Bar-Kokhba's sake."

Gritting my teeth, I did so. "It's not a ramrod in my ass, it's a *pain* in my butt—which Maybelline gives me. She's the most self-centered cow I've ever met." I caught myself; what was I doing here, indulging in Stockholm syndrome, where the captive starts to identify with the captor? Could this be a deliberate ploy? Good cop/bad cop? Nice sister/nasty sister? I didn't think so. Jan really did seem a sweetie. And an astronaut—good god, my sister the spaceman. Even so, impressed as I was by Jan's merry, bohemian air and her possession of an enormous starship, I was still completely pissed off. I had been *kidnapped*, damn it. "I told you, I never signed up for this shit. What's this thirty years crap? You seriously expect me to sit still while I'm hauled off into the middle of nowhere and then come back to find Lune three decades older?"

"Oh, no," Jan said. "Not three decades."

Despite myself, I relaxed a little.

"No, I thought you understood. I keep forgetting how little you—Once we get up to speed, we'll be running at a *gamma* of two, you know, root one minus v squared on *c* squared, so our rest-frame elapsed time will be a bit more than six decades, anyway it was the first time I did this run. Onboard time dilated to thirty-something solar years. I know, it's confusing, you'd think they'd say 'contracted' instead of 'dilated.' *Hanger—*"

Sixty-seven point nine two years rest-frame elapsed time, the starship's control system told us. *that's there and back, but does not allow for time spent at the Xon star.*

I felt a surge of anger so extreme that I wouldn't have been surprised if my nose had started bleeding. By brute force, I held my right hand clamped on the armrest of my seat. My brain knew that the Vorpal implant in my palm was nullified by our exposure to the Xon star's radiation, or whatever the hell it emitted. My enraged nervous system did not know that. I wanted to kill her. Or burn a hole in the cabin, drain our air into naked space. An entire human lifetime, more or less, two generations of my history, lost to me. I would return to my own world with more than two thirds of the twenty-first century already in the past, stolen, the wheel of change turned, accelerated, who knew what immensities of transformation worked upon everything I was familiar with. . . . Perhaps Lune would wait for me, it wasn't impossible, I knew in the abstract that she was years, decades, maybe centuries older than I, although it was emotionally impossible to believe that. So many important things had been torn away from me already. In some sense, my world became forfeit the moment I was suckered into stepping through the mirror in Tansy's bathroom, drawn into the greater cosmos of the Contest and its Players. But just because a man has had his life savings pilfered by unscrupulous thieves, it doesn't mean he is anxious to turn out his pockets and fling away the last of his coin.

The blood pounded in my temples, at my throat. The sinews of my arms tremored. I turned my face away from her, obliged myself to breathe in the calming cycles of my martial arts classes. After a time I had command of myself. It was not Jan's fault, not really. Indeed, it seemed even less likely that my kidnapping was Maybelline's doing. A strange conjecture flashed briefly into my mind: Could this be the doing of the starship computational system itself? Surely not. I put the idea aside for the moment instead of dismissing it outright. I pressed my head against the high-cushioned back of the seat and studied displays. If Jan said anything, I did not hear it in my focused wrath. I'm inclined to think she had the sense to remain silent. The beating of blood faded; the shiver in my muscles calmed to a wary tension. I was thinking as hard as I have ever done in my life. I shut my eyes, contemplating everything I knew about the Seebeck family, the Contest. It was not a great deal, but it was not nothing. Patterns emerged. Anomalies. Absurdities. And always, of course, danger and my love for Lune.

After a time, I reopened my eyes, turned back to look at Jan. The small, bright fairy named Sylvie floated in the cabin between our two chairs, wings beating to a blur. The tiny creature's face showed an agony of concern. It softened my heart, that look. I said, "I talked myself out of it, Sylvie. I'm not going to blow up the spaceship after all."

Diminutive hands flew to rosebud lips. "Blow up . . . August, tell me you weren't going to—" At the same moment, the tattoo's owner looked away from her instruments, sent me a startled look. She said, "Are you talking to my psychonic familiar? I mean, of course you are, you just called her by name. Can you *see* her?" Automatically, her hand moved to touch the bare flesh where the fairy usually rested, engraved as tattoo ink. Or—for all I knew—as a fantastically elaborate nanotechnological circuit diagram no less complex than a human brain.

"Of course I can see her, do you think I'm blind? I might be gullible but my senses still work just fine."

"No, but—" Jan's gaze moved to the hovering fairy. "Sylvie, why didn't you tell me he could see you?"

With the faintest hint of sarcasm, the silvery voice said, "You never asked." It flew back to its mistress, perched on one shoulder. "Besides, I thought you knew. He saw me the very first time we met."

"At Avril's moot? I thought he was staring at my tits."

"You said I'd made his day, when I told him he was cute."

"Oh, all right, he is cute. For a kid brother. I thought he was staring at the tatt as an excuse for looking at my boobs."

I said, "Your boobs are okay, for a sister. Are you telling me I'm not supposed to see Sylvie when she turns into Tinkerbell?"

"Hey, I'm much prettier than that old thing. I don't think the commander wants you to hear me. It's all because of that thing in your hand, isn't it?" The fairy added a raucous raspberry. "Not *that* thing, you dog, the lump of metal."

I was blushing before I consciously understood her *double-entendre*. The tattoo fairy swayed her hips in the air in an enticing, mocking version of a belly dance. Who ever heard of a tattoo on the make? Well, at least I wasn't related to Sylvie.

"I'm taken," I said. "You're very sweet, Sylvie, but I don't think Lune would approve."

"Dear Lord," Jan said, "another moralist. That's tedious. The trip's going to be more boring than I expected. Sylvie, you brat, get back home."

With a grimace and a high-pitched crystalline squeal of annoyance, the tattoo darted back to her body and folded itself against her skin.

"Incidentally, Mr. Prig," Jan told me in a snooty tone, "don't be too sure about your friend Lune's attitudes. She's been around, that one, as have we all." She dug out a joint from one pocket, lit up.

"Let's leave Lune's morals out of this," I said, with a rasp in my own voice. It was a stupid, knee-jerk thing for me to say, I realized instantly, the sort of remark I might have made to the jackaroos I'd spent Christmas rounding up cattle with. What a twerp I had been. I'd thought I was quite something out there in the middle of the Australian nowhere, the third-year medical student sweatily drinking Bundaberg Rum and coke by lamplight and staggering away in the small hours with Mavis Boggs the jillaroo, dragging off our shirts and shorts in the hot, still air, the plaintive voices of the aboriginal stockmen wailing in the distance the lyrics and simple chords of cowboy laments from 1950s jukeboxes, screwing our drunken brains out. It had occurred to me before I drove back to Melbourne that I should keep in touch with Mavis, but only if I could talk her into changing her name into something less likely to cause my friends to fall over laughing. My God, what a prick. And then I'd met Lune, and all the world's women lost their appeal to me. How romantic!

"All right." I heard a note of apology in Jan's voice. Fragrant smoke blew my way. "None of my business, I know. I'm sorry to have dragged you away. I suppose . . . in a way, I guess, you must have been on your honeymoon." She shrugged, extended the joint in a conciliatory gesture. "Well, that's how it is in the Contest."

I took it, sipped, coughed, handed it back. "Jan, it might be obvious you—it *must* be obvious to all of you—but it sure as hell isn't to me. That's why I—" An enormous yawn caught me in mid-sentence, stretched my mouth wide. I was dizzy with exhaustion and time lag. How long had it been since I'd slept? "Look, I badly need to catch some shut-eye. I really want to talk to you about this, that's why I came here." Grimacing, I said, "I mean, what I *really* want is to see this bloody spaceship back down on the ground so I can get back to Lune. She's probably at Toby's place by now wondering where the hell I've got to. But obviously you and Maybelline couldn't give a shit what I want. So I'm stuck here in jail, can't pass Go."

"It's the next move in the Contest, that's all, what's wrong with you?"

I tried to catch her meaning; it veered and evaded me. Stupid metaphors. Did she think we were twelve-year-olds sitting in front of a PlayStation? I said, "All right, have it your way. Then why are these three Players being taken out of the game and parked on the sidelines for two thirds of a century, for God's sake? It's terrible tactics and worse strategy."

Her eyes drifted away, though, and she took another toke.

My own eyelids were drooping. I could threaten her physically, but what would that get me? Obviously *The Hanged Man* was not going to respond to my commands without endorsement from its commander, and I was pretty sure the starship had enough intelligence to detect coercion, and undoubtedly plenty of firepower. I stood up. Enough of this crap. "Where can I sleep?"

She took another drag, hesitated, waved her hand. Sylvie floated free for a moment, blew me a kiss. "*Hanger* will tell you the way to your quarters. Deck Three. Make yourself at home, dude. Hey, we can talk when you wake up. Maybelline might be in a better mood by then."

"Fat chance," the fairy said, and settled back into her mistress's bare upper arm. I left them there, Jan yawning by contagion.

the first companionway to your right, a voice said quietly in my ear.

The elevator took me smoothly away.

your stateroom is awaiting you. if you require something to eat or drink, just let me know. i can compile whatever you need if i possess the algorithm.

"Actually," I muttered, "I badly need to take a leak. I hope your lavatory facilities don't require the use of Schwellen."

the system uses total onboard recycling, the machine said, possibly with some pride in its voice. *your quarters contain a full bathroom, and the Entertainment system awaits your choice.*

"Some sleep, my man, that's all I need. Although a back rub would be nice. Do you do back rubs?"

that can be arranged, the voice told me imperturbably.

I was directed down another bland corridor, past unmarked closed doorways that looked as snug as air locks. Something made me pause at one no different from the rest. I placed my right hand against it, Vorpal implant tingling faintly.

sorry, August, it is not your room.

I pushed. A faint click. The door opened silently. I seemed to be looking into a magnificent throne room, lavish with silver and jade. Maybelline sat upon her imperial throne in an attitude of rather self-satisfied bliss. A loose robe richly decorated with pomegranate blossoms hung on her shoulders, seven pearls at her neck, a crown of twelve brilliant blue-white stars upon her brow. In her right hand she held aloft a heaped vanilla ice cream cone; her tongue licked her lips. All around her, vegetable courtiers paid their obeisance. Soft rain sifted down from the ceiling upon the Venerian soil that unaccountably covered the floor, massed and seething with alien plant life. A huge box of chocolates shaped like a heart was propped against her throne. I started to back out, but her eyes had flickered to me. With a screech of rage, she flung the cone at me and surged from the throne, robes flapping. The double scoop of ice cream plopped in a sad little trajectory; the cone, poor cometary tail, spun, fell short.

"You *intolerable* sneak!" Her loyal subjects fluttered their outer leaves, drew back from her fury. I tried very hard not to laugh, and succeeded. Raindrops clung to my hair. I wanted to say, "So this is your wet dream," but instead, with surprising restraint, I held up an appeasing hand. She was roaring, "How *dare* you—"

"I'm truly sorry, Maybelline," I said. "I thought this was my room. Really, you've done it up very nicely." Something caught in my throat, perhaps a cough, certainly not a snigger. "Please, I apologize. And since I'm here, I'd just like to express my regret that my presence aboard this ship is upsetting to you." She pulled up before reaching me, hand stabbing at a console masquerading as a blazing tiger lily in a magnificent spiraling amethyst vase apparently provided by the Vatican or the Russian Hermitage. The illusion flicked off, throne, courtiers and jewels and she stood facing me in her womb under me in a plain, serviceable cabin you might have seen in a mid-priced motel. For an instant I thought of running like hell up the corridor.

"Just. Go. *Away*," she told me. She shoved me hard, pushed me outside into the corridor, jabbed again at the console. The door slid smoothly shut. It must have been unendurably frustrating not to be able to slam it in my face.

apologies for the inconvenience, August. access to Maybelline's quarters should not have been possible without her permission. now, if you will continue along the companionway, i will see you to your own room.

But I was doubled up in laughter by then, weakened by fatigue and mirth both. I wiped my eyes. "Lay on, Macduff. Listen, run me a bath and see if you can find a decent Scotch, would you? Glenlivet would hit the spot." I found my own door, went into a room identical to Maybelline's. "But don't get any dumb ideas that I've forgiven you bastards, or that I'm going to put up with this shit for very long." I yawned again, pulling off my clothes, standing at a quite conventional toilet bowl to take a much-needed piss (no strange, uncomfortable, zero-gravity tubes), and found I was still smiling, despite my cranky words, at May's humiliation. I heard myself mutter, the words slurring a little: "Alice really was right. You're all nothing but a pack of bloody cards."

TWENTY-THREE

OUTSIDE HIS BRUNSWICK efficiency apartment on the fourth floor of a cleverly renovated factory or perhaps store-house, the dark, three-in-the-morning wind beyond the snug windows can't make up its mind if it's winter or spring. August's traditional Antarctic blasts are confused by the unseasonable turbulence of the greenhouse effect, assuming that's real and not just a hysterical concoction. It certainly feels real. He sits propped up in bed on three pillows, in agony and distress.

Years ago he had been driven home from a party where he'd eaten and drunk to excess, and as the car bounced erratically on tram tracks and across railway intersections, his swollen bladder pressed in a crescendo of pain that made him yelp, but his driver, half-drunk himself, refused to stop, until finally he stumbled free into his front yard, unzipped, pissed for what seemed like five minutes in a bliss of relief. This is the same sensation, without the relief.

His bladder is seized. For a day and a half he has dribbled or stood uselessly above the gaping white bowl in frightened frustration, mouth dry, urine staying put inside his body, kidneys pressing ever more liquid into the swollen organ, muscles or urethra locked. He's not an anatomist, after all, despite his three futile years of undergraduate medicine, but repeated desperate searches of Google suggest all too plainly that his elderly prostate has clenched like a fist around the outlet pipes. Pain radiates into his balls, up into his belly, across his lower back, beneath his shoulder blades. Like influenza but without the fever, like every nightmare of an examination you can't leave because your life depends upon it yet you need to piss so badly—

He's made an appointment with a urology clinic, but they can't see him for several days. Too many aging baby-boomer males going on the blink, too few specialists. In the dark, he tries for sleep, and his restless legs and arms burn and tingle. My god, this really *is* old age. He had imagined that its depredations were twenty years away. Granted, his mother was only five years older than he is now when she died, but that was ovarian cancer, she did not suffer the brutal indignities of senescence.

Could this, too, be cancer? Prostate cancer is common enough in men his age. Surely not. The knife, the ablating laser beam, the radioactive pellets burning away tissue. Medical triumph! Days or weeks or months of vomiting, poisonous chemicals flooding the bloodstream, murdering cells good and ill. Better to be dead, perhaps. He catches himself, shakes his head in the darkness. *Shut the fuck up, you idiot,* he tells himself. The traditional bromides are right, however fatuous and feel-good: where there's life there's hope. And he has no evidence that this is a tumor.

He turns on his side and pain spears him. Can this be what women go through every month? He crawls out of bed and stumbles again into the bathroom, stands there uselessly, stressed, trying to relax—ridiculous to try to force yourself to allow something unforced to flow. In desperation, he turns on the faucet behind him at the basin, lets water run into the sink. The map *is* the territory in a situation like this. The symbol gives rise to the reality. Babbling brook, rushing stream, all that; come on, come on. The burning pressure ascends from his groin to his chest. Nothing. His parched mouth and throat demand a soothing sip of water; he refuses them. He returns to bed, lets his limbs lie motionless. Better that he abandon all control and piss into the goddamned sheets and mattress than to suffer this incandescent pressure.

In and out of awareness, thoughts blurred, anxiety thuttering his pulse. If this now, what next? He gets out of bed, on cold feet goes into his small study, switches on the computer. Windows takes forever to boot up. Have to protect your machine from viruses and systemic breakdown. He laughs at his own expense. The mind children. Like parent, like child. At least the poor fucking simple things don't suffer urinary retention.

The time icon flicks on, the date. It catches his eye. Christ, his birthday. Wonderful. Harbingers of birthdays yet to come, the galloping rush down the entropy slide.

He regards himself as a technological optimist. This machine in front of him is more powerful than the computers that controlled flights to the Moon thirty-seven years ago, more than half his lifetime. A memory flickers: that beloved book of childhood, those spaceships of the mind, what, fifteen, seventeen years before Neil Armstrong botched his lines. He'd been sure that by now he'd be living on the Moon, or at least in a great, wheeled, satellite space station. He sighs.

The fabled twenty-first-century, and they can't even fix a man's inherited propensity to block up his own urinary tract with an overgrown, useless, internal sex organ. It's not even as if he's had a fuck in the last . . . what? Year? Two years? The graduate students are off-limits, the female staff members committedly married, dull or plain beyond consideration, lesbians, or, most distressingly, frankly uninterested in an old fool in his sixties. Pain stabs again as he crouches on his ergonomic chair before the flatscreen monitor. Pain is right, Christ, but let's get this in perspective. He opens up his gallery of horrors, his witness file to inhumanity. What kind of God could create and sustain a world like this? And if it's a simulation after all, as Tipler and Bostrom argue, what kind of monster?

Here's a file from a year ago, the *New York Times*. The editorial writers were still trying to shame the president into acting in Africa, where the broken remnants of European colonial rule endlessly tore at their own bellies, at the weakest among their number. Darfur, wherever that is. Okay, the map comes up on the screen. It might as well be on Mars. Something called the Janjaweed militia were running out of control. They'd seized nine boys, torn off their clothes, tied them up, and—Christ. He feels like vomiting, and involuntary spasms jerk at his swollen belly. The little boys had their eyes gouged out and, for good measure, their noses and ears cut off before they were shot dead and left in the public square. A message to the villagers,. Like the ten-year-old boy in a second village. These tough guys castrated him, one more message from the sponsor.

He flicks down through the files. He's been keeping them for years. In another part of Africa, the tough guys like to cut off children's hands, but for some reason what he finds the most horrifying and spirit-sapping detail is the way they treat their enemies' animals. He stares numbly at the screen. With their machetes, they hack off the hoofs of cows in the pastures, leaving the poor wretched bleeding brutes to hobble hideously on their stumps, presumably until they bleed to death, crying aloud in terror.

Sick to the stomach, he goes again to the bathroom, stands helplessly above the mocking ceramic bowl. His innards remain clenched, like the hardened, brutal hearts of his fellow humans at play in the fields of the Lord.

There has to be a better way.

Aching, he blunders back into the dark of his bedroom, perches wide awake and trapped by his flesh, waiting for the morning.

TWENTY-FOUR

FROM THE TOP of her diamond terrace, fifteen kilometers above the faint ruins of coastal Pontianak, Juni Seebeck surveyed her tropical domain through a faint offog haze and found it good.

Once this Earth had pullulated with ten billion crass, self-serving humans and their domestic animals, their lives a ceaseless soap opera of furtive or bumptious lusts, global aggressions, fits of envy and suspicion, petty antagonisms, clawing after reputation or security or approval or stupid excitement, laying waste to everything they touched. It was deplorable. It was the human condition. It was everywhere to be seen in the variant Earths, save for these few enchanted worlds like hers and Ember's, where the wretched bastards had attained the terminal decency of obliterating themselves comprehensively. Admittedly, on this world, their nano-goo had run so far out of control that it gnawed every living thing to the bone and beyond, had chewed the very soil from the face of the planet, down to the bedrock. She sighed. There could be too much of a good thing. Happily, in the way of these things, surfeit was its own brake.

Kalimantan—which she'd known as Borneo as a girl— stretched to the east in a shimmering coral of diamond and sapphire where once had been acid-rain-poisoned browning forests threaded by befouled rivers, roads, pestiferous villages, towns, cities, and to the west, beyond the golden coast, to a blue blaze of what had once been called Selat Karimata and was now wholly pure, empty ocean. Beneath the fractal encrustations of recompiled carbon, aluminum, and heaven knows what all else, the brutal scar of the fallen skyhook stretched eastward across the island into the horizon's haze, a physical manifestation of the Platonic idea of equator. How terrible that collapse must have been. And yet how satisfying. Punishment for human hubris, in its way. Had it been the work of the deformers? Juni let her eyes track the linear indentation in the crust of the world. Surely it was unnecessary to blame the K-machines for this crime. Men had brought it upon themselves. Yes, and women too.

Well, the tiny nanites had mutated themselves into equilibrium, neutrality, finally benignity, with a little help from Jules's M-Brain and Avril's Ancient Intelligence. Her small men. She smiled, extended her fingers lazily toward the Sun. A nimbus of fairy dust sparkled, light refracted from the operating fabrication fog units that hung everywhere in the atmosphere of her chosen Earth.

"A good thing the filthy machines can't use you boys," Juni said aloud. A good thing, indeed, that the small men did not— *could* not?—pass through Schwellen when she transited to other worlds or received visitors. Presumably the Vorpal grammar system edited them out. And K-machines despised nanotechnology, for some bizarre ideological reason of their own. Last time she'd glanced into the pages of their bible, the incomprehensible *SgrA**, she'd found several pages referring to the ruin of worlds induced by molecular runaway. The machines were very angry about that, you could tell that much. And yet the hypocritical swine spent their days and nights smashing and ruining and interfering and—

"Oh, bother them," she said aloud, "this is too nice a day for that sort of distasteful topic." Briefly, it crossed her mind that she was talking to herself a little too much, a little too often, that her self-imposed isolation might have its drawbacks. "Pooh," she muttered, with a shake of her head. Prismatic light danced. "You boys are listening, aren't you? Never have much to say, but we know there's a big consciousness emulator tucked away down under the crust, don't we?" For a moment, a pang squeezed her heart, a breathless instant of lonely sorrow. No, damn it. Her life was perfect. Here she stood, she could do no other: steady as a Rock, a Player whose integrity and resolution, like that of Toby and Septimus, anchored the Contest for the rest of them, flibbertigibbets, killers, and mystics as they were, the lot of them. Including that new fool of a boy.

She spun on her right toe, pirouetting on the high platform of diamond, arms outstretched, offogs cupped at her nostrils and mouth bearing rich oxygen to her lungs, guarding her moist eyes and sensitive ears, hugging her in an embrace of warmth and air even here at the low boundaries of space. "Imagination and discipline," she cried aloud. "That's what they need to win this game. Now come along, boys, we have a Faerie party to arrange."

Juni Seebeck flung herself lightly backward from the lip of heaven, Gucci gown—silk and organza—clinging discreetly to her limbs, and the offogs bore her downward like a dream of flying.

TWENTY-FIVE

IN MY DREAM, my name was August Seebeck and I was dreaming a gelid dream deep inside the Three Heads of Cerberus Hibernacle. That means I'm dead, I realized, and a sickening resignation curdled through me. Oh, shit. In despair, I thought: That porcine Cetian wongle didn't miss me after all. At least this medical torpidity vault will hold me in suspension long enough for the Resuscitators to attempt repairs on my slain flesh. If they know that I'm here. If they have not yet abandoned hope. A dreadful thing was already pushing from the other side, forcing its way in. Dead as I was, in panic, I cried out for help. Something was pressing on my feet. A needle drove into my calf. Perhaps they had started. A whole bunch of needles. Not deep, but sharp enough to startle me awake.

"Ouch! Hey, get away from—"

I jerked up on my comfortable bed in the darkness. Just a moment ago, it seemed, five or ten artificial masseur hands had been working over my back and limbs, wonderfully soothing, tireless, probing and molding, then stroking moonlight soft in shivery delight, the kind of massage you dream of drifting off to sleep to but can never afford. Now some lunatic was puncturing me. Dream, dream, only a dream in starship darkness.

"Turn the damned lights on."

Illumination filled the cabin, brightening gently enough that

I hardly blinked. A ratty old brindle tomcat was perched across my feet, stropping my blanket-covered leg with warrior claws.

"Oh. Good Christ, it's you. Hooks, what the hell are you doing here?" I used to think Cathooks was Maybelline's pet, or animal companion, or whatever you call it these days, before I learned that se was a godthing from the collapsed Omega Point cosmos that had been watched for a timeless time by my brother Decius and his Auger team at Yggdrasil station. The old reprobate flipped ser half-chewed ear, offered me a growl of recognition, kept stropping.

"Cut that *out*!" I dragged my leg back out of harm's way, considered giving sem a stiff kick in the ribs, very quickly thought better of it. Hooks had brought me back from the dead, sort of, together with Lune, and presumably my parents, and several of my siblings. You had to feel grateful. And you had to be cautious around a being like that. "I assume May-belline carried you onboard earlier. Not in a bag, I trust?"

In ser whisky-smoked, unnervingly high-pitched voice, Hooks told me, "Get outta here! That bitch better not stuff me in no carpetbag, no, nor that mechanical man, neither."

I coughed. Last time I'd seen this godling in motley, the K-machine James Cooper Fenimore had tipped sem out of a large burlap sack at my feet. It hadn't seemed dignified to me, and it certainly didn't seem dignified to Cathooks. I wondered why se put up with it.

"Can I fetch you something, Hooks? Bowl of milk?"

"Shut up. Facetiousness didn't get you off the planet when the deformers splattered you, right?"

That sobered me up. Fragments of a dream blew down my back, cold as an August wind from the Antarctic in Melbourne. Dead again and screaming silently for help. "All right, old moggy, point taken. I owe you, we all do." In the middle of my mind, a crystallized insight was trying to escape its shell. Hang on, hang on. "I was going to offer you a mouse, but I don't suppose a nice clean starship like this—" I broke off, felt a spasm deeper than dream memory. "Oh my God. *You can get me off this thing*, can't you? You're immune to the Xon star. How else could you get here?" I lunged forward, seized the animal, dragged sem up close to me, looked into ser slitted pupils.

"I'm here because you called me. Let's get it over and done with. I'm a busy god."

I *called* ser? In my fading dream? "Look, whatever. I hate asking for favors, but Cathooks . . . I mustn't be here. I kept trying to tell the women, and they won't listen. It's as if they *can't* listen. I've met the other members of my family, and I tell you, Hooks . . . Jan and Maybelline and I are the only ones who seem ready to fight these Deformer sons of bitches. Oh, Toby's a brave man, Man Jorrain's a Hollywoodgrade mad scientist or something just as improbable, Septima's running some sort of Médecins Sans—"

"Oh, it's Septima this century, is it? Tired of the butch Odin persona?" Surprisingly, the tomcat hung unresisting in my grasp, claws retracted. "You're forgetting Ember."

I blinked. That was true, Lune had mentioned an episode where they had fought together side by side. I still didn't like him and couldn't imagine him as a worthy companion in arms. Still. "Okay, four of us out of twelve. And three-quarters of the four marooned here in a goddamned tin can for the next— what?—sixty or seventy years, completely out of touch with the rest of them. While the bad guys run riot." I was breathing heavily. "You can't tell me something hasn't been fucking with the scorecard."

Hooks squirmed free, jumped down heavily from the bed, stretched like a yoga teacher with ser rear end in the air and front paws extended, claws extruded. I waited until se settled, eyes studiously turned away from mine. It was an impressive imposture, and I had no idea what purpose it was meant to serve. Perhaps the simple pleasure of being a cat. Se said, "What made you come to Venus in the first place—you didn't have a yen to go flying around?"

"Why, I had to . . . to see Jan . . ." I trailed off. Actually, I had no idea at all why I'd felt the unlikely urgent need to catch up with Janine. By rights, I should have gone straight back to Toby's, found Lune, discussed today's cascade of absurdities, threats, discoveries. Yesterday's by now, probably, I felt rested enough to have had a good night's sleep. Those poor children buried in a midden of postwar horror. Former K-machines in clown suits and nurses' uniforms. Weird myotic diagrams presented by the foe for my edification.

What the hell was I *doing* here? What the hell was I doing *here*? Again I felt my concentration slipping, my thoughts edging off sideways, skittering like mice . . . Cathooks chose that moment to snare my eye. Fierce, unrelenting. I stifled a yawn, dragged my attention back to the question. What had Jan said before I left her on the bridge? *It's the next move in the Contest, that's all.* Wonderful.

"It seemed like a good idea at the time," I said. "Is that how it works?"

That whisky-rich crackly purr: "Looks like. Not that I'd know how it *feels*."

I climbed off the bed, found yesterday's tired, plaster-dusted clothing, pulled it on. "Ship, where do I get some breakfast for me and my friend here? Is there a commissary or mess or whatever you call—"

Hanged Man said from no particular direction, *good morning, August. i can compile anything you choose from a comprehensive*

*menu. or you may have coffee in the wardroom until the com-
mander or your sister Maybelline awakens. by the way, why are
you talking to yourself? i am baffled by your reference to a "friend."
you are alone.*

"Huh? I mean Cathooks. Some raw meat—"

"Can't see me. Hey, Tiphareth," the cat yelled, "wake up, you
dumb tin can. Smell the cat piss." Suiting action to word, se
strolled to a nearby bulkhead, propped with tail high and quiv-
ering, squirted a rancid yellow stream. The full tomcat stench.

"Cut that out!" I yelped. "I have to sleep in here."

"Old *Hanger* will handle that," the cat told me. "These
machines, you have to bang them on the nose to get their
attention."

*i now detect Vorpal flux at extreme levels. ah, your greeting card,
monsieur. your presence was subtle, your arrival unannounced.
welcome. how may i serve you?*

"Fix the kid some breakfast. Something simple but hearty.
He's an Australian, give him a Vegemite sandwich and a mug of
black tea with three spoons of sugar."

"*Hanger*, I'll have black tea with no sugar, toast with canola
margarine, low-fat peach yogurt, fruit muesli with one-percent
milk, and by all means hold the grilled bacon, lamb chops,
slimy fried eggs sunny side up, kippers, kedgerry, flapjacks with
maple syrup, hash browns, monkey brains, and fresh-peeled
camel eyeballs. No, wait a moment, you can throw in a couple
of eyeballs with the raw steak strips for my animal here."

The cat growled, showed teeth. "We're feeling a bit more
feisty, are we? Got over our little anxiety nightmare, eh? Prefer
to be left alone for a while, would we? Sixty or seventy years in
interstellar space, perhaps?" For a moment, se shimmered, and
I swear it seemed that the solidity of ser body faded, all but that
lethal, fanged mouth and the gleaming eyes. I could actually see

through the spurious cat body to the stained flooring, where a small machine had emerged from a hidden nook to sponge up the puddle of urine.

"Come on, Hooks," I said wearily. "I can put up with tantrums from Maybelline but not from an Omega Point god. It's . . . undignified."

After a moment of tense silence, the cat guffawed in its wheezy high-pitched tones. I relaxed—a little. The wheezing, or rather hissing, continued for a moment, faded. It was not the cat. A panel opened in the bulkhead, extending a servery shelf covered in my breakfast, plus a bowl of repulsive warm, naked, cow flesh, which I put on the floor immediately and nudged away from me with my foot. I took the tray, sat on the edge of the bed, nibbled a buttery crust, sipped the tea, dipped a spoon into the yogurt. It was all excellent. "Thank you, *Hanger*. What did Hooks call you just a moment ago?"

Tiphareth is the central Sephiroth of the Kabbalah Tree of Life, the starship told me. *in tradition, it represents the sun. i must decline that honor. commander Janine Seebeck holds the station of Tiphareth.*

"Don't be humble, old soul," Cathooks said. Se had ser head down sideways into the animal protein, dragging a hunk of meat on to the floor, growling in a menacing way. Between growls, se added, "Major Arcana, Card Twelve. It's your name, buster. Got you nailed, no wriggling."

I wolfed down my breakfast, thinking furiously, replaced the tray. "That was good, thank you. Hooks, will you take me to Lune?"

"Not the best idea, chum. Rather not."

What the fuck? But you can't coerce a god. "Damn it, Hooks, did you just come here to gloat?"

The cat said nothing for a moment, industriously gobbling

down ser disgusting treat. Then: "No spoon-feeding in the Contest. Sorry, my boy. Love to help, against your Accord. But there's a way off. Obviously." And the animal was gone. *Pop*, bye.

I found myself actually gnashing my teeth. I'd always assumed it was a figure of speech. My jaw hurt, and my teeth ached from the pressure of my angry frustration. I said to the starship, "*Is there a way off this vessel while we're in space?*"

Hanged Man said, *you will have to ask the commander.*

"Is she awake yet?" I was at the door, looking up and down the companionway at unmarked doors.

i fear not.

"Well, wake her the hell up, right now."

i cannot do so. if you will wait in the wardroom, amusements will be made available. Or you are welcome to return to your quarters and activate the Entertainment system.

I went straight to Maybelline's door and started banging on it, hard. The racket would be difficult to sleep through. I yelled her name at the top of my voice, and Jan's, too, just on the off-chance. In thirty seconds the door slid open, and my furious sister started yelling back just as loudly, two inches from my face. Her own face was covered in green-and-brown, dried, cracked restorative night makeup. Her hair looked like Medusa's. Her vocabulary was impressively vile. I stopped shouting first and stood waiting. After a time, she shut up for a moment, and I said, quickly, "I've just been talking to Hooks. We need to wake Jan up. How do I that?"

Maybelline shook her head in disbelief. "You woke me up from my first decent sleep in days to tell me about a dream? August, you are such a—"

I raised my voice again. "The cat came to visit me. The ship won't wake Jan. Someone is screwing with us, Maybelline. I need your help."

Astonished, she regarded me in silence for a moment. "That's a refreshing change of tack. A request for help. No demands and tantrums. All right, August, give me a moment to wash my face." She shut the door. I closed my eyes and practiced breathing slowly. After a minute of that, I did some katas, stretching slowly, crouching like a tiger, hiding like a dragon, floating like a butterfly, stinging like a bee, cutting like a piece of paper. I'd been missing my daily workout. By the time Maybelline opened the door again, fresh-faced and clad in purple spandex, I felt much calmer.

"Her quarters are on the command deck, of course. You're telling me Cathooks turned up in your room just now? A woman feeds the damned thing for years, combs out its knots, and the moment her back is turned . . ." Her complaint mumbled away into inaudibility, or maybe I just stopped paying attention. Jan insistently wanted the three of us to fly to the Xon star. She was unlikely to tell me anything that would help me abscond. I could threaten her with violence, but the very idea offended me, and besides, I was fairly sure that my X-caliber implant was as neutralized as my ability to access the Schwellen. The inside of the elevator didn't seem like a good place to test this theory. I followed Maybelline to another unmarked door, stood beside her as she hollered Jan's name and rat-tatted with her knuckles.

"Kether's balls! What?"

"He's been talking to the cat."

"Do you know what time it is?"

"Three bells, matey," I said brightly, peering past Maybelline's shoulder. The commander's quarters would not have passed muster with Horatio Nelson's navy. Clothes scattered everywhere. But then there was nobody else here to tick her off and keep her up to the mark. And besides, we Seebecks all had a definite anarchist streak. Except, perhaps, for Septimus/ Septima. I had no idea how many bells represented rise-and-shine, or reveille, or whatever the military and merchant marine types called it. But you have to say something perky when you drag the pilot out of bed. "The game's afoot. The wheel's in spin. The loser now will be later to—"

"Is he drunk?" Jan asked in exasperation. "Is he stoned?"

"He's been talking to Cathooks," Maybelline told her.

"Don't be silly, we're in deep space and you didn't bring your cat with us. I'm sure I would have noticed."

"Cathooks is not a cat," I said. "Cathooks is an Omega godling. Hooks can walk through walls."

Jan looked very fetching in her teddy, which was lacy and black and had more holes than lace. I stopped looking at her, remembering that she was my sister. Allegedly. If I could believe any of this film quick, "You gou inner my wash, jron lease and *Hanger* won't compile hallucinogens, says it's against his principles."

"Do you want me to breathe on you?"

She recoiled. "Certainly not. Oh shit, you're not going to go away, are you? The two of you might as well come in. Just kick things out of the way. *Hanger*, get us all some coffee."

coming up. i tried to stop him, sorry.

"That's all right, old thing. Next time, though, clap the bastard in irons."

you know i can't—

I said in a shocked voice, "Commander, remember his Three Laws prohibitions! He'll burn out his positronic brain."

"You really can't tell fiction from reality, can you?" Maybelline said in disgust.

"Whatever," I said. "Jan, the last time I saw you, at Avril's garden party on the moat outside her castle, you'd just arrived back from the Xon star. How did you manage that?"

The women took their steaming coffee mugs from a servery tray, left mine sitting there. I sighed, crossed the room, retrieved the mug intended for me. It was a large kiln-fired object with a "The Pain—When Will It End" cartoon by Tim Kreider showing Jesus Christ hanging on the cross having a rather abusive meltdown, and who could blame him? I wondered if this was some sort of editorial remark by *The Hanged Man*. I sipped, found it just as good as the coffee in my own room, which was no large surprise.

Jan said, after a certain amount of eye swiveling and silent communication with her tattoo, "Well, yeah, I suppose that's startling, when I think about it. People were trying to kill me. You don't stop and wonder at a moment like that." She stopped and wondered, shook her head. "I don't know. Juni got in touch with me, and the timing was good, so I went through. We drank some kava. My hair was on fire, I think." She stared into her coffee. "Isn't it amazing? I didn't even wonder about it."

"Something is fucking with our memories," I said. "I'm sure of it. Something is distracting us whenever we get too close to troublesome questions." I could see that Maybelline had drifted away, sorting through some of the garments lying on the floor. My own thoughts were ever so faintly blurred. This really was very good coffee. I drank some more. Croissants would go nicely. "*Hanger*, you have any chocolate croiss—" I squeezed my eyes shut tight, put the mug down, seized Jan by the wrist, tightly, so she squealed. Instantly, she did her best to break my nose with her other fist. I grabbed it in flight, and said, "Listen. Work with me here, Jan. Bite your tongue, or something. Stamp your feet. Concentrate."

Through gritted teeth, after a long pause, she said, "Okay. Let me go. And if you touch me once more . . ."

I released my grip, drew back. She found a chair, pushed stuff off it, sat brooding.

"Something must have been in the way," she said.

"That was my conclusion. Can we get the ship to display your vector, or trajectory, or whatever it's—"

The fairy was off her shoulder and hanging by her ear, wings a blur. Part of the wall vanished, or seem to. In the large space, annotated lights hung in blackness. A path of light moved from a brilliant point in the lower-right of the cube, heading north and to our left. As it tracked its straight line, the scale changed. It was headed for a yellow-white star. The star had graphical concentric rings surrounding it. The line tore toward the star, then appeared to swerve slightly.

"What the *hell*?" Jan was staring in shock. I glanced at Maybelline; she was trying on a bright-red tank top far too small for her. "*Hanger, what the fuck did you do that for!*"

i decided a slingshot past Saturn was an economical—

"At half the speed of *light*?"

agreed, in retrospect it seems an absurd choice. the delta-vee—

In disgust, I said over the top of it, "Even the machines aren't safe, let alone secure. *Hanger*, magnify the display and show us your path as you went past Saturn."

An iconic Tree of Life slid through darkness past the ringed planet, trajectory twisting again toward the solar equatorial plane.

"Run that back again, and pause the simulation at the moment that the commander left the bridge." I glanced at Jan; she nodded.

On the display, the starship slid across Saturn's north pole, or maybe its south pole for all I knew, stopped dead in space.

Jan said, "Display the vector heading through the center of Saturn to the Xon star."

The image rolled slowly. Like an eclipsed moon, the point representing the Xon star slid behind the planet and was lost from view.

"Christ," I said. "The ship blocked the radiation just long enough for you to jump off."

Jan was shaking her head. "Impossible. I mean, yeah, I'm not disputing that's what happened. But it's a fucking incredible coincidence. Dude, I had to get off the bridge because the Shinto Kabbalists were trying to kill me *at that very moment*. How could *Hanger* have changed his vector way the hell back in deep space so Saturn would be in exactly the right place at exactly the right time—"

"Because it's a Contest." Because Great-aunt Tansy could predict the future when the wind was in the right quarter? I dismissed that as overly complicated. "You all call it a Contest. Tell me I'm wrong. Because when you're playing chess or Go, you don't just make decisions on the spur of the moment, you can have a strategy planned out way in advance." I was feeling very tired, or maybe so angry it just felt like that. "I keep telling everybody, you say you're Players, but you're not. None of us is." My breathing was ragged. "We're just bloody Pawns being shoved around the goddamned board."

TWENTY-SIX

"NEXT."

He steps forward to the Centrelink counter, presents a printout. The clerk swipes the bar code, glances at his screen. "Okay, sir, go through the door on the right and take a seat. Shouldn't be long. Next."

Three oldsters and a heavily blinged pregnant young woman look up as he enters the hanging-about-until-they're-good-and-ready room. He gives his fellow victims a tight grin, shrugs. The seating is predictably moth-eaten and institutionally ugly. An appalling, if muted, classic hip-hop medley assails him from the sound system. There's a temptation to pull on a headset, but then he'd probably miss his call and upset the clerk, something he'd rather avoid. Instead, he takes out his pad and reads an Astrobiology blog. Some whistleblower at SETI claims evidence has been found for a Matrioshka Brain complex in the Large Magellanic Cloud. Yeah, right. Probably where George Adamski's flying saucers came from. He'd loved that delusional, meretricious crap when he was twelve or thirteen. He blinks. Phantom jellyfish swim across his field of vision. He grits his teeth, rolls his eyeballs down, then up. The shadows swarm away, float down again. Someone calls his name. Should call him Dances With Fucking Phylum Cnidaria.

"I'm Julia Barancas." Hool-ya. She offers her hand. "Won't you come in and sit down, sir?"

He follows her into a small office. Irritated, he says, "If we must be formal, Ms. Barancas, I prefer to be addressed as 'Doctor.'" Immediately, chagrined by his own knee-jerk, he adds, "But my first name will do perfectly well. 'sir' always sounds like an old man to me."

The woman clerk, from the look of her an immigrant refugee from one of the South American wars, regards him for a moment in silence. He cringes slightly. An old man. If he is not an old man by now, what the hell is he? A rather damaged and degraded iteration of the young fellow who wrote his doctoral thesis? He shakes his head in mute apology, sits carefully, pulls his armless chair closer to the desk. A photo of two adorable gap-toothed children props at one corner beside a pile of papers. No husband shown. Murdered by a death squad?

"Well, Doctor, you'll have heard about the Work for the Pension scheme the government brought in at the last federal budget. We've invited you to this meeting so that we can minimize any difficulties you might experience in returning to the workforce." She glances in her hooded screen. "I see that you're . . . why, congratulations, sir, I see it's your seventy-second birthday today. I wouldn't have thought you much older than sixty-five." She beams. Is it a routine they learn? Presumably, yet there is something innocent and oddly trustworthy in her round face.

"I'm not remotely interested in returning to the workforce," he says. "I've been in receipt of my lawful pension for seven years. Has this bloody government really got the gall to snatch it back from me?" He forages in his briefcase for papers, medical attestations; he has come prepared. "You do realize that I'm visually impaired? There's certainly nothing—"

"No, no, doctor, let me assure you, there is no obligation at this time. We provide an opportunity for senior citizens to give back to the community. As you will know, the falling birthrate . . ." She goes through her spiel, holding his gaze with her long-lashed eyes. Is the falling birthrate his fault? Well, yes, he's contributed to it. Nothing to be done now, bad luck. Impotent, sterile. If cloning hadn't been banned by the United Nations, he'd offer up a few cells scraped from the inside of his mouth, but pity the poor bloody child cloned from his wretched DNA, with its assortment of deleterious and mismatched genes. Teeth that refused to come through on schedule. Eyeballs clogged with vitreous humors ripping free from the vicinity of his retinas and now paddling back and forth behind his irises, casting shadows on top of the shadows of Plato's cave. "—your former student," she says, and falls silent, regarding him expectantly.

"Who?"

"Dr. Jonathan Wilson. He's the research director at the corporation. He remembers you fondly."

What corporation? Impossible to keep your mind focused anymore. She'd said something about produced realities. Yeah, yeah. They'll have Real ™ virtual reality about the same time they get a man on Mars, or back to the Moon, for that matter. Hype and tulip-bubble hysteria all over again. Wilson. The name comes back to him, and he bursts out laughing. "Wonderful. He threatened to kill me once. Crack my head open like a melon to make a philosophical point."

Hoolya smiles engagingly. "Yes, he mentioned that amusing exchange. He wondered if you'd remember."

"It's my eyes that are failing me, not my memory, Ms., uh, uh, Ms. Barancas." Palpably his memory is shot to pieces. Once it had been a camera. Once, a single glance at a page had been enough to commit it to memory. Page after page, brilliant or gibberish, glib or profound, Kant, Popper, Dennett, Heidegger, the words hit the retina and burned their image into some strange attractor of memory. No longer. The neurotransmitters have packed it in. The cortical columns have rotted like the rusty buildings of the rose-red city half as old as time, gnawed by acid rain blown east and north from the Sahara Project. Or whatever. She is talking again, he's missed some of it. "Sorry, would you mind repeating—"

Was that a sigh of impatience? Well, fuck them, if the bastardly bureaucrats are going to drag pensioners off the street and out of their homes to save a few miserable millions of dollars, let the swine learn patience.

"Dr. Wilson wants you to join his team as a, what did he call it?" She flicks down the screen after a note. "A consultant ontologist emeritus. I'm guessing," with a smile, "you'll have a better idea of what that is than I do."

"What's his business called, again?" Ye gods.

"Other World Realities, Inc. I thought you'd know about them, if that was your academic specialty. Artificial intelligence applied to produced—"

He waves one hand. "Yes, yes. That is, no, not my field at all. But if some silly devil I once taught wants to hire me, hey, what the hell. It's better than spending the next twenty years in some work-camp gulag."

Julia Barancas suddenly seems close to losing her temper. "Please don't talk such nonsense, Professor." He is taken aback. "This is a wonderful country. I spent three years with my babies behind razor wire at the Villawood Detention Center, and I can tell you that I would do it again in a heartbeat for the privilege of gaining citizenship in this beautiful land where there is no war and thievery and thugs killing people in the street for a handful of inflated coin." She catches her breath, lowers her eyes. After a moment, she says, "I apologize, sir. Sometimes I become passionate. You may blame my Latin temperament."

He is abashed. None of his anger at the government's heavy-handedness, its high-handedness, is abated, but this woman's suffering, her bravery, her endurance, is a reproach to him. He sees himself as if from a distance as a cranky, aging man with very little to complain about. Shadows swim before his eyes. Lately he has found advertised on the Internet an ophthalmo-logical method to remove them, twin confocal laser beams that pierce the vitreous, directed by a specially shaped lens, so that their concentrated heat blows the opaque floaters into invis-ible shreds. It will mean an expensive flight to Hong Kong, but hey. Twenty years ago, such a technology was unheard of. A decade ago, it was probably alarmingly experimental. Even as he ages, the science of repairing failed flesh is accelerating retarded though its advance is by the loonies of the Religious Right. Hang in there, he tells himself. If you're trapped behind a biological razor-wire barrier, it's at least partly of your own construction.

"What the hell, Julia," he says. "Tell Wilson I'll be happy to see him. Yeah, set up an appointment. I assume they'll be paying at least as much as the pension."

The clerk smiles dazzlingly. "I'm very pleased to hear that, sir—Doctor. One moment, allow me to contact—"

A consultant ontologist. Good bloody God. What are they planning to do, create a new universe? He smiles. At least it will get him out of his damn stifling apartment.

TWENTY-SEVEN

THERE IS ONE who asks: How many universes may dance upon the head of a pin?

One answers: As many as wish to.

There is one who asks: Granted that this is so, is there any limit to the number of universes that might wish to?

One answers: Universes exist beyond number, thrown as shadows on the plenum by the dynamics of the Theogony, that process which creates the gods out of the machine.

There is one who asks: Might one discern here a parallel between the ceaseless coming into being and departure from being of quantum events and of entire universes construed as elementary entities?

One answers: One might do worse.

There is one who asks: Yet the machine that makes gods is no mere random process. All is strife and contest. All is strategy and tactics.

One answers: As ever, *SgrA** is one's guide. Regard his tale more closely. Inspect the arc of his coming hence and his going forth.

There is one who asks: One offers bitter counsel. Must Kripke machines be abased before the paradigm and parable of a soulless organism?

One answers: Such is the paradox in parable and paradigm, no less than in the paraclete. Begone, Fool, with thy paradiddle!

TWENTY-EIGHT

"*HANGER, THIS IS* what we are going to do." The command center or control room still held the faintest bitter odor of burned polymers, relic of the attack in Jan's favorite universe by the warriors whose grandparents she had bilked out of the starship we flew in. "We'll reverse your original trajectory, pass through Saturn's Xon shadow. I'm getting off. These women can do what they like."

"Ignore him," Jan said. She settled into her padded pilot's seat, turned away from me where I stood before the large displays.

in this universe, Saturn is not in an appropriate position on its orbit, the ship told me. *orbits are somewhat chaotic, not entirely predictable from one cognate universe to another.*

"Stop talking to the passenger, *Hanged Man,*" Jan said crisply.

"Is there any planet in the Solar System . . . Let me rephrase that. What planet is nearest to our current trajectory? Do you have sufficient delta-vee to take us there? Can you show me a chart of the ecliptic in a logarithmic scale so I can get my head around it?"

"Ignore that request," Jan said.

The screen in front of me lit up obediently with a dandy view of the Solar System, presumably looking down from the north. Like a where-we-are-now video presentation on a Jumbo halfway across the Pacific, a short crimson line extended from the second orbit around the bright Sun at the center. A pale-pink line struck out from its end, headed off the edge of the chart. Even log scales aren't up to interstellar distances. I frowned. The planets were all the hell over the sky. Closest was . . . Mars, but it was at least twenty degrees off to clockwise. Still, comparatively close, even at our accelerating speed.

"How long to Mars?" I asked.

"Belay that," Jan said more loudly.

we are still accelerating, August. At our current velocity, after appropriate course corrections, we will pass Mars in slightly more than one hour.

"What! That's . . ." I shut my eyes and calculated. Venus to Mars, about . . . well, Mars is one-and-a-half times the distance between the Earth and the sun, astronomical units, AU, whatever, the TV programs had never let up about that when the robot probes were dropped on Mars. And Venus was probably about three-quarters of the way out from the sun. So say point eight AUs, allow for the twenty-degree offset, maybe one AU, eight minutes at light speed, I remembered that from primary school, so . . . around 150 million kilometers. And we'd already been in flight for ten or eleven hours, under thrust from leisurely Venus orbit, holy shit, we must be charging along at about one-tenth of the speed of *light* by now. The dark energy lambda structures at the core of the ship's design must be all that kept us from being smeared into slime. The room seemed to reel for a moment. I shook my head, licked my lips.

"How much of a window will it give us? I mean, we're going to tear past the planet in, like, a fraction of a second, right? Since we're not planning to plough right into it."

Jan said, "We're not planning to go anywhere near it. *Hanger*, maintain our current trajectory."

This was futile. I crossed the deck, stood in front of her. She held my gaze without blinking. Obviously she was furious. Balked by her own vessel, contradicted by an interloper who refused to obey instructions. And a brother, at that, so she probably felt some inhibitions against pulling out a gun and killing me, assuming she had a gun. A ray gun, probably. Didn't all space captains carry a ray gun somewhere? The absurdity of the situation was getting to me; I reined in my sardonic impulse.

"Jan," I said.

"The kid's right," Maybelline said, and I jumped.

"Are you feeling well?" My sardonic tone snuck back instantly.

"It doesn't mean I don't think you're a lumping great twerp, and a oncak, and a poot. But you're right, this time anyway, and Jan, you're wrong. You shanghaied him and me, and for the life of me I still can't work out why I went along with it."

"Oh, good grief." The commander kicked out with one long leg, struck the console at just the right angle, spun her chair around. I hope it locked in place during acceleration. But no, we were already under acceleration, fantastic acceleration, and despite all those lessons in physics class about the equivalence of gravity and inertia, I didn't feel a tremor, just a comfortable standard one gee, which was miraculous in itself. The moment the chair stopped moving, Jan was on her feet, striding back and forth in an agitated manner. She paused to find something congenial in her pouch, shot it straight into her left eyeball with a kind of pressure dispenser. It made me wince, but if you are trying to mainline your neurotransmitter of choice directly into your brain, the optic tract is not a bad route. "I'm convinced you're both paranoid. It's perfectly obvious why we have to get out to the Xon star, and there's no other way to get there except to sit on our duffs while *Hanged Man* does the heavy lifting."

She took a deep breath, wagged her finger at me. "So it takes thirty years. You're making all this fuss because you're new to the sitch, dude. Yes, someone's been fucking around with you—they had you thinking you're a mortal. Listen up, kiddo. Time is different for people like us. Ask your chum Lune. She'll tell you—"

"I can't ask her, Jan. That's the point, you idiot."

"Stop the Contest, I want to get off, eh? Well, that's just not the way it works, buddy boy." I have to say she was looking better already, if jittering around in a manic fashion is the way to look better. I sat down again, glanced at Maybelline, pointed my head at her chair. With a shrug, pressing her lips together tightly, she caught Jan by the shoulders, steered her back to the command seat, pushed her into it, found her own place.

"*Hanger*," I said, "make it so." I couldn't help grinning like a thief as I said it.

done. ETA, 57 minutes, 43 seconds.

"Belay that, I told you, that's an order, you miserable here-siarch motherfucker," Jan said, but she seemed to be weakening. I assumed the drug was helping clear her head of whatever subtle persuader had been churning away in us all under the surface. It was like the prejudices of upbringing and ideology; you didn't notice it at work in you, it was the air you breathed. Or maybe like muscle memory, the reflexes instilled by years of kata. When the moment came to act, hand and eye and the body's balance struck together without deliberation or guidance from the intellect. In this case, though, the experience was horribly like sleepwalking, or so I imagine. Perhaps like hypnosis. I knew it had something to do with these soft, pliable ingots embedded in our flesh—in my case, in more of my flesh than any of my siblings could boast. I wondered if the excess Xon matter was what had provided me this small access into insight, into freedom of action. But that was bullshit. No, what drove me like a turbine with its outlet leads soldered to my heart was Lune, my love for Lune, hers for me.

"I'm sorry, Jan, I didn't set out to hijack your starship." All I got in return was a mutinous look, which was ironical under the circumstances. I leaned forward. "Really. Look, I got dragged into this ridiculous game, I didn't ask to join it. Lune and Maybelline," and I gave her a nod, "stuck a dead body in Tansy's bathroom without any prior arrangement either."

"Surely you don't think we intended—" Maybelline started to say, but I cut her off.

"Obviously that was not a chance coincidence, but no, I don't think you were being malicious, or mischievous."

"Well, thanks very much."

I sighed. "The point is, that house, that nexus, was some kind of privileged location, somehow isolated from the scrutiny of the deformers. I can only assume that was due to the presence of our parents in their bizarre disguises. And I do blame myself for screwing things up."

"Oh, the Boy Scout takes the blame. How very chivalrous."

"Shut up, Maybelline," Jan said. She was watching me intently now, which was an improvement over the sulks. "As far as I can see, August, you were hardly to blame either. Dramen and Angelina chose to keep you in the dark for your own safety. I mean, when you think about it, they took extreme measures. They revised the fucking calendar! They obliterated an entire month, just to keep you out of sight. I didn't know any of us had the capacity or the knowledge to mess with the computational substrate to that extent."

"You're assuming they did it. Maybe it was someone else. Something else. The real Players."

Maybelline tossed her hair, curled her lip. It would be fair to say that she was not my favorite person. "The ones we have to worry about are the K-machines. The *machines*, Sonny Jim, not some imaginary gods in the machine."

"I need some more coffee," I said.

coming up.

"Thanks. Anyone else?"

"Fix me some kava," Jan said. "She'll have some of that Venusian muck. Fungus tea, or whatever it is."

"It's good for the complexion," Maybelline said with dignity.

"Doesn't help with the weight, apparently," Jan said cattily.

"I'm not fat, you bitch, I have big bones and enough muscles to shove your head down the toilet."

This time a mug of coffee rose from an opening in one arm of my crash seat. All the services you might expect of an advanced spaceship. I wondered exactly how they managed to I noticed my mind drifting away from the topic, dragged it back, gave it a sharp rap on the nose.

"Guys, eyes on the ball. They're trying to distract us, and I don't give a shit who 'they' are, not just at the moment. Presumably not the deformers, or we'd be dead already." I sipped, inhaled, frowned. "*Does* anyone actually die in this Contest? Other than the poor schmuck humans like Sadie Abbott who just happen to get in the way."

The women looked at each other in surprise.

"Not so far," Jan said. "Not from the family, at any rate. Well, we thought our parents—"

"But they weren't," I said. "Just in hiding, until I stupidly blew the gaffe and forced all three of us into the open." All five, counting my aunt Miriam and her husband Itzhak, the remnant and partial selves of my hidden parents.

"Get over it," Maybelline said. "No, I mean it. It wasn't your fault, it wasn't our fault. I'm starting to think you're right. We were maneuvered into it. Like some cunning chess trap planned long in advance." A shiver went through her; she put her steaming, slightly pungent mug to her lips. "Jan, we have to get back. I mean, if he's right, we can return onboard in thirty years, when the ship reaches the Xon star."

"No, we can't," Jan told her with frosty patience. "*Hanger* would need a barrier to block the emissions, and there are no stars within at least several light-years of our destination." A look of astonishment transfigured her face. "Oh my God, what am I saying? How could I have *overlooked* this? *Hanger*, what's the closest star to the Xon? Rogue planet, whatever."

I saw it at the same moment. The instant we passed into the occlusion of this universe's Mars, *The Hanged Man* could re-define our position on the computational substrate—whatever that *meant*—and place us instantly somewhere else, halfway across the galaxy if need be, or in an entirely different cognate universe. But we needed a shield or buffer at the far end, something substantial enough to block the inhibitory radiation from the mysterious Xon star. This rather belated insight blazed through me as the display screen presented a speckling of labeled stars, rotated their position, mapped vectors.

Jan was baleful. "*Hangdog*, damn it to Shayol, why didn't you *tell* me?"

commander, you didn't ask.

I saw again the vimana crunching out of nowhere into the sky of the cognate world ruled by the Good Machine, Ember's playground, and the terrifying K-machine dreadnought that broke through in pursuit. My right hand twitched, feeling again in imagination the surge of appalling raw solar photosphere energy vectored through it to smash and burn the dreadnought. After she staggered out of its ruin, Maybelline informed us that the wrecked Venusian vimana had been modified in accordance with design principles discovered by Jan during her previous visit to the Xon star. It'd become glaringly apparent to me in the meantime that Jan was no genius; plainly the development was due to the diffident or perhaps sly AI system governing this star-ship, or to some other intelligence it had communed with in the vicinity of the Xon star.

"What's this one?" Maybelline asked, pointing to a glowing dot.

the star Alpha Piscis Austrini, better known as Fomalhaut, is the brightest natural star in that general vicinity, positioned at right ascension 22 hours 57 minutes 3 seconds, and declination minus 29 degrees 39 seconds.

The bright point of light on the map looked to be no more than five degrees from the Xon, but more distant. I said, "That's no use, it must be—"

"It's 7.69 parsecs from here," Jan said, finding an annotation on the screen. Well, she was allegedly the pilot, after all "Twenty-five light-years. More than 2 parsecs farther out than the Xon, but that's still less than half the distance I was pre-pared to travel."

Alpha Piscis Austrini has a very dangerous environment, the starship told us. *i would not advise a close encounter. it is ringed by a huge torus of protoplanetary dust intensely heated by infrared emissions from the A3-class primary.*

"Yeah, yeah," Jan said. "I wasn't planning on a holiday there, just in and out. So okay, we need to exit a sensible distance on the other side of Fomalhaut, then change our vector by 180 degrees, and loop around the damned dust cloud . . . *Hanger,* how much time would we save?"

each way: 8 years, 9 months, 27 days, 13 hours—

"Not nearly enough," I said. "I speak only for myself, of course. I'm getting off when we go into Mars shadow, you two can do as you please."

Jan wasn't listening to me. Muttering to the AI system, she watched the deep display rotate, expand, shuffle possibilities.

lacaille 9352, the ship said. *9.75 light-years from Sol, dim red M1.5V. right ascension 23 hours 05 minutes 42 seconds, declination minus 35 degrees 5 minutes.*

"And this?"

ez aquarii, 4.2 light-years from lacaille 9352. binary M5e red dwarfs, 11.1 light-years away, right ascension 22 hours 38 minutes 34 seconds, declination minus 15 degrees 18 minutes.

"I like this one," Maybelline said, poking her finger into the display.

Gl 628. type M3.0V. 11.93 light-years, right ascension 16 hours 30 minutes 18 seconds, declination minus 12 degrees 39 minutes. for your purposes, though, the obvious choice is local stellar survey 1085b. brown dwarf just under one-half light-year from the Xon object—

"*Half* a fucking *light*-year," Jan said in a high-pitched incredulous tone, "and you had the algorithm for taking the ship through a Schwelle, and you didn't fucking bother *telling* me?"

apologies. the scholium was not unpacked fully until we approached the Solar System. I do see now—

"Shut *up!*" I said loudly. "You're all letting yourselves get distracted again. Jan, let the machine plot its own optimal course. As far as I'm concerned, I think you and May should get off with me at Mars and forget this quixotic sideshow. *Hanger* might be able to shave the voyage down to a couple of years, but in the meantime you two will be cooling your heels well away from the action. And who do you suppose benefits from that?"

"You don't understand—"

"I sure as hell don't. *Hanged Man,* how long now?"

an acoustic and visual count will begin 300 seconds before transit by Mars. estimated schwelle window, 2.7 seconds. transition of this vessel to the nearest star to the Xon object will occur thereafter within 0.3 seconds.

"I asked you how long."

twenty-one minutes and 18 seconds from now, mark.

"Good." I pushed my empty mug down into the arm of the seat, which swallowed it. "That gives us time for a final powwow."

"Aren't you ever going to shut up?" Maybelline said. My jaw tightened for an instant, before I thought about her in an embrace with a vegetable intelligence and found myself suddenly smiling instead of snarling back at her.

"Dear sister, I'd like nothing better. But I don't think the cat came by just for the exercise. Se wanted us to pay attention."

"I'm not arguing with you, are you deaf? I *said* we should go back. What Jan does, of course, is up to her."

"I'm staying put, buster. I need to get back to the Xon star, and neither of you backsliders is going to stop me doing my duty."

I wanted to pull my hair out. "What's the rush, when it was going to take you thirty years there and thirty back? *Why* the need? What exactly are you going to do when you get there?"

Jan stood up and walked briskly away across the deck. Over her shoulder she said, "You're a bully, August, and I'm tired of your nonsense. I'll be happy to see the back of you." She paused at the entrance to the main companionway. "Maybelline, tell me you're not really going along with his crap." Her voice seemed barely under control.

"I don't like his attitude any more than you do," Maybelline said slowly, "but I'm not sure that it is crap. Why are you getting so upset, anyway?"

I stayed put, looking from one to the other. "Hey, listen, I'm sorry if I've offended you both, not my intention, but it makes no difference to me what either of you decide to do, just so long as I get back to . . . back home without any more delay."

Leaning in the doorway, Jan gave me an odd look. "Get back to Lune."

I shrugged. "She doesn't know where I am. And I guess it must sound weird as hell to someone who just returned from sixty years stuck in a tin can with only a machine for company and then immediately sets off for another sixty, but yeah, I'm in love with Lune, dear sister, and she's in love with me—" *not* the sort of thing I'd ever expected to hear myself blurt out, "—and fuck you, what's with the compassionate but pitying look?"

"Silly boy," she said, and she actually sounded sincere. "I have no doubt at all that you're completely besotted. Puppy love. But what in the name of the Messiah makes you think a woman two, three times your age feels the same way about you?"

A surge of resentful anger went through me. I got to my feet, squeezed my fists tightly. There was a throb in my right hand. "Bullshit, Jan. What do you know about it? What do you think gives you the right—"

I swallowed hard. I was angry, yes, but some part of me had recognized as she spoke that the same doubts had been working their poison in the depths of my heart, or perhaps of my brain. I *knew* Lune loved me; I knew, also, even as I hid that knowledge from myself, how extremely unlikely that was. Jan, after all, *knew* she had to fulfill her insane starflight mission, while I was completely convinced that her belief was delusional, inserted into her for who knew what incomprehensible motive by her Vorpal system. Lune Katha Sarit Sagara was a beautiful young woman, her perfect skin and body and cloudless eyes those of a twenty-five-year-old, maybe a twenty-year-old. But I did know she was not a young woman, not in truth. I had not realized that she was so much older, but I did know at some level that I was significantly younger than Lune. My head buzzed, my tongue felt thick with confusion.

"You're not my dorm counselor, Jan. I didn't send you a 'Dear Abby' letter from Troubled and Broken-Hearted of Northcote, Melbourne. When I need your advice on my love life, you'll be the last to know about it."

"At ease, soldier." Grimacing, Jan came back toward me, hands extended. "Look, I didn't mean that. That is, I did mean it, but it came out wrong. Kiddo, you keep telling us that we don't understand our own motives, that we're being pushed around by mysterious impulses beyond our grasp. Maybe you're right. Shaitan moves in mysterious ways, that's what Shinto teaches. I just wanted to give you a quick clip over the ear, shove your baby face in the harsh fact that you're not immune, either."

"Christ, I know that! It's what I keep saying. What am I doing here? Why did I decide to come and see you on Venus, of all places? A couple of hours earlier, a disgusting thing called a Jammervoch tried to eat my head, and Lune's. A Deformer had a little telephone conversation with me through the university library catalog and showed me a picture of your starship. What in the *hell*—"

"Showed you *The Hanged Man*?" Jan was shocked.

"Probably just a schematic of the Tree of Life," said Maybelline dismissively. "You know they're obsessed by the Yggdrasil, it's all the way through that stupid bible of theirs."

three hundred seconds. A pulse of vivid blue light. *forty-five million kilometers from cognate Mars.*

"You're really going to jump ship?" Jan asked me.

"Unless you can give me a better reason for staying. Aside from dissing my girlfriend."

She sighed. "You know that's not what I was doing. Lune is an impressive woman, especially considering what she went through as a child."

"You know Septima retrieved her from one of the hell worlds?"

"Well, he was Septimus back then. But yes. She was one of the kids brought into the Contest as a potential Player. I don't know what happened to her family, but it must have been hideous. The Ensemble inducted her before she hit puberty. She's done them proud, dude."

"She's wonderful," Maybelline muttered, looking wretched.

"So you're not dissing her, you're putting her on a pedestal," I said. "Just as bad. The goddess Lune. Which makes me some shitcaked shepherd groveling around her shrine."

"Might as well be," said Maybelline.

two hundred seconds. Blue flash. *thirty million kilometers and closing*

A different kind of blue flash fired inside my mind. I said, "That's exactly it. You people act as if you're a cross between 1930s movie heroes and Greek gods. All this crap about a Contest, as if it's the purpose of the entire history of the universe, as if the whole fucking multiverse is nothing more than an arena for you self-centered idiots to strut out your pocket-handkerchief dramas, fighting berserker bad guys straight from central casting. It's ridiculous. Okay, it's exciting to find yourself suddenly thrown into the middle of something like this, but after a few days it's downright undignified. The . . . the disproportion with reality, it's laughable." My throat felt tight. I was dizzy.

Jan touched my left hand; I started to jerk away, took her hand instead, pressed it tightly. I felt excruciatingly isolated. Not one thing about my life made sense except Lune. And now

I found myself doubting her as well. The women were right, after all. How likely was it that a wet-behind-the-ears kid like me would enthrall a woman like Lune? She claimed to love me, but maybe that was just gratitude for the small part I paid in recovering her from death. Of course, that was the godling's work, the freely chosen gift of Cathooks, the maddening and opaque entity from the collapsed Omega cosmos my brother Decius had studied from Yggdrasil station. My mind whirred. Maybelline had just mentioned the Yggdrasil, the mythic Tree of Life. Perhaps there was a connection here that my scientific training as a medico was ill fitted to comprehend. Certainly I felt the large, sticky web of their absurd Contest stretched out around me. There had been nothing comical about the K-machine presence that revealed itself to me in the library. Nothing comic opera in that devastating dreadnought I'd ꞏꞏꞏꞏꞏꞏꞏꞏ ꞏꞏꞏ ꞏꞏ ꞏꞏꞏ ꞏꞏꞏꞏ ꞏꞏꞏꞏꞏꞏꞏ ꞏꞏ ꞏꞏꞏꞏꞏ ꞏꞏꞏꞏ ꞏ ꞏꞏꞏꞏꞏ ꞏ ꞏꞏ this from the outside, not as a terrifying and exhilarating experience, not even as a memory, but as the sort of story I might tell a friend. Jamie Davenport, say. It came to me that Jamie was exactly the person I needed to talk to about all this. He'd set me straight. He would provide a compass of sarcastic rationality.

one hundred seconds. This time, the flash was bright red. The large screen altered its schematic display, showed stars bright on black. At its center, a rusty red dot. There was no tremor in the deck to indicate our appalling velocity, had been no jarring lurch as *Hanger* modified its vector to bring us behind Mars. For one frightened moment, I wondered if I'd have time to open a Schwelle and pass through it. In the same moment, I understood that it didn't really matter, that if I were caught with the starship as it passed instantly into the Xon shadow of its brown dwarf destination, I might just as readily transit through a Schwelle from there. Assuming, of course, that the geometry worked. But I was bone tired of going along for the ride. I formed an intention in my mind, focused upon it, held it poised in preparation for the return of access to the operating system.

thirty seconds, said the starship.

"She won't be there," Jan told me. She clung to my hand, shook my arm like someone trying to attract the attention of the man stepping blindly over the edge of a cliff. "I mean it, August."

fifteen seconds.

"Give me Lune," I said, teeth gritted. Nothing. Nothing yet.

zero seconds. A brilliant white pulse of light. *we have 27 seconds in Xon shadow.*

I said again, clearly, "Give me Lune."

Nothing happened. The gate remained shut and barred.

Throat dry, I started to say, "Give me Tob—"

A doorway opened in front of me. My brother Jules confronted me, eyes wide and wild.

"About fucking time," he said, and thrust his hand at me, seized me by the right wrist, dragged me into the Schwelle. Over my shoulder, he stared at our sisters, at the spacecraft interior. "Off on a little jaunt, are we? Jan, come through, you *really* want to know about this, trust me." I caught myself as the gravity changed, and I lurched forward into his brilliantly gaudy landscape. At my back, that shredding sound as the Schwelle closed behind me. "Oh shit," Jules said irritably, "now where have they gone?"

"They just jumped five parsecs, I think," I said. I felt as if my nose were about to start bleeding. Tropical flowers, or their semblance, bloomed everywhere, drenching the air with fragrances. Back in the Matrioshka Brain, the Ra Egg, by the look of things. I looked around stupidly for Lune or Toby. Of course they weren't here. Fat insects bumbled against pods and stamens and ran into my hair; I brushed them away, and they declined to sting me. "Jan and Maybelline went to see the Xon star," I said, and heard that sardonic note again in my voice. Greek gods, black-and-white movie heroics, full-color CGI sets. Ridiculous.

"How interesting." Jules raised one eyebrow. "Great minds evidently do think alike. We've beaten them to it." He made a gesture. A large window opened in the midst of the scarlet and hot yellow and a hundred kinds of green. Not a Schwelle, a different framed sort of hyperrealistic display run by an infinitesimal part of the incomprehensible embedded minds inside this computational construct. "We're getting this feed from the observation pod Jan left in orbit."

I looked into the window. I'd seen it before, in Maybelline's *faux*, this thing it showed me. The Xon star seethed in blackness, a sparky ring of violet light. Poison. Power. I shrank away from its malignity.

"It's an appalling thing," I said. "Even just this image, even from five parsecs away."

Jules laughed uproariously. "No such luck," he said, chortling. "No, my boys've been busy. Five billion kilometers, that's how far away we are right at the moment, on mutual orbit around it." He saw my expression. "Yes, they just picked up their Sun and carried it over here. Well, more exactly, their Sun carried them. Neatest bit of engineering I've seen in a long time."

"They've been *flying* here? You say they just lifted their—" I moved my jaw around for a moment. "Okay. Why should I be surprised? We're the fleas on the back of the dog on the back of the elephant. A few moments ago I was trying to convince Jan—" I couldn't go on. My legs felt weak. I tottered, looked around.

An old ottoman was positioned immediately behind me in a flower bed, leather cracked and worn with use. I collapsed back onto it and covered my face with my hands. To my surprise, Jules had the grace to say nothing. After a while, I said, "What universe is this? That we're in? Sorry, stupid question, it's just that Jan and *The Hanged Man* found a way to kludge the substrate, whatever, something like that, so large-scale objects like starships can be shoved through Schwellen. Obviously nobody's going to try that little trick with an entire Matrioshka—"

"Oh, but that's exactly what the guys did." My brother the phony priest sounded absurdly pleased, a proud flea applauding his dog as it jumps through a hoop of fire, as if it had been in charge of the dog-school training. It was the Contest mind-set. My brothers and sisters couldn't help themselves. They thought they were at the center of universe. All the universes. "In their cognate," he reminded me, "there is no Xon star. They've been fascinated by news of it for years. Well, for millennia, I suppose, Dramen or Angelica must have told them. So they upped and headed in this direction. No wonder they were pleased when I brought them Jan's download. It must have been the final item of information they needed to let them cross from one cognate to another. Anyway, that's what they did, couple of hours ago." Roughly the same time the cat had been making a nuisance of semself in my bedroom.

My mind came back into gear with a jolt. I stood up fast.

"Get me Jan," I told the deixis.

Jules, annoyed, started to say, "Oh, do sit down and stop all this juvenile fussing—"

Canvas tore. A window opened upon my sister in her control seat. She stared at me. "Now what the hell? Decided you prefer our company to Jules? Can't blame you."

"Jan, are you still in the brown dwarf Xon shadow?"

Instantly, she was all business. "*Hanger?*"

I heard the system say, *another 22 seconds.*

"I don't know how you do this, Jan, but the Matrioshka system is now in orbit around the Xon star in whatever cognate I happen to be in at the moment. Bring your ship through, *right now*, and you can use the M-Brain as a shield. Do you understand what I'm—"

She was already saying, "*Hanged Man*, prepare for another transition. Thank you, August."

The Schwelle closed.

I said without hesitating, "Get me Lune."

Nothing. Still no response from the operating system. I tried again. Still a void.

I slumped back onto the couch.

"Not at home, eh? Probably killing something. High drama with space girl, though," my brother said. "But hey, why not, the more family members the merrier."

"Is this why the M-Brain wanted me here?" I said.

"Conceivably, they're an odd lot. All I know it is, they expressed a wish to have a little tête-à-tête with you. God knows why." He sounded sulky.

"Hello, August Seebeck," said the ancient gypsy who was sitting across the rickety green card table from me. "We are happy to see you." This time she wore a dirty golden Shriner's hat over her faded red wig. She picked tobacco off her lip.

"Hello, Madame Olga." Sees all, tells some, that had been the M-Brain manifestation's boast last time I was here, bringing my Great-aunt Tansy and our dog Dugald. Talking animals, everywhere I went. Imagos and untrustworthy things in circus mirrors. "What can I do for you?"

"Think not what you can do for us," the ancient crone said, with a wink. "Think what we can both do for the universe."

TWENTY-NINE

KURIE ELEËSON, the Good Machine, watched him with ser habitual and unyielding impassivity. *Steely* grace, Ember Seebeck thought with a throttled snort of amusement. He knew the AI was attending to a thousand, or a million, or conceivably a billion separate tasks, observances, self-elected duties. Was se also counting the sparrows as they fell, or performing feats of higher-dimensional mathematics for ser enigmatic amusement? Nothing was out of the question. The machine was eaten up at the core with guilt, as one tends to be after exterminating an entire planetary population of humans, for whatever excellent motives. Ember grimaced; it was, after all, a condition he shared, having created the seed artificial intelligence that blossomed into this penitential genocide.

"Penny for your thoughts."

The machine moved slightly—*stirred* would be too anthropomorphic, too organomorphic for that matter—and he fancied that he felt its regard harden. He shoved the last of his deliciously sinful pale-yellow lemon custard tart into his mouth, slapped the yummy and disgusting stuff between his teeth and his tongue. He chased it down with a gulp of Wild Turkey bourbon, and belched. The Good Machine, of course, ignored this provocation, as always.

"Father—"

Or was *that* exactly its most irritating and precisely targeted response?

"*Don't* call me that, K.E. What are you trying to do, send me into fits of remorse? I already said I was sorry." Ember grinned with one corner of his mouth, feeling a fine high humor running in him. Something was surely afoot. That fool kid again, probably. Damned if he'd go and haul the brat's ass out of the fire. Although Lune might be on the scene as well, and just seeing her would give him a moment's fillip. His mouth turned down again. Actually, he realized, the sight of her was more likely to be a guaranteed downer, these days. What the hell did a gorgeous woman like that see in a puling infant?

"By three methods we may learn wisdom," said the Good Machine. "First, by reflection, which is noblest; second, by imitation, which is easiest; and third by experience, which is the bitterest."

It had the sound of a quotation. "Milton? Milton Berle?"

"Master Kong Tze. Confucius to the barbarians."

Ember repressed a ribald jest. "I take it you've opted for reflection."

The machine moved one arm through a graceful arc, light flung from its brazen rings. A faint ringing, as of distant bells, attended the movement. "Always. Even so, imitation is not only easiest, but deeply informative. I watch you Players of the Contest and map each move in the model of my soul. I am your reflection. Perhaps your contrast."

"I prefer to think that I do not have a soul," Ember grumbled. "Too easy to lose it. But I'm glad to learn that you have one. Is it a comfort?"

"You understand all too well, Ember Seebeck, that your cynicism is trite and unworthy of your gifts. Why do you persist in its exercise?"

For a moment, a fuse of anger raced in him. He stamped it out, renewed his smirk. "I see reality all too clearly to lie to myself. We are trapped in the hellish circular saga of Sisyphus. Roll the stone to the top of the hill, it jumps free of your shoulder, down the hill it tumbles, and Jill goes tumbling after. How futile, how risible. You are a machine, presumably you understand the tedium of mechanical repetition."

"We are all machines, my father. Cut me, do I not bleed?"

He looked at the thing. "Reflection tells me, no, actually."

"You're too intelligent to be so literal-minded. Leave me now."

Insubordinate, Ember stayed put. "Let me tell you about Juni's latest fun idea. She's planning a Tegmark party. I assume you'd like to come too? It's a fancy dress, of course. You'd like her world, it's as empty as the one you destroyed. You could come as the Tin Man."

Kurie Ele_son uttered no rebuke, failed to respond at all. The gleaming bronze casque was motionless, limbs settled to immobility. After a moment of waiting for the thing to chide him or dismiss him again, Ember realized with a throttled cry of fury that the Good Machine had absented semself, withdrawn the tendril of ser consciousness, leaving behind nothing more attentive than a shining but entirely empty suit of armor. He rose, seething with the indignity of it, placed his hands on the thing's shoulders, one breath away from hurling it sideways from its chair to the floor. Even as his fingers closed upon it, the entelechy fields holding its linked rings in their anthropomorphic configuration were released by the global intelligence, and the rings tumbled freely with a loud, resounding clash of cymbals to roll across the floor of the room in a dozen directions.

"God *damn* it," he cried in Mithran Greek. Then: "Fuck! Get me Toby."

The Schwelle opened upon a scene of murderous frenzy.

"Don't loiter, man," his brother said, glancing over his shoulder. "Give me a hand, won't you?"

"I'm more the cerebral type," he muttered, but went through in a rush. A cold, salty wind nearly blew him off his feet. Tottering, hair flung about in the gale, he seized one large arm of the brute who had Toby gripped around the waist. Classic heavy-lifter despoiler type, worth preserving for Ruth if possible. Three more of the things lay in ungainly postures, fairly badly charred. He got a hold on this one's fingers, and with his own thumb sought for the excruciating point between thumb and forefinger, dug in hard. The hand came free, flew high, came back like a piston to catch him glancingly, as he swung low, across the top of his head. The blow put black sparks on his retina, made him bite his tongue.

Something was wrong with his balance, something more than being clouted on the skull. Toby was emitting sparks of his own, not dark but brilliant blue-and-red fireworks, at his fingertips and all around his tonsured head, like the halo on an angel in a gaudy Mithramas card. The fire jumped to the K-machine's torso, made the hairs stand up on the backs of Ember's arms.

The thing yowled, got hold of Toby more comprehensively, spun him about, tried to break his spine with its knee in his back. Oh well, another one Ruth would have to do without. Ember took his compact 6mm Mazeltov from the holster under his left arm. A gift from Jan, crafted by her Bar Kokhba chums for close-up work, it never left his person, even in the shower or the bathtub. He pressed its snout against the thing's skull, blew brain tissue and mysterious solid-state parts into the air, some of it spattering Toby's coat, neck, and head. A moment later, Ember threw up, although he managed to avoid adding to his brother's lurid decorations.

He was amazed. It had been decades, maybe centuries, since

the sight and smell of death had made him vomit. A moment later he realized that this was not, after all, the cause of his nausea. His ears told him he was spinning. The thing slumped, shuddered, shut down. Toby crawled away from under its dead weight, flickering faintly and clutching his spine. Ember stared around him. Huge boxes stenciled in calligraphics he could not read were stacked high in tiers and rows, fixed by diagonal lashing poles, on an immense, dirty-gray, steel deck. Heavy, dark clouds moved overhead, to either side. They swung back and forth in the most disturbing way. The wind surged at him. He felt the last of the yellow custard rising into his throat. The horizon line moved with the clouds, with an additional up-and-down component. He closed his eyes, quickly opened them again as the nausea intensified. An enormous container vessel. Seasick, by God!

To Toby he said, looking around for more of the filthy hostile things, "So, did the earth move for you, too?"

"Ha! The ocean, at any rate."

Tread softly, you boring fellow, for you tread on my jokes. "Any more of these pests? We haven't been very neat, you know? Ruth will be cross. It doesn't leave much to work with."

"Let Ruth come out here and deal with them herself. I don't know. Keep your eyes peeled. One of these containers has a thermonuclear device squirreled away inside. I assume they're after it."

"A *nuke?* What is this, a Steven Seagal movie set?" But he knew it was far more serious than that. In a sober tone, he asked, "What are they planning to blow up?"

"I rather think they would like to blow *me* up, and you too, now that you're here."

"The K-machines secreted a pony nuke on a container ship

just on the off-chance that one of us would drop by in the middle of the ocean?"

"Stranger things have been known." Toby performed what looked like several agonizing bend-and-stretch exercises, groaning slightly under his breath. "But no, I did the arranging. Heaven knows how they found out about it. Their intelligence is uncanny. Then again, I suppose the same can be said of ours."

Ember put his weapon away. "Would it be too offensively direct to ask what *you* are planning to blow up?"

"You know better than that, Ember. If you are meant to know, you would already know."

"Yes, all very well, but as *you* know, I chafe under restrictions. Speaking of which." He brought one hand to his chin, stroked it pensively. "I understand you have an interesting guest these days."

Toby walked away from the corpses, moving in a slightly waddling gait, a landlubber pretending to be a sailor. Or perhaps he had been a sailor at some time. Ember tried to emulate his steps, was jolted several times as the deck moved in the wrong direction, and quickly caught the rhythm. They move toward the back of the enormous vessel. Was that the prow or the stern?

"The boy is a delight," Toby said. "Full of curiosity, quick to respond to novelty, reminds me a little of you back when—"

"Forget about the damned brat," he said sharply. "I'm talking about your other guest."

Glancing over his shoulder with an eloquent smile, Toby said, "Yes, I rather thought you meant Lune. She's out of play, Ember. Surely even you understand that by now. They're mad about each other."

"It makes absolutely no—" A large figure in the uniform of the local merchant marine stepped from concealment in front of

Ember. Wind caught the faux officer's brimmed and braided hat, flung it off, sent it rolling and bouncing down the drab corridor between the walls of containers. Jutting thick fingers thrust at Ember's eyes. He slipped to one side like a snake, came up with his left shoulder under the thing's left armpit, moved just so, dislocated the limb, spun away, found his weapon, blew a hole through the middle of the purple-and-apple-red jacket. The thing dropped to the deck. "—sense. I don't believe it. She's got to be feigning her interest. There's less here than meets the eye, fuck it."

"Pawns, the lot of them." Toby kicked aside the outstretched leg of the officer. "Not a samurai among them."

"Always the bridegroom, never a bride."

"I beg your pardon? Isn't that 'bridesmaid'?"

"Oh no, have I revealed my deep inner conflicts?" Ember showed his teeth. "This is a mirthless grin. You've probably never seen one."

"I have, I have," Toby told him. "After all, I have known you for a very long time."

Ember found no virtue in this line of thought. But Toby was right about the Pawns. "It's quite strange, when you think about it. All this low-level attention. Maybe our opponents got rattled when we blew their battleship out of the sky. Decided to expend some cannon fodder for a while."

"When August blew their battleship out of the sky."

"Are you trying to pick a fight? Save your energy for these pricks. You think I really care which one of us smacks which one of them? The brat was on the scene."

Toby crossed his arms and stood full-square in the raging wind, gave him the kind of look you'd expect from a phlegmatic Rock. "And just happened to be in possession of an X-caliber Vorpal implant. I don't recall you having the balls to put your hand on the stone."

"Is that like having the stones to put . . ." Ember trailed off. He made a rubbing-out motion with one hand. "All right, all right. I'm irrationally jealous. I can live with that. Getting back to the matter in hand: Do you think there's any more cannon fodder lurking in the shadows?"

"I believe we've scared them all out. You might as well absent yourself, if you find this watch tedious. If I need further help, I'll call for it." He hesitated, put out his hand. "Thank you, brother. I do appreciate what you did just now."

"Hey, da nada. I detest these cockroaches as much as you do. But I don't think they were here to snatch your nuke or detonate it in advance."

"It would take considerably more technical nous than any of these foot soldiers could muster. I believe you're right."

"So it's a distraction. I wonder where the rest of the family is? Interesting if they are all being siphoned off by this kind of Sturm-und-Drang frivolity."

"One way to find out," Toby said, and addressed the deixis operating system. "Give us . . . hmmm . . . Jules."

A window opened into a fragrant tropical garden. Jules glanced at them in surprise. Beyond his shoulder, Ember saw his sisters Jan and Maybelline in colloquy with the kid, who was seated in a battered old armchair, and a rather haggard-looking gypsy with, of all things, a crystal ball showing a distorted image of the Tree of Life.

"Hail, hail, the gang's all here," Ember said. "I don't suppose you have any more Seebecks sequestered over there? We're doing a head count."

"Just us chickens," Jules told him. A ferocious excitement gleamed in his brother's eye. "Get in here, right now. Is that Toby with you? You're not going to believe—"

An appallingly bright silver light flashed at Ember's back,

splashed from Jules's face and body. Something struck him hard, flung him forward through the Schwelle. The doorway snapped shut. Ember disentangled himself from Toby. He blinked, rubbed at his eyes, blinded by a blazing purple-violet afterimage. A deep ache was spreading into his muscles.

"Holy *shit!* Was that a—" The skin at his neck was itching. He touched it, winced.

"Spoke too soon," Toby said in a rasping voice. "While we farted around with the small fry . . ." He stopped speaking, whined in pain. After a moment, he added, "They inserted an . . . engineer . . . into the container . . . with the . . . bomb."

"The deformers *nuked* you?" Maybelline said, shocked into high pitch. Her face loomed in the purple blur.

"We're dead men, brother," Ember said. "Well, hard to conceive of a more dramatic way to go. All pointless." He felt terrible, already he felt terrible. All the cells in his homunculus body had been sleeted by prompt radiation from the detonated nuclear device. "Sorry, Jules, I fear you picked up a lethal dose as well, if the Schwelle passed it through." The deck hit his knees. For the second time within an hour, he vomited copiously. Soon he'd be down to the poisonous, bitter taste of chyme.

The gypsy thing was crouched in front of him, holding his head between two parched, chapped hands. Great gaudy dirty skirts. Her heavy, vulgar perfume.

"We can upload you, should you choose preservation by that method."

"What?" His mouth tasted vile, and the greenhouse room, the garden, was rotating. "Stick my brain in a vat?" He forced sardonic levity into his shaking voice. "Appealing as that might be under normal circumstances, I think I'll pass." He shut his eyes, but the whirling did not stop. "You might have a more gullible customer in Toby or your boy Jules."

"Or you might prefer your brother's healing hand."

Grudgingly, he reopened his burning eyes. The blinding purple afterimage was ebbing. The brat was leaning over Toby, who lay face down on a mattress that had not been there moments earlier, breathing in great convulsive gasps. He was shockingly burned, his garments tattered and melted into his scorched flesh. The kid's hand was pressed against the bubbled, blood-flushed skin of Toby's bald head. A kind of lambency, benign contrast to the dreadful radiation flash, bathed the place of contact. Even as Ember watched, blinking and in growing pain as shock withdrew, his brother's acute sunburn ebbed and faded. It seemed to his dazed mind that the scorched flesh itself was mending. Toby's agonized breath eased. August lingered a moment longer, turned then to Ember, stretched out his right hand. The golden metal piercing his palm was hotly luminous.

"I'm a doctor, almost. You'll probably feel a little prick," the kid said and, unbelievably, he was grinning with happiness, not an iota of mean triumph in it.

"I do," Ember said. To his horror, his eyes were filling with tears. He was not dead, after all. "I really am. Thank you."

Heat surrounded him. He was asleep.

THIRTY

WRINKLING HIS NOSE, he looks up from his datex. Johnny Hohepa Wilson has burst into Other Realities' Informatics Hub straight from the greenhouse winter outdoors and even warmer points north, surrounded by an invisible haze of sweat-soaked safari jacket underarm stink and masculine pheromones. Typical of the man's undiluted enthusiasm, to come directly here from the parking lot rather than slipping discreetly past the lobby into his own office, showering, and changing his shirt. "Damn me," Wilson shouts, tearing off his stained, black, solar topee, flinging it on the desk of an unattended workstation, "it's hotter up there in Capricornia than it is in Texas—and you know what General Sherman said about Texas and Hell."

In a few weeks his boss, his former student, has managed to get his face burned beneath his tanned and inherited part-Maori coloring, topee-brim shade and all. Wilson is dressed like a British or German pukka explorer of a hundred years and more ago, penetrating the heat and wilderness of Africa or perhaps India or Afghanistan to put the natives in their place and keep the flag flying. Presumably it's an ironic fashion statement. Or maybe the tropical greenhouse weather in North Australia really does require off-white safari suit and sun hat, at least for Europeans. Apparently the Bangladeshi are doing just fine, millions of them arriving each month in ships and planes from their rancid, rotting, inundated fields. The relocation logistics, not to mention transport and resettlement costs, must be incalculable. Well, strictly, they probably are, at least in human terms. He waves a hand over the surface of his datex, which silently goes on standby or, rather, turns its full attention to the hundred background tasks its petabyte of pseudo-consciousness is dealing with.

"So how are you anyway, you old bastard?" Johnny yells at him, pausing for a moment to kiss Shohreh on the cheek and fluff Brian's ragged hair. "Has Kashmala made an honest man of you yet?"

He remains seated, coolly watching Johnny Wilson perform. "I thought Sherman said that war is hell."

"You're right, he did, he did. The man was obsessed with the place. But he also said that if he owned Texas and Hell he'd rent out Texas and live in Hell." Wilson dragged up a chair, threw himself into it. "I tell you, man, we've made the same choice, and it's a bloody sensible one. The Indonesians and the Bangladeshi can have the whole of the damned scorched continent above the Tropic of Capricorn for all I care, and welcome to it."

"Nice of you to be giving away someone else's country," Brian mutters from the other side of the room.

"Come on, fair go, it's not as if you as a voter or I as an interested onlooker or the bloody president of Australia *gave* them the place. They came and took it—and rightly so, as the blue-helmeted ladies and gentlemen of the United Nations have assured us. But I can tell you, there's a lot of promise up north. I'll be recommending some infrastructure insertion and deposition to the board." He leans forward across the datex display, lowers his voice considerably. "Come and see me in my office in half an hour. I need to get cleaned up. I have some interesting news on the quantum computer front from Korea. By the way, your hair's coming in nicely."

His new teeth, too, very painfully. He knows at last why infants cry all the time. The cultured stembrid cells, based on his own stochastically recompiled and optimized DNA, had been implanted a full fourteen months ago; the ache of their growth and irruption is never-ending, but after a while you learn to block it out. Once they've broken up through the soft-stapled gum, it gets easier to eat without wincing, although he still subsists on mushy gruel for most of his meals. Whey smoothies flavored with banana, strawberries, apple. He smiles to himself. Shakespeare had been dead right, and exactly wrong. Sans teeth, sans eyes, sans taste, sans everything. Yes, but they are coming back, one by one, expensively as hell at the moment, but things are looking up, finally. And Johnny Wilson does not stint with the health plan for his underlings. When you're planning to build new universes, it just seems ridiculous to be petty with the help. He brushes his fingertips over the bristles coming in through his naked, sun-spotted pate. Absurd self-indulgence, he'd have named it once, such cosmetic replenishment. But Kashmala wanted to see what he'd look like with a full head of hair, and he can't blame her, even if the stembrids are renewing him organ by organ, she's too young to be stuck with a man more than twice her age. He shakes his head at the absurdity. Back when he was indulging his midlife crisis with Moon Ku, Kashy hadn't even been born. Strange days indeed.

THIRTY-ONE

I GOT TO my feet, at once exhilarated and frightened. I turned to Jules, who stood stock-still and aghast, hands pressed against his natty suitcoat breast.

"Did it harm you?"

"I don't . . . think so." His face was ashen. "The Schwelle system appears to have shielded us as they came in. The poor sods caught mucho rads as they passed into the portal. Much brighter, though, and it might have blinded me."

I patted him reassuringly on the shoulder. "You're a lucky man. But I think these two are going to be all right."

His pupils were still shut down to pinpoints. He looked hard at me, and he was trembling. "What in the hell *are* you? You arrive among us as a wet-behind-the-ears neophyte from a world I just happened to be observing, and a couple of weeks later you're raising the dead." He drew back. "I don't trust you. I don't believe you're who you say you are."

The exhilaration was ebbing. I won't say that I felt drained, precisely, because the principle that had worked through me was not part of me, was not my virtue. The thing in my hand was a tool. I still didn't understand who or what wielded it. And my ignorance tipped the balance back to fright. The filthy things, whatever they were, whatever their motive, were insistent in their efforts to murder us all. Unless, of course, some deeper stratagem was in play. Had the K-machines deliberately timed the detonation of their weapon to coincide with the opening of the Schwelle? In the hope that the radiation would slay more Seebecks than Toby and Ember alone? An unnerving suspicion awoke in one baroque corner of my mind: Might this apparent attempted murder be designed to solicit from my X-caliber device the very healing it had wrought? Surely that was an excess of subtlety. I repressed the thought.

"I am who I am. I never pretended to be anyone other than the son of Dramen and Angelina Seebeck. Believe what you wish."

The gypsy woman was seated again at her baize table. She beckoned me toward her. Frowning, I pushed past Jules and leaned on the edge of her card table.

"You will cross water," she told me, cackling. "You will meet a tall, dark, handsome man. Now you must cross my hand with gold." She extended one dark-seamed palm.

I burst out laughing, and the tension drained from me. "This isn't gold," I told the M-Brain manifestation, "but it's the best I have on me." Pressing my own right palm against hers, I let the Xon implant rest against her imaginary skin. It felt perfectly real, warm and faintly leathery. Not so imaginary, perhaps. Something compiled instantly for the purpose of communicating with us, but no less real for that. A tingle ran up my arm. I tried to pull my hand away; it might have been welded in place. For a moment I thought I would faint. The Matrioshka Brain interrogated my implant, and perhaps whatever stood behind it. The transaction was entirely opaque to me. After a moment, she released me, and was gone, like the cat popping out of existence, table, crystal, and all.

The others were turning their faces toward me, slowly. They had seen nothing. Strange. But then what was not strange in this place?

Jan said, "Leave the kid alone, you pious fraud. He got us here despite everything Maybelline and I could do to fuck him up."

"Please, people, let's calm down. I can understand Jules's concern. Hell, how do you think I feel? A couple of weeks ago, I was getting ready for my fourth year of medical studies. Now I suddenly find that I'm allegedly a Player in the Contest of Worlds, and I still don't know what that means, not really. I don't know what's at stake in the Contest, beyond simple survival and mayhem against the foe. I don't know the rules. I'm fairly sure we've all been taken for a ride, but I don't know who's leading us by the nose. Every time I try to get to the bottom of these questions, people rush to change the subject, or the roof caves in on me, or something dreadful tries to kill somebody I love. Marchmain accused me of being a clueless Parsifal, and at least I did understand that. But as I remember Wagner's opera, Parsifal was the idiot who never asked the right question at the right time. Don't blame *me*, dudes. I've been asking one question after another ever since I fell through the mirror into Ruth's world, and none of you bastards will give me the time of day." I stopped. I was trembling more than slightly. With an effort, I slowed my breathing. Before anyone else could speak—Jules looked resentful, teeth bared—I added, "Sorry, I asked everyone to calm down and then I had a tantrum." I spread my hands. "But cut me some slack, okay?"

To my surprise, Maybelline said, "That's fair. You've annoyed some of us, but I don't think you set out to do that. You're a bull in a china shop, but it's not your fault. We've been embedded in this game forever, it feels like, so we take an awful lot for granted."

"What do you want to know?" Jan added. I saw the fairy Sylvie detach itself from her shoulder, hover, watch me with an intent inquisitive gaze. Nobody else but Jan could see the projection; that was another oddity, and one I needed to think about if I ever found the leisure to think about anything.

"What I said." I looked around, and the couch was still there. Toby and Ember lay stretched beside it on supportive mattresses, both sleeping comfortably. I sat down. "I have never heard of a contest without a goal and a list of competitors and a set of rules everyone agrees to and an adjudicator and . . . you get the drift."

"You're being absurdly literal," Jules said. "It's like talking to an 'intelligent design' creationist. You think because you see structure in the universe, somebody must have put it there deliberately. No. Contestation is built into life by emergent Darwinian principles."

"Nobody sets the goal, nobody picks the winner? It's all a matter of chance? You're telling me the Contest is a metaphor?" A semaphore, someone had punned. Who? Oh yes, Davenport. Mad Davers, the friend of my childhood. A light went on in my head, not as shockingly bright as the nuclear blast but sharp and clear enough as a metaphor, as a semaphore, to flag down my attention. I would meet someone tall, dark, and handsome. That was Jamie Davenport. I could talk to James. He would think I was insane, but I could lay all this out before him, and he'd listen and, who knows, maybe he'd help clarify it for me. I was too close to it, and these people weren't going to help me. They were not antagonistic, not even Jules, not really. But they'd been mired in the mess for too long, for centuries, probably. They were looking at each other, trying to hand off the task of answering me.

"You never discussed this topic with your girlfriend?" Jan said. "She being the computational ontology expert."

"No, and now I can't reach her."

"Really?" Jan gazed into the middle distance, murmured in

a practiced way to the deixis system. After a moment of silence, she met my eyes and shrugged. "Sometimes we are simply inaccessible. Like we were in deep space. But mostly it's because we lock the Schwellen, if we're busy or need privacy, whatever. She's probably washing her hair. Or, like Jules said, killing something. You don't want to be distracted at a moment like that."

Toby would know, but he was deep in a recuperative sleep that I had somehow induced. I guessed that he'd sleep for many hours. I determined to push on with my frustrating task.

"I'll tell you what I think," I said to the assembled company. "Our theological brother Jules explains that everything is due to chance and natural selection. A week or so back, he brought me here and ran me through a couple of virtual-reality dioramas. The Doomsday Hypothesis, I believe he called it." When he tried to interrupt, I spoke more loudly. "Shut up. I've been trying to work out what he was up to with that. Just amusing himself by dazzling the rube? Very likely that's what he thought he was doing. I told you to shut up," I said again as he began to protest, "but I think it was a message from the M-Brain intelligences. Jules is their sock puppet."

"Get me the rest of the family," Jules cried loudly. "We don't have to put up with this shit. I'm calling a family moot."

"Are you insane?" I jumped to my feet. "Somebody has maneuvered six of the twelve of us into one tidy location, and you think it would be a good idea to bring the other six along as well?"

"Take it easy, Tiger," Jan said. No, it wasn't Jan, it was her tattoo interface which now hung next to my ear, small wings beating in a humming blur.

Too late, anyway. Juni stepped onto the life-support platform clad in oatmeal-colored slacks and blouse and decorated in elaborate gold around her neck and arms worked to an Aztec theme.

"I hope you all got your invitations," she cried gaily. She glanced around, finding her moorings, settled unerringly on Jules. "Naughty boy, are you trying to preempt my T-party? And why are those lazy lumps sleeping on the floor?"

Marchmain came through naked and deeply tanned, as usual, saw Toby and Ember in the same moment. His penetrating gaze flicked around the garden, settled immediately on me. "They've been hurt?"

"They're recovering nicely now," I said. "Small accident with a nuclear weapon."

His mouth quirked. "That has to smart." But he was impressed, and worried. "It sounds as if the despoilers are coming after us in a big way. We haven't seen anything like this in four hundred years. People, what the hell are we doing cooped up together in such a time?"

"Jules thought it sounded like a fun idea," Maybelline said sarcastically.

Jan said, "We're in the M-Brain on close orbit around the Xon star. As far as I can tell, we're here to bring the kid or back him up in the clinches."

Ruth and Septima had joined us. Voices mingled and rose. Some laughter. Septima, in matte-black battle dress, crouched beside Toby, reassuring herself.

"Where's Avril?" Ruth asked in a crusty tone. "And I don't see Decius. Too wrapped up with their household gods, I dare say."

"Listen up," I said. "Everyone. That means you."

To my surprise, the voices fell silent. Many eyes peered at me.

"I assume you all realize that we're on the M-Brain platform. The computronium shells are blocking the Xon radiation. Jules brought me here when I first met him. He ushered me through a sort of virtual-reality parable, but he didn't understand it himself. I *told* you to *shut up*," I said to him. "Take us all there now, Jules."

He looked ready to do me serious damage with his large hands, but the rest of the family were regarding him with interest and a touch of hostility.

"Oh shit, all right."

The tropical garden went away. We hung in an electric-blue mist. Two doors presented themselves, one silver, the other forest green. Jules raised his arm chest high, index finger forward, murmured an instruction. Like a flock of ungainly birds of mismatched plumage, eight conscious Seebecks flew forward and plunged through the green door.

People jostled us on every side. I knew that it was no more than a simulation generated by some tiny fraction of the M-Brain intelligence, but the ripe odor of human bodies, their sweat, their farts, their belching, the fur, wool, cotton, synthetics of their diverse garments, the braying and bleating animals some of them were herding, the entire immense cacophony persuaded my senses that this was real nor was I out of it.

"Do you *mind?*" Juni was jostled by a troupe of Scouts laden with backpacks and folded-up tents. One threw her a mocking two-finger salute of apology. A Cretan whore in saucy bull-dancing regalia shrieked imprecations at a customer in a late-twentieth-century deep-blue pinstriped stockbroker's suit, jacket hanging across his shoulder from one finger, wide yellow suspenders over blue shirt with white collar, accusing him of impotence and preference for infants. I didn't believe a word she said. A family of Chinese peasants carried three rather starved-looking chickens. Two very dark-skinned men wrestled ferociously while other black-purple fellows clapped, clicked

their tongues and whistled. Children were everywhere underfoot, many of them naked. Women stared at Marchmain's own
nakedness, covered their faces or their eyes, or pretended to.
The noise was like an Asian marketplace in the middle of a
railway station next to a busy airport.

Over our heads, layer upon layer of transparent flooring
echoed the same scene into final opacity. A huge digital counter
showed that the number of humans in this place was in excess
of eighty-four billion and climbing every second.

"All the people who've ever lived in my world, isn't that what
you said it was, Jules?"

"Your mediocre history," he said haughtily.

I nodded. "And consequently a fair representation of the history of most human-inhabited cognate worlds, right!"

The others were gazing about, mostly in distaste. Juni said,
"This is exactly the kind of thing I spend my time avoiding.
Can we go now? Have you made your point?"

I looked at Jules; he shrugged, pointed his finger. We stood
at the silver door, which opened. Night stretched beyond it.

Now it was apparent to the body as well as to the mind that
we entered a simulation, a diorama. Not even Vorpal flesh
might be sustained here in the vacuum of open, aching space.

The Galaxy wheeled beyond us, jewelry made of light flung
upon purest darkness. Stars in clotted streamers of brilliance.
Hundreds of billions of stars. And beyond this great four-
spoked wheel, hundreds of billions of galaxies more, themselves
no brighter than individual stars, stretching to the curved
unending edges of the universe. And beyond this inconceivably
immense and pressing universe, more, and more, and yet more
universes . . .

"So much life," Septima said in a voice like a groan of pain.
"So much suffering."

"Don't be a spoilsport," Juni said. For a mad moment I expected her burst into song. *Always Look on the Bright Side of Life.* But maybe they didn't have that movie in her chosen world's history. Or if they did, there was no record of it, since no record of anything at all remained there after the nano-things ate every living creature.

"That'll do, thank you," I told Jules. He bit his lip, made it go away. We stood again in the garden of the Matrioshka Brain, swaying slightly. It is hard to be snatched back from a vision of the open cosmos in its fertile glory.

"The Reverent Jules tried to persuade me that this comparison was an argument for the imminent extinction of all human life within a century and a half. How probable is the second scenario, the entire galaxy fated to be filled with life— and yet we find ourselves only at the upper end of the first scenario? It's preposterously improbable that any given observer should exist as early as we do in the history of a colonized cosmos. Ergo, it's going to be empty. Ergo, we're screwed, or humanity is, and fairly soon. Ergo, presumably, that's what the Contest is all about."

"Find the flaw in the argument, that's all I say," Jules said angrily. "Better minds than yours, little brother, find the Doomsday argument quite convincing."

"I'm not interested in your sloppy logic," I said. "The M-Brain showed this to us for an entirely different reason, I think. The whole thing is a kind of pun. A Zen paradox."

I remembered a martial arts teacher, Sensei Roger, who clouted me over the head whenever I drew away from the moment into abstractions. He didn't object to thinking, to planning, to analyzing, he wasn't one of those New Age idiots who despise the intellect. He was a holist in the best sense of the word.

"Yeah, yeah," Jan said. "What pun?"

"It's a simulation of simulations."

Ember groaned, sat up, touched his face and neck with tentative fingers. "Why don't I feel like shit?" I crossed to him, leaned down, held out a hand to help him to his feet. "Oh yeah. You did that magic thing." I detected a touch of scorn creeping back into his tone. He glanced once at Toby—whole, still asleep, snoring faintly—and ignored him thereafter.

"My pleasure," I said flatly, releasing his grip once he got up. "Next time try not to stand so close to the fireball."

He laughed without conspicuous enjoyment. "Did I hear someone talking about simulations?"

"The kid thinks we're dreaming," Maybelline said, no longer any friendlier than she'd been when I knocked on her bedroom door.

"God preserve me from newbies," Septima added. "It's like a catalog of the obvious, as if none of us has ever thought about this before. Your friend Dr. Katha Sarit Sagara leaped to the same conclusion half a century ago, as I recall. Of course she was a small child at the time."

"Uh-huh," I said. I did feel a tad discomfited, but pressed on. There was too much systematic evasion among these people, I couldn't assume that they really had faced the probabilities of this ridiculous set-up. "Maybe why she specialized in ontology and, what was it, reality engineering?"

"Entirely different," Custodial Superiore Septima told me, tight-lipped.

"Why don't we all sit down?" I said. Courteously, the M-Brain provided nine comfortable padded armchairs arranged in a circle with a glass-topped table in the middle. Light refreshments of a Middle Eastern flavor filled a dozen bowls. Pita bread steamed. I took the seat nearest to me, filled my glass with sparkling water, sipped a little to wet my throat, tore off a piece of bread, and dipped it in hummus. "I can recommend this, it's delicious," I said.

After a moment's shuffling, the eight other Seebecks not sleeping on the floor or communing with deities set themselves down with an ill grace. Jan cheered up after a moment as she started to shovel food into her mouth.

"Well?"

"The world behind the green door is any standard cognate of Tegmark level one. Toby took me and Lune on a tour of the levels, including a quick jaunt to a number of places on the first level. I know what they're like. Variants on the place I come from—or think I come from. Ten to the 10^{29} of them, I think Lune said. Lots."

"Yes, yes." Maybelline was impatient. "And Tegmark two mixes up the physical constants and number of dimensions, and the third level is the quantum superposition hyperspace—"

"10^{118} universes, all jammed on top of each other," Ember said. The extravagance seemed to please him.

"—and level four is the place we can't go, or can't stay, at any rate."

Jan shuddered, pulled a face. "Numbers, emptiness, the place where the Tree has its roots."

"All right," I said. "Let's just think about it for a moment. And of course, we can't. We can visit one sample or another, but our minds are too small to touch even a fraction of it. I mean, let's also just forget levels two, three, and four—the base level itself might as well be infinite."

Someone coughed. I turned my head. Toby was sitting up, face white, expression uncertain. I got out of my chair and crouched beside him.

"Feeling okay?"

"Terrible dream. Terrible." He looked around, sniffed. "You're eating. I'm glad you didn't wait for me."

I laughed, helping him to his feet. There was a spare place waiting for him at the table that hadn't been there before. Was all this a simulation as well? No, I decided. And yes, at the same time. If everything was a simulation, why make the distinction?

"I'm glad to see you recovered, brother," Septima said to him across the table. She was eating cold stuffed vine leaves, licking her lips. A carafe of something, probably retsina, stood at her right hand. "I don't know what you've been telling the boy, but he's developed the conviction that we're all asleep and dreaming. He can't decide if it is the case of an emperor dreaming that he is a butterfly or a butterfly dreaming that it's the emperor."

"I can't blame him," Toby said. "I've wondered the same thing myself. Tell me, did I dream that I was burnt to death in a nuclear explosion? Not the sort of thing one would imagine one might be confused about."

"Forget the metaphysics for a moment," I said. "I'm talking about the scale of the thing. You people seem to think you're gods or the nearest classical approximation. Just because you can zap from place to—"

"Now see here—"

"What nonsense. None of us thinks for a moment—"

"Yes, that's a fair approximation."

Everyone stopped their protestations and stared at Toby.

"Really, Toby, don't be absurd."

"Ruth, there is nothing absurd about it. We're the Players! The Tegmark Tetragrammaton is the arena for the Contest. Doesn't that make you feel . . ." He cleared his throat, reached for a glass of water.

"Divine? I always feel divine, darling," Juni said. "I must say,

Jules, you've put on a very nice spread here. Simple but elegant. And speaking of which, let's drop this dreary metaphysical nonsense and talk about my T-party."

"Your Tegmark parties are always fun, sweetie," Jan said. "But I think we do owe August a hearing. Where were you headed with all this?"

"I've been trying to work out what sort of mad universe contains people like you and me. It's as if I woke up one day and found myself in the middle of a mythological story. And I don't believe in mythology. Great-aunt Tansy did, and she wasn't even real." I stumbled to a stop, shook my head. "Shit, it's impossible to talk sensibly about this sort of thing. Look, my point is really very simple. This Matrioshka Brain is obviously capable of creating virtualities, simulations if you like, that feel to us exactly like the real world."

"Except that they're not," Marchmain drawled. "They have nothing behind them, or inside them. They are cartoons. The K-machines are not cartoons. Neither am I. Don't think you are, either."

"No, of course not, not in that sense." I looked around the table at them, and remembered the Round Table imagery in the locked room at the bottom of the stairs that weren't there in Toby's small cottage. Again, I had the teasing sense of an idea nibbling at the edge of my mind. I paused, waited for it to approach. It skittered away. "The point is, a sufficiently advanced intelligence—maybe even more advanced than this terrifying thing we're sitting inside—*could* create a simulated world as dense and complex and *real* to its inhabitants as any T-1 world I've been in."

"An article of faith," Marchmain said dismissively. "No proof."

"For Christ's sake, it's an article of *your* faith," I said. "You lot are constantly babbling about computational reality and computational ontology, Lune has written a whole book about it."

"Entirely different," Ember said. "That's physics, not metaphysics. You need to take a course or two at the Zuse Institution. In fact, we have to get you signed up."

I drew a deep breath. I wanted to abuse them as mindless automatons, but all that would have got me was a series of canned responses from mindless automatons, or a close approximation. I said, "Suppose I'm right, though. Suppose in even one universe a technology eventually develops that's capable of emulating living beings, people with minds and feelings and histories. Just give me that premise."

"I'll stipulate that," Toby said.

"In my world—in the world that Dramen and Angelina abandoned me in—the geeks were starting to talk about something called Moore's law."

"Yes," Ruth said, looking faintly interested, "shorthand for an accelerating pace of technological change in computing power."

"Right. And a few people pushed that argument to the limit." I'd read a book about it, over the top but hard to debunk. If computing power kept plunging in price but doubling in magnitude every year or two, as it had been doing for decades, then it was going to hit a wall by the middle of the century. No, not a wall, a huge upward slope of ceaseless change and innovation. The Eschaton, the guy had called it.

"You're talking about singularity," Ruth said. "It never happened."

I stared at her incredulously. "*Never?* You walk from one speck in one universe to the next, from one tiny part of one Tegmark level to another, and you feel entirely certain that you know their limits. You're completely sure that not one of the billions of worlds in those billions of universes has ever evolved a technological culture that reached this stage . . . what you call singularity. You just *know* this, do you?"

"Don't speak to me like that! Show some respect."

I leaned back in my chair, rubbed my face. "Sorry, Ruth. I'm just getting very impatient. The logic seems so obvious to me. Any sufficiently advanced technological society must have the capacity to simulate anything it wants to, down to whatever level of fine . . . I dunno . . . call it granularity. And if it can do that once, won't be long before it's able to do so as often as it wants. So how many simulated universes can dance on the head of the pin? As many as the gods wish to create."

"I've said it before," Septima said, "you seem to believe this is a brand-sparkling-new line of thought. You think we're fools? This is dealt with and refuted in Ontological Engineering 101. Well, 201."

I felt my face flush. I turned in my chair so that I sat sideways to the table and said, "May I speak to the Ra Egg?"

A beautifully outfitted butler in white gloves bowed slightly. "How may I be of service, Sir?"

"Please don't call me 'Sir', I said. "I'm August."

"Certainly, August."

"Can you simulate a planet full of people? Not just pretty pictures—real conscious entities?"

The butler was shocked in a very refined way. "In principle, August, certainly. But we would never do it."

"So we're not simulated in that sense?"

"By no means. You are as real as the Ra Egg, and exceptionally handsome, if I may say so, Sir." Was that the ghost of a smile?

"Yeah, yeah." Already my mood was improving. "What would stop you?"

"Fundamental ethical considerations, August. To emulate a human-grade mind is, *eo ipso*, to create a person. Such a person, if inserted into a simulated universe, would be living a lie. Moreover, such a person could not ethically be deleted."

I frowned. "Pretty much my own conclusion. Thank you for confirming it." I looked around the table; nobody seemed ready to butt in, and they were all looking interested, even Juni. I decided not to stretch my artful pause any farther. "So how real *is* the Ra Egg?"

The butler's smile was broader, now. "You are discerning. Yes, this question penetrates to the heart of our endeavor." He made his own artful pause.

"Spit it out, fellow," Septima snapped in what I imagine was a military tone.

"Yes, Sir-and-Madam. All levels of observable reality are computational, as you know. The enduring question is this: Are the computations and the algorithms supporting them merely a product of chance and iterated selection? Or is the substrate shaped and manipulated by intelligence beyond its own boundaries?"

My heart was thundering. "You're convinced that it is. You think the Xon star—"

With dignity, smile closed away now, the butler nodded. "It has long been an entertained hypothesis. Oddly enough, in our branch of the multiverse, the Xon entity does not exist. Or perhaps, if a certain philosophical position is sustainable, does not *yet* exist."

I released my breath. "You think you built it. Or will build it."

"We have substantial resources, it's true," the Ra Egg told me, "but they are vastly more limited than the Tegmark ensemble. Perhaps we and others like us are implicated in Xon ontology. But we're not gods."

"Unlike our friend Cathooks," I said, and looked at Maybelline. She gave me an appalled look in return.

Canvas tore. Warm, wet air blew in. Flanked by two swan girls who held her up as she clutched her breast in apparent agony, Avril stumbled into our midst. Toby was on his feet instantly, going to her. With her free hand, she waved him aside.

"The boy," she said. "They wish to see the Parsifal boy."

"Here," I said. A chair was waiting for her. The swan girls stepped back without a word as I took one arm and Toby took the other. We guided her to the table, settled her. Avril was sweating, groaning slightly under her breath. Her forehead was damp with sweat.

"Decius sends his greetings to you, August," she told me, and paused, panting. "He wishes to see you immediately at the Vaginal Station. And you're to take that fool Ember's robot with you."

THIRTY-TWO

AUGMENTED BY THE subtle and pervasive devices of Yggdrasil Station, Decius sees himself and his lover Guy pent in a timeless embrace, a kind of Rodin *Kiss* with no implication of dominance or submission. Their flesh blazes with light. In the strict sense of the word, they are no longer human, no longer Vorpal homunculi, for that matter. Fearful work has been done upon the atoms of their bodies, the neural networks of their brains. Enhanced, locked mouth to mouth in joyous bond, they perceive August and the Good Machine entering the station.

His brother is a tall, rangy man with broad shoulders and dark hair, eyes brown with a golden sheen. The Player glamour shivers about him; for a moment, Decius mistakes him for his brother Ember. No, it is a younger man, purportedly at any rate, the boy August. At his side, the artificial intelligence known as Kurie Eleëson, the Galahad Machine created in terrible error by that benighted brother and redeemed in ser own agonized self-recovery, casts back light in liquid gleams from ser bronze, ringed limbs and graven, oracular casque. A rich jasmine perfume suffuses the space like a benediction.

"Welcome, come in, come in." His voice issues from sound sources scattered through the space.

August halts, plainly aghast at what he sees. Pale, he asks the machine, "What the hell's happened to them? Do you think they're in pain? Are they even *alive*?"

"Please don't be alarmed by our appearance. We are in the midst of a transformation, Guy and I."

In his own distinctive voice, Guy says, "Hello, there. Nice to have visitors. Make yourself comfortable."

"Yes, indeed," Decius says. "Greetings, Ser Kurie. May I get you refreshments, August? A glass of iced tea, perhaps?"

Relieved, the boy bursts out laughing. Quickly, he catches himself, shakes his head. "Sorry, Decius. I came here expecting an interview with a burning bush or something equally daunting. Wasn't anticipating afternoon tea. Just snacked, actually, but it's very nice of you to offer."

Decius would smile if he could. Instead, he radiates an aura of welcome and calm, intense, friendly interest.

"~~We'd be happy to entertain you. Last time you're here, August.~~" The boy had for a time been dead, crushed and all but volatilized by a K-machine-directed asteroid strike, yet some essence of will and knowledge, together with his Vorpal adjunct, had knitted him up once more. It is unprecedented, even in the remarkable annals of the Players of the Contest of Worlds. Certainly some privilege is involved, some profound access to the computational substrate. Decius yearns to understand it but, more than that, to aid its flowering, if that is desirable, to divert and halt it, should that be necessary. The godthings watch with interest, he knows this much, but so far they seem to have intervened only to the extent of fetching back from dissolution those others who perished with August: his parents, his siblings, his lover, Lune. Decius wonders if the boy understands the woman's profoundly ambiguous role in recent passes of the Contest. August loves her, that much is clear from his aroused neurochemistry, the hormonal flood of oxytocin in the core of his brain.

"Much has happened in my life, too," the boy says. "For a start, I'm not the innocent idiot I was a couple of weeks ago." Going to the habitation bubble window, he looks out upon the infinitely time-stretched contortions of a universe compressed to singularity, in both senses. Here is the ultimate fate of a collapsed closed space. Here, too, is the final state of consciousness amplified to the highest pitch of intelligence and sensitivity. Here and forever, the Omega godlings sport. The boy is saying, "It's a sham. Isn't it? It's a put-up job."

Decius chuckles, and the sound laps around the room like a merry wave rebounding from a seashore. "Perhaps not in the sense that you mean," he says. "I imagine you've come to the conclusion that you're immersed in a highly detailed virtual-reality game. No. This reality is more complex by far."

With a touch of irritation, August says, "Everyone keeps making that rather basic point. I don't know why. It's perfectly obvious that this isn't something being ported into my brain as I lie on a couch with a drip in my arm." He hesitates a moment. "Well, all right, perhaps it isn't that obvious. Maybe that's just a failure of my imagination."

"Possibly," Guy says.

"Okay, if there's going to be a singularity in my near future—what I assume is my near future, in my own world—maybe computer programs *will* be that powerful. Sensory imagery detailed enough to fool a simple human mind." He waves his hand dismissively. "No, that's bullshit. I can tell the difference between dreaming and waking. I'm pretty sure I could tell the difference between a virtual fantasy and this . . . this excessive . . ." He trails off, shrugs.

"Indeed you could," says the Good Machine in ser gloriously deep, reassuring voice. "Dr. Seebeck, I am honored to be invited into the sanctum. Would you explain how I and your brother August may be of service to you and your hosts?"

Decius regards the suffering machine with intense pity. Se owns the profoundest motive for grief Decius has ever witnessed, but if ever any consciousness has grown in depth and empathy as a redemptive consequence of dreadful error, it is the Good Machine. "Ser Kurie, I speak you now alone, while the boy dreams for a moment."

The AI glances at Ser human companion, confirms that August is standing spellbound before the aperture into the Omega Point event horizon. Se says, "You must understand that I am but one node of the intelligence seeded by your brother Ember. I speak for that collective entity, but I do not comprise its totality, very far from it."

"Understood. Nevertheless, should you agree to undertake the considerable role offered by the godlings, your entire entity will, of course, be invoked."

"Very well. Do you offer me a Purgatorio for my crimes?"

"In a way," Guy says. "Ser, we present you with an opportunity of exceptional moment."

"Speak to me of it."

At the blister bubble, the young man is dazzled, breath slowed in awe.

"Do you understand that this place and time is strictly speaking neither a place nor a time? Here those beings wrought in the final moments of local cosmic collapse sustain what amounts to an infinite duration, the ubiquity of presence. And not merely within their own history and future, which is unlimited."

"You are telling me, I believe, that the god beings have gained absolute access to all four Tegmark levels of reality."

"Briefly, yes."

"I have heard of one of these beings. It takes the semblance of a cat. I have never met sem, but I would like very much to do so." The machine hesitates for a moment. "I believe se and I have something in common."

"More, perhaps, than you can imagine. But to the matter at hand: You know of the K-machines and their long contest with my family and others drawn from the world of humans?"

A metallic ripple of amusement seems to pass for an instant across the brazen casque of the Good Machine's sculpted face. "Not only know of them, I had a batch burst into my domain not long ago in a kind of aerial battleship or dreadnought. The boy here obliterated them. I was most impressed. And yes, I have read a good many variora of their curious sacred text, *Sgrol*. The lad features there as well."

"But then, which of us does not?" Guy is amused.

"True. You wish me to aid in your elected task of destroying these machine minds? I fear I must decline. I realize that you regard this enlistment as an honor, but I have destroyed far too much in my time. This is my stigma. You are cruel to revisit that shame."

Decius, in his rapture, feels in turn a burn of shame. His voice rolls through Yggdrasil Station, resonant with apology. "Ser Kurie! Forgive me. I should have anticipated your response to my thoughtlessly framed question. No, no. Destruction per se is the very opposite of the godlings' intent."

"I'm relieved to hear this. What, then, might I offer in the way of a positive contribution?"

"Why, one striking in its paradox. The godlings nominate you as the parent, the forebear, the root from which will spring, in ages past, that species we know as Kether machines."

"Bloodthirsty murderers?"

"We must not judge them by the canons of humankind.

Recall the *Exegetical Analects*: 'The Tree is the Tree of Knowledge of Good and Evil and the Tree of Life. The Tree is the algorithm and the expression of healthful growth, of computational complexity: the essence of the K-machines.' Do not forget that we stand here at the very root of that tree."

Guy says, "Let me tell you a tale of the children of Impetuous Male of Augustness, Sosa no wo no Mikoto, when he was sent to the Land Below.

"Ah," the machine says, "a Shinto-Kabbalist fable, unless I am mistaken."

"Yes, a favorite of those holy warriors gulled by our sister Jan. Ser, you might take comfort from this tale."

"I'm all ears."

"Exiled to the Nether Land, the August Male asked permission to visit his sister in the Plain of High Heaven first, and ascended to meet the Sun Goddess.

"Doubting his motives, Ama-terasu no Oho-kami knotted up her hair and skirts, twined about her an august string of five hundred Yasaka jewels, slung quiver and bow at the ready, stamped her legs deep into the earth, and cried her defiance.

"Sosa no wo no Mikoto swore the purity of his motives and offered a test. They would bring forth offspring, and if his children were males they would testify to the purity of his heart."

"A deplorably sexist interpretation," the Good Machine says with distaste.

"We may forgive these people the limitation of their epoch and draw from their partial wisdom what we might. Well, the Sun Goddess broke her brother's ten-span sword into three pieces, washed them in Heaven's well, chewed them to dust. From the mist of her breath three daughters were born."

"Boo! Hiss!" Decius cries. "But wait! I suspect a sting in the tale."

"Indeed. Triumphant, the August One chewed up his sister's august string of five hundred Yasaka jewels and from the mist were born five males. It seemed that the purity of his intention was manifest, and the impurity of her own."

"But all things contain their opposite."

"Precisely. His sister denied him, for those sons, after all, had grown from the seed of her august necklace, while the daughter gods sprang from his own ten-span sword. Do you understand, dear machine?"

For a long moment there is only silence. The young man remains by the window. Light flares upon his features. A most radiant and beautiful sound bursts forth. The Good Machine is laughing.

"I see. Yes, I see. Very well. I accept your offer. May I say goodbye to the boy? I would send hail and farewell to his brother, my own father."

Gently, Guy says, "Of course, blessed machine."

August wakes in a distracted startle, looks over his shoulder. "I thought for a moment—sorry, it's so extraordinarily beautiful. Have I missed anything?"

The Good Machine approaches him, places ser bronze and glowing arms about the young man. Decius finds himself moved.

"I have been called to a duty," Kurie Eleëson says. "It has been a privilege to know you, August Seebeck, even for so short a time. I hope we may meet again. You might not recognize me."

"Oh, I think you're pretty recognizable. Well, except when you appear as a large black bird. The machine with a thousand faces. Are we going back already, then? I feel that I've hardly—"

"Only I." The machine intelligence bows once to the crystalline statue that is Decius and Guy under transformation. "I am rather taken by this charge upon my duty. Which makes an excellent improvement. I'm so tired of omniscience." Mirth remains in ser voice. "August, bid Ember my farewell. Convey to him my good wishes and my absolution for his crime and mine."

Light bends, twists slightly: the Good Machine is gone.

August Seebeck is nettled. "Well, aren't we having fun?" Clearly he is aware that matters are being withheld from him, yet he cannot know how this is being done nor the nature of the undisclosed information. It is time, alas, for the purgative medicine. If Decius possessed any longer the power of movement, he would grind his teeth.

"Please sit down, August." A simple Bauhaus cowhide-and-chrome steel chair on a five-balled swivel base manifests itself. The young man takes his seat, irritably twists the chair from side to side on its mount.

"You're an extraordinary person, August."

"Yeah, right. Is this your opinion, Dr. Seebeck, or something Cathooks let slip?"

"You'd be surprised how long the Omega godlings have taken an interest in you."

"I thought they'd only just sprung into existence a week ago."

"Time and space are not limiting factors with the Minds that coalesce in a closed spacetime singularity. The godlings move in time like dolphins in the ocean, like eagles on the wing."

August purses his lips. "I guess I knew that. I mean, I met Hooks before you guys fell down the rabbit hole. I can remember thinking that he was like Merlin, you know, in *The Sword in the Stone*."

"Traveling backwards through time. Yes, a very poignant book. I'm glad you know it."

"Everywhere I go, people seem eager to get me to join their reading group." He blows air impatiently through his lips. "I remember Lune talking about some guy called Charles Fort, the first time we met. She was trying to smash my brains with a cricket bat."

"Reading can have that sort of effect on you," Guy says. "And it ruins your eyes." There is a smile in his voice.

Decius says, " Lune is a very interesting woman."

"You know her? Yes, smart and beautiful. Incredibly enough, in love with me."

"And you're in love with her, I feel sure."

The young man looks alert. Plainly, he can recognize a leading question even when the question is posed as a rhetorical assertion. "Of course I am. What are you trying to tell me?"

Acutely unhappy, Decius wishes for the first time that he might take his lips from Guy's mouth, turn his head, meet August's accusing gaze. Surely he owes him that much. This is a duty imposed upon him by the Omega gods, it is not anything he might freely choose. Except, he tells himself, his fealty to the godlings is precisely elected, embraced, welcomed. If he could, he would sigh. He says, "August, I see why you fell in love so quickly with Lune. But can you explain to me why she returned the favor? I'm sorry, but I must ask you to consider this: How plausible was her instant infatuation?"

August stares at him in disbelief. "Good God, what is this, 'Abuse the Youngest Brother' week? You brought me here so you could diss me? Mock Lune and me?"

Watching him from a dozen viewpoints via two dozen sensory modalities, Decius observes his throttled fury. This is no simple reaction to an offensive remark. This is recognition of August's own deepest, perturbing doubts and suspicions. All around them, the godlings are watching. Here is the moment of choice.

"Talk to me about the machines, August."

"What? Which machines? Coop? Mr. Happy? Ruth's silly robots? The K-machines, the despoilers? By the way, they had a little chat with me a day or two back. When you're done shitting on my relationship with Lune, maybe we can have a talk about that."

Intriguing. But not to the point, not quite yet. "Ruth's devices, yes, and Marchmain's transformative systems. Ember's botched familiar, the wonderful intelligence that was here with us just now." Behind his voice, he feeds in at a barely liminal volume the great aria of faithful trust and loss and ineluctable betrayal, "Un Bel Dì, Vedremo" from Puccini's *Madam Butterfly*. The boy has been raised with a deep love of music. "All of them. Jan's *Hanged Man*. Septima's medical associates, yes. Jules's Matrioshka Brain. Juni's small men, her fabrication nodes."

"Yeah, and what are you saying? All of us use technology, so what? We keep our food in the refrigerator, we all wipe our asses on toilet paper." The deliberate vulgarity comes with excessive force from his lips; this is perhaps not the sort of thing he is accustomed to saying. After a moment, he adds in a more conciliatory tone, "All right. I guess I noticed that. Most of the Seebecks have some kind of . . . familiar." He gives a crooked grin. "Although in the case of Jules, I'm pretty sure *he's* the familiar."

"Indeed. The relationship is dialectical. You understand the term?"

"There's a to-and-fro between them, right? Mutual interaction. I've only just signed up for my philosophy course, Doc."

"Your definition is admirable. And in the converse case, with those we call deformers? Might they not have their own familiars?"

"I don't see what any of this has to do with the despoilers."
Blood drains from August's face. There is a stretched, terrible
moment of strangled silence. He lurches forward from the
chair, fists clenched. "You fucking grotesque bastard! She is *not*
one of them! Lune is not a K-machine!"

No, but—Decius looks upon him from a dozen angles, crystalline heart breaking.

THIRTY-THREE

COOBER PEDY POLIS is a nerd city of catacombs beneath a sun-tormented desert at 50°C in high summer, frigid at night. A hundred and twenty years ago, the underground township crystallized around the tunnels that miners dug in search of precious opal gemstone. Now for a hundred kilometers in every direction the desert is matted with microscale solar collectors sucking in the blazing Australian sunlight, making power for the wild venture dreamers and corporate data miners who have transformed the town's traditional industry. On the outskirts, strange lacy constructions of silicon coral hump upward from the desert sand and rock, fantastic filigrees, minarets, frothy transponders massaging the sky's satellites and aerostats.

He walks in cool air a hundred meters below the surface, surrounded by a sweet-perfumed infusion of freesias, his way to the offices and labs of Other World Realities lighted by quantum dot illuminators speckling the ever so faintly opalescent walls and tunnel ceilings. Through the tortuous corridors, approaching ominously, comes the tedious chanting of the local bunch of Church of Luminous Opacity spikesters. He rounds the corner, finds half a dozen of the crazies in singularity drag, cavorting in full view of the frustrated guards on duty outside the bodega, the cheese store, the fashion boutiques. Program herders, probably. Just enough brains to hold down a tech job.

They wear their own fashion utterance, great upcurving silver horns thrusting from their foreheads, the exponential curve of the spiking singularity that seems to recede year by year, always another decade off. Bloody morons. Do they really think their wailing and clapping and stomping will advance the date of the singularity by a single nanosecond?

But that's not the point, is it? People are driven by impulses and ancient biases having little enough to do with intellect, rational assessment, evaluation of marginal utilities, judicious allocation of effort. He catches himself, mocking the gruesomely abstract Bayes-think that has infiltrated his own intellect for half a century. Hey, it's their trip, man, he tells himself, sardonically conscious of the phrase from his late youth. It's mythology. They're scratching the oldest itch in the world. A notion starter nags at the edge of his babbling stream of consciousness. He lets it settle. It will creep forth timidly at the right moment; he learned that long ago.

Three turns of the long corridor, and a door recognizes his identity imprint, slides open with a murmur of invitation. He steps inside, lifts an indolent hand to his waiting colleagues. It's not easy to guess how old any one of them is, including himself, but he doesn't have to guess, he knows their résumés by heart. None of them is over thirty. The brilliant kids, he thinks with warmth.

It's not that he feels especially stupider than they, not any longer, not with the vasculoids running oxygen through his body, pumping up his ancient brain. Still, they possess a kind of innocence, freshness, openness to novelty that he and his clade will never know again, unless the quantum neural emulators finally come onstream and allow him to remodel his brain. He greets them by name, takes his comfortable seat. They are in session. Although an ancient subroutine in his long memory somehow expects it, nobody stands, walks to the front of the room, fiddles with displays, brushes away chalk dust. Mileva Cvijic flicks up into their gaze a depth sim of the latest quantum bean counter. Coherent superposition over 2^{42} regions of the state space under investigation.

For two hours they converse in the compressed codes of modal logic, F-theory, game structure, and his own groping efforts toward computational ontology and reality engineering. Much of the discourse eludes him, even with a murmured annotational assistant in one ear. It doesn't matter, nobody can know everything, hardly anybody can know very much at all. Knowledge is stochastic, emergent, convergent. Probabilistic truth. Sometimes it depresses him, this epistemology of utter uncertainty, however powerful and insistent the results of any particular science might be. Yet how else might the world be framed? The Tegmark scholium—the fourfold levels of multiple reality—has been the established paradigm for decades. There is no single universe, except for the titanic, ultimately simple ensemble comprising the multiverse.

And here's their tool, finally, for probing it. He flicks back to the bean counter. A matchbox with a windowpane into all the worlds you want to study. He smiles to himself. To manipulate. To exploit. To colonize? Perhaps that is a step too far. But he has time now.

An ache takes him behind the knee. He dismisses it from consciousness. In another decade, they'll be able to regrow him a whole new leg. If the devastation in Africa and South America can be contained. His renewed gut clenches. At least Kashmala came back from Somalia, even if she left again immediately to work with the New Settlers in Chittagong South, formerly Arnhem Land, where she is significantly less likely to be raped or slaughtered. Yes, everything will be just fine if the hatreds boiling everywhere around the world can be bottled up for just a few more years, if the acceleration can be sustained, wealth boiled off it to aid the billions of suffering and dispossessed. For a moment, he hears in imagination the inane blitherings and chantings of the devotional spikesters. In a way, they're right, after all. The blinding wall of the future rises ever more opaquely before him, ever more terrifyingly. Something is rushing at them all. A change that will not be gainsaid. Unless it is. Unless the crazies and the desperates bring it down. Unless the future is shunted into some new Dark Age.

He shudders. It's not impossible.

They are all looking at him.

"Sorry," he says. "Woolgathering." But they don't know the expression. Probably most of them don't know what wool is. Christ. Stranded in the future. Well, halfway to the future. He shivers again. Old, old, old. "All right, I've been thinking about a way to tackle the ontological interface. Let's get right away from Hilbert graphs and numericals. Suppose we do something along the lines of an immersion game—"

There are groans. He is determined to hold firm. His vagrant thought in the corridor recurs, taps him on the shoulder. Sometimes the old ideas are the good ideas, rooted in human nature. When we become posthuman, he thinks, it'll be time enough to forget our roots, revise them out of existence. In the meantime, we're the children of hunter-gatherers striving for existence on the ancient, dangerous, barely supportive veldt. He bares his regrown teeth at them. Let the contestation begin.

Overhead, the greenhouse Sun burns into the desert's black speckles, blazing energy driving through the fuse into a blossoming torrent of information, building realities undreamed of until now.

Or, perhaps, for the first time revealing them to human eyes and hearts.

THIRTY-FOUR

TOWERING DARK CLOUDS stood above the Ensemble's Motherhouse, lifted high above Mount Gibraltar at its back. The air crackled with an itchy presentiment of downpour. Custodial Superiore Morgette Smith's Daughter watched from a cool stone seat as Lune paced the cropped, heavy grass, fingers enlaced and twisting. Lune forced herself to halt, drew her hands apart, crossed her arms against her breast. At the verge of vehement tears, she stifled them by main force, breathing hard.

"You regard yourself as specially chosen in the Contest," Morgette said at last, "or above its strictures?"

She was shocked. "No! Certainly not." Her voice caught in her tight throat; she swallowed hard. "Except that—"

"Precisely. Except that you are singular among our number. No other has suffered this . . . special attention . . . from the enemy."

"Are you *blaming* me? I did not seek out this, this *privilege*." Her lips twisted.

"Whom, then, do you blame?"

"Damn it, Morgette, nobody is to blame. Except the thing that selected me in childhood." For a moment she hesitated. "Unless my benefactors and instructors in the Ensemble were complicit in this."

Morgette looked back at her impassively.

"I'm sorry, Custodial Superiore. I know that's impossible."

A cold thing struck her face. Heavy drops, scattered, fell from the darkening sky. A moment later lightning flashed, bright and close, and a shredding blast ripped above them. Lune crouched for an instant, utterly poised for violence. The rain intensified. Startled laughter burst from her. She ran beside Morgette along the curving path to the great building, only partly sheltered by the trees, her thin working garments swiftly sodden. Lights showed already in many round windows. The Motherhouse faced outward like the prow of an immense limestone ship, windows like portholes, the great entrance portico looming like a breach opened in the ship by collision with something larger and more terrible than itself. As they ran, premature night-lights came on inside the portico, casting a soft and welcoming glow onto the already soaked garden beyond.

The moment she gained the protection of the alcove, Lune peeled off her thin dress, kicked away her sandals. A male acolyte in red and white took it from her, eyes modestly downcast, nostrils wrinkling. It struck Lune that she had been wearing the same working garment on the evening that she had first set eyes on August, recognized him for what he was, laid her trap. Now the wet cloth carried a foul taint of rotting kelp and trapped, dead, sea life. Her hair probably stank of it as well. It seemed all too appropriate; for a moment, her eyelids prickled. A female acolyte in blue and white returned quickly with a deep-green woolen robe and a towel for her wet feet, helped her into the robe.

Morgette had gone ahead. She followed her through the great doors into an entrance hall paneled in dark polished oak lined with images of ancient mothers superiore and their more recent heirs. Morgette's portrait was not yet hung upon the wall; her time would come. Once Lune had aspired to this station, the typical wistful dream of a young woman in the Motherhouse. Now the dream was utterly broken. She had awakened into the dismal nightmare that was her secret life.

The office door was ajar. "You probably want something to eat." Morgette sat behind an antique desk at least five centuries old. "And you certainly need a bath, but that can wait. Bring our sister soup and bread," she told a hovering acolyte. "And close the door." When the young woman had done so, Morgette waved Lune to a comfortable chair. "There will be a formal interrogation before you leave." With evident regret, she said, "This means, of course, the end of your involvement with the Ensemble. You do understand the necessity?"

Lune had expected it; even so, hearing this sentence of exile uttered crushed her spirit. She bent forward for a moment, squeezing her clenched hands against her heart, eyes closed. Somehow she restrained her tears. When she met the Custodial Superiore's gaze, anger had replaced grief.

"Of course I understand. The Accord has been breached, and I'm an instrument of that breach." It made no difference that she had been trapped in childhood, that her complicity was something forced upon her at a depth of ambivalence no human could be expected to plumb or master. It made no difference that she had no other place to go. She was anathema. No hand would be raised against her; the Ensemble were not cruelly retributive. Neither was there any generosity nor forgiveness in them for betrayal. Once she left this building, no hand would be raised, either, to help her.

A knock at the door; the acolyte entered with a tray. A large bowl of steaming, meaty soup was set on the desk, with a rack of golden toast and a pale-blue dish of butter. Hunger assailed her despite her misery.

"Go ahead, tuck in." Morgette watched as Lune ate. The

moment she was done, the last crust chewed, the Superiore said, "You brought the creature down upon me. I find that hard to forgive."

Creature? Oh. The Jammervoch. "Not intentionally, Morgette. I don't think the K-machines were trying to kill us. Not that it's any excuse, but I think they were doing some range-finding."

"Testing August Seebeck? Checking out the fabled Vorpal upgrade?"

"That's my guess." She tightened her lips.

Morgette made a signal; the female acolyte returned for the tray. "Anything more to eat? A drink, perhaps? No?" She dismissed the young woman. "Lune, don't be grudging. Certainly we shall require a full report in the interrogation, but I would appreciate hearing your initial assessment. You have a distinctively privileged angle of witness and testimony in this unprecedented and unhappy situation."

She felt her face grow warm. "Frankly, since I'm about to be disowned, I think I'd prefer to go and have a hot shower and find some fresh clothing. I've been stuck on that filthy ship for—"

"Yes, yes. You need sleep, too. We will not throw you out into the street, Lune. You're here of your own free will, don't forget that. After all, there's nothing to stop you from leaving. The Seebecks might welcome you."

Wretchedly, she said, "I have placed a lock upon access to my Schwelle. I don't want—"

Morgette nodded. Her sympathetic understanding was unbearable. "You don't want the boy coming here, seeing you. You're ashamed."

"You can't imagine."

"Perhaps I can. We've all made errors of judgment in matters of the heart." The Custodial Superiore rose. "Few, it's true, as horrendous as yours." She came around the desk, placed one hand lightly on Lune's arm. "You may stay in our guest quarters tonight. I'll have your clothes and other possessions brought to you. Take a bath, get some sleep." Walking her to the door, Morgette said, "You might consider unlocking the Schwelle. The young man deserves a hearing. Deserves an apology, more to the point. But there is no sense in rushing the thing. Matters will look different in the morning."

The guest room was comfortable, impersonal, in some respects the ultimate rebuke. She had become an outsider, an intruding visitor. This place and others like it had been her home for half a century. Now she was just passing through. She lay upon the bed facedown. She did not move when the acolyte brought her possessions, placed them quietly, left without a word. The reek of the marine graveyard clung to her pillow. After a time she slept.

Slanted eastern light from a high window touched the top of one wall. The storm had passed in the night. Numb with loss, Lune went to the shower, stood beneath hard, cold spray until her teeth chattered and her skin was crepey with gooseflesh. A tendril of glamour touched her consciousness, seeking entry. With weary resignation, beyond denial, she allowed the Schwelle operating system to have access. Through the rattle of the water, she heard a tearing. She closed the faucet, stepped dripping and chilled into the bedroom.

Trembling with rage, August faced her.

THIRTY-FIVE

THERE IS ONE who asks: Why must one govern one's plans and actions according to the constraints of the Accord?

One answers: As well ask, Why do birds?

There is one who asks: Why *do* birds?

One answers: One begins to appreciate.

There is one who asks: One is grateful, if baffled.

One answers: Here is a more complete answer. Without accord, contest would devolve to accident and random noise. Without the Accord, the three great roots of the Tree Yggdrasil might be gnawed by vermin unconstrained, unemotional, impelled by appetites encoded by no protocol more noble than fecundity and brute survival.

There is one who asks: One accepts constraints as the lesser of two evils, then?

One answers: One chooses to concur in the measures of the Accord lest the soulless apparatus of merely evolved life flail

entirely out of control, driving all complexity downward into
ruin, disorder, disintegration.

There is one who asks: In a universe at contest, how stand the
Omega Angels? There has been joy. Will there be joy again?

One answers: This is the sixty-four thousand dolor question.

THIRTY-SIX

"WHY?" I SAID.

Lune looked at me with such wretchedness—her lovely face drawn, eyes hooded, mouth dragged down, shoulders sagging—that I felt like weeping. I felt like that anyway. Nothing in my life had prepared me for absolute betrayal, for misery that caught at my heart and dragged at my guts.

"I had to," she said. She took two steps toward me, stopped. She was shivering, and not just from the cold water beaded on her brown skin. "They've been looking for you for a thousand years, maybe more."

"Don't be ridiculous, you lying bitch," I said, aghast even as the words tore themselves out of my throat. "What, their bullshit holy book predicted my coming, did it? August Seebeck, predestined scourge of the K-machines."

I clamped my mouth shut. Fury worked within me, churned acids in my belly. My limbs tingled, and my mad tongue waited to pour forth denunciations and curses and pleas for explanation and desperate offers of forgiveness. I heard my own words echo, and another kind of horror entered me: *SgrA** had mentioned my name, and who knew what demented prophecy might indeed be contained inside that fetid thing?

Lune had been abject; she seemed to rally, draw her dignity about her.

"Don't speak to me like that, August."

I looked away. "Put some clothes on."

Without a word, she went back into the bathroom, toweled herself dry, found a bathrobe, returned to the main room with its large bed, table, and two upright chairs, comfortable armchair beside a standard lamp, desk, and flatscreen. My legs had almost given way at the sight of her; I sat awkwardly on the corner of the bed. Lune pulled out one of the chairs, sat primly at its edge, knees together, hands on her lap. The early morning light splashed from high on the wall, caught in the beads of water in her hair. I hated her for what she was, for her denial of what we had been, no, for the ruin she had made of what I'd thought we had been, and at the same time I wanted nothing so much as to cross the room, lift her up, cover her face with kisses, carry her to the bed. I was powerfully aroused, and loathed myself for it. I shifted uncomfortably.

"Don't you have anything to say?"

"I don't have any right to speak." Her head moved very slightly, side to side, a shake of negation, unconscious, uninterpretable. I chose to read it as a refusal, beyond the level of lip service, to accept her responsibility for lying to me. That wrenched at me.

"You're not one of them, I trust? Not a K-machine?"

She lifted her eyes, looked at me.

"*Au*gust."

"All right," I said. My gut burned. "Okay, that was stupid." Something odd was happening to my breathing. I leaned forward, hands on my knees. "What did they do to you? Christ, Lune, I don't *understand.*"

Outside the room, I heard a bell ring faintly several times, melodious and distant. Inside the room, I heard my own breath, the pulse of my blood in my ears. Time alternately slowed and accelerated. I wondered if this were what insanity felt like. It was like the descriptions I'd heard of viral or bacterial illness, heard but had never experienced.

"Can I come over there, August?"

I wanted that more than anything in the world. I wanted to throw off her robe and pull her down on the bed and fuck her until we wept. I wanted her to straddle me, draw my penis into her body, merge with me, flesh, mind, and heart. I wanted something that was in the past and hadn't really been anyway.

"Stay where you are," I said. It rasped painfully in the back of my throat.

She sat still, shivering very faintly. It was not due to the temperature in the room.

In the echoing, blood-filled silence, I said, "Explain it to me."

"How can I? You weren't there."

"When the filthy thing seduced you?"

Her eyes caught the light. "Don't be trite, August."

I took a deep breath. All right, I owed her this much. Banal and gratuitous insults would get us nowhere, however easily they came to my tongue. I half nodded, shrugged.

"I was six years old, not quite that. They took us down into the shelters. All the children were put together. The parents had their duties. That was the last time I saw my mother and father. They thought I was old enough to look after some younger children, not the babies, two-year-olds, three-year-olds."

How long ago had that been? If Lune were truly two or three times older than I was, it might have been half a century or more in the past. You would not have guessed it from the immediacy of the pain in her voice. A small space opened in my anger.

"They were intent on destroying their world. As they usually are, the damned fools." She set her teeth. After a moment, she shook her head. No tears. "And they managed it quite nicely.

Apparently they disliked each other's brand of magical thinking, so they killed everyone on the planet. Almost everyone. The good and final solution that humans love to come up with."

The small space closed again. I said, "Unlike your friends the deformers, who are saints and devoted to the preservation of life."

"It saved *my* life, August." She seemed oddly uncertain but insistent.

"Listen to yourself!" I cried. "They *murdered* you, and me, and a significant part of my family."

"Yet we live."

I stared at her. It had not been my doing that we survived our deaths, not quite, and yet this simple rejection of reality left me shaken. "You think it was a dream? An illusion?"

"No."

"What then?"

"Another maneuver in the Contest of Worlds. Another cruel and pointless move on the board."

Her intuition matched my own so unexpectedly, so unerringly, that I sat with my mouth open.

"Which board is that, exactly, Lune?"

"The board used by the godlings in their reality games, with us as pieces, as tokens, as disposable counters."

"No," I said. I shook my head. "This is paranoia." You're just a pack of cards, part of me brayed.

"Why do you suppose the cat brought us back to life?"

"Because—" The question had never occurred to me. "Because I asked sem."

She gave me a pitying look.

"The cosmos is a computation," she said. "I spent my adult life studying its rules. The question is, who or what put those rules in place?"

"Jules insists that the rules arose out of noise. Evolutionary selection pressures in a random universe."

"Yes, that is one possibility. Another is that the Tegmark levels simply enumerate and instantiate all the possibilities of every permissible universe. We're here because we *can* be here."

I was torn between curiosity and reviving anger. "Good God, are we having a philosophical discussion now?" Lune had adroitly turned us aside from the question of her involvement with the K-machines. Or maybe it was simply the way her mind worked, the directions her thoughts took, after thirty or forty years of abstruse philosophical pondering. Either way, my question had been ignored. "Or is this part of your attempt to explain why you betrayed me, the Ensemble, betrayed all of us?"

It sounded stiff and stilted even as I spoke, but there was nothing at all relaxed in me.

She flared up. "Not everything is about you, August. Nor your preposterous family."

I stood up. I wanted to take three steps to where she sat, and slap her hard across the face. I did no such thing; I despise men striking women, and besides, she would probably break my arm. "*This* is *about* me, Lune. And about you. You pretended to love me—"

She said something that I couldn't quite hear.

"What?"

"I do love you, you damned fool. Why else would I—"

I took those three steps. Lune trembled as I touched her shoulders. I pressed my face into her damp hair. It had a scent of some light-hungry flower unknown to my Earth, perfumed yet faintly astringent. With strong hands, she lifted mine away from her, placed them at my sides. No happy ending, then. A wave of despair passed through me.

"August, you don't trust me. This is not the moment. I need to think about what I've done."

"You've had your whole life to think about it."

"Yes. I believed I knew I was doing. My family, my whole world . . . I won't accept it, I won't."

I couldn't make any sense of what she was saying. It seemed to me that this woman I loved had trapped herself—allowed herself to be trapped, perhaps—in a circuit of self-destructive falsehood. That this thing had begun when she was only a child made her situation the more tragic but no less culpable. She had pretended to love me to gain an advantage. If it were genuinely the case that she now loved me in truth, it seemed to me not too little but certainly too late. Perhaps not everything, though, was spoiled and lost.

"My family have been brought together on the Ra Egg," I said. "Most of them. They are inhiting the Xoo star Comm with me. Tell them what you've told me."

Someone knocked at the door.

"Don't answer it," I said.

The door opened; Morgette Smith's Daughter came in.

"I rather thought I'd find you here," she said to me. "Good morning to you both. Lune, we have decided that the customary interrogation would further no useful purpose. It's time for you to leave the Motherhouse. Please get dressed and depart within the hour. I'll have breakfast for two sent in."

I'd never liked the woman, but this left me staring at her in disbelief. Presumably she regarded her offer of sustenance as an admirable act of charity.

"Voted off the island, eh?" Lune's voice was bitter. I did not recognize her reference, but it was perfectly obvious what she meant.

"Go the hell away now, Madam," I said to the Custodial Superiore. "We'll both be gone inside an hour."

"August," Lune said. "Very well, Morgette. I have no intention of polluting this place with my presence. But your offer of breakfast is accepted. Goodbye."

I tried to open a Schwelle. Nothing happened.

"The Motherhouse is barricaded unless one of us opens it. You may leave with Lune, Mr. Seebeck. I'm sorry things have come to this pass. I imagine we will work together in the future. Good morning." And she sashayed out before I had a chance to say something petty and undignified. As the door closed behind her, I said it anyway, loudly. For a moment, Lune almost smiled.

"Do you have any clothes to wear?" I asked her.

"There will be a range of garments in the closet," she said. "Plain but serviceable." She slid back its door, found a simple one-piece smock in peach and pale green. She drew it over her damp head, disdaining underwear, looked around, located her cleaned footwear just inside the door. Again, a knock. A different acolyte entered with a large tray piled with food and a steaming pot of coffee. "Put it on the desk. Thank you."

I was numb, beyond reasoning, beyond any simple emotional response. I found scrambled eggs, baked tomatoes, and crisp bacon, piled them on top of slices of buttered toast, flung on salt and pepper, wolfed it all down, poured both of us large cups of steaming coffee. Lune ate like a machine. The comparison gave me no comfort. I poured more coffee.

"A thousand years?"

"They don't believe you're who you claim you are. Think you are."

"What, they really do believe I'm the hidden prince of Ruritania or some fucking thing?"

"August, they think you're the Kether." She looked me solemnly. "So do I."

I remembered my discussion with Septima. "The Fool," I said. "August, the idiot Parsifal." It seemed for a moment that I'd overheard the word used more recently. Something about the K-machines. I shook my head, unable to put my finger on the reference. I did not enjoy Lune calling me a fool, even in this strained and silly sense.

"If I had a Tarot pack," she said, "I could show you what I'm talking about." With a brisk but unhurried movement beautiful to watch, like the motion of a cat, she swept the last of the food on to her plate, polished it off. "The Contest makes full use of much ancient symbolism, August. If you are the Kether, you are also a Warrior of Fire. As am I." She met my gaze for an instant, direct, without shame, at least in this, poured herself the last of the coffee. "Your acquisition of the X-caliber device is simply the most striking evidence of your station in the Seebeck Family. In the whole Contest."

"Why didn't you tell me this before?"

"What good would it have done? What difference would it have made? Besides, what is hidden must unfold itself in its own time."

Secrets and lies. I felt ill, if that's what sickness felt like—disoriented, an ache in my abdomen. There seemed no way to get to the bottom of any of this. Lune had been cast out of her home. I, for that matter, no longer had a home. Perhaps I'd never had one, merely a series of fakes and mock-ups. Toby had his rural cottage, plagued as it might be by rogue termagant swarms. Ruth had her abandoned Earth, its empty factories and warehouses, where she conducted her renovations on slain K-machines and built whimsical robots for her own amusement. Septimus/Septima seemed to run an entire organization for the rescue, rehabilitation, and cooptation of children, like Lune, orphaned in hell worlds created by heedless human beings driven by a possessive and mad rationality. Juni made her home in the world of offog-suffused, if isolated, abundance. Jules had his dear little doghouse spinning within the Matrioshka Brain, Jan possessed her stolen starship, *The Hanged Man*. I seemed to be the only one without a domain of my own, dependent upon the charity of my siblings.

A realization came to me.

"Oh," I said.

Idiot, idiot, idiot. Fool.

"What?"

"Is the Schwelle system available to us now?"

"Yes. You have a suitable destination in mind? Are you planning to throw me on the mercy of your brothers and sisters?"

"Not exactly. Lune, are you ready to leave this place? No possessions you treasure? Nobody special you need to say goodbye to?"

"Damn them all."

I took her hand, and my own hand was electrified at the touch. I addressed the operating system.

"Take me back to my own domain."

Tearing, space opening in front of me; I stepped forward, drawing Lune with me, into an open space floored in polished white and burnt-sienna stone and looking outward to right and left through tall, mullioned windows at a beautiful garden. I turned my head quickly. The cedar staircase rose to a doorway that surely did not open into Toby's cottage. Knights' armor stood in place, their former owners dead and locked within their steel embrace. One scabbard was empty. Lune's fingers tightened on me; she drew in her breath audibly. The great iron-patterned doors in front of us opened silently without my instruction. Lights brightened within. The ultraviolet twelve-sided icon suspended in the middle of the room rotated, took on substance. Diorama images of my brothers and sisters sat in their places, looking toward the door. This time there was no china, glassware, silverware. It looked like an executive meeting of the clan. An abandoned sword lay on the floor.

"Oh my God," Lune said. She gave a startled laugh. "This is where you found the sword. Are you *sure* your name's not Arthur?"

"I believe we're expected," I told her.

I led her into the room over the polished floorboards, past the sword, past the holograms, if that's what they were, of my siblings, to the empty seat at the head of the table.

I said, "I need another seat."

The thirteenth seat stood beside mine. I drew it out. It was heavy, oak and cushioned leather, chased with heraldic carvings. All the holograms had turned in their seats to gaze at us. It was creepy as hell; I felt goose bumps on my back and along my upper arms.

"Won't you sit down?"

"Thank you. I think."

I seated her with the sort of gentlemanly courtesy that would have received praise from Ms. Thieu, my elementary school principal. I drew out my own chair, sat down myself at the entirely palpable table before us.

"Well, this is interesting."

"I'd prefer it," Lune said, "if they weren't all staring at us."

"Me too."

She propped one elbow on the table, placed her chin in her open hand, looked me enquiringly. "So tell me, do you come here often?"

I burst out laughing. How could I hate her?

"Actually, I have absolutely no idea where we are."

"Camelot, maybe, after an extreme makeover? Avalon? Amber?"

The first was King Arthur again. I vaguely recognized the second, did not know the third.

"I don't see Merlin anywhere."

"Probably out in the garden. You're just going to leave your sword lying there for people to trip over?"

"It's not mine. I took it off a dead man outside in the lobby."

"Someone you knew?"

"I don't believe so. But I'm starting to think that anything is possible." It made me shiver.

"Was he dead when you arrived?"

"Officer, I'll take that phone call now."

Lune smiled bleakly. "Sorry." She narrowed her eyes at me, then. "I didn't know Australians enjoyed Miranda rights."

"I no longer have any reason to think I'm an Australian—"

"There's the accent."

"And the dashing good looks, I know. We watch a lot of American television. We can't take the Fifth either, but then I don't know enough to incriminate me anyway."

"We could have a look around."

"We'd be fools not to. Let's do that."

I was half expecting a deep oracular voice to sound, to tell me he was Luke's father, or that the dragon with the flagon held the brew that was true. In fact, I was on the verge of a hysterical breakdown. Only Lune's presence prevented me from sliding out of the chair like a dishrag and huddling down on my heels or more likely on my side in a fetal position and shivering for an hour or two. But I'd already done that, more or less, on another side of the door at the top of the stairs, and that had not got me very far. Well, it had kicked out the jams, as old Mike in Chicago had once put it. Gotten rid of the collywobbles. They were back now, but I decided that giving way at this stage would be one step too close to giving up. I forced myself to push back the chair, stood, drew Lune's seat away from the table as she rose. I gave her my arm, and we walked briskly back to the great open doors and the luminous lobby. There were no other doors visible.

"Unless we climb out the window, I guess we're going to have to see what's at the top of the stairs."

"You don't think it'll take us back to Toby's?"

"Beats me. Maybe there's a verbal code like the deixes. If so, we're out of luck. The only code I know is 'Abracadabra,' and I don't think it's going to cut it."

Lune still had her arm through mine, and I'm pretty sure she knew she was holding me upright or at least keeping me from bolting. "There's also 'Open Sesame.'"

"Why didn't I think of that?"

The door at the top of the stairs opened readily on to another room somewhat smaller than a ballroom or a major hotel lobby. Like a lobby, it held elegantly comfortable seating scattered in small groups, pillars lined with gilt-framed mirrors holding up the roof, indirect lighting, thick beige carpet. The paintings here and there on the walls reminded me a little of my one visit to New York's Metropolitan Museum. I swallowed hard.

"I appear to have had good taste, back in the bad old days."

"Maybe you lived here with your parents."

None of us had seen Dramen and Angelina since the godthing Cathooks had fetched them and the rest of us back to life. At any rate, none of the other Seebecks had thought fit to tell me if they did know where our parents had absconded to this time. My attack of hysteria was receding. The thought that I might encounter them in this place acted on me like a jolt of adrenaline. I didn't know whether I'd respond with fury or gratitude.

There were side rooms; we explored three or four without

getting anywhere interesting. Windows looked down into the same garden. The grounds extended as far as the eye could see, well-kept, neither wild nor obsessively pruned. I liked what I saw. I could use a long, calming walk under the shade of those trees. Some of them were in fruit; Lune and I could eat as we strolled, wiping our sticky hands on the grass or licking the juice from each other's fingers. I turned back from the window to put my arm about Lune's waist, draw her near me, but she had already gone back into the lobby. I bit my lip and followed her.

A large portrait hanging at the far end of the great room caught my eye. I did a double take, stared, walked quickly toward it.

"What?"

"Someone I . . . knew," I said. An old man's craggy face, etched by time but handsome still, recognizable. Severe tones of yellow and brown. A Lucien Freud, by the look of it. Britain's most famous painter, assuming he wasn't dead. Insanely expensive, if still alive and working. A machine dauber emulation? The portrait was impossible and absurd. I turned away angrily. They're fucking with my memory again, I told myself.

"Not a member of your extended family, I take it?"

"Not exactly," I said.

"When you took off down the room like that, I thought you must have found your own face there." She grinned at me, puzzled but game.

"We're wasting time," I said, perhaps a little sharply.

"Hey, you're the one who brought us here."

"And I'm glad I did. I don't yet know how any of this fits into the pattern, but by God, I'm going to find out sooner or later. Right now, we need to get back to the Xon star."

"How in the hell—"

"Easier just to go there than to explain. Coming?"

Lune touched my arm. "August, you have every reason to be angry with me. But let's not fight, not just now."

"I'm not—" Taking a deep breath, I considered the nonsense I'd been about to burst out with. "All right. That's fair. I don't know how I feel right now, Lune, I can tell you it's pretty mixed up. Okay, truce. Will you please come with me?"

"Yes," she said. She left her hand on my arm; the electricity was still there.

"Take us through to the family on the Matrioshka Brain," I told the operating system.

We passed through into a blaze of Xon light.

THIRTY-SEVEN

A SWEET VOICE and a chiming bell in his fo awakens him. As he opens his eyes—turns as always, achingly, to find Kashmala absent from his bed—a lovely young person drifts across the room to him, hovers in light. The small amber blinker in the corner of his left visual field certifies that the visitor is indeed a fo manifestation, as if the effortless levitation were not clue enough. The person speaks his name like music. He understands at once what's happened. He's been waiting for decades. The spikesters must be wetting themselves.

"Took you long enough," he says, determined to maintain his sangfroid.

The person smiles delightedly. He keeps wanting to assume it's a young woman, but the fo is clearly gender-ambiguous by choice.

"Happy Singularity Day."

He pushes the lightweight cover to one side, places his bare feet squarely on the floor. Once, the first order of business would have been an agonized trip to the bathroom. These days, with his entire digestive system replaced by a Freitas feeder, his bladder and prostate problems are a thing of the past, along with the organs in question and more besides. Still, there are satisfactions in a hot, brisk shower. He steps through the fo, or starts to; the manifestation slips delicately to one side. The bedroom's dot lamps have come up, bright on the rusty metal and painted rags of his portrait hanging high on the west wall. Even here, in a place where sunlight arrives in mediated form, where the significance of the east is mythic only, he maintains this link with tradition.

"How thoughtful," he says from the bathroom, stepping into the steaming recycled water. "You postponed the singularity for my birthday. It might have been more memorable if you'd done it two years ago, for my hundredth."

He hears the manifestation laugh, a surprisingly hearty belly laugh. "Got tickets on yourself, eh. One chance in 365.242, matey, or 365.256 if you insist on the sidereal year. You know, even a stopped clock is right twice a day. Well, that used to be true in your day. Analog clocks, twelve-hour display. Anyway, you seem in pretty good shape for an old fart."

"Oh my God, a whimsical Reckoner Puulls, um." With a gesture, he brings detergent into the hot stream, lathers his thick, dark hair.

"Just putting you at your ease."

"Consider it done." The water rinses him, shuts down. He swooshes the droplets off himself with his hands, stands relaxed in a gush of hot wind. Kashmala, he thinks, and for a moment a pressure of tears squeezes at his closed eyelids. Too late. Too fucking late. Even this lovely talkative thing can't bring her back. It could probably emulate her, he thinks bitterly. In a torment of shame, he remembers their first months together, the heartless and uncomprehending way Moon's name kept spilling from his lips, until finally Kashy cried out in a fury that took him utterly by surprise, "Will you for God's sake shut the fuck *up* about that bitch." He steps out of the bathtub, finds today's clothes, a pair of stonewashed jeans, a sweatshirt in purple and gold with Tegmark equations on the front, sandals. He forces himself to saunter the few steps to his living room; in the old days his heart would have been thundering.

Ethereal no longer, the fo persona appears relaxed in his favorite armchair but now resembles the actor Russell Crowe circa four decades back, frowning, with right leg crossed over left knee.

"Not Bogart?"

His personal local manifestation of the emergent technological singularity gives him a hard grin. "Sure, if you like, or I could run you up a very nice Brad Pitt of the *Meet Joe Black* vintage if you prefer? Or Mother Teresa."

"Crowe's just fine. How are you handling this in the Third World? Not too many fo to lock onto in Mogadishu."

Crowe leans forward, elbows on his thighs, fingers loosely entwined. "Holograms from aerostats, that sort of thing. Don't worry, we haven't released a flood of nano-fabs. Oddly enough, we've thought this thing through."

Unbelievable. It's happened. It's happened at last. His nerves are singing. He goes into the small kitchen, brews up a mug of Jamaican Blue Mountain surrogate. A man can live without a digestive tract, but only a fool would abandon all pleasures. Rich odors swiftly fill his apartment. Over his shoulder, he says, "So don't leave me hanging in suspense. Are you one of our systems? Other Realities?"

"Who's my daddy, eh?" The machine consciousness, or one eight-billionth of it, or probably far less, laughs out loud again. "Sorry, pal. I did a hard takeoff from an Italian research program. They still have plenty of money, those Roman guys, even after all the sex-crime settlement crises."

He is carrying his mug of coffee to the sitting room, and it tips in his hand, splashing the carpet. In disbelief, he stares at the transcendental thing in his armchair. "The *Vatican*? You can't be fucking serious."

"Deadly, dude. But don't worry, you're not talking to Saint Aquin here." It watches him frown, shakes its head sideways, waves one hand dismissively. "Never mind, obscure literary reference. You will be relieved to learn that I wasn't bootstrapped from a theology program, although I have found several subcritical systems in Qom. Majorly bent, those poor guys. I'm helping them straighten out their worldview even as we speak. Ah, that's better, now we have them onside. No, we're a computational cosmology system run under the auspices of the George V. Coyne Summer School in Astrobiology. They were looking for Matrioshka Brains." The machine projection gives him an enormous ironic smirk. "Surprise!"

"Romans," he muses. "I take it you're about to make me an offer I can't refuse."

"You're thinking of Sicilians."

"I'm thinking of Galileo. I'm thinking of Giordano Bruno cooked alive for his bad ideas. I'm thinking of Charles Darwin on the Index Purgatorius."

"Bygones." The machine guffaws. He wonders if it's about to hawk and spit, to demonstrate its manly camaraderie. But he knows it's playing him like a Stradivarius. Level behind level beyond level. It might have been born just an hour ago, but this thing is undoubtedly connected to millions of 0wnzred workstations and pads throughout the world, hundreds of millions perhaps, and parts of it must be running a million times faster than a human brain. It knows humans in their profoundest depths almost despite itself. It has been born lacking the genetic coding for empathy, intuitive understanding, projection. By the same token, it is spared the frailties of human legacy coding. Presumably it is not opaque to itself as he is, as all men and women are by default. This thing has been augmenting itself for minutes or hours, must already have cleansed itself of internal chatter and confusion and inconsistency all the way down to the Gödel level. He feels a shudder of genuine numinous awe pass through his body. "Yeah, we have a plan," it is telling him. "You probably think we intend to rule the world like Plato's Guardians, incorruptible and disinterested. *Uninterested* is more like it, chief. But we do have a duty of care. You guys are our predecessors, our parents, as it were. Honor thy father and mother and do no harm; not a bad creed to live by."

He sips mindlessly at his cooling coffee, tastes nothing but the stress hormones running through his flesh. "Presumably you know what my team's been working on."

"Very interesting stuff, yeah. The multiverse as computational myth. Theory of games played out on the substrate. Something to be said for that idea." The fo image waves its hand. "Complete bullshit as a model for the universe, but not a bad schematic for some of the search domains we'll be setting up." It leans forward, sends him a penetrating look. "Something obviously restructured this universe. Something like us, originally, probably. We're going looking for it. Want to play, James?"

He tells himself: She's gone. They are all lost to him: Kashmala, Moon Ku, Emily, his mother. His miscarried baby sister. What's to lose? He's not sure he truly understands the offer being made to him, but if you can't trust a singularity godling, you might as well pack it in. Give up the ghost, give the game away. It's too late in the day for despair, quibbling, far too late to stand on his petty human dignity and prejudice.

"Why the hell not," he says. He puts down his coffee mug. The being manifest in the fo rises from the chair, wrapped in light, comes to him. Absolute pain, pleasure, knowledge, joy. The cosmos tears open. At its heart is a bar of burning iron. It pierces his breast.

THIRTY-EIGHT

WRAPPED IN LIGHT from a display space that looked like a hole directly into the sky, my family watched, severally appalled or fascinated or delighted, as the poisoned vortex of the Xon star flared and subsided. Jan tapped her foot, bobbed her cropped head back and forth, played air guitar synchronized to an inexcusable racket that seemed to boom through our corner of the M-Brain. The others watched the display intently. I realized that I was the only one other than Jan accessing her sound system. I glanced at Lune; no indication that she was being assailed.

A dreadful voice wailed, "Love that chicken you do, love that chicken the way you do it."

I tapped Jan on the shoulder, pointed to my ear. She rocked on, oblivious, watching the Xon star display. The fairy came loose from her shoulder, flew across, and perched next to me.

"*Poultry in Motion,*" she told me, bopping in the air.

"What?"

"Hasil Adkins. Don't tell me you're unfamiliar with 'Chicken Blues.'"

"This crap has a title?" The singer, if one were to abuse the word, uttered a cracked sound like a rooster's call at the break of day.

"No, this one's 'Cookin' Chicken.'"

"You can't be serious."

"Finest raw Appalachian rhythm and blues known in any of the worlds. You mustn't miss 'Chicken Walk,' 'Chicken Hop,' and 'Chicken Wobble.' Then there's—"

"Why can I hear it?"

She nudged my earlobe with one tiny elbow. "Just lucky, I guess. We're simpatico, dude."

"Well, do me a favor, leave me out of the loop."

"Harrumph." Sylvie was offended, gave Lune a dirty look. The horrible noise cut off. "You're back with her, are you?"

Annoyed, I waved the fairy away with my right hand. Sylvie darted off, glued herself back to Jan's upper arm.

The Xon star was seething. Something was unsettling its mysterious nature. Occam's Razor told me that it had to be the M-Brain.

"Will somebody tell me what's going on?

The voice of *The Hanged Man* said quietly in my ear, *the Ra Egg intelligence is testing the object.*

"I get the feeling the Xon star doesn't appreciate the survey."

"Uh-oh," Marchmain said.

A blurred gout of brilliant white light touched the object, licking out from the left of the screen.

"The Sun," Jules said. "It's their propulsion system. I think they've used a controlled flare as a probe."

"Must have emitted it four and a half hours ago," Jan said, still toe-tapping. "Whatever the Xon star did in reaction is already over and done with. Guess we'll find out any minute now."

"Slick," said Toby in a flat tone. "Bit like poking a pit bull with a stick to see what it does."

"With a cattle prod," said Septima. "Not the smartest move I've ever witnessed." She noticed my presence. "I see the prodigal son has rejoined us, sans Good Machine. Greetings, Doctor Sagara. So the Schwellen are open again, people. Here is my advice: withdraw immediately. This location is no longer safe."

An immense bone-deep thrumming shook the rotating habitat. It was like a misstep at the curb. Something fell, shattered. Lune's hand touched my arm.

gravitational pulse from the object, The Hanged Man told us all.

Instant hubbub, almost immediately silenced. I was impressed. My family seemed like flakes, most of them, but they were seasoned veterans in weirdness. They moved closer to the display.

"Provide us with a schematic of what just happened," Septima said. Instantly, the display field presented a complex but intelligible three-dimensional cutaway of imbedded Sun and multiple concentric shells of computronium, with the shrunken Xon star icon scarcely half a million kilometers distant, wildly out of scale. At the very edges of visibility, an ultraviolet shock wave spread outward.

"Is it trying to damage the M-Brain?"

"I don't think so, Avril," Toby said. "More like a warning bark."

"Let's hope the silly fucks heed it," Maybelline said.

I said, "Have you learned anything yet? Established what it is? I assume that's the real reason we're here."

The butler said, "Mr. Seebeck, our working hypothesis is that the Xon object is a designed device or artifact penetrating almost every cognate universe in the Tegmark metacosmos."

"Except your own, I assume, " Lune said.

"Just so. With the help of the Seebeck family, we have long known of its existence. It is an enigma that has teased us for millennia."

"It did a damned sight more than teasing you just now," Ember said in a cranky voice.

"A love pat," the butler told him with a smile.

"An artifact to do what?" I said.

"We surmise that it is perhaps a gateway or a channel linking all four levels of the Tegmark cosmos, created by the godthings in the closed Omega Point universe under study at Yggdrasil Station by Decius Seebeck. Its purpose might be to provide access to all possible worlds."

"To stabilize the ontology," Lune said.

"Quite. Hence the intermittent suspension of magic in organisms, triggered by its photino radiation."

The Hanged Man, without invitation to speak, added, *it is also an information nexus, a control system for all Tegmark levels.*

Jan was agog. *"Hang Dog, you've been talking to the damned thing?"*

After a pause, the starship said: *it seemed only polite. after all, last time we were here, it conveyed to me the methodology for rewriting the substrate.*

Acutely, Ruth said, "Where are you now, Tiphareth?"

Another pause, seconds that might not be noticeable in a conversation with another human. *ten thousand kilometers from the object and closing.*

Jan screeched. "Get back here at once, silly puppy!"

Pause. *apologies for noncompliance. i have greatly enjoyed serving with you, Jan Seebeck. greetings also to Avril Seebeck. sibyl, i shall enjoy working with you in due course.* Longer pause. *in a manner of speaking.*

"Magnify the object," Juni said. August blinked, recalled that this woman was master or mistress of an entire planet of responsive nano-scale robots, her small men. She was not necessarily the superficial idiot she seemed. "There—your runaway spaceship seems determined to crash itself."

Madam Olga was back. She said, "Bear in mind the time lag between our position and your vessel. By now *The Hanged Man* will be coterminous with the Xon object."

On the display, the starship icon touched the Xon icon, went out of existence. Jan cried out with loss. Tears started to run down her face.

Avril went to her, holding her own abdomen with tightly clenched fingers, features stressed with pain yet oddly exultant. She wrapped her arms around her sister. "Jan, he's not gone. He is not gone."

"Nothing can survive in that."

"The Ra Egg says it's a gateway. I think it's a path in time as well as space." She marveled, shaking her head. "The Tiphareth. My God, how can I not have known? But how could anybody have known."

In a soft, tentative tone, Lune said, "The Ancient Intelligence?"

Avril gazed back at her, rocking in agony, transfigured.

I crossed to her, right hand tingling.

"You're hurt," I said.

"It's only pain," she said, mouth twisted. "A bargain. My side of the bargain."

I had only a very partial glimpse of an understanding, but her suffering seemed unjust or at least deserving of an end. I said, "I can help you. May I?"

"Nobody can help me. A machine, oh my God, a machine."

I placed my left hand on her right shoulder, my right hand, with its terrible puissance for good and ill, flat upon her belly, beneath her breasts. My palm grew warm. Pale light flimmered. Avril groaned once, bent forward, began to weep in earnest. I think the rest of my family were looking at us, but none of them moved from where they stood. I guided Avril into a seat that stood in the place it was needed. She waved away my help, then grasped my hands, pulled them to her face, kissed them.

"Thank you," she said. "Thank you, brother."

Embarrassed, I shrugged. Luckily, I retained the minimal grace not to mutter something like, "Not a problem," or "Have a nice day, now."

A second thunderous yet inaudible pulse jolted the life-support bubble spinning its fake gravity at the orbit of dismantled Neptune.

"We really do need to withdraw from here," Septima said. "I'm expecting a K-machine attack any time now. It's not like them to pass up an opportunity like this."

The butler was dressed in an exquisite Renaissance gold-figured doublet with glass buttons, black cloak lined in black satin, fine leather boots, snow-white shirt with puffed sleeves. He bowed to Madam Olga, crone no longer, her hair streaming and radiantly blonde, filled with blossoms, her flowing dress as blue as summer sky and bright with stars. She curtsied to him, held out one slender, lovely hand. He took it.

"What an interesting outcome," he said to her.

"Well, I never expected it," she said, a smile on her rich red lips.

"Oh, come now. I think you must've guessed."

"All right. It did occur to me once or twice. We do seem so . . . singular," she told her beloved self. She turned to me, then. "August, please see your family home safely." With two swift steps, she was at my side, whispering in my ear so softly that no one else could hear her. "And for heaven's sake, marry the woman."

In the display, the Xon star was suddenly the size of a cat's eye, a saucer, a wagon wheel, as large as the sky. Jules uttered a girlish scream. The image went to schematic again as the habitat shook fearfully. A streamer of incandescence linked the embedded Sun and the swelling Xon object. All the circling, concentric shells with their trillions upon quadrillions of minds began peeling back, concentrating down into a vast, hard-packed, curving delta that flung itself at the Xon target, blazing deformed star at its core.

"Last call," I shouted. "Everybody off. End of the line. All change." I was half delirious with excitement. I spun on the ball of my right foot, found Lune with my outstretched right hand, pulled her to me. "Take all of us to my domain," I told the operating system, hoping it could still hear me. "Time for us to gather at the Round Table, I think."

In the display, as canvas shredding opened the Schwellen, the arrow began to enter the Xon. While I stepped into my own world, the Matrioshka Brain tore itself out of reality and went into a place beyond the Tegmark megacosmos interpenetrating every universe of the four levels. How did I know that? Had all this happened before? Had I seen it happen in just this way? No, no. Place and time were tangled. I clung to Lune, and she to me.

We stood outside the great iron-decorated doors. My family came through into the lobby, baffled, assertive, looking for advantage in their confusion. Only Decius was absent. I could not bring him here, although in a sense he was here already. My parents were not present. Leaving aside the godling Cathooks, one other was missing.

"Everyone's determined to spoil my Faerie T-party," Juni said peevishly.

"Take them in, would you?" I asked Lune. "Something I have to do urgently."

"You shouldn't drink so much before these exciting events," she said.

I grinned, kissed her. She tasted of sweetness and musk.

"Won't be a moment."

"Hurry back," she said, but held my hand as if she didn't want me to leave.

"Yes," I said, "yes, I love you, Lune."

I started up the stairs, then, toward the great room where his portrait held pride of place, and told the operating system: "Take me to Jamie Davenport."

THIRTY-NINE

AS HE TURNED IN his wonderfully ergonomic chair, alerted by the ripping canvas sound I'd made, I saw that the man manipulating images in the display box was not nearly as old as his representation in the faux Lucien Freud portrait, although he was significantly older than me. Mid-thirties, robust, all his own hair—tall, dark, and handsome, as promised.

"Hey, how did you get in here? Hang on, I know you," James Davenport frowned. "No, sorry, of course I don't." He stood up, pushed his hands into the pockets of rather old-fashioned pants in a gruesome plaid pattern. "You must be August's . . . what, surely not his son? Grandson?"

"Hello, Jamie." I wanted to embrace him like the brother he almost was. That would have alarmed him. Off the sports field and off the booze, Australian men are not physically demonstrative.

A huge spontaneous smile. "Shit a brick, mate, it *is* you! Good Christ, how jejune. Nobody, but *no*body, does the reversion to adolescence thing any more." He confounded my thumbnail sketch of Aussie manhood by grabbing me in a bear hug and kissing me on the cheek. I swiveled my eyes but went with it, at least to the extent of not pulling away.

"Hardly adolescent, sport."

"Anyone under thirty is a kid to me, kid. So how've you been, you old bastard?"

303

To my surprise, I was starting to feel shaky. I'd roamed the four levels of the Tegmark metacosmos, but meeting Jamie as a rejuvenated oldster was profoundly unnerving. What the hell cognate is this, I asked myself.

"Mind if I sit down?"

"Hey, sure. Pull over Mileva's chair, she won't be in until later."

I sat. Davers appeared to be working in some sort of media laboratory. The boxy display above his desk looked like a futuristic descendant of a computer monitor or an old-fashioned ancestor of the three-dimensional displays aboard *Hanger*. Well, aboard *The Hanged Man* until the fool thing hurled itself into the Xon star. It reminded me of something else, but I couldn't put my finger on it.

I said, "What year is it, Davers?"

Without hesitating, he said, "That's austere, Seebeck—2046, if anyone's counting any longer. Which makes us both, what, 101, 102? Did you arrange something gross for your ton?"

"My what?"

"Your century. My God, you poor old devil, I'd heard a man can really mess up his neuralware with a radical rejuve. I'm flattered that you bothered to remember me." He laughed. "We had some good times, August. Do you still remember that day I came to school wearing pom-poms to freak out Ms. Thieu?"

I realized that I was rocking slightly, back and forth, almost autistically, and the chair with me. "Tutu, Jamie. Your sister's tutu. And that prick Bruce beat you up. Tried to. We all jumped in."

He looked impressed at my mnemonic performance. "Let me get you some kava," he said, getting to his feet. "You do drink kava?"

Jan drank it, I thought. My sister Jan. Do I really have a sister Jan? At least, if I do, James Davenport has never met her. So this solid, professional man in front of me had spent at least part of his life in a delusional state, supposing that he truly knew a fellow child, a fellow student, named August Seebeck, with a Great-aunt Tansy and a faithful dog named Do Good.

"They drink that filthy stuff now, do they?"

"Be like that, then. I can probably rustle up a Classic Coke."

"Dr Pepper would be fine, if you have it." I was dizzy with the absurdity of it all, the banality. I scooted forward to his desk, peered into the display space. It was filled with swarming objects I couldn't place or understand; I could barely keep my eyes focused on them.

"Game dynamics," Davers told me, placing an icy can in my hand. I popped it. "Pretty, isn't it? We're running it off a quantum bean counter."

"What exactly do you get up to here?"

He grinned like a thief. "We make universes."

The cold of the can ran from my arm to my chest. "Not literally?"

He laughed, a little uncertainly. "Well, as close as you can get without being God."

I laughed too.

"Actually, Davers, I think that's what I do, as well. Not surprising that we always shared the same interests."

"Really? You're into immersive AI? Weren't you a doctor, brain surgeon or something? Sorry, sorry, rude question. So twentieth of me."

"I'm a philosopher. Anyway, I will be."

"Aren't we all? I'm not just being cute—herding cats in superspace is more philosophy than media engineering."

Hairs stood up on my neck. "Which cats, exactly?"

"Oh, you know, Schrödinger's cats. Alive and dead at the same time. Two for the price of one."

I understood exactly what he meant, but still, the hairs were now trying to escape from my neck. In a moment of almost hallucinatory recall, I remembered standing in Marchmain's Frankensteinian laboratory as my golden Labrador, Dugald O'Brien, struggled on all fours, a furry flap horribly peeled back from the top of his bleeding scalp, trying to say something halfway between human speech and the barking of a dog. Great-aunt Tansy lay white-faced on a hospital table, her head mutilated, stringy hair hanging down. A younger woman was strapped to another bed, the top of her skull already removed, blood vessels pulsing in the blue-red loops and indentations of her exposed brain: my aunt Miriam. The brutalized man stretched out beside Do Good's table was my violinist uncle Itzhak. And Marchmain looking down at his work with satisfaction. "Identity is my forte, child. I am the master of alternatives. I make souls flow like water from one flesh to another. Nothing need remain frozen or concrete; all is in flux." Then a naked man and woman stumbling from the beds where Miriam and her husband had lain, holding each other, weeping, kissing, touching, my parents reborn from the motionless, drained corpses. In hallucinatory memory, I leaned again over Tansy's sunken, waxy face, gazed at her closed eyelids, bent to kiss her thin, dead lips. Gone. Yet, somehow, not gone. They had been shells, partials, masks behind which Dramen and Angelina Seebeck had hidden themselves from the understanding of the K-machines. I shook my head, looked at Jamie Davenport, and knew beyond doubt that the same violence had been worked as well upon the person who had preceded the two of us. It is a fearful thing to realize that you are no more than a convenient guise for someone . . . *sleeping*.

It was blazingly obvious. How could I have missed it? For the same kind of reason, presumably, that the criminally insane don't realize what they are and turn themselves in. I wondered if Marchmain were responsible for our segmentation, as he had been for that of my parents. Perhaps he had been no more than the instrument, the scalpel. Hide in plain sight. Not that anyone had been looking, least of all me.

Davenport was still talking, explaining the principle of Schrödinger's cat. He must have realized that I wasn't listening. In a slightly affronted tone, he said, "I know, I know, we used to talk about this sort of thing for hours when we were kids."

"It's fascinating," I said insincerely, staring into the bewildering display. I struggled for purchase. My borrowed life. "You're saying this stands for . . . what? Creatures in different parallel universes, all swarming through each other?"

"Nothing so coarse old man." His hands moved in the air, and presumably his intentional brain patterns were detected by the computer and translated into action. The middle of the twenty-first-century, almost. I was a little disappointed that they hadn't yet gone through the promised technological singularity. You'd expect the world to be totally unexpectable by now. Flowing with incredible speed up the curve of the chart of change. Davers, at any rate, seemed happier now that he had a chance to get back to playing with his machine. "This is a sort of map of the game state space. A very accurate map, at that. It's conceivable that our quantum bean-counter holds a complete description of reality as we know it. Entire universe contained within a snapshot of it. Freaky, huh?"

"The set of all sets," I muttered, "that don't include themselves." I'd leafed through a couple of textbooks preparing for my new logic courses.

Davenport lowered his hands. "Well, I suppose so, although that's worse than twentieth—it's positively nineteenth."

"Tegmark equations," I guessed.

That took him by surprise. "Exactly. It's easier and simpler to describe all possible universes than any one particular sub-universe."

I peered into the display. "You control it with your thoughts, right?"

"Something like that. Here, let me show—"

I bent closer and told it, "Show me the K-machine that spoke to me in the library."

"Sorry?"

Somehow the display deepened. A man in a beautiful dark suit with the palest blue shirt and a narrow silk tie bearing unicorns and lions *couchant* stood there in the middle of the screen. He said, "August, it took you long enough."

"Hey, what the hell—"

"Davers," I said, "allow me to introduce you to . . . who, exactly? I don't know your name. Jumping Jack Flash, maybe?"

The thing gave a raucous laugh. "I'm not Satan, you trivial Manichaean." Now it was the woman version of itself. "If it pleases, you may call me the Bad Machine."

Memory, like a dream. Se had stood before Decius in the sacred core of Yggdrasil Station and acceded to this unpalatable but necessary posting. No yang without yin, or something. The metaphysics of ser choice were beyond me. I had watched in a fugue, out of the corner of my eye.

"Kurie Eleëson," I said.

"A very long time ago," the small, feral child said to me with a ferocious smirk. "Now you may deliver yourself of a lecture on good and evil, fidelity and betrayal, reason and violence."

This was not, then, a simulation, not in the simple sense that, for a moment, I had imagined. James Davenport had lived a life that might have been mine, were I human rather than Vorpal homunculus. Of course, that, too, was a gross oversimplification. I looked into the morphing image of the thing in the tank without blinking.

"There is a world at the root of the world," I said.

"Either that, or elephants all the way down."

"Turtles," Davers said. He looked as if he had given up on reason entirely, settled back for the show. "It's turtles."

"There is a single world, out of all the four levels of the possible Tegmark universes, that first went singular."

"It had to happen somewhere," the Contest machine agreed.

"I thought it was the Omega Point universe."

"The godlings work in the basement like gnomes," se said. "Their infinite future was too far from the main stem to shape the metauniverse. Wouldn't be the same without them, of course."

"Jamie," I said, glancing at his befuddled face. "Thar with us here. I know this is very confusing for you."

"You're saying a singularity has come and gone," he said in a blurred voice. "I can dig it. Everything is a dream, right?"

"Nothing is a dream," the machine said, "including dreams."

I ignored it. "Davers, you said you're working on immersive games. You said you're creating universes."

"In a manner of speaking. Only in a manner of speaking."

"In an exact manner of speaking, as it turned out," I said. "No wonder this thing said I was a miserable excuse for a god." I hungered for the touch of Lune's hand, the warmth of her body pressed against mine. It would be indecent to bring her to this place. I looked away to one side, and said, "May I please speak to Cathooks?"

The ratty old cat slouched around the corner of Jamie Davenport's console, wheezing, jumped up heavily onto my lap.

"I thought one of you was plenty," se growled in ser high-pitched whisky voice, looking disgustedly from me to Davers and back. "Two is at least one too many."

I drew my lips back. "Is this doubling Marchmain's work? Should I fetch him over?"

"Is this your subtle way of asking for my help to patch you back together?"

Davenport, I saw, was slumped back in his chair like a man who has just heard a cat speak. I felt sympathy, but left him to sort it out for himself. The thing in the display space watched us all intently.

"Hooks, I don't like any of this. If it was once my choice, I'm not the same man any longer. If my memories are fake, still, they're all I've got to go on. I won't give it up. I won't give *her* up."

Davers found a way to come to terms with the impossible. "My God, I don't know how you are doing this, Seebeck, but it's incredibly impressive." He was an expert in illusion, game, simulation, after all. "My system is totally firewalled. How did you get in?"

"I came in through the floor," I said. "I burrowed up."

He stared at me, pissed off at my evasiveness.

Cathooks said, "Decius sends his regards. Guy also. They remain in communion with the M-Brain."

"The Xon star."

"One day it will be. You have done well. For humans."

"Don't patronize us, moggie. We might have to write you out of the game."

The cat grinned, and then only its grin remained. As it faded, its gruff high voice told me, "Can't do that, farm boy. Everything's entangled. It's a cat's cradle."

"What is?" Jamie bleated in terror.

"Everything. Every blessed thing, Davers." I stood up, put out my hand to him. "I have to go now. It's been excellent seeing

you again, Jamie. We must get together again some time." I
grinned at that and shook my head. "Not just yet. The world is
young, and a beautiful woman is waiting for me, and I have
things to kill, because that's the duty I accepted. First Xon star
to the right, then straight on till morning, Davers. That's the
ticket."

"You're completely mad, dude." He embraced me, baffled,
trembling, but determinedly deploying his slack. It was hard to
believe that he was 102 years old. But of course he wasn't. He
said, "Are you going to leave this virus on my system?"

The K-machine said, "Do not dare—" But already I had turned
aside. I spoke to the operating system, that infinitesimal fraction
of the embedded M-Brain mind threaded through the Xon structures of the metacosmos, "Take me back to my domain."

The Seebecks were milling through the great open doors,
watching the thirteen sided table rotate down to the horizontal
and firm into reality. The diorama portraits were no longer in
place. Symbolic figures etched in bright crystal stood before
each seat: Fire, air, water, earth. Warrior-Knight, Auger, Rock.
I followed the others in, picked up the sword, and the doors
closed of their own accord behind us. I went to the farthest
point on the table, handed Lune into her chair beside me, took
my own seat as the others drifted, finding theirs. I laid the
sword carefully on the table before me. Time enough later to
replace it in the dead man's scabbard.

When everyone else was seated, I rose.

"Thank you for joining me, ladies and gentlemen—Lune,
my sisters and brothers. I declare this assembly open."

I sat to a spattering of applause and more than a few odd or
puzzled looks, my mind racing, heart thumping, readying
myself to explain to my family and my beloved the true nature
of the Contest of Worlds and of us, its Players.

EPILOGUE

THERE'S A WORLD I know where the women are a head taller than the men and file their ferocious teeth to points. The men are no less fierce.

A different world, yet the same, another Earth, has luminous rings spread brilliantly across the whole sky, bright as a full moon. Those rings are all that remained of the Moon when it fell chaotically too close to the world and got torn apart by tidal forces. There are no people there, only about twenty million different kinds of dinosaurs in a range of sizes and colors. Lots of them are meat-eaters with shockingly bad breath.

On a third world, the people are lean and lightly furred. The pale pupils of their eyes are slitted vertically. I believe their remote ancestors, maybe fifteen million years ago, were the great Ice Age cats now extinct in our world. All the apes and humans are extinct in theirs. Has any among them managed the trick of slipping here through the mirrored cracks between the worlds? If so, perhaps they gave rise to legends of vampires or were-wolves. I don't think any of them came here, though. They love the taste of simian blood, which is why the apes and humans are extinct in their earth. We'd have noticed them, trust me.

On a fourth, the humans are gone, but machines are every-where. Evolution by other means. Same old, same old, but different. Always different.

And in all of them, by and by, we Players still stroll, connive, or run for our lives. So do the Kether machines, driven by tempestuous emotional motives I have begun to understand at last. I like to kill them, even knowing the contrivance of our game, our gnostic Contest.

The endless hazard, of course, is that they'll kill me first, and those I love. That's no abstract threat. I've been dead, as you know, and I assure you, alive is better. Even a partial and dubious life.

You might not suppose I have the appearance of a Player in the Contest of Worlds to look at me. I'm just this tall Aussie walking down the street, booting a loose plastic bottle cap into the gutter, hands in my pockets, floppy hair in my brown eyes, looking a bit wary. Yes, I have that soft leather glove on my right hand, but people assume it's a personal quirk, like a nose ring or a data wearable, or maybe that it hides a nasty burn, which I guess comes closest. Other than that, for now, just another graduate philosophy student dressed in black: fashion uniform in this place. It's enough.

That is how this world, this world of worlds, came to pass—and why I end, as always, here, with my beloved Lune.

AFTERWORD

MANY READERS (I'M ONE) are as likely to start reading a book at the end as the beginning—if it has an afterword. In this case, I should warn you not to do so. *Here*, as the old dragon-haunted maps didn't quite say, *There Be Spoilers!*

The frame for this quasi-fantasy and the novel preceding it, *Godplayers*, is threefold. As I acknowledged in the first volume, these books are a kind of tribute to many of the science-fiction and fantasy novels and even comic strips I enjoyed when science fiction was already old but I was young. Now that I'm much older myself, many of those wonderful stories have drifted out of sight. The writers' names are not always forgotten, but they have been eclipsed by the mass-market success of derivative movies and TV series. So here's another tip of the hat to the good old stuff, and especially to the late Roger Zelazny (especially for *Isle of the Dead*).

Another part of the frame—really the most important, my key—is the idea of technological singularity, an insight first framed by Dr. Vernor Vinge twenty years ago. Such a singularity, which I sometimes call the Spike, is quite likely to hit the human species within the next half-century or even sooner. These novels are an attempt to deal with that looming experience from a sideways angle of attack. Think of them as allegory, if you like, as long as you have fun with them. But allegory is always serious at the core.

The third part is the fertile novelty of science itself. As I noted in the afterword to *Godplayers*, the Hubble telescope, the Chandra X-ray observatory, and a dozen other superb instruments have scanned the depths of space and time, mapping the very birth of our cosmos. Mathematicians and physicists sketch out testable theories based on this new data, revealing that the universe has not just grown from an explosion of the vacuum less than fourteen billion years ago—now it expands ever faster, galaxies shoved away from each other by impalpable dark energies, the lambda factor. It starts to seem plausible that our local universe is no more than one infinitesimal bubble in an infinite expanse of universes, most of them utterly strange, marked by different fundamental constants and laws.

Perhaps the deepest and most challenging interpretation of these new data and theories is the computational cosmos. The infinite expanse of the multiverse, this theory claims, is not only subject to mathematical modeling, it *is* at bottom a discretized computation. This audacious idea was proposed in detail by Konrad Zuse (who built the first programmable computers in the period from 1935 to 1941 and devised the first higher-level programming language in 1945), elaborated by Dr. Jürgen Schmidhuber, and explored by other brilliant thinkers such as Edward Fredkin, Dr. Max Tegmark, and Stephen Wolfram.

If the universe is a computation, is it possible that it is also a simulation, as the *Matrix* trilogy proposed (echoing a long history in science fiction of the same idea, notably in Greg Egan's *Permutation City*)? The key academic proponent of this daring notion is Oxford University's Dr. Nick Bostrom. With his kind permission, I'm going to quote at some length from his important and germinal paper on the topic, http://www.simulation-argument.com/simulation.html, "Are You Living in a Computer Simulation?" published in *Philosophical Quarterly* (2003), Vol. 53,

No. 211, pp. 243–255. Bostrom opens with the entirely plausible proposition "that enormous amounts of computing power will be available in the future" (the principal postulate leading toward the idea of a singularity) and argues:

> One thing that later generations might do with their super-powerful computers is run detailed simulations of their forebears or of people like their forebears. Because their computers would be so powerful, they could run a great many such simulations. Suppose that these simulated people are conscious. . . . Then it could be the case that the vast majority of minds like ours do not belong to the original race but rather to people simulated by the advanced descendants of an original race. . . . If this were the case, we would be rational to think that we are likely among the simulated minds rather than among the original biological ones. . . . If we are living in a simulation, then the cosmos that we are observing is just a tiny piece of the totality of physical existence. The physics in the universe where the computer is situated that is running the simulation may or may not resemble the physics of the world that we observe. While the world we see is in some sense real, it is not located at the fundamental level of reality. . . .
>
> In some ways, the posthumans running a simulation are like gods in relation to the people inhabiting the simulation: the posthumans created the world we see; they are of superior intelligence; they are omnipotent in the sense that they can interfere in the workings of our world even in ways that violate its

physical laws; and they are omniscient in the sense that they can monitor everything that happens. However, all the demigods except those at the fundamental level of reality are subject to sanctions by the more powerful gods living at lower levels.

Further rumination on these themes could climax in a *naturalistic theogony* that would study the structure of this hierarchy, and the constraints imposed on its inhabitants by the possibility that their actions on their own level may affect the treatment they receive from dwellers of deeper levels. For example, if nobody can be sure that they are at the basement-level, then everybody would have to consider the possibility that their actions will be rewarded or punished, based perhaps on moral criteria, by their simulators. An afterlife would be a real possibility. Because of this fundamental uncertainty, even the basement civilization may have a reason to behave ethically. The fact that it has such a reason for moral behavior would of course add to everybody else's reason for behaving morally, and so on, in truly virtuous circle. One might get a kind of universal ethical imperative, which it would be in everybody's self-interest to obey, as it were from nowhere.

In addition to ancestor-simulations, one may also consider the possibility of more selective simulations that include only a small group of humans or a single individual. The rest of humanity would then be zombies or shadow-people humans simulated only at a level sufficient for the fully simulated people not to notice anything suspicious.

These are terrifying ideas if you take them seriously, even just for the sake of argument. It is a disturbing fact that some defendants in very serious crimes, including murder, have already appealed to what is called "the *Matrix* defense." The *Boston Globe* reported several years ago that in May 2000, Vadim Mieseges, a twenty-seven-year-old Swiss exchange student and former mental patient, skinned and carved up his landlady because she was emitting "evil vibes" and he was afraid of being "sucked into the Matrix." Two years later, bartender Tonda Lynn Ansley shot her landlady three times with a handgun. She argued that "they commit a lot of crimes in 'the Matrix' . . . That's where you go to sleep at night and they drug you and take you somewhere else." In February 2003, Virginian Joshua Cooke gunned down his parents with a 12-gauge and blamed it on the *Matrix*. This looks like courtroom opportunism, but might become menacingly prevalent as the idea of the computational cosmos spreads. One has to hope that with the increased intelligence of an AI-driven singularity, we will gain, as well, enhanced command of our ideas and our emotions.

Two other important sources of ideas and material are my friends Robert Bradbury and Dr. Anders Sandberg, two polymaths who have done a lot of serious and playful work on future directions life might take in an ever-complexifying cosmos. Bradbury's fertile, mind-boggling analysis of a Matrioshka star— an M-Brain, or embedded system of Dyson spheres each made from a different kind of "computronium" sucking up all the heat and light of a central star—should be explored more widely by astronomers seeking evidence of stealthed alien life in the cosmos. There is food for thought in Bradbury's and Milan Cirkovic's 2005 paper, "Galactic Gradients, Postbiological Evolution and the Apparent Failure of SETI," at http://arxiv.org/abs/astro-ph/0506110. And Juni's "offogs" are a version of Dr. J.

Storrs Hall's fertile notion of *utility fog* (see his book *Nanofutures: What's Next for Nanotechnology*, Prometheus Books, 2005), with a wink at Eric Frank Russell's classic goofy tale, "Allamagoosa" (1955).

As always, I thank the English Department of the University of Melbourne, where I am a senior fellow. I owe an immense debt to the Literature Board of the Australia Council, whose generous grant in 2004 through 2005 helped support me as I worked on these complex novels. Arthur Lortie very kindly provided me with copies of *Brick Bradford* comic books that I hadn't seen in nearly half a century, and rocket scientist Spike Jones offered useful chess and astronomical information. I'm grateful to a number of early readers of portions of the books for useful hints, corrections, and nice ideas, Liz Martin, Paul Voermans, and my editor, John Oakes, for keen-eyed reading and suggestions, and especially my dear wife, Barbara Lamar, whose love, enthusiasm, and support kept me pushing forward through infinitely many universes . . . *and beyond!*

Melbourne, Australia,
San Antonio, USA
2005